The

Shepherd's

The Shepherd's Man

by

David F. Gray

New Leaf Press

First printing: November 1995

ISBN: 0-89221-258-6
Library of Congress Catalog Number: 93-87253

Dedication

Dedications are fun. It gives the author the chance to thank the special person or persons who have been instrumental in the creation of a book. When that person also happens to be the wife of the writer, it is doubly satisfying.

It takes a very special woman to live with this particular writer. She tolerates my moodiness. She smiles when I come home grumpy from a long day's work, makes conversation as I gulp down a quick meal, then kisses me cheerfully as I disappear into the bedroom for a few more hours to wrestle with a reluctant chapter. She listens to the ramblings about my characters and story lines, and nods and smiles when I tell her all the things I am going to do for her once I have "made it" as an author.

She is a mother, a teacher, a confidant, lifelong companion, and lover. She is also the best friend I have ever had. For some reason I will never understand, yet always be grateful for, God brought her into my life. To that end, it is with deepest love and gratitude that I dedicate The Shepherd's Man to my wife,

Heidi Powell Gray.

Acknowledgments

One of the most precious gifts a friend can give to a writer is the gift of encouragement. It is a gift that can lift one's spirit and renew one's determination. Over the past few years, I have received many such gifts, and would like to give a heartfelt thanks to those who gave them.

To Rick and Sylvia Powell, who are not only the best in-laws anyone could have, but who have become best friends as well.

To Mark and Sheryl Greenlee, sister and brother-in-law, for always being there when I needed you.

To my brother Danny and his fiancee, Stephanie, whose enthusiasm for *The Shepherd's Path* went way beyond the line of duty.

To Warren Wiersbe, under whose ministry I was saved, and whose letters of encouragement have meant a very great deal.

To Sandra Sims for delivering a good kick in the pants when needed. (And when not needed, for that matter!)

And to the following, whose friendship means more to me than I can ever say: Leo Martin, Bill Rowan, Lon and Bill Barclay, Marcia Pugh, Arthelene Rippy, Linda Brown, Herman and Sharron Bailey, Tim and Susie Hopkins, and Pastor David and Dottie Rice.

To all of you, my deepest and most heartfelt thanks.

David Gray

JULY 2, 2002

"Henderson."

"Henderson here."

"See anything?"

"Nothing, boss. All's quiet."

"Hmmm. All right. Stand by. We go in 10 minutes."

"Roger that."

With just a touch of frustration Paul Sinclair, crack agent for the Bureau of Religious Affairs, flipped off the vid-screen of the car communicator. His mood was quickly going from bad to worse as the wait lengthened.

Leaning back in the leather upholstery of his sleek, black sedan, he forced himself to relax. To keep from fidgeting, he carefully smoothed his rumpled gray suit. The graceful, precise movements of his six-foot-plus hardened frame brought to mind a panther on the hunt. Every muscle was tensed, awaiting the coming action. The uniformed sergeant sitting behind the wheel glanced over and grinned.

"This is the hardest part, eh sir?"

"Yeah," Paul replied briefly. He did not like to indulge in small talk before a bust, especially with an underling.

"Not to worry, Mister Sinclair," the sergeant continued, oblivious to Paul's mood. "We might have got here late, but we'll get them. Everything's covered. They aren't going anywhere." Paul merely grunted. The sergeant, finally getting the point, lapsed into silence. The lateness of their arrival was another sore spot in this operation. Bungled paperwork at the local office had resulted in their being sent to the wrong location.

For the tenth time in as many minutes, Paul raised his macro-binoculars to his dark eyes. Even in the fading twilight, they gave him a clear picture of the surveillance area.

The dirty streets of downtown Covington stretched out before him. The surrounding buildings, most of them abandoned, stared darkly back, ghosts remembering better times.

The object of his attention, a used furniture store, sat, squat and ugly, just a few hundred feet away. They had parked across the street and about a half a block down. Paul fingered a control and the image before him zoomed in quickly. Now he was looking through the display windows and into the back of the store. There was only one occupant — a bald, sturdily built man sitting at an old fashioned high top desk. He was unaware of the fact that his world was about to come crashing down about him. Once again, Paul flipped on the vid-screen. The young, excited face of his second in command appeared before him.

"Henderson."

"Right here, boss."

"I don't think anyone else is going to show. Prepare to go. On my mark."

"Roger that, boss. On your mark."

Paul paused for a moment, willing his rapidly beating heart to slow. His Zen training came into play almost automatically. After a tension heavy moment, he hit the all-page button on the communicator so he could address his whole team. When he spoke again it was with absolute calm. "All right gentlemen, let's round them up."

The sergeant muttered a soft "Ye Ha!" and started the car. Checking the area, he gunned the engine. The car surged forward, the tires squealing in protest. Within seconds they jolted to a stop in front of the store. Two other cars and a van joined them, effectively blocking the entrance. As he jumped out, Paul knew that the rear of the building was being covered as well.

There was no need for words. Paul and his team had done this dozens of times. At his wave, half of the agents fanned out, drawing their weapons and training them on the store. It only took them a few seconds to deploy themselves to his satisfaction. Then, drawing his own pistol, he charged into the building. Five members of his team, two in the dark black uniform of the bureau, three others in plain clothes, followed him. He suppressed a smile as he sprinted past rows of dilapidated furniture. The poor fool at the desk barely had time to paste a startled expression on his pudgy, bald face before Paul was on top of him.

Quickly and easily, Paul reached up and grabbed him by the scruff of the neck. Yanking hard, he pulled him off his high stool and threw him onto the floor. The bald man cried out in pain, and Paul heard the unmistakable sound of a bone breaking. Not his problem.

"Cuff him," he said to the nearest agent. "The rest of you, with me." Turning, Paul led his team through a dirty curtain and into a dim stock room. Shelves reached up into the darkness above, piled with broken and discarded tables and chairs. Pausing, he pulled a small but powerful flashlight from his jacket pocket. Switching it on, he panned it around the room. Their informant said the group would be meeting in the basement.

His eyes lit on a rickety, locked door about halfway to the back wall.

"There," he said, and pushed forward. He reached the door and pushed against it, testing. Then, glancing back and nodding, he brought his leg up in a powerful forward kick. Rotting wood splintered as the door flew open. Before him appeared a rickety wooden staircase. Without hesitation, he started down. He made it halfway when his foot reached out and found empty space. Desperately he grabbed the handrail, feeling splinters dig into his palm. His outstretched foot slid harshly onto the next step, twisting his ankle in the process. Pain lanced through his leg. Only his lightning fast reflexes saved him from plunging into the darkness. Cursing under his breath, he stopped his pitch forward and brought himself to a stop. The pain in his ankle made his already foul mood even worse.

"Move it," he whispered savagely to the agents behind him. Disregarding the throbbing, he continued down the stairs. At the bottom, a sharp left brought him to another locked door. He brought his fist up and pounded on the rough wood.

"Peace officers!" he shouted. "Open this door at once!" From inside there was a muted shout. Paul gritted his teeth and rammed the door with his shoulder. There was no room for a strong kick. The door shuddered, but held. Paul focused every ounce of his strength into his shoulder and rammed again. This time, he was rewarded with a solid "crunch" as the door gave way. He bulled his way inside, followed by his team. A dim, naked light bulb hung from the ceiling. The dim light it cast revealed twelve frightened faces staring back at him. There they were, gathered in a circle on their knees, holding hands — quite a pretty picture.

They called themselves an underground church. Paul called them traitors. Moving forward, he suppressed a smile. This was the part of his job that he loved. A little nest of malcontents, ripe for the taking. Several of the group were women. So much the better.

"Everybody, against that wall!" he shouted in his best "take command" voice. "Let's go, get up off those knees. Move!"

The tiny group was still stunned that they were discovered. They began to rise slowly — too slowly to suit Paul. The back of his hand swung out like a striking snake, connecting with the temple of the woman closest to him. Her cry of pain was music to his ears. He took a moment to notice her. Dark hair, dark eyes — not bad, Paul decided. He opened his mouth to say something, but was interrupted when one of the group, a big man with gray hair, stood up and spoke.

"Everyone, be calm," he said in a powerful voice. Paul did not bother to suppress his grin this time. He knew a leader when he saw one. The idiot had just given himself away! "Do what they say. We knew that this might happen. We are in God's hands. Don't fear!"

"Yeah, right." The sergeant standing at the door elbowed his way into the cellar. "I got yer 'god' right here." His fist came up and connected with the leader's chin. The big man collapsed with a groan. The sergeant turned back to Paul for instructions while Paul swallowed a rebuke. For all of his crudeness, the sergeant was a good man. *Let him have his fun,* he decided. He turned his attention back to the frightened group, looking for one particular person.

"Well, isn't this special," he said in a mocking voice. "What a nice cozy group." As he spoke, he looked at each captive carefully. There! One of the men had his fingers crossed in a pre-arranged signal. There was their informant!

"Sergeant, cuff these traitors and get 'em into the wagon. Looks like a good night, gentlemen. This is quite a haul, a real feather in our cap. It'll look good to the higher ups."

"We have to take them all now?" leered the sergeant. He moved to stand next to a young blonde and ran his hand down her back. Another man, obviously the woman's husband, started to turn, but was slammed back around by one of the other agents. "This one here, we could have some fun with her." The woman let out a groan that was nothing but pure despair.

"Sorry, sergeant," replied Paul. "Orders are that none of them are to be damaged. They got a little trip ahead of them." The orders had come in that day. Any underground church members arrested within the next 24 hours there in the greater Cincinnati area were to be immediately shipped to some place in California.

"Too bad," said the sergeant, real regret coloring his voice. He turned to the rest of the group. "Okay, let's go. Come on, MOVE!" He started to herd the tiny church out of the cellar, but the big man Paul pegged as the leader stopped. He had a dark purple welt on his cheek where the sergeant struck him.

"What about our rights?" he asked calmly, looking Paul right in the eye. His gaze made Paul uncomfortable. *The fool should be on his knees right now, begging for his life.*

Abruptly, Paul realized that most of the church members he arrested acted much the same way. He wanted to smash that calm face, to wipe the serenity right off of it. Instead, not quite understanding why, he answered. "You have no rights," he said flatly. He put every ounce of coldness he possessed into his voice. "When you decided to have your little meeting, you automatically became a traitor to the state. That means you forfeited any rights to be treated like a citizen — or even like a human being, as far as I'm concerned." He turned away. "Sergeant!"

"All right, enough talk," the sergeant growled. "Let's go." Roughly he pushed the shattered group out of the cellar and up the stairs. From the sound of things, he was not too gentle. Paul shrugged to himself. Again, not his problem. He turned back to face the one remaining church member — the man who had given the recognition signal. He jerked his thumb toward the door, indicating that he should proceed him. One of the agents handed him the informant's ID. *Allan Meyers,* he read to himself. Satisfied, he returned the small piece of plastic to its owner. Reaching up, he switched off the single hanging bulb, then followed his flashlight's beam out the door where Meyers waited.

"Nice work," he said shortly. He disliked informants, although he recognized their necessity. One could never trust a man that turned on his own. "Thanks to you, we got the whole bunch." The smaller man squirmed at the compliment. Feeling guilty, Paul knew. After all, he had just destroyed 11 people who trusted him. Frankly, Paul did not care, as long as the results were good.

"Look," said Meyers, "You got what you wanted. Is that it? Can I go now?"

"Of course," Paul nodded. "Just as soon as you assure me that we got all of them. Wouldn't want to miss someone, now would we? It wouldn't look good for you — or your family." He allowed a threatening tone to creep into his voice. It was quite effective. Meyers had the look of one totally defeated.

"Two others left just before you got here. You must have seen them." His voice almost broke as he spoke.

"Nobody came out the front," Paul replied evenly. "There's a back entrance, but we had it covered. Are you sure they left?"

"Where else would they go?" snapped Meyers. He was obviously feeling the strain, but *nobody* talked to Paul like that.

"Don't use that tone with me, mister," he replied, putting a dangerous edge into his voice. "What were their names." Meyers drew a deep breath.

"Scott and Beth Sampson," he answered after a slight pause. "They live on this side of the river, somewhere in Fort Mitchell, I think." Quickly, Paul reached for his communicator.

"Sergeant!"

"Sir!" The reply was instantaneous.

"There are two other suspects. They left just before we came in, so start a search of the immediate area. Their names are Scott and Beth Sampson. Call that in to central and get an address on them, and put out an APB to the local agencies. Let's find them, sergeant!"

"Yes sir!" The sergeant clicked off.

Paul turned his attention back to Meyers. "Now," he said, "Is there anything else you need to tell me?"

Meyers seemed to collapse inward. Paul knew he was looking at a totally defeated individual. "No," he finally replied, his voice almost a whisper.

"Then go on home, but don't leave town, and be sure to stay in touch. Got that?" Meyers grunted in assent and started up the stairs. Paul hesitated for a moment, feeling that he was forgetting something. He could not figure out how the two people Meyers had mentioned might have escaped. He let his flashlight wonder around the cellar entrance, the tight beam probing the darkness. For just a moment, he thought to check under the staircase, just in case they missed something. He started forward, shining his light through the steps. Then he noticed that there was nothing there but moldy, decaying boxes. He stood there, pondering his next course of action. Then, shrugging off his misgivings, he started up the stairs to coordinate the rest of the raid. All in all, he decided, it had been a *very* good night.

* * *

August 2, 2002

Call him Wolf. It was a name he fancied, even cherished. It signified power, and cunning. It spoke of control. *That* was the one thing he craved more than anything else — control — and dominance.

His old identity had long since been submerged deep in his subconscious. Harry Belmont, for all practical purposes, was dead. He had begun to die when his drunken father would lock him in a dark closet for hours and hours, just because he spilled his milk at dinner.

"Had enough, Harry, boy?" The taunts would come through the closed door as the cringing seven year old hid his face against the darkness. "Not too dark in there, is it? Watch out for snakes, Harry boy!"

He continued to die when a sadistic marine drill sergeant took a perverse kind of joy in demonstrating the various kinds of pain the human body could endure. He had gasped his last breath when, in the desert of Iraq, he had pulled out his .45 caliber pistol and, egged on by a few "friends," calmly, deliberately, shot a helpless and starving prisoner. From there, it was no big deal to kill a Black, or Jew, or another Arab.

Harry had been a weakling, a nobody. He was one of the controlled, one of the dominated. Wolf was a hunter, and a warrior, strong and in control. Belmont was a middle-aged, balding fool. Wolf was a cunning giant. While most would call him a terrorist, deep in the polluted bowels of his mind, he thought of himself as both judge and juror, dispensing justice equally and fairly. After all, a bomb did not differentiate between the rich and poor, or the good and bad. It took all, no matter how strong or weak.

Wolf was a man in love with his work. The one person he took orders from literally ran the country. He liked the idea of being close to that kind of power. Jacob Hill, he thought, knew how to get things done. He got results. Like this current assignment, for instance. Just now, Wolf was browsing sleepily through the science fiction section of a large bookstore in a mall on the outskirts of Washington, DC. He was dressed nondescriptly in denim jeans, plaid work shirt and beige windbreaker. His eyes had that hooded look that he thought a cobra must have just before striking. Indeed, right now he felt more like a cobra than a wolf, for he was ready to strike. Maybe, he mused, he would change his name to "Cobra" after this job — or Viper. That had a nice ring to it. Probably Hill would say no, but he could try anyway. It was too bad Hill had not allowed him to be part of the bombing of Flight 407 last month, he thought. True, it had the desired results, but Wolf felt he could have done it better — with a little more finesse.

Glancing around to make sure that no one was watching, he pulled a thick paperback book out of his inner jacket pocket and placed it on the shelf in front of him. It was a new copy of Clarke's *2001, A Space Odyssey*. He stood there looking at it for a moment, frowning. The old classic was as popular as ever, and there was a chance that it could be picked up by a customer. Carefully he pulled out several other paperbacks and placed his book all the way in the back. Then he replaced the others, effectively hiding his little surprise. That was better. Results, they were the only thing that mattered.

"Can I help you with something?"

In spite of himself, Wolf jumped. Turning, he saw one of the sales people, a bright looking young man of about 20, smiling at him.

"What?" he snapped back, upset that he had not heard the young man's approach.

"Can I help you find something special?" asked the sales person, oblivious to Wolf's mood. "I saw you looking behind the books, and I thought you might be having trouble finding what you were looking for."

"No," said Wolf shortly, wanting the young fool to leave. "I'm just browsing," he added on an afterthought, trying to sound like a customer. He tried to hang a smile on his face, but it came out as more of a grimace.

"You never know what you might find hidden away somewhere."

"I know what you mean," said the attendant eagerly. "Why, just the other day, I was looking through a secondhand bookstore and found a copy of an original *Wizards and Warlocks* game book. Can you believe it? It even had the original spell sheets with it! Ever since the role-playing games got linked up with the national computer networks, you just can't find them anymore. Nobody bothers with the books when everything's right there on your home computer. In fact, I think the only place you can find them now is in the public school system, but that's just the entry level stuff, you know. Why, one of my friends told me. . . ."

"Excuse me," Wolf interrupted bluntly, "But I've got to go. I'm late." With that, he shouldered past the bookseller and headed out of the store. The young man stared after him, blinking in confusion. "Jerk!" Wolf said under his breath. "I hope you stay right where you're at for the next 20 minutes. The world can always use one less idiot." Actually, it did not matter. The explosive nestled tightly in the book he had left behind was more than powerful enough to take out the whole area.

He made his way through the highest level of the crowded mall, looking for others of his group. By now, they would have left similar packages in another dozen stores. The combined explosives would not be enough to level the building, but it would certainly cause untold damage in property and lives. Just the thing to draw the right kind of attention to the right kind of people.

Inwardly, Wolf smiled. He smiled at the milling customers, blithely going about their business. There was an elderly couple sharing a soft drink seated a few yards away. Leaning over the railing, he looked down into the lower levels, watching as a pair of teenage boys strolled by, talking heatedly to each other. Directly underneath, a mother with two toddlers in tow swept past him, not even bothering to glance his way. *If only you knew, little mommie,* he thought to himself. *If only you knew who you just passed, you would have a little more respect.*

Glancing back up, he saw the rest of his group coming toward him. They were a local gang, more in to drug dealing and street warfare than this sort of operation. For the right price, however, they were more than willing to try anything. They were also easily recruited and easily disposed of. He nodded as the leader, who called himself Bliss, leaned on the railing next to him.

"Done?" he asked briefly. The youth merely grunted an affirmative, not bothering to look at him. He was a tall black man, thin and haggard looking from a lifetime on the streets. He might have been 18, but the haunted eyes and tired countenance made him look twice that. Wolf looked back at the rest of the gang, who waited on their leader patiently. They were an odd looking bunch. Three Blacks, two whites, and a Hispanic.

While gang violence in this city was drawn mainly along racial lines, there were a few exceptions. This particular gang, the "Black Death," did not care about skin color. These boys were more interested in the money they could make off drug sales, particularly the newest thing to hit the streets — black ice. A derivative of "crack" cocaine, it was ingested directly through the skin. It had the two characteristics of practically bypassing the blood stream and affecting the brain directly, and being 100 percent addictive when taken only once. Law enforcement agencies had lost count of the number of pre-teenagers who had been addicted without their knowledge by casual contact with a "friend." The number of fatalities from the drug was skyrocketing. It had almost reached the level of deaths due the killer plague AIDS II.

"Good," said Wolf, after studying them for a moment. "You head out to your van and I'll meet you in a few minutes. I've got a call to make." He started to move, but Bliss caught him by the sleeve.

"My mon," he said, in a low, quasi-Jamaican accent, "Don' even think about leaving us behind. I think you better pay up now. Know what I mean, mon?" Wolf looked at the leader, his eyes narrowing. He took in the mocking smile and murderous eyes, then glanced down at the dirty hand on his arm. The youth was strong, stronger than he looked, but Wolf had a few surprises, thanks to his marine training.

Reaching over quickly with his other hand, he grabbed Bliss's thumb, twisting up and back. Bliss let out a gasp of surprise as he was forced up against the railing. His lack of leverage made it impossible for him to retaliate. The other gang members moved in, but Wolf was quicker. He slid his hand into his jacket pocket. The harsh click that sounded a second later stopped them in their tracks. They knew the sound of a pistol cocking.

"Don' push it, mon," said Wolf through gritted teeth, his voice low and dangerous. "You'll get your money when I'm ready to give it to you, and not a second sooner. Got it?" Bliss hesitated, and Wolf applied more pressure. Unwillingly, the younger man gasped in pain. A few passers-by glanced in their direction, then looked rapidly away. Finally, the leader nodded, his eyes burning with hatred. Wolf smiled his coldest smile and released the leader's hand. "Get out," he growled, motioning with his hand still inside his pocket. "Wait for me in the van. I'll have your money then."

Sullenly, the Black Death moved off. They kept together, constantly glancing over their shoulders at him. They resembled a pack of whipped dogs, beaten, but still very dangerous. Wolf knew that they would be waiting to make him pay for the humiliation they had just suffered. Not that it mattered. Like any hired help, they were expendable.

As soon as they were out of sight, he found an elevator and moved down to the lower level of the mall. Once there, he found a row of pay vid-phones. Making sure that no one else was in earshot, he selected one and inserted the proper change. Activating the video lockout, he pulled out a small, flat, circular object and placed it on the audio pickup. The little gadget would effectively disguise his voice. Then, he dialed a three-digit number. The instant a connection was made, he started the timer of his watch.

"Nine-one-one," came the professional voice over the tiny speaker placed next to the video monitor. There was a pause. "Would you please activate your video link. Federal and state law requires both audio and video transmission on emergency vid-phone calls."

"Listen carefully," said Wolf, in a prepared speech. "This is Wolf, of the Christian Liberation Front. In five minutes, several bombs will explode in the Washington Galleria Mall. This is done in response to the increasing government harassment of Christianity. The government must bear the responsibility of the deaths that will occur. We demand an end to the persecution of organized religion and an immediate release of all prisoners held because of their beliefs. If these demands are not met within one week, another bombing will occur."

Quickly he broke the connection. Retrieving the voice modifier, he checked his watch. Twenty-two seconds since he began the call. By now, the emergency service would be notifying mall security of the threat. They would know that the call was made from the mall itself, although it would take another few seconds to trace the exact location — seconds he had better use to his advantage. Without seeming to hurry, he set a brisk pace to the row of glass-enclosed elevators located in the center of the mall. One was waiting, its doors open. Without hesitation, he stepped in and started up. Looking down, he saw a half-dozen armed security guards rushing over to the row of phones. He smiled grimly, knowing that there was no way they were going to identify him. Again he glanced at his still running stopwatch. Just over a minute had passed. He cocked his head, waiting.

"Attention," said an impersonal female voice over the public address system.

"Right on cue," muttered Wolf under his breath.

"This is an emergency," continued the voice. "The Washington Galleria is closing immediately. Please go to the nearest exit. Do not — repeat — do not hesitate. You must exit the mall now. If you need assistance, please come to the information booth in the center of the mall. Again, this is an emergency. The Washington Galleria is closing. Please go to. . . ."

The elevator bumped gently to a stop and Wolf got out. He could see that many of the shoppers were merely standing there, staring stupidly at each other in confusion. So much the better. The greater the loss of life, the greater the public outcry against Christianity. Actually, that did not really concern him. He really could not care less that a few fools were meeting in secret, praying to a God who was obviously too busy to listen. What really mattered was that Jacob Hill would be pleased with the results. That meant he would get another assignment. He would get to kill again. Three minutes to go. Wolf walked leisurely to the exit he had planned to use. The mall security force was now beginning to usher people out of the building. Many were protesting indignantly. He grinned as he stepped out into the humid evening air. It would take at least 20 minutes to evacuate that crowd. Far too much time.

Two minutes to go. There, across the lit parking lot, was the van. He could see the Black Death standing around, waiting for him. He could imagine their plan. They would let him give them the money he promised, then drag him into the van and drive off. His body would probably be found somewhere in the Potomac the next morning.

"Sorry, boys," he said in a low, emotionless voice. "Nothing personal. Just business, you understand." He pulled out a tiny transmitter from his hip pocket and pushed one of the two buttons situated on one side. A tiny telltale light glowed green. He looked at his watch one last time. One minute. He took a breath of the stale air, enjoying the moment. Wolf considered himself a craftsman — an artist. This would be one of his finest concerts to date. He held the transmitter loosely in his right hand, carefully counting the seconds. Timing, after all, was everything. When his count reached 10, he smiled a shark's smile and pushed the other button.

The explosion was deafening. The van disappeared in a ball of yellow-orange flame. The Black Death were incinerated instantly. Wolf watched casually as one body (Bliss, he thought), went flying across the lot, coming to rest a good 30 yards away. There wasn't enough left of the rest to worry about.

Quickly he averted his face as the blast of heat reached him. It was so strong that it actually knocked him down. He lay there for a moment, listening to the screams of bystanders. Evidently several had been injured. And it was only the beginning. Quickly he picked himself up. It would be bad form, after all, to be trampled at one's own bombing.

He moved away from the mall just as the explosions began. The ground beneath his feet thudded with the shock waves. Twelve well-placed explosives went off in perfect precision. The sound of the blast jarred him. He reached the rented car he had parked across the lot from the van and looked back. A glow of flame was starting to rise above the mall, quickly spreading from end to end. Wolf allowed himself a full-fledged grin. Perhaps those explosives would be enough to level the place after all! He stood there for a moment, watching his handiwork. The brightness of the fire, the screams of the frightened and of the dying, all were a flawless concert to his ears. He could hardly wait to see the newscasts tonight, or the newspapers tomorrow.

Taking one last loving look, he opened the car door and got in. With the coming traffic jam, it would probably take him a while to get out of the immediate vicinity. No matter. No one could identify him, and it would give him more time to enjoy the fruits of his labors.

"Pretty good, Wolf, old man," he whispered gleefully to himself. He was unaware of just how much he sounded like his father. "That's one for the books." All in all, he decided as he started the car and headed for the exit, it had been a *very* good night.

* * *

OCTOBER, 2002

"Ayres Two, you are cleared for docking. Stand by to release to central control."

"Roger that, Liberty. Awaiting your command."

"Ayres Two, on my mark. Five . . . four . . . three . . . two . . . one . . . release."

"Liberty, you have control."

"Roger, Ayres Two. You are in the corridor. Sit back and enjoy the ride, folks. We are bringing you in."

Christine Smythe settled back into the acceleration couch in the passenger cabin of the modified space shuttle. Reaching up, she switched off the monitor that allowed her to listen in on the pilot's conversation. She closed her eyes and willed her heart to slow and her body to relax. Ordinarily, she was icy calm, but this was her first trip into space. It made her feel a little like a school girl waiting for her first date. At 48, she still retained her youthful good looks and lithe figure. Her dark hair held just a hint of gray, and the wrinkles around her eyes were barely visible. Not bad, she knew, for one of the world's most wealthy and powerful women. The thought caused her to grimace. Even she could not shake the "male oriented" thinking that had dominated the previous century. The fact was, she was one of the world's most powerful *people*, gender not withstanding.

Carefully she tightened the straps that held her firmly in the couch. The unaccustomed weightlessness was making her feel vaguely nauseated. The injection she had taken before liftoff should have prevented that, but she still felt decidedly queasy. Hopefully she would get over that before her meeting.

With a gentle lurch, the shuttle's maneuvering thrusters came on. The slight acceleration pushed her sideways in her seat as the sleek shuttle rotated on its latitudinal axis. Docking was seconds away. Leaning forward, she touched the control that would cause the viewport next to her to go from opaque to clear. As it slowly became transparent, space station Liberty came in to view.

In spite of herself, Christine gasped. She had seen the plans, of course, and had been instrumental in its construction. Cooperations under her direct ownership had designed and built many of the systems. She knew its dimensions, its total tonnage, and the staggering cost to put it all together. Still, nothing prepared her for her first look at the completed product. Stretching out before her, it filled the darkness. A masterpiece of twenty-first century engineering, it was begun in the late nineties and had just reached completion this past year. She could still see much of the original design, particularly near the center of the structure. Over the years of construction, though, that design had been greatly modified.

At first, specially built sections were hauled into orbit by NASA's small fleet of shuttles. With the continuing problems that plagued the original shuttle, the process had been cost prohibitive and agonizingly slow. Then, Carl Potter, one of her own engineers, had run across an old science fiction story written in the late eighties. The idea gleaned from it had been rejected as unworkable a decade before, but caused Carl to raise his eyebrows. A few elaborate equations and a simple proposal had resulted in a space station 10 times the size of the original at a fraction of the cost.

The result now floated in orbit above the earth. It ran the length of over five football fields, reaching across the sky like a giant, segmented earthworm. The huge, cylindrical sections that made up the station used to be the external fuel tanks of the shuttles. Once allowed to fall back to earth after launch, they were now kept attached to the orbiter. When the shuttle reached Liberty, the tank was disconnected and placed into a holding orbit by small, mountable thrusters. Once prepared, it was attached to the station and, at a fraction of the original cost estimate, a major addition was made possible. Powerful solar screens were added to each section, providing cheap and efficient power. Liberty was now fully operational, and Carl Potter was station manager. Already plans were under way for space station Freedom. Construction should start within the next year. It made her feel proud, and just a little smug. As far as the general public was concerned, Liberty was under the complete control of the United States government. She knew better.

A barely perceptible bump told Christine that the docking had been completed. There was a hiss of air as pressure was equalized, then she could hear the main hatch on the pilot side of the shuttle open. A moment later, the pilot himself floated into the passenger cabin.

"Ma'am," he said, inclining his head in a gesture of respect, "If you are ready to disembark, I will assist you."

"That will not be necessary, pilot," replied Christine coolly. "Please return to your duties." The pilot blushed slightly, either with embarrassment or anger, and returned to the control cabin. Christine followed him out with her stare, then allowed herself a grim smile. She would *NOT* allow herself to be helped up from a chair like a helpless invalid! For the past three-and-a-half decades, she had been on her own. She wasn't about to place herself in the control of *anyone*. Carefully she released her safety harness and pushed herself up. An instant later, she almost regretted her decision. She found herself hovering near the ceiling of the cabin like a wingless fly. It took her a moment to orient her mind.

Choose a reference, she told herself quietly, repeating the instructions she had been given earthside. *There is no up or down in a weightless condition. I can choose my own reference.* Hovering inches from the ceiling, she decided to let that be "up." Once that was settled, everything else fell into place. Up and down and left and right ceased to become mere concepts and took on real value.

With just a bit of clumsiness, she reoriented herself and pushed her way out of the passenger cabin, grateful that she was its only occupant. She was always careful to never allow anyone to see her in situations in which she was not in complete control. Passing through the small passageway that separated the passenger cabin from the control cabin, she caught the eyes of the pilot. The two locked gazes for a moment. Then, the pilot turned back to his work, but not before Christine caught an amused smirk. He had obviously seen what had happened. Christine stared after him for a long second, then turned to debark. She knew how to deal with insolence.

Waiting for her as she emerged from the airlock was Carl Potter, the station manager.

Through long practice, she hung a warm smile on her lips in greeting. The truth was, she did not really care for the engineer. He was too narrowly focused on Liberty itself. For him, the station was the end, not the means. It existed for its own value. For Christine and others, it was a tool. Nevertheless, Potter was important. His ability to translate theory into reality boarded on genius. He returned her smile with a wide grin.

"Welcome to Liberty, Miz Smythe," he beamed, extending his hand in greeting. Carefully, remembering the results of her last sudden movement, she returned the grip.

"Thank you, Carl. You and your people certainly have something to be proud about here. I didn't realize just how big this thing is until I actually saw it." Potter nodded eagerly.

"It hits everyone that way," he replied. "I'll be happy to give you the grand tour later, if you like, but right now I'm instructed to escort you to the main conference room."

"Fine," said Christine shortly. "By the way, who was the pilot that brought me up here?"

Potter frowned, confused by the unexpected question. "That would be Jack Stryker. Is there a problem?"

"As a matter of fact, yes," said Christine, remembering the pilot's smirk. "He was rude and insolent. Would you please see that he is no longer assigned here?"

Potter's frown deepened. "Are you sure that's necessary, Miz Smythe? Stryker is one of my best. That's why I assigned him to Ayres II. I wanted my finest people to bring you up here."

Christine allowed her smile to disappear and her voice to chill. "The gesture is appreciated, Carl, but nevertheless, I want him gone. I will not have people with that kind of attitude working for this complex. Understood?"

Unhappily, Potter nodded, then turned to lead her through the station. She could tell that he was quite unhappy at losing one of his best people, but that was not her concern. *No one* laughed at her — ever.

Without speaking, Potter led her to the station taxi. They had docked on one of the end sections, about halfway down. This particular section was divided into smaller rooms that dealt with shuttle maintenance as well as passenger transfers. Carefully leading her "up" a narrow access tube, they reached the taxi in a matter of minutes. It was actually an open-air monorail that ran along the axis of this and every other section. Four separate rails were grouped together and served as rapid transportation through the enormous station. One could also use the smaller hatches at each end of each section, but for traversing the entire station, this was the preferred method. A similar system ran along the outside of the station, used for equipment transfers.

Potter slid behind the control panel and waited as Christine settled in beside him. Then, using the touchpad, he keyed in their destination. Within seconds, the taxi started moving. The trip took less than a minute. Christine had little time for sightseeing, but what she did see impressed her. Research facilities, crew and guest quarters, even an open-air arboretum that contained hundreds of plants growing in weightlessness. She would have to examine Liberty in detail later. She was especially anxious to inspect the nuclear arsenal, part of the old "Star Wars" program. That would have to wait, however. Right now she had a very important meeting to attend.

The taxi slid to a halt in the nerve center of the station — ComCen. As she emerged from the cab, she saw a tall, young, dark-skinned man floating there easily, obviously waiting to meet her.

"Miz Smythe, I'm Derrek Robinson," he said. "If you will come with me, the rest are waiting." Christine merely nodded and moved to follow. A series of handrails placed alongside of the access tubes allowed relatively easy mobility. She kept her eyes on the young man's feet as he floated in front of her. They reached a point where the tube widened out into what legitimately could be called a corridor. Off to one side was a door-sized hatch. Her guide indicated that she go through, and opened it for her. Carefully, so as not to appear clumsy to those waiting beyond, she pushed into the room.

"Ah, Christine," said a deep, powerful voice. "You are the last to arrive. Please take your seat, and we will begin." Christine knew that voice.

It belonged to the one person in this world that could instill a sense of fear in her. He was sitting there, across the main conference room. Even in weightlessness, he held a definite aura of power. He sat at the head of an oval table, held into place by the curving arms of his cushioned chair. A big man with a broad, strong build, he seemed to have stepped out of a Roman museum. A strong, aquiline nose blended with a mixture of Anglo-Saxon and Arab features to form a face that bespoke strength and power. To Christine, it seemed as if the statue of Apollo, the sun god, had come to life. Handsome was too weak a word to describe him. He appeared both old and young, wise beyond normal human years.

All this, one noticed later, however. It was the eyes themselves that spoke of this man's power and disposition. Dark, they were, black and shining. Deceptively calm on the surface, like twin pools of cold water that hid something — something both powerful and destructive. Once his gaze locked on, there was no escape. He had gone by many names in the past, some famous, some infamous, and many unknown. Just now, he preferred to be addressed as "Brennon."

Like a willing servant, Christine found her seat and slid in, pulling the arms protectively around her. She barely glanced at the five men already there. They were part of Brennon's ruling elite — his Sextuaget, as he called them. Each person represented one of the major world powers — United Europe, the African States, the Asian Cohort, the Middle East, the United Baltic States, and the Americas. Christine, representing the Americas, had just become a part of that circle, thanks in part to the clumsiness of her successor. Brennon eyed her a moment longer, as if gauging her commitment and character. Then he turned back to the others.

"Very well. Let me say first, that this represents a momentous occasion. This is the first time that the entire Sextuaget has ever been physically gathered in one location. The fact that we are meeting in person for the first time aboard this station is significant. No one single power block stands out among the other. Each of you are equal. In this room are gathered the great powers of the world. Let the dictators, the party chairman, the kings, and the elected officials continue in their self delusion that they are in power. The real authority lies here with you and your own "inner circles." Brennon swept his gaze across each member of the Sextuaget.

"Make no mistake," he continued, his voice conveying the power he wielded, "Each of you has been groomed and trained for the position you now hold. Each of you, and the people you command, is vital to ushering in the new world order." Here he paused.

"However," and his voice took on a menacing note, one of barely veiled threat, "You are not irreplaceable. Let the lesson of Jacob Hill serve to remind you of that. Thanks to his incompetence, our plans have suffered a minor setback. Failure will not be tolerated." With that, Brennon touched a control in front of him, and the large view screen on the wall behind him came to life. It took Christine a moment to realize what she was seeing, then her heart began to thud heavily in her chest. There in front of her was a large white room containing six large, man-sized clear cylinders. They were about seven feet in length and were lying horizontally. Each was filled with a blue liquid that had the consistency of gelatin. She knew it for what it was — an interrogation chamber. A person was placed into the cylinder, which was then filled with the blue liquid. The liquid was an oxygenized, nutrient solution that could sustain life indefinitely. Once the subject was placed inside, probes previously inserted into his or her brain were activated. The subject could be made to see and feel anything the interrogator desired. The results could be translated to video and played on any monitor. The subjects very thoughts could be watched. No secrets could be kept from the interrogator. The only catch — a patient went in, but did not come out. To this date, no one had survived even limited exposure.

As Christine watched the monitor, the technicians drained one of the cylinders and pulled out a body. The camera zoomed in to the face of the victim. The look of pure horror frozen permanently on the face made it difficult to identify who it might have been, but Christine knew it anyway. It was the face of Jacob Hill. Judging from his features, his end had been unspeakable. This man had been her leader. She had been part of his inner circle, and he, in turn, had been part of the Sextuaget. This man had literally run the United States. Now, he was just another body.

"I trust this lesson will be taken to heart by all of you," said Brennon, switching off the monitor and turning back to face everyone. "Failure will *not* be tolerated, no matter what the excuse." He paused for a moment. "Cyclops!"

"Yes sir." The cultured male voice of Brennon's master computer system came from the speakers set into the ceiling of the conference room.

"Display Brennon Alpha," replied Brennon. Christine suppressed a smile. Cyclops was a work of genius. For years, rumors of a giant "super computer" had popped up again and again. Depending on who you listened to, it was either buried under the Vatican or orbiting the earth. The truth was far more astounding. Cyclops was a conglomeration of *many* separate systems, linked together across the globe. As such, he could never be shut down. Brennon had given him a personality that made him seem human — at times *too* human.

In obedience to Brennon's command, Cyclops immediately activated the monitor, showing a computerized graph. The white grid glowed vividly in the dim room. A series of blue, red, and green lines ran horizontally across the grid, stretching from the beginning to almost the end.

"This, as you are all aware, represents our overall plan," said Brennon. "Obviously, it is almost complete. Centuries of work and planning have gone in to it. We stand at the brink of a new age on the earth, one that can scarcely be imagined by humanity. An age of peace, prosperity, and a united world government. All that remains is to put the final pieces into place." He switched off the graph and again turned to regard the Sextuaget.

"Christine," he said, bringing those riveting eyes to rest on his newest member, "We will start with you. Please make your report."

Surprised, Christine struggled not to appear nervous. Suddenly she felt every eye in the room on her. She started to stand, then remembered her weightless condition. Clearing her throat, she began.

"As you said, sir, we have suffered a setback." She fought to keep her voice level and emotionless. "The Mentasys affair, and the awkward mess with Senator Jack Kline, not to mention the bombing of Flight 407, brought to light too many of our activities. As a result, the Bureau of Religious Affairs, our "muscle," so to speak, has been discredited and severely limited in its activities. There was even talk of easing off government control of organized religion. Fortunately, we own too many key Washington figures for that to happen. Also, we have been able to place the blame for everything else squarely on Jacob Hill's shoulders. We have successfully painted him as a power mad schemer with delusions of government control."

"And the underground churches that Jacob tried so hard to stamp out?" asked Brennon, his voice soft, yet demanding.

"They still exist, sir," said Christine, her nervousness growing. "We have destroyed hundreds, but they still keep popping up." For a moment, she hesitated, dreading to give this next piece of news. There was no avoiding it, however. "This so called 'Shepherd's Path,' that links and unites them is also still in operation. We are in the process of hunting down the leaders, but they still function. As for the political area. . . ."

"Christine," said Brennon, his voice rising ever so slightly, "Understand that the church is not a 'minor irritant.' It must be your top priority to destroy it. It is the one thing that stands in our way. Disregard the bureau and deal with it directly if you have to, but eliminate it. Do I make myself clear?"

Lips pressed tightly together, Christine nodded.

"Very well," nodded Brennon. "Please continue."

"In the political arena," she said, "Everything is on schedule. The United States is financially stretched as far as it can go. Another monetary disaster like the banking industry collapse four years ago will plunge the country into a major depression that it cannot recover from. There will be only two courses of action possible. First is government seizure of private holdings. This will move the nation closer to a totalitarian rule. Second, the U.S. will have to join the United European market. Already several key people are pushing for this. At your command, the necessary steps will be taken to begin the depression.

"And the implants?" asked Brennon.

"Many are already in place. The rest will be ready by the end of the year." She paused, gathering her thoughts. "I would like to implant a few underground church members we apprehend," she began. "If we could gain control of their minds directly, we could. . . ."

"Absolutely not." Brennon's voice did not raise in pitch or volume, but his tone lashed at Christine. "Understand this, all of you." And here he addressed the entire Sextuaget. "No one professing to be a believer is to be implanted. That is final. Do I make myself clear?" Everyone, including Christine, nodded.

"Now," he continued, "The stage is being set for our final victory. Again let me warn you, Christine, destroy the Church. I will accept no excuses if this is not accomplished. That is your priority. Do you understand?" Christine merely nodded, and Brennon turned to the African member of the conclave, asking for his report. Inwardly she sighed, relieved to have those dark eyes off of her. She thought about the steps she would have to take to accomplish Brennon's demands.

She would start with stepping up Wolf's activities. That would be a beginning. Threats made to random families, bribes to the greedy, all would help. Still, she needed a break. She needed someone who could track down and destroy the "Shepherd's Path." True, that would not destroy the underground church, but it would certainly put a dent in their activities.

As the meeting went on, she searched her mind for a solution. There had to be a way to bring these people under control. It was maddening, in a way. Before the government crack down, Christianity had consisted of a lazy, barely committed bunch of hypocrites. Now that it was deadly to be a believer, they seemed to be thriving. It did not make sense! Fools who, 10 years ago, hardly ever attended church now risked their lives to meet secretly. When caught, they stood proudly before judges and interrogators and reaffirmed their faith in a man who had been dead for 2,000 years. Madness!

One thing was for certain. Christine had better find a solution to this, and in a hurry. Brennon would not tolerate failure, and delays only made him angry. She had no desire to see those eyes turned on her in anger. She had better think of something soon, or Jacob Hill's fate would be her own. With a feeling of gloom settling over her, she turned her attention back to the meeting. All in all, she decided, it had not been a very good day.

1

Paul Sinclair slumped dejectedly in his uncomfortable plastic chair and studied his tiny office cubicle. The cubical itself was devoid of any personality or warmth. It was a clone, a drab piece of sameness that blended in to obscurity next to its neighbors. Plain gray chest-high partitions made up its walls, and the dull gray carpet was wearing thin on the floor. It contained only a small desk, computer terminal, vid-phone, and a few plastic chairs, differing little from its many brethren. It was one of 20 squeezed into a medium-sized room that served as offices to the operatives of Davis and Ross, one of the largest and best-known investigative agencies in the greater Cincinnati area.

Just in from an excruciating day of useless leg work on his current case, Paul stared into the imperfect infinity of the featureless partition. He twiddled a pencil in his right hand while his left beat an abstract rhythm on the desk top. Eyes wandering, his attention came to rest on a small coffee stain caused yesterday by the agent using the cubical next to him. The stain marred the otherwise perfect grayness, making everything a little less bland. For some odd reason, that irritated him. Bland was the order of his life these days. It was only fitting that his "office" should reflect that.

Unconsciously, he gritted his teeth. How far he had fallen! Four months ago, he was the hottest, sharpest agent the Bureau of Religious Affairs could boast of. He had had a staff, his own office, an official government vehicle, and a great deal of influence. Now, this depressingly tiny cubical was it. He was one of many faceless names that worked for Davis and Ross. How could so much have happened in so short a time?

"Sinclair!" The high-pitched, nasal voice worked a remarkable change in Paul. Instantly, his back went ramrod straight and his jaw clenched even tighter. The pencil he was holding snapped like a dry twig. Over the partition in front of his desk appeared the mouseish face of his boss, Wesley Blaine.

"What's the matter, hotshot?" mocked Blaine. "You too good to report in to your supervisor when you get back? I know it's only standard procedure, but we lowlifes would all appreciate it if your high and mightiness would follow the rules." Blaine's last three words were spat out in a hiss. There was no love lost between the two men. It had been instant hatred from the start. Blaine considered Paul an arrogant, conceited snob, while to Paul, Blaine was the quintessential wimp. Even his name sounded wimpy. Wesley? What kind of name was that for a private investigator? The fact that Blaine was several years younger than him did little to help. Paul took a deep breath and forced himself to answer in an even tone, "I haven't reported in because there is nothing to report. I spent the afternoon questioning supposed witnesses, and everyone of them had the same line — "Go talk to somebody else." Paul's calm, sarcastic tone caused Blaine's cheeks to flush slightly.

"Mrs. Whitney is paying us good money to prove that her husband is having an affair," he shot back. *"We* are paying you good money to do just that. You prove it by investigating, get it? You're a private investigator." He spread his hands in mock wonderment. "What a concept! A private investigator. So, Mr. Hotshot Investigator, investigate!"

That did it. Boss or no boss, *nobody* spoke to Paul Sinclair in that manner. "I investigated," he snapped back. Unconsciously, his body assumed an aggressive stance. If one of his old staff members had been present, they would have warned Wesley to back off. Even seated, Paul was easily capable of killing the smaller man with a single blow. "I'll even give you the results in one syllable words, so you can understand," he continued, practically spitting out the words. He sounded something like a tommy gun with a stutter. "I talked to every man, woman, and child that Whitney has had contact with the past year. I have followed the man for two solid weeks, and he hasn't strayed once. I think Mrs. Whitney is wrong. You want my report? That's it. She's wrong. End of report." With that, Paul folded his arms and looked back defiantly at Blaine. He didn't think it possible for the man to get any madder, but Blaine accomplished it. As he watched, Blaine's face went from pink to bright cherry red. Paul found himself perversely enjoying the show.

"That does it," growled Blaine through clenched teeth. "You're out of here. I don't care if I have to go all the way to Mr. Davis himself." He pointed a shaky finger at Paul. "The only thing that's kept you here is the fact that you are a halfway decent operative, but that won't cut it any more. I want you gone. Count on it, Mr. Bureau Hotshot. Mark it on your calendar. By the end of the week, you'll be history." With that, Blaine turned and stormed off.

Paul stared at the top of the partition for just a moment. He knew that, this time, Blaine meant it. More than that, he might just be able to pull it off. He was certainly mad enough to try. Paul had finally pushed him too far.

"Blast," he snarled under his breath. Had it come to this? Was he going to have to kiss up to Blaine so he could keep the only job he had been able to find?

Four months ago, he had been at the top of his profession. He was the best. Expert investigator, third degree black belt martial artist, a working knowledge in physical and computer sciences — he had everything going for him. Then things had started to go wrong.

It had begun with that bust at the furniture store. He had let two people slip through his fingers. Scott and Beth Sampson — those names were burned forever into his mind. How could two insignificant people could cause him so much grief? Because he had not caught them, the lid had been blown off of bureau activities. Beth had shown up in some kind of futuristic torture chamber called "Mentasys" out in Los Angeles. If that wasn't bad enough, Scott, along with a former FBI man and a turncoat bureau agent, had rescued her. Then the agent, Stephen Lynch, had gone right to the media. The resulting outcry had almost shut the bureau down. Massive firings occurred, and Paul was one of the victims. Overnight he had gone from key personnel to unemployed.

For two months he had kicked around the country, trying to find work, but suddenly, former bureau agents seemed to have the plague. No one was hiring. Then, he had hit upon a plan. He would return to the place where all his troubles had started. Perhaps he could pick up the pieces of his shattered life there. Pounding the pavement in Cincinnati, he had finally found work at Davis and Ross. It was on the lowest rung of a large company, but it was a paycheck. It also gave him the resources to pursue his own investigation — one that would get him back in good with the bureau and put him back on top. Of course, being fired would put a major crimp in his plan.

Paul let out a slow sigh that sounded like steam escaping from a boiler. Shaking his head at his own folly, he quietly allowed the tension to drain from his body. Carefully he allowed himself to relax. His anger shifted from Blaine to himself. Why couldn't he just play by the rules? Would it kill him to simply do his job and let that be that? Now, if he couldn't calm Blaine, he would have to start over somewhere else, although it was doubtful that anyone would hire him after this fiasco.

Massaging his temples to soothe the coming headache, he turned to his terminal. *Might as well enter my official report on the Whitney case,* he thought. *No sense in leaving loose ends.* He started to type, then noticed the small, flashing icon in the top right corner. For a moment he blinked in confusion, then took a sharp breath. The tension he had released was suddenly back, and in spades. Something was demanding his attention — something important. The search program he had covertly entered into the agency's computer net was displaying its "Hey, I have something interesting" signal. He had set it up within a week of being hired, but this was the first time it had flagged his attention. It was programmed to scan both federal and state government networks for anything related to the raid on the furniture store. Evidently it had finally found something. Eagerly he punched in his identification code and accessed the proper program. There was less than half a second's delay, then the information flashed on the screen.

"All right!" he whispered fiercely. One of the church members he had arrested in that raid had finally surfaced. Since the bust, everyone in that little group had disappeared so completely, it was if they had never existed. He knew that many had been shipped out to Los Angeles for further interrogation, but had not been able to track any of them down. Now, finally, the computer had located one of them. "Susan Ferguson," he read to himself. He toggled a button and her picture and biography appeared before him. He recognized her instantly from the arrest. Blonde, pretty, good figure — she had been the one the sergeant had taken a special interest in. Carefully he scanned her recent history. It was not a pretty sight. Just 24 hours ago, she had been admitted to the psychiatric ward of a state-run hospital in Sacramento. Someone claiming to be her uncle had left her there, then had disappeared.

Paul frowned as he read her diagnosis. The physician in charge described her as traumatized . . . almost catatonic. According to her bio, she was close to being a vegetable. He toggled another key, and a current picture replaced the one already on the screen.

"Good Lord," whispered Paul, staring at the image. She was unrecognizable. Her once long blond hair was cut short, in a butch style. Her eyes were sunken and hollow, and her face had lost any trace of life. She lay in a hospital bed, curled into a fetal position. Judging from the thinness of her arms, she could not have weighed more than 90 pounds.

Additional information flashed on the screen. Her husband, Timothy, was listed as deceased, and she had no other living relatives. Her whereabouts for the past six months were "unknown." Understandable, thought Paul. Chances were that she and her husband had ended up at Mentasys. That would have been right before everything fell apart. When the FBI raided the place Susan was probably secretly evacuated. Her husband was either already dead or else killed outright. Since Susan, in her current condition, was no danger to the people behind Mentasys, she was dumped into a state-run hospital and left there to eventually die. Judging from the picture before him, that would not take too long.

Paul sat and stared at the screen for several minutes, thinking hard. Was it possible that she could be of use, he wondered? He had to admit that it did not look promising. Frankly, he did not care one whit for Susan

Ferguson's condition. She was a possible tool, nothing more. At this point in his life, he had but one goal — to regain all that he had lost. To do that, he would have to pull off a major coup.

It was no secret that there were hundreds, maybe thousands, of underground churches in the country. Their existence was inevitable, given the fact that religion was under tight government control. What was not common knowledge, however, was the existence of some sort of network that linked many of these churches. He had gotten wind of it just before the Mentasys incident. A group of people, calling themselves the Shepherd's Path had banded together to link hundreds of these underground cells of dissidents. From what he had heard, they did everything from move church members across the country to safer locations to provide the local groups with banned literature, Bibles, and so forth. Some likened it to the underground railroad used during the Civil War to transport slaves to freedom.

It was also Paul's ticket back to the big time. If he could infiltrate the Shepherd's Path, discover who its leaders were, and find out how it operated, he would not only get his old job back, but he could have his choice of assignments. The entire bureau, under the direction of the powerful Jacob Hill, had not been able to break up this network. If he could pull it off, he would be a hero!

There was only one problem. The people behind the Shepherd's Path knew what they were doing. They were smart and crafty, and could operate under the collective noses of the different branches of federal law enforcement. There were no leads at all — until now.

Paul chewed the inside of his lip absently. Susan Ferguson was the first break of any kind he had come across in four months of searching. The question was, was it worth pursuing? She had been in the hands of the Bureau of Religious Affairs, and they had discarded her. True, it had obviously been in a hurry. They may not have had time to thoroughly interrogate her. Even if they did, she might not have any relevant information. Then again, he thought, she could be his ticket into the Shepherd's Path.

At the moment, he had just enough money stashed away to buy a one-way ticket to Sacramento. That was the extent of his resources, and it was not even close to being adequate. To pull this off, he would have to have backing — lots of it. The only place he knew where to get it was the Bureau of Religious Affairs. True, it did not have the power and influence it once had, but if he could reach the right people. . . .

Paul's neck suddenly cramped from sitting too long and he stood. As he stretched his tired muscles, he glanced around the room. It was full of private agents, all going about their business. Divorces, child custody cases, blackmail — the normal, everyday poison that humanity inflicted on itself. Across the room, he saw Blaine conferring with another agent. For just an instant, Blaine looked in his direction. Their eyes met, then Blaine turned away, but not before Paul caught the smug, self-satisfied look he tried to hide. That did it. He was probably out of here anyway. Might as well try to end it on his own terms.

Sitting back down, he ordered his terminal to print out the information on the Ferguson woman. While that was happening, he activated his vid-phone and punched a certain number, one that he had not used in six months. The screen of the phone lit up in a test pattern, while a feminine voice answered. The video was being blocked from the other end.

"Bureau Of Religious Affairs," said the flat, unemotional voice.

"Kyle Donavan," replied Paul shortly.

"I'm sorry, but Mr. Donavan is in a meeting. May I take a message?"

"Just tell him that the Master wants to talk to him — immediately." He held his breath, hoping that whoever it was would relay the message and not hang up.

"Just a moment," was the short reply. Impatiently, Paul waited. So many things could stop him this early in his gambit. If Donavan . . . abruptly the screen cleared and the man himself stared back at him. Kyle Donavan was an older man. The deep lines in his face hinted of the harshness of his life.

A veteran of two wars, Donavan was a hard man. He demanded absolute dedication from his people, and drove them mercilessly. Since the death of his son from AIDS II five years ago, and the subsequent suicide of his wife, he had poured his life into the bureau. He was one of the lucky ones who had survived the recent purging. Just now, he was looking at Paul with something akin to amazement.

"Sinclair? What the deuce are you doing calling me, and using your old code name to boot? That alone is enough to get your butt hauled in for questioning." Paul allowed himself a thin smile. At least this man had not changed!

"Good to see you too, Kyle," he replied dryly. Donavan frowned at the familiar way Paul addressed him. When Paul was with the bureau, they were equals, able to deal with each other on a first name basis. Now, as far as Kyle was concerned, Paul was a nobody.

"This had better be good, Sinclair," said Donavan flatly. Paul recognized the coldness of his tone and swallowed. Paul had been a ruthless agent, squashing traitorous churches with a kind of gusto and joy. Donavan, on the other hand, did his job with no emotion, no feeling. To him, those he relentlessly pursued were "non-people." They were to be eliminated, period. It made him a very efficient, but also a very dangerous man.

"I think it may be," said Paul. "I've got a lead on this Shepherd's Path your people have been trying to break up for the past few months." At that, Donavan's eyes actually widened a fraction of an inch.

"Okay," he nodded, "give. If it pans out, I'll see what I can do for you." Paul shook his head negatively.

"No way, Kyle," he said, matching Donavan's flat tone. He had no delusions about the man in front of him. If he gave Donavan his ideas, he would take them for his own, and Paul would not hear from him again. "This one's mine — completely. I'll give you the whole package nice and neat, but the bust is mine." Donavan regarded him with a shark's eyes.

"Mighty big talk from a 'has been,' " he remarked, putting a slight sneer into his voice. Carefully Paul controlled the look on his face. He did not want Kyle to see how much that remark had stung. "Have you forgotten that you are no longer bureau personnel?" he continued harshly. "In fact, you are," and here he paused to look at something off screen, "a third-rate private investigator for some local yokel company there in Cincinnati. You don't have the authority. . . ."

"And I don't have the time," interrupted Paul savagely. "I didn't call to talk to you, Donavan. I want you to relay a message." Donavan's face went completely blank. Paul knew that inside the man was seething. For just a moment fear settled into his stomach. He was pushing hard, maybe too hard, but he had gone too far to back out now. "Tell whoever is running the bureau now that I can give them the Shepherd's Path on a silver platter, but I'll need bureau backing. An expense account, travel priorities, security clearance, the works. I'll need an answer within two hours. You can reach me at station 555-4432. Its an audio line only, but I'll be the only one answering." He paused and regarded Donavan, mentally holding his breath.

"Mighty big talk," Donavan repeated after a moment. He regarded Paul with his lifeless eyes. "Think you can do it?"

"Yes." Paul's answer left no room for doubt.

"All right, Sinclair," said Donavan after another lengthy pause. "I'll deliver your message. You might even get what you ask for, but know this, my friend." Donavan leaned forward, emphasizing each word. "If you blow it, you are mine. I will personally see to it that you wish you had never started this. Understand?"

"Understood," replied Paul. He could not resist a final jab. "Better be nice to me Kyle. When this is over, I could end up being your boss!" With something akin to a snarl, Donavan broke the connection. For just a moment Paul sat there and stared at the blank screen, marveling at his unsettling ability to make the wrong people angry at him. Then he gathered what few personal belongings he had, piled them into his briefcase, and headed toward the door. His former depression gave way to a happy determination. He finally had a purpose, and was starting to feel very, very good. This was the break he had been working so hard to find. He was sure he could make it pay off.

"Hey big shot! Who told you you could leave?" Blaine's voice sounded across the crowded office. Paul stopped short, hiding a smile. He had been hoping that something like this would happen. Blaine came storming up to stand less than 12 inches from his face. The fact that he was a good head shorter than Paul did not seem to bother him. He was too full of his own self-importance.

"Where do you think you are going, Sinclair?" he asked belligerently, hands on hips.

"Out," replied Paul shortly.

"Wrong answer, mister," snapped Blaine, leaning forward. "As of now, you are on probation, pending a full personnel evaluation. You don't go anywhere without my say so. Got it?"

Paul couldn't help himself. His hidden smile turned into a full-fledged grin. That alone caused Blaine to back up half a step. Unfortunately, he didn't back up far enough. To the utter dismay of his former colleagues, Paul was a devoted Three Stooges fan. Anyone who had the misfortune of spending an evening with him usually ended up seated in front of the vidscreen watching 80-year-old reruns of the slapstick trio. They came to Paul's mind now, much to Blaine's misfortune. Paul's hand shot out and grabbed Blaine's nose between the thumb and forefinger. With an even bigger smile, he began to squeeze.

"OWWW!" screamed Blaine in surprise and pain. "Let go, Sinclair!" His hands flew up, desperately trying to dislodge Paul's grip, to no avail. Paul was far to strong for him. Casually, Paul watched as Blaine twisted, trying to free himself. It had suddenly grown quiet in the office, and he realized that he had an audience. Fair enough. With the practiced ease of a master, he swung his leg in a low, roundhouse kick, at the same time releasing his hold on Blaine's nose. Blaine's legs were swept out from under him and he sat down — hard.

"Offff." The grunt slipped involuntarily from Blaine's lungs. He sat there, not quite believing what had just happened.

"Consider this my letter of resignation," Paul said to his former supervisor. He went on with mock formality. "I have enjoyed my time at Davis and Ross immensely, but feel that it is now time for me to move on. I wish you every success in the future, and thank you for the privilege of working here. Sincerely, Paul Sinclair." With that, he turned and once more headed for the door.

Abruptly, the other employees watching the scene play itself out broke out in applause. It surprised Paul for a moment. He had never realized that Blaine would be as unpopular with them as he was with him. Evidently Blaine's office tyranny had alienated most of the staff. He turned back, letting his eyes cross the room. He had never gotten to know any of them, except by name. Surprisingly, he found himself regretting that fact. There might have been friends here. Now he would never know. Like a performer who had just finished his act, he raised an arm, accepting the ovation. Then, for a final time, he turned toward the door. Blaine was now on his feet, shaking in anger, and maybe just a little fear.

"I'll get you for this, Sinclair!" he screamed shrilly at the top of his lungs. "You're nothing — a useless has-been! I'll put out a report on you so bad that no one will hire you!"

"Please don't say it," Paul pleaded under his breath as he continued to walk. "Surely even you would have more class than to say what I think you're going to say."

"I'll see you in court, big shot!" Blaine continued, screaming at Paul's retreating back. "I'll have you up on assault charges so quick you won't get out of the building!"

Maybe he isn't going to say it, Paul thought with relief. *Maybe I misjudged him.*

"YOU'LL NEVER WORK IN THIS TOWN AGAIN!!!"

That did it! Paul could no longer contain himself. He broke out into the biggest belly laugh he had had in years. He could not remember when he had laughed so hard. For a moment, he actually could not get his breath and had to lean against the door. Blaine just stood there, unable to say anything else. The ridiculous look he had on his face caused Paul to laugh even harder. It was contagious. An embarrassed titter escaped from somewhere in the back of the room, followed by a loud guffaw. Soon the whole room was laughing at little Wesley Blaine, who stood there in utter disbelief. Feeling like a victorious gladiator, Paul waved at his admiring audience and left the offices of Davis and Ross Investigations forever.

* * *

It took Paul just a little over an hour to reach his run-down, one-room efficiency apartment across the Ohio River in downtown Covington. There were few worse places he could have chosen to live. Business was practically non-existent, and the entire area was given over to a combination of gangs, transients, and the homeless. Most of the buildings, including the one he lived in, were fire hazards, and it would take only one arsonist's fire bomb to set the whole block ablaze.

Paul swung down off the rickety bus that was now his only transportation (he had been using an agency car). Wrapping his overcoat tightly around him against the biting November wind, he walked the few hundred feet to his building. Across the street a few members of the Butta Heads, a local Chinese gang, eyed him warily. He had run into them a few months back, when they had demanded "insurance money" from him in exchange for protection. Paul had merely smiled at them, then had proceeded to break an assortment of bones, mainly arms and legs. They might be tough, but Paul was the result of years of intensive physical training. Now they left him alone, although he was sure that it was a temporary truce. When they felt brave enough, or got stoned enough, they would try again. No matter. If things worked out, he would be out of this dump by the week's end. Cheerfully he waved at the gang members as he entered the front door to his building.

Thirty years ago the Carson Arms might have been called "quaint." A three-story brownstone, it would have been the type of place a doctor or lawyer might have lived in order to be close to his practice. Now it was a death trap. Rotted wooden stairs and paneling were just waiting to go up in flames. The aged mortar that held the bricks together was crumbling, and in some places had disappeared entirely. As he made his way up the stairs to his second-floor dwelling, he winced at the stench of human waste that seemed to cling to everything. The plumbing was of so little use as to be practically non-existent. His fellow residents had long ago given up any kind of hope of a better life. Now they either preyed upon those who were even less fortunate, or were themselves preyed upon. Chances were that one of them would wake up tomorrow morning dead.

If Paul Sinclair had been a caring man, he might have felt something for his neighbors. Such feelings, however, had long ago been locked away, buried so deep inside of him that it was unlikely that they would ever resurface. The only thing he cared about was getting out of this place once and for all. He wanted his old job back with the bureau. More important, he wanted to be back among his own "kind." He considered himself to be as far above this human refuse as humanity was above the cockroach.

He reached the door to his apartment and fished out his keys. Before entering, he peered carefully over his head. The single human hair, held in place by his own dried spittle, was still there, resting delicately between the door and the frame. No one had entered during his absence. It was a crude method of detection, but effective.

His apartment was just as he had left it. If possible, it was even more depressing than his former office. Where his old cubicle had been merely sterile, this place reeked of decay. Peeling yellowed wallpaper covered the four stark walls. Above, moldy plaster barely held itself in place, while the plain wooden floor creaked dangerously as he stepped on it. A dozen roaches the size of his fist scattered in all directions as he entered. He had taken one of his few days off and tried to clean at least some of filth, but it was too firmly entrenched to be completely evicted.

There was no air conditioning, so even with the current cold spell, the place was stifling. He debated for a moment, then crossed over to the single window facing the street and pulled it open. The stench of the dying inner city was slightly less offensive than the stuffiness of the apartment. He stood there for a moment, shivering, and staring out over the rooftops across the street. The late afternoon sun cast impenetrable shadows across them, making them seem more desolate than the harshest desert. Just a few streets over was the furniture store that had signaled the beginning of all his troubles. It was the main reason he had chosen this location. He wanted a constant reminder of what he used to be.

Angrily he shut down his train of thought. Thinking about better days would only put him into a quiet rage. He would be unable to think clearly, and he needed all of his cunning for what lay ahead — assuming, of course, that he had managed to draw the attention of the right kind of people. Carefully, bringing his emotions under tight control, he shut the window and moved over to the barely-functioning refrigerator. He put his hand on the handle, then paused. The fact was, he was too keyed up to eat. Instead, he switched on the oversized space heater that sat on the floor next to the bed and set it on high. Then he moved the cheap plastic furniture that came with the apartment against the far wall. Breathing deeply, he began a series of stretching exercises designed to let the tension flow out of him. Gradually he loosened up and began to relax. After about 10 minutes, he began to feel focused. He had reached that state where, as he had been taught, mind and body were one. Sitting up in a cross-legged position, he entered into a light, self-induced trance. The sounds and smells that surrounded him faded into the background, and a sense of well-being flooded into him. He could remain like this for hours, if necessary.

Somewhere in the back of his mind he breathed a sigh of thanks to the Yogi Shah. It was he who had taught Paul the techniques of effective meditation, sitting with him for hours, guiding him in his quest for inner peace. Paul counted himself lucky indeed, for there was no doubt in his mind that the holy man had saved his life.

A memory tugged at the back of his mind, trying to force itself into his trance. Unconsciously, he gritted his teeth, suppressing it. He did not need to dwell upon the time his father had not come home from work. He did not need to remember how his mother had cried night after night, closeting herself in her room, leaving Paul and his sister to fend for themselves.

"Mommy, when is Daddy coming home? He promised to finish reading to me." Unbidden, the voice echoed in the back alleys of his mind.

It was the voice of a child, the voice of a stranger. It was his own voice when he was all of eight.

"Concentrate," he admonished himself out loud, banishing the voice. "You are in a beautiful meadow, walking up a hill." Gradually, the voice faded, and with it, the tiny shred of memory. With something akin to relief, he continued his mantra. "You come to a tree. Someone steps out from behind that tree. Who is it?" In his mind's eye, Paul could see everything clearly, as if he really were present in that beautiful meadow. He stood by his tree, waiting to see who would emerge. Sometimes it would be his sister, sometimes it was his mother. Once, it had even been his father. Paul would see them in sharp detail. To him, they were real. No words would be spoken, but when it was all over, he would feel better. Many times, he even felt another presence there beside him. He liked to believe that it was the spirit of the Yogi, still guiding him. It made him feel a little less lonely.

As Paul watched, a figure did indeed emerge. For a moment, he stared in surprise. The person before him was a stranger. At first, he was clouded and indistinct. Paul squinted, trying to pierce the shroud of darkness that seemed to surround the enigmatic figure. A sense of deep disquiet began to gnaw at him.

Suddenly, there was a blinding flash of light, as if lightning had struck nearby. For just an instant, the face became clear, and Paul began to scream. It wasn't the chiseled, Anglo-Saxon features that filled him with horror, nor the fact that the man was a total stranger. It was the eyes. Paul looked into those dark, deep-set eyes and saw his own death — a death that was not just final, but never ending. It was the death of his very being — his own soul.

Shaking uncontrollably, he stumbled away, down a hill that suddenly became stark and lifeless. The meadow was gone, replaced with brambles and thorns that crawled with unspeakable horrors. He ran, heedless of the danger, knowing in his soul that he could never outrun the stranger with death in his eyes. He stumbled and fell, crawling madly forward. Darkness settled over him. He opened his mouth for one final scream . . . and jerked back to full awareness, still seated cross-legged in his tiny apartment. He sat there, half-dazed, aware that he was sweating profusely. The apartment, which before had been merely stuffy, was now stifling. Gradually his heartbeat slowed, finally reaching a steady, hard "thump thump, thump thump." The sound thudded in his ears. He took a few deep breaths, trying to clear his head. Already the memory of the trance was fading, settling into the depths of his subconscious. The fear that had reared its terrifying head sank back into dormancy, waiting for another chance to come forward. Gingerly he rose and stretched to his full height. Tiny rivulets of sweat ran down his arms, cooling him. Without warning, he shivered violently.

"What . . ." he began out loud, but could not finish the thought.

Nothing like this had ever happened before, not even in the deepest of trances. Even as he concentrated he felt the memory of the whole episode slip away, leaving him feeling empty, and strangely enough, used. Once more he took a deep breath, expelling the negative energy.

"Stress," he said aloud to himself. "It's got to be stress." With that, he shrugged it off. He even allowed himself a little laugh. *What would the Yogi think of that,* he chuckled to himself. *Probably not much. He'd tell me to start over, and this time do it right.* For just a moment, Paul considered doing just that, but discarded the idea. There would be plenty of time later, when things got back to normal. With one last effort, he swept all of the negative feelings he had "under the rug." He could feel them lurking there, liked caged animals, but he could ignore them for now. He walked into the bathroom and pulled a semi-dry towel off the rack. Wiping off the remaining sweat, he came back into the living room. Between the events of the day and his botched attempt at meditation, it was understandable that when his phone buzzed, he nearly had a heart attack.

"Oh man, oh man, oh man," he whispered to himself fiercely, over and over. "Get it together, Sinclair, and fast." With his eyes shut tight and his jaw clenched, he forced himself to calm down. The phone rang twice, three times, then four before he finally felt ready for what was coming. He took a step forward, and carefully, as if it were a snake ready to strike, picked up the receiver.

"Sinclair," he said quietly, grateful that his voice did not crack.

"Your message was relayed," came a flat, male voice from the other end. "You think you can pull this off?" Paul did not recognize the voice.

"Yes," he answered, forcing himself to use the same flat monotone.

"You get one chance at this, Sinclair. You know the price of failure." Somewhere in his mind, Paul's sense of humor flared up. It helped to erase the remnants of fear left over.

How "cliché," he thought. Anger followed the humor. He did not like being talked down to like this.

"I only need one," he answered back, putting as much confidence into his voice as he could.

There was a pause, as if someone were sitting in judgment on him. "All right, you've got a shot. What do you need?"

Carefully, Paul explained his plan. He left out specific details, such as Susan Ferguson's name and current location. He was not about to let anyone take this away from him. There was silence on the other end of the line when he finished. Then the voice spoke once more.

"All right, its worth a shot. Give me this woman's name and where she's at, and we'll get her released into your custody."

"No," Paul said adamantly. "We do this my way. Just get me to

Sacramento and provide me with an expense account. For this to work, I've got to spring her myself. It's vital that she trust me implicitly. I'll need support and back-up, but other than that, leave me alone and let me do my job." Again there was a pause.

"Your job, Sinclair, is to get to the root of the Shepherd's Path." The voice now rose above a monotone, taking on a threatening tone. "Don't get cute, and don't get the idea that you're the only one who can do this. The fact is, you're completely expendable. It's the only reason you've got this chance. Blow it, and you're a dead man. Got it?"

"Yeah," snarled Paul, adding some menace of his own to his voice. "So how about that support?"

"I'll get you booked on a direct flight to Sacramento. Hang on." The line went silent for a few moments, then the voice was back. "All right, you've got two hours to get to the airport. It's Flight 411. Your ticket will be waiting at the check-in counter. A driver will be at your place in 45 minutes. He'll have a uni-card, cash, and instructions on how to contact me."

"Fine," Paul answered, impressed in spite of himself. A uni-card! Only a select few had them yet. It was literally a passport to just about anywhere. "I'll be waiting," he said, and moved to hang up the phone.

"One other thing," said the voice, stopping him with the receiver halfway down.

"Yes?" said Paul, bringing it back to his ear.

"You make regular reports to me. You miss calling in once, and the deal's off. Just once, bud. Remember that."

"I'll remember," replied Paul in the same tone. "How do I make contact? I'll need a communicator."

"Your driver will have all the details," came the reply. "As far as a communicator, forget it. They're only for official bureau personnel. You will have to use the Omninet." Paul frowned, not liking the sound of that. If he were to get into a jam, there would be no quick help. His contact seemed to sense his hesitation.

"Sorry, Sinclair, but you know the rules. For what it's worth, if you make this work, you'll get full reinstatement. That's what this is all about, isn't it?"

"That's my price," acknowledged Paul.

"Then enough talk. Get going."

"Just a second," said Paul. "What do I call you?"

"I'm surprised at you, Sinclair," replied the voice mockingly. "Haven't you guessed yet? I was famous enough a few months ago. Who else would the bureau trust with this?" There was a moment's silence. "Call me Wolf." With that, the line went dead.

Paul stood there, staring at the receiver he was still holding. Those last three words caused a thrill of fear to surge through him. It was an unaccustomed sensation, and he found that he did not like it much. He started to shiver, and this time, it had nothing to do with meditation or the cold.

* * *

Twelve hours later, Paul stood outside the Rollings State Mental Institution in Sacramento. It was a newer building, erected within the past five years. Very little distinguished it from the many other similar structures in the surrounding area. Like most constructions of the time, it was a glass and steel non-entity, without charm or character. Only the triangular sign at the entrance gave it any identity.

Paul stood patiently there at the entrance, watching. The temperature was in the eighties, a nice change from the frigid Midwest. Carefully he consulted the information he had been given at the start of his trip. According to it, Susan Ferguson was located on the fourth floor of the five-story building, in a high-security section. She was in a ward that held 18 other patients, ranging from hopelessly insane to mildly paranoid. She was allowed no visitors and had no privileges normally given to the better-behaved patients.

For the last time, Paul mentally reviewed the plan he had formed during the long flight. His task would be threefold. First, of course, was to get Susan out of the hospital without getting caught. Paul was reasonably sure that he could accomplish that. Although security here appeared to be relatively competent, he had beaten better. The other two parts of his plan were not as easy. Second would be to alert Rollings security to the escape — before he left the building, but too late for them to stop him. There had to be a commotion big enough to gain media attention.

Finally, he had to make sure that they knew, or thought they knew, who was responsible. That was vital. Evidence had to point to one of Susan Ferguson's co-conspirators, and yet could not outright implicate the Shepherd's Path. If he could sell the media on that, then he was sure that he would not have to contact the underground network. *They* would contact him. Once that happened, the battle was half-won. All he needed was a starting point, a beginning of a trail. When he got that, he would follow it to the ends of the earth, if necessary.

Taking a last look at the sheet of information the driver had provided him, he folded it neatly and placed it into his jacket pocket. It was time to go. He paused to glance at his reflection in the glass door, checking his hastily assembled disguise. A heavy fake mustache and dark glasses stared back at him. It would not do if he were to be recognized by local or federal agents. Checking to see if anyone was paying undue attention, he pushed through the double glass doors. A large reception desk stood directly in front of him, running the length of a two-story high lobby. It was manned by assorted nurses, orderlies, and a single receptionist. He pasted an "off the rack" smile on his face and moved forward. The receptionist, a rather plain looking middle-aged woman with dark hair and a look of permanent boredom, ignored him while she spoke on the vid-phone in front of her.

"I'm sorry, Mrs. Franklin," she was saying, "But Dr. Lykes' orders are specific. Your son is to have absolutely no visitors, including family members. Yes, I know that you are his mother, but once you admitted Roger into our care, you forfeited certain rights. He is now a ward of the state, and is in its care." A pause. "Mrs. Franklin, I'm afraid that you will have to take this up with Dr. Lykes. He *is* the physician in charge. Yes ma'am. I know that his fanatical belief in a supreme being is a serious aberration. I can assure you that he is getting the best of care. I'm sorry, but Dr. Lykes will have to answer those questions, and he cannot be reached until tomorrow morning. Yes ma'am. I'm sorry, but I have to disconnect. Goodbye." With a casual flick of her index finger, the receptionist terminated the conversation, leaving the unseen Mrs. Franklin to her own means. She busied herself with a stack of papers for a moment, with the self-important air of a polished bureaucrat, then shifted her dull look to Paul.

"May I help you?" she asked, her tone making it clear that she really did not want to.

"Can you tell me what room Susan Ferguson is in?" Paul replied evenly, assuming a casual pose. Without replying, the receptionist, whose name tag proclaimed her to be Miss Delmarco, consulted her computer terminal.

"I'm sorry," she replied, returning her attention to Paul, "But I cannot give out that information. Mrs. Ferguson is in a restricted ward and is not allowed visitors. May I ask your name, sir?" Her voice was barely civil.

"Paul Simpson," said Paul, using the name on his new identification. "I'm a friend of the family and just heard that she was here." Mrs. Delmarco's eyes narrowed in suspicion.

"Susan Ferguson is a ward of the state," she said, using the same phrase she had used on the unfortunate Mrs. Franklin. "That means, according to laws established in 1998, she *has* no family or friends other than what the state allows her. You will have to register with our office and undergo a thorough security check. That will take a minimum of 48 hours." Her frown increased. "I must warn you, however, that you still will probably not be allowed to see her. Dr. Schmitt has specified that she be allowed no visitors."

"Dr. Schmitt is the physician of record, then?" asked Paul, and received a nod of affirmation. "Where do I go to register?" he said. The receptionist pointed off to the left.

"Through that door, and down the hall. Third door on the left. Do you have your federal identification?" Paul pulled out his wallet and displayed his uni-card, a plastic enclosed identification that included a drivers license, credit card, bank card, and emergency medical information. The receptionist was suitably impressed.

Uni-cards were still relatively new. While they were common in the European Federation, the United States had just started using them. With it, Paul could travel to over 80 percent of the world and still have access to his bank account, credit rating, or emergency medical care. In time, each citizen would be required to carry one. The United States government, in fact, had set the end of next year as a deadline. By then, everyone would have to pass a rigid security check in order to receive their card. Without it, an individual would be unable to perform any kind of business transaction.

Rumor had it that the cards themselves were only a transition for something else. Paul had heard something about a computer micro chip that could be imprinted with the same information as the uni-card, placed under the skin, and read with any ordinary scanner. It would make printed money obsolete. For now, though, only an elite minority were allowed to have the uni-cards. Having one marked Paul as favored.

The receptionist nodded, now just a little more respectful. "That will do fine, sir," she said. Paul suppressed the mocking smile that threatened to leak out. Mrs. Delmarco was a true bureaucrat. Turning down her nose at anyone she considered beneath her, she was nevertheless cowed by someone who could get her into trouble. He replaced his wallet, and walked off, not bothering to acknowledge her change of character. Let her sweat awhile!

As soon as he passed through the indicated door, Paul lost his smile and replaced it with a look of intense concentration. He was now in the administration section of the hospital, where security was almost nonexistent. That would change as soon as he headed toward the more restricted areas. He had decided on a lightning strike rather than any hint at subtlety. The faster he worked, the greater the confusion, and the better the chances for success.

The layout of the hospital was relatively simple. An east and west wing stretched out in either direction. This hall ran all the way around the first floor, accessing various offices and examination rooms. With the exception of the security section, the other floors were identical. Setting a firm, "I know where I'm going" pace, Paul passed the office he had been directed to and headed toward the end of the hall where a set of swinging double doors barred his path. Without pausing, he pushed his way through and entered a section marked "employees only."

As he walked, he pulled out his uni-card and, using a small magnetic clip he had bought earlier, placed it on his shirt pocket. It wouldn't get him past even a cursory security check, but Paul knew that the average person would not even glance at it. He had considered obtaining a doctor's credentials for this little job, but had discarded the idea. Simplicity was his greatest ally. A confident stride, and an official-looking badge would get him where he needed to go.

Glancing into each room as he walked by, he finally found what he was looking for. A youngish-looking doctor stood alone in the center of an examination room, studying a clipboard. He barely looked up when Paul entered the room, then saw that this was someone he did not know.

"Can I help you?" he began, then noticed the uni-card on Paul's chest. "Hey! You can't be back here! This is for . . . ." He never finished. With the fluid, fast motion of a master choreographer, Paul flipped the door shut with one arm. With his other, he jabbed two stiff fingers into the solar plexus of the unfortunate doctor. Caught completely off guard, he fell back onto the examination table, gasping for breath. Paul did not hesitate. His attack would leave the doctor helpless for just a few minutes. Effortlessly, he grabbed his arms and swung him around. Putting his hand on the back of his neck, he forced the doctor's face down hard onto the table.

"Where is my sister?" he hissed, pressing hard. The doctor gasped for breath, not able to respond even if he knew the answer. Paul did not really want one, anyway. This was all for show. "Where is my spiritual sister?" he repeated. "Where is Susan Ferguson? I want her out of here." The doctor shook his head frantically, still unable to breath normally.

"Bah," spat Paul. "You are no help to me." With that, he struck the back of the man's neck just hard enough to cause unconsciousness. The doctor slumped limply against the table, and Paul let him slide to the floor. He regarded him critically. The man was considerably shorter than he was, but had a stocky build. The white medical jacket he wore should be a close enough fit.

Paul listened carefully to see if anyone had noticed his attack. Then he knelt and stripped off the jacket. Shouldering it on, he took a closer look at the examination room. Besides the table, there was a counter holding several medical instruments, and a small closet off to the side. Stepping over the inert form of the doctor, Paul opened the closet and smiled. There was just enough room to put one short, stocky doctor. It took just a few minutes to squeeze him inside. Then, making sure that the room showed no signs of struggle, he opened the door and headed down the hall in the same direction as before.

He had only gone a few yards when he came upon an elevator. A rather pretty woman in a white smock was there, standing in front of the doors, waiting. The stethoscope hanging casually around her neck marked her for a doctor. Holding his breath, Paul nodded and moved to stand beside her, making sure that she could not see the name identification tag on his stolen jacket. Chances were that she would know the doctor he had cold-cocked. The elevator arrived moments later. As the doors closed behind them, the woman eyed Paul critically.

"I don't think I know you," she said in an even voice. There was no trace of suspicion yet.

"Paul Simpson," replied Paul in the same tone. "I'm here from Children's, across town."

The doctor frowned.

"Strange place for a pediatrician to end up," she remarked, glancing up at the floor indicator.

Paul shrugged. "Don't really want to be here, myself," he said, putting a touch of frustration in his voice. "Evidently there's been some mix-up, and one of my patients has been referred here by mistake." The doctor's eyes widened.

"That's some mistake," she said, looking back at him.

"Yeah," said Paul. "Sixteen-year-old kid, stoned out of his mind on Black Ice. Highly schizophrenic. They brought him here by accident." He would have elaborated further on his lie, but the elevator bumped to a stop and the doors opened. The pretty doctor glanced at him, looking the question. He shook his head.

"Next floor," he said. For just a moment, a slight frown creased her forehead. Then it cleared and she smiled.

"Goodbye then, Doctor Simpson. Maybe I'll see you again some-time." She stepped off and Paul pushed the close button, careful to keep his badge turned away from her.

"Until then," he smiled as the doors shut. The elevator continued on its journey and he breathed a mental sigh of relief.

Less than 30 seconds later, he reached the next floor. The doors slid open and Paul found himself staring down at a standard security gate. One single guard sat at a gunmetal gray desk, in front of a transparent, dura-glass door. Although frail seeming, Paul knew that the door had a tensile strength that approached steel. Brute force was not going to work here.

Just on the other side was a chest-high counter that formed a cubical. It combined both a guard post and nurses station. A single orderly stood next to the two security guards that occupied it, chatting idly. Paul sized them up professionally. Competent but complacent was his assessment.

The guards in the cubicle, one male, the other female, did not even glance his way as he emerged from the elevator, their attention centered on the orderly. On either side of the door, a security camera monitored the entire area. He would have to put on a good show.

The man at the desk thumbed through a magazine, a slightly bored look on his face. If Paul moved fast enough. . . . Confidently, he stepped forward. He put his hand into his pocket, gripping the one piece of special equipment he had obtained for this job. As he approached, the guard at the desk looked up. His eyes flicked to Paul's face, and then to his badge. A puzzled look replaced the bored one for an instant, but that instant was all Paul needed. In one smooth motion, he pulled the object from his pocket, concealed in his palm, aimed and fired. The dart gun responded as it was designed to. The drugged projectile struck the guard's neck and instantly dissipated into his bloodstream. His back arched, then he slumped into his chair as the drug took effect. The entire incident had occurred so fast that the two guards on the other side of the door were only now turning to check out the new arrival.

"Open the door, now," said Paul in a low voice as he approached the desk. The guard, forced into compliance by the drug, obeyed. He reached over to the wall where the control to the door was placed. To confuse the security cameras, Paul held up his stolen ID, as if he were asking for admittance. The guard hit the control, and the door slid open with a soft whoosh. Paul pocketed his ID and stepped through.

"Hey!" exclaimed one guard, the female, starting to her feet, "You can't just walk in here like that, Harvey," she said, speaking to the sedate guard through a microphone. "Since when do you let someone through without clearing with us? You know the. . . ." It was all she had time to say. With an effortless, fluid motion, Paul shot her with the dart gun and she slumped back. Before the other guard or orderly could react or set off an alarm, he had tranquilized them as well.

"Remain here at your station," Paul ordered softly. "Do your jobs. When you see me again, open the door. Do you understand?"

"Yes," said the male guard, echoed by the other two. Paul, knowing that somewhere inside the building someone was monitoring this station, again presented his bogus ID, pretending to chat with the drugged guards. Then he glanced down at his clipboard, nodded to his victims, and headed down the adjoining hall. Casually he put the dart gun back into his jacket pocket. It was definitely handy to have around. Besides, the men who rescued the Sampson woman had used the same type of equipment — one more item to link him with the underground Christian movement.

Ignoring the wards that opened on either side of him, he headed toward the end of the hall. A wheelchair was parked haphazardly off to his right and he commandeered it. Pushing if before him, he glanced over his shoulder, back towards the station. Everyone was still there, sitting quietly.

He passed other nurses and doctors, none of whom gave him a second glance. If he had been cleared by security, then he was no concern of theirs. As he moved deeper and deeper into the high security section, the noises and smells of the place began to assault him. Wails of grief, sorrow, and rage resounded down the hall, echoing against the hard surfaces. The stench of human waste, barely covered by the ever-present hospital antiseptic smell, grew stronger. He had thought the stink of his old apartment was bad, but this was far worse. He passed single cells holding the violent, and could feel murderous eyes staring at him.

He had to hurry. It would not be too much longer until someone checked in at the security station. When they did, the area would be sealed off, along with any hope of escape. Finally, after an eternity, he reached the end to the hall and the ward he was seeking. Under a full head of steam, he pushed through the door. It was a typical hospital ward. Ten beds lined either side, only two of them empty. White walls and a white, tiled floor banished any character the room might have had. A single nurse stood there, reading the chart of the comatose patient on the bed in front of her. She looked up and saw Paul, her face registering surprise. Paul did not hesitate. There were no cameras in this particular ward, so he did not need to waste one of his few remaining precious darts. He started toward her. Somehow, she sensed the danger he represented. She backed away, her lips forming into a shout of warning or a scream of alarm. Whatever it was, she never finished it. Paul was not gentle—he could not afford to be. He shoved the wheelchair at her, catching her off guard. The wheelchair and the nurse crashed to the floor together, making much too loud a noise. Paul was on her instantly. A quick blow to the neck knocked her unconscious. Rolling her to the side, he righted the wheelchair and moved further into the ward.

It took him only seconds to locate the woman he had traveled so far to find. Susan Ferguson was lying curled into a fetal position in the last bed in the room. Paul parked the wheelchair at the foot of the bed and moved to the side, examining her. Despite what he knew he would find, despite what he had seen in the computer file back in Cincinnati, and despite even the professional coldness he had worked so hard to develop over the years, Paul was not prepared for what awaited him. If he had not known where to find her, he would never have recognized the woman lying there before him.

Susan lay on her side, a blank stare hanging haphazardly on her shrunken face. Dark, almost black circles ringed her eyes, and her once full blonde hair was cut short, matted and thinning. A thin dribble of saliva ran down the corner of her mouth. That, and the very slight rise and fall of the thin sheet covering her, were the only signs of life.

Quickly Paul stripped off the sheet, his jaw clenching. Her stick-like form could not have weighed more than 90 pounds. Effortlessly he scooped her up and carried her to the wheelchair. With an uncharacteristic gentleness he set her down. She was so frail that it would be easy to break a bone. Paul was no doctor, but he had had basic paramedic training. Everything he observed in the limp form of Susan Ferguson told him one thing — this woman did not have much longer to live.

Anger welled up inside of him, not from the way she had been treated, but from the fact that in this condition she would not be any use to him at all. He had sacrificed much on this gamble. Worse, his own freedom was now contingent on his success. If he could not find a way to bring her out of this stupor, then he would have lost everything.

Grimly, he shoved thoughts of failure out of his mind. The priority at this moment was to get her out of the hospital. Then he would worry about the rest. He knew, in fact, that there might not even be a "rest" to worry about. His planned escape route was not easy. It was possible that this frail human being would not survive.

Slowly, but with increasing speed, he began to wheel Susan out of the ward. He reached the hall and began the long trek toward the security station. Now that he was accompanied by a patient, he was beginning to draw unwanted stares. Doctors and nurses looked up as he passed by other wards. Soon, someone would start asking dangerous questions. With an effort of will, he forced himself to maintain a slow, steady pace.

"Excuse me, doctor," said a voice from behind him, "but could I see your authorization for removing that patient from. . . ." Swiftly, Paul pulled out the dart gun and shot the nurse that had appeared from the ward he had just passed.

"Go back to your duties," he said in a commanding voice, and she disappeared back inside. Now Paul did quicken his pace. He glanced over his shoulder and saw a doctor staring at his back step into the ward the nurse had just entered. The game was up. Now it would be a race against the Rolling's security staff. Just as he heard a shout behind him, he reached the security station. Everything was as he had left it.

"Open the door," he said to the female guard.

"The door must be opened from the outside," she replied in a dull monotone. Paul cursed at himself for not realizing this earlier. Of course the door would be designed to keep patients out, not doctors in. Ignoring the running footsteps behind him, he moved to stand beside the transparent door.

"Open the door," he repeated to the guard at the desk. Immediately the drugged guard obeyed. Once again the door swished open, just as the running footsteps thudded to a halt behind him.

"Shut that door," said the frantic voice of the doctor Paul had seen a few seconds ago. "Seal off this area...." Paul's leg lashed out in a hard kick that caught the unfortunate doctor in the ribs. This was not the time for finesse, Paul decided. He felt something give under the doctor's jacket. The unmistakable crunching of bones was heard, and the doctor dropped to the floor, crying in pain.

"Stop!" Paul shouted at the guards. The disadvantage of the drug he had injected them with was that they would obey any voice unless otherwise instructed. The guard froze, and Paul grabbed the wheelchair and pushed it through the door. Now other staff members were beginning to emerge from the hall, running toward him. He was almost out of time. Halting on the other side, he turned and grabbed the dazed guard by the collar. Yanking hard, he pulled him down onto the floor. Quickly he hit the button that would shut the door. Then, focusing his energy, he drew his hand back to striking position. He took a moment to center himself, then let fly. The door control crunched beneath the flat of his palm. It was too strong to give way with just one blow, but enough damage was done to insure that no one would be following from that direction for at least several minutes. Now all he had to worry about was the rest of the hospital.

Three quick steps brought him to the elevator. Ignoring the pounding on the door behind him, he punched the button, summoning it. The lights above indicated that it was on the ground floor, and would take a few moments to reach him, moments he could put to good use. Forcing himself to remain calm, he moved Susan carefully out of the way. Then, he hopped onto the desk. Grabbing the camera with both hands, he twisted hard. It held for a moment, then gave way and came off its mount. Throwing it aside, he jumped back down. Security was now blind, as far as his next few movements were concerned.

Taking deep, energizing breaths, he faced the elevator, knowing that he would have to move hard and fast as soon as the doors opened. He watched as the floor indicator moved steadily and inexorably closer. There was a soft "ding," and the doors slid open. Paul jumped forward, right into the center of the four guards who had responded to his intrusion. They were caught unprepared. They had been expecting a fleeing foe, not someone on the attack. They were fairly well-trained, but none of them was a match for Paul. Within moments, they were all down. Breathing hard now from the exertion, Paul dragged them out next to the security desk. Then he retrieved the wheelchair containing Susan and got back into the elevator. By now, others would be coming, probably from the emergency stairs off to the left. Knowing that those pursuing would be expecting him to head for the nearest exit, he punched the button for the top floor.

As soon as the doors closed, he straightened his jacket and finger combed his hair. It would take only minutes for the alarm to spread through the entire building, but he could use those minutes to his advantage. Within seconds he reached the top floor. Once more the elevator doors slid open, and he found himself facing a crowd of worried, anxious staff members. So, the alarm had spread to this level after all. He had only one hope. He knew that pure brass, of the non-metallic variety, could often get one further than the most impressive credentials. Without hesitation, he pushed the wheel-chair containing Susan forward.

"Get somebody down to the security level now!" he snapped, moving away from the elevator. The nearest person to him, a male orderly, looked back in confusion. "What?"

"Get somebody down there, now!" shouted Paul, raising his voice and using his command tone. "Some idiot has just tried to break a patient out of ward six. The guards are trapped behind the security door. They're sending reinforcements from downstairs, but they need help with the patients. This mess has got them all stirred up. Now move! I've got to get this one into therapy before we loose her altogether!" Paul was so convincing that four large men immediately boarded the elevator. Just as the door closed behind them, he heard one of them exclaim, "Hey, wait a minute. Therapy's on two!" Then they were gone. The rest of the group stirred uneasily, unwilling to get further involved. They were still there when Paul reached the end of the hall and turned the corner.

He had studied the layout of the hospital carefully, thanks to the efficiency of the bureau. It took him only a moment to find the west end staircase he was looking for. Just as he opened the door, two more guards barreled out. He backed away, giving them room to get by. They started to dash down the hall, then stopped short, realizing their mistake. Too late. Paul's dart gun sang out one final time, expending the last of its ammunition. They went rigid, then froze. Leaving Susan by the door, he moved over to study them closely. Like the rest, they were equipped with stun sticks, pistols, and hospital communicators. Noting the name badge on the shorter guard, Paul commandeered his communicator, activating it.

"This is Rand, on four," he said, hoping that whoever was listening was not a close personal friend of the guard.

"Central here," came the reply.

"We've got them," Paul replied, sounding excited. "They just headed into the east wing. I think they're heading for the staircase there!"

"Roger that, Rand. Good work! All units, converge on the east wing. Repeat. . . ."

Grinning, Paul replaced the communicator. That should give him the rest of the time he needed. He retrieved Susan and shouldered his way through the door into the staircase. There, just as he expected, was a ladder that led to the roof. As carefully as he could, he slung Susan over his shoulder in a fireman's carry and began to climb.

Paul was in excellent shape, but no one carries 90 pounds up a 15-foot-high ladder without feeling it. By the time he reached the top, he was sweating with exertion. The hatch was bolted and locked, but he was prepared for this. Shifting Susan's weight as gently as he could, he pulled a tiny pick out of his pants pocket. Ignoring the protest of his overworked muscles, he inserted the pick into the lock. With the ease of a master, he soon had it open. He shoved the pick back into his pocket and pushed the hatch up. The spring mechanism responded easily and he was soon standing on the hot asphalt roof. Carefully, he laid Susan down. She groaned for a moment, then lay still.

Paul surveyed his surroundings, giving his cramping muscles a chance to rest. Before he had begun his assault on Rollings, he had done a quick but thorough survey of the outside of the building. From the ground he had noted the satellite dish that squatted on the east side of the roof. It was a huge dish, over 40 feet in diameter. Although it was large enough to support itself, since it was on the roof it was secured with thick, metal guide cables. Two of these cables ran from the building all the way down to the parking lot at about a 30-degree angle. The descent would be dangerous, but possible.

Knowing that time was running out, he returned his attention to Susan. She lay there on the roof, frail and weak. Briefly, he wondered if she would be of any value at all to him. Then he shook his head. He was way too far along in this little game to wonder about that now. Scanning the area for trouble, he unbuckled his belt and stripped off the white jacket he had stolen. Then he fastened the belt tightly around Susan's chest, under her armpits. Carefully he eased her to her feet and again slung her over his shoulder. He put his arm through the belt and eased it toward his neck. A hard jolt would cause him to lose her, but otherwise she should stay put. Then he trotted over to the satellite dish and chose the proper guide wire.

There was no activity in the parking lot yet, but that would not last too much longer. The nondescript white van he had rented was still there, waiting. He took a deep breath, willing himself to calm his rapidly beating heart. Sweat rolled down his forehead and stung his eyes. He rolled the jacket up into a tight cord and threw it over the wire, testing it for strength. Just as he moved toward the edge of the roof, another hatch on the far side of the building popped open. A guard peered over the edge, spotted Paul, and yelled something unintelligible to his unseen comrades below him. Then he jumped out of the hatch and began to run toward him. Paul wasted no more time. Gripping the jacket with both hands, he jumped hard and threw himself over the side. He rocketed down toward the parking lot, Susan balanced precariously over his shoulder. They reached the bottom in seconds. Paul threw out his feet and caught the pole the wire was attached to, breaking their forward momentum. For a moment, they dangled there, three feet off the ground. Then he let go and dropped to the pavement. He fell hard, unbalanced by Susan's weight, and landed on his knees. Pain shot through his legs, and he forced himself to his feet. Nothing was broken, he found, only bruised.

Quickly and carefully he unslung Susan from his shoulder and gathered her up in his arms like a child. The van was just a few yards away, and he staggered toward it. He had left it unlocked, and it did not take long to secure his charge in one of the back seats. He did not have time for an examination, but miraculously she seemed unhurt. Then he jumped in the front and started the engine. People were starting to emerge from the entrance as he squealed out of his parking space. They were waving and yelling wildly. One of them, an armed guard, pulled his pistol out of its holster, aimed, and fired. There was a loud "clang" as metal struck metal. Paul gunned the engine. The van barreled out of the parking lot and into the street. Just as he turned the corner of the nearby intersection, he heard another shot. There was no sound of it hitting, and he kept going. In seconds, the hospital was out of sight.

Three blocks ahead was another rented car he had left there, this one a blue station wagon. He pulled up behind it, thankful that it was not rush hour and traffic was not too heavy. Someone behind him probably saw his escape from the hospital and was even now noting his license number — not that it mattered. He had left yet another vehicle just a few blocks further on.

He jumped out of the van and ran to the other side, opening the door. Susan was still comatose. If she understood anything that was going on around her, she gave no sign of it. He pulled her out and half-walked, half-carried her to the wagon. Just as he got her inside, he heard the wail of a police siren. Rollings security had finally swallowed their pride and called in the real law. That meant that the media would not be far behind. The story of Susan's escape would be all over the air within hours. Excellent! He got behind the wheel, started the engine, and took off. It took him less than five minutes to reach the third car, a silver wagon, where he repeated the process. Once he was on his way, he headed north. He drove slowly, searching for any signs of pursuit. Nothing materialized, and he began to relax. He had succeeded in the first part of his mission. Now he could only hope that this woman would somehow lead him toward his real goal — the annihilation of the Shepherd's Path and the underground church.

2

"Now, my children, relax. Breath in. Let me take you into the deeper mysteries of true Christianity. Not the silliness practiced by so many, but the power of real godhood! Feel the energy of the cosmos surround you. Feel it penetrate you, and bind you to your brothers and sisters. This is the power that makes us one — the power of the universe — the 'Christ Consciousness.' This is the power of 'God'! Take it inside, become one with it. Become part of 'God.' Indeed you can now become a 'god' yourself. Feel the flow of power. . . ."

Christine Smythe stood in the back of the circular lecture hall and watched with a perverse fascination as her associate Rajijah Indres hypnotically lectured the 200 top teachers in his sect. He was standing on a raised dais in the exact center of the hall, with his students gathered around him. They came from all over the world, and represented every religion, every system of belief from Shiite Moslem to Southern Baptist. They were his elite. These 200 formed his "inner circle." From here, they would take his teachings to thousands of others under their discipleship, who would in turn take it to tens of thousands, and so on.

"Master?" One of his disciples, a young woman of about 25, raised her hand.

"Yes Rachel," answered Indres, smiling.

"You have spoken often of one who will come after you — a great teacher and prophet. When will he come? Will this really be Jesus himself? And what will become of you?"

Indres chuckled softly. "Daughter," he said gently, "I will *always* be with you. Never fear about that. And yes, another *is* coming — and soon! Will it be Jesus? Not the 'Jesus' you learned about in Sunday school! No, this one will be filled with the Christ consciousness. His thoughts will be those of God! He is coming to set the world on its proper course, and you, his eventual followers, will be the true Christians."

Again Christine smiled. Indres was a master teacher. He played his disciples like a finely tuned Stradivarius. He was also a shrewd businessman. In the past five years, his movement, called the "Many Paths to God," had spread across religious, cultural, and national boundaries. Millions subscribed to his beliefs. Even the United States government seemed to be in his corner. New laws and restrictions had placed a stranglehold on most of the established religions. Possessing a Bible or other non-approved literature was considered an act of treason. Most church services still held in public were monitored by a government official. All sermons were scrutinized and okayed by government representatives.

Indres, however, was left alone. Denominations who embraced his teachings were allowed to operate in relative freedom. He promoted unity — unity of thought, unity across denominational boundaries, and unity of belief. His teachings also endorsed an absolute, almost fanatical loyalty to the government. He was, indisputably, THE single most powerful religious figure in the world.

Although she would never understand it, Christine knew that there were multitudes of otherwise normal people hungry for spiritual guidance. They *needed* hope for an uncertain future, now more than ever. The decline of Christianity over the past few decades, thanks in part to the highly publicized scandals in the nineties, had left a void that needed to be filled. Indres filled it.

From an economic standpoint, he was equally as powerful. His organization was the proud owner of one major television network, assorted news services, and more than a handful of congressmen and senators. Daily, even hourly, his message of unity coursed through the airwaves. News events were constantly slanted to show his movement in a favorable light. At one time, the IRS had thought to audit the "Many Paths to God." Hundreds of millions of dollars poured in from no apparent source, and not a penny was being paid in taxes. Nothing had come of it. Rumor had it that those pushing for the audit had changed their collective minds when several of their number had turned up missing.

Christine worked closely with Indres. He was a vital part of Brennon's ultimate plan. Together they, and a few select others, labored to bring about Brennon's vision of the New World Order. Privately, Christine believed that it would not be long before Indres joined Brennon's Sextuaget. Brosolov, her Baltic States counterpart in Brennon's circle, had dropped some hints the last time they had spoken. He had mentioned that the Middle Eastern "overseer," Rhys, was not fulfilling his duties adequately, and would probably soon be replaced. Indres was the logical choice to bring in. It made Christine wonder just how great a turnover there was in Brennon's elite group. First Jacob Hill, now Rhys. Would there come a time when he decided that *she* was not doing her job? The thought worried at her subconscious constantly.

"Now, reach out with your senses," Indres was saying in a soft but commanding voice. "Your spirit guides await you, to take you further into the great mysteries. Listen, watch, and learn." He let his voice trail off, and silence dominated the hall. Christine found herself covered with goose pimples, half mesmerized. While she herself believed in no "higher power" or "supreme being," she still felt something there in the hall. An undeniable, powerful presence permeated the place. Senses that she barely knew of or understood reacted to it, causing her to shudder ever so slightly. Resolutely she shrugged it off, telling herself that it was merely the result of the group hypnosis Indres was practicing.

The Indian "holy man" surveyed his people for a moment, then continued. "Use this time for personal meditation and communion with your guides. In time, I will return." With that, he stepped off the dais and moved toward Christine. When he reached her, she nodded, then followed him out of the hall into a small anteroom just outside. A large window dominated the room, and they moved to stand next to it.

Before them, the city of New York spread out in every direction. It was a surprisingly clear day in the "Big Apple," and they could see all the way to Manhattan. They were on the sixty-first floor of the Smythe Tower, the central headquarters of Christine's huge, multi-national corporation. The two colleagues stood there in silence for a moment, both thinking of the task each of them was responsible for. Then, finally, Indres spoke.

"All proceeds as planned?" he asked in his soft, almost feminine voice.

"Yes," was Christine's simple answer. There was another moment's silence.

"And the Christian church? The underground movement called the Shepherd's Path?"

Christine hesitated, then answered. "Everyday we stamp more of them out. We no longer use the Bureau of Religious Affairs as our primary tool. Instead we are taking direct action against them — direct and violent."

"That does not answer my question," replied Indres, turning to look at her with his placid stare. Christine frowned at this, not liking his insinuation. At one time, just a few months ago, they had both been a part of an elite inner circle headed by Jacob Hill. Now Christine was the head of that same circle, and answered only to Brennon. For now, at least, Indres was subordinate to her, not the other way around. It was time to remind him of that.

"It doesn't concern you," she snapped. "Let me worry about the underground groups. You see to it that your movement is recognized as the official national religion." Reacting to her tone, Indres put his hands up in a calming motion.

"You misunderstand me," he said, his face showing nothing but sincerity. "I do not mean to criticize. I only wish to know your status, so that

I may better determine mine." On the outside, at least, he was all but dripping humility. Mollified somewhat by his subservient tone, Christine allowed herself to relax.

"The Shepherd's Path still operates," she admitted reluctantly. "However, we may have a breakthrough. One of the bureau's former agents has contacted us. He believes he has a plan to infiltrate and destroy the entire network. If he is successful, not only the network, but many churches should fall as well."

Indres frowned at this information. "This agent," he inquired, "is he reliable?"

"When he was with the bureau," replied Christine, "he was considered one of the best."

"And you believe one man can accomplish what the entire Bureau of Religious Affairs could not?"

"As a matter of fact I do," answered Christine. "I approved his plan just a few days ago, and he has already begun. His initial success is promising." Indres nodded, allowing a faint smile to show through his normally calm demeanor.

"I hope it will work, Christine. Of course, you have my full support. The battle we fight together is both physical *and* spiritual. Anything you ask of me, I will do."

"I know that, Raj," she said, returning his smile. Her initial anger at his presumption disappeared. "Now tell me, how is your end of things coming along."

"Quite well," answered Indres. "My people have established themselves in every major religious group — at least the ones officially recognized by the United States government. The rest, of course, do not matter. There is growing public support of the idea of making 'The Many Paths to God' the national religion."

"Interesting name," murmured Christine.

"Indeed," agreed Indres. "It is what my teaching is all about. Tolerance of other beliefs is a vital element of the new world order. One may say, 'My faith is *a* way to heaven, but not the *only* way.' "

"Of course," said Christine. "That's an interesting little exercise you were doing in there, by the way." Indres nodded.

"Useful," he replied. "It puts them in the right frame of mind. The major breakthrough comes when they actually make contact with their spirit guide." Christine felt a skeptical smile start to worm its way onto her face, and suppressed it. Indres, observant as always, noticed anyway.

"Do not dismiss the supernatural," he warned. "It *does* exist, Christine, and can be used to dominate and control."

"May the force be with you," she said, not bothering to hide her smile now. Indres matched it with one of his own.

"There is more truth in that old, worn-out statement than you realize. The 'energies of the spirit,' as I call them, cannot only control our minds and bodies, but can be made to obey our commands as well. You would find them a valuable ally."

"No thanks," said Christine, starting to walk away. "I'll let you deal with the metaphysics. I'll see to the more practical side. In fact, it's time I was doing so. Things begin to roll today."

"Really?" Indres actually looked surprised. "I did not realize that you were putting things into motion so soon."

"No choice. The rest of the Sextuaget is ready. I don't want to be the one they are waiting on."

"Until later, then," said Indres, bowing slightly. He turned silently and disappeared back into the lecture hall. Christine allowed herself to relax just a little. While she respected the diminutive Indian, she did not particularly like or trust him. Not that it mattered. He was brilliant and charismatic, a natural leader. His ability to sway people was just as important to the overall plan as Christine's economic and political movements.

It took her just minutes to reach the hub of her financial empire three floors above. She smiled as she entered the large open space. This was where she felt the most at home. The place was bustling with activity, and she was always reminded of an ant farm when she entered. She was the queen, and dozens of her workers were scurrying about, carrying out the day to day details of running her corporation. Rows of desks were linked by computer to offices all over the world. Her work force controlled the various and diverse aspects of her empire with skill and imagination. Each man and woman in here was hand-picked — the "best of the best."

Walking through the organized chaos, Christine glanced up at the New York Stock Exchange read-out that was zipping by on the far wall. It was programmed to show only those stocks that were relevant to her operation. Her smile grew larger as she watched the numbers go by. All of her businesses were doing quite well, while many of her competitors struggled. The large chain of women's clinics, for example, were growing daily. Her defense plants were booming (she chuckled at her own pun), and even in these hard times the millions of citizens her corporation employed were enjoying high salaries and good benefits. It was too bad, she thought to herself, that it all had to be destroyed.

Carefully she threaded her way through the frenzied activity. On the far side of the huge room was her private suite of offices. A palm reader was placed next to the entrance, and she placed her hand over it. There was a soft white glow and a slight hum as the reader scanned her palm print. It recognized her immediately. The door slid open and she stepped in. A small outer office held a desk, a couch, and one of her many executive assistants. Gary Small looked up from the vid-phone he was speaking to and nodded. Christine drew an index finger across her neck, indicating that he should terminate the call. Obediently he said goodbye to whoever he was talking to, and turned his full attention on his boss.

"Get me a video link to Los Angeles now," ordered Christine shortly. He nodded, and she walked past him, through another door, and into her private office. In appearance, it was much like her old suite in Mentasys. Decorated in mauve and gray, it was large enough to hold a small house. Furniture imported from all over the world was placed with the expertise of an artist, and the deep plush carpet added both comfort and beauty. It was designed to be both functional and aesthetic.

Crossing to the large ornate desk on the far side of the office, Christine frowned slightly. The thought of Mentasys still aggravated her. She had put a lot of time and money into that little project. It still hurt to lose it. If not for Jacob Hill's stupidity. . . .

Sitting in her overstuffed leather chair, she thrust thoughts of Jacob and Mentasys away. It did no good to dwell on the past. Patiently she waited for her call to come through. Gary did his job competently, and within moments she was rewarded with the gentle chiming that signified there was a call waiting. Reaching over, she activated her monitor. The face of Matthew Riever stared back at her. He was an older man of about 50, with gray hair shot with black and a stern, commanding face. He looked every inch the top executive he was. He also knew why Christine was calling. His face betrayed his emotions. Fear, uncertainty, and apprehension played with his features like a cruel pianist.

"Christine." His voice was a deep baritone, obviously used to giving commands rather than taking orders. "Good to hear from you. Your assistant said it was urgent. What can I do for you?" He was seated at a desk much like Christine's. She leaned forward, her face now intense. Matthew's casual banter did not fool her. He was dreading what was about to happen. He, more that anyone else she knew, had poured his life into making Smythe Enterprises the economic giant it was. While Christine directed the corporation, and decided on long-range goals, it was Matthew who turned those goals into reality. The board of directors, all of the presidents and vice presidents, were so much window dressing. Christine held the power, and Matthew provided the drive and muscle. What Christine was going to tell him was going to be harder on him than anyone else.

"It's time, Matthew," she said softly. Privately, Christine considered herself the ultimate entrepreneur. Business decisions were made with the good of the corporation — and Brennon's ultimate plan — in mind, not the individual. Concern for the "human element," as she called it, only slowed things down. Nevertheless, she had a soft spot for Matthew. The man was energetic, motivated, and completely loyal to her and to Smythe Enterprises.

"Time?" he asked in apparent confusion. Christine was not fooled. Matthew knew very well what she meant.

"Time," she repeated firmly. "You know this has been coming, Matthew. In fact, you knew it was coming from the first day we started working together." Matthew slumped back into his chair.

"I know," he said softly. "It's just that — well, I guess I never really believed you would actually go through with it."

"Then you really don't know me," replied Christine coldly. Soft spots regardless, Matthew Riever was still a tool to her, useful, but not to be confided in. "I want you to implement 'Thistledown' immediately — today. Understood?"

Matthew hesitated just a beat, then nodded slowly. "A lot of people are going to be hurt," he remarked.

Christine nodded in agreement. "It can't be helped, Matthew. This is for the greater good." She allowed a touch of concern to come across her face. Forced and pretended, it was nevertheless convincing. "Don't you think I know that millions of ordinary people are going to be ruined by this? Believe me, if there were any other way, I would have thought of it." Matthew continued to stare back at her, not responding. He was not privy to her inner circles, and therefore did not understand the ultimate plan.

Enough of this, thought Christine. "Just do it, Matthew," she said, adding the forcefulness to her voice that had made her one of the most powerful people on the planet. "Implement Thistledown."

Matthew stared a moment longer, then, very reluctantly, nodded.

"Good," replied Christine. She allowed herself a small smile. "Don't worry, Matthew. You'll still have a job. The country is about to be flushed down the toilet, but it won't affect you."

Abruptly Matthew nodded. "I'll put Thistledown in motion, then." He started to say something else, but then decided against it.

"Good," replied Christine shortly. "Report back to me as soon as you are able. Keep me informed. Remember, it's Thistledown that's going to get me in to see the president on very short notice."

Matthew snorted at that. "I won't have to report," he said grimly. "Just listen to the newscasts. Watch for the stories of Wall Street executives jumping off the top of Smythe Tower. That'll let you know how things are going."

"Report to me anyway," said Christine, ignoring his sarcasm. "I'll be here in New York for the next few days. Then, if all goes as planned, I'll be heading for Washington."

"Watch yourself out there," Matthew warned. "A lot of powerful people still blame you for Jack Kline's death. He was shot on your property, after all, and by your security force."

"You let me worry about that," replied Christine briskly, wanting to end the call. "Just take care of your end. I'll talk you to soon, Matthew." She reached down to terminate the call.

"Goodbye, Christine," he replied softly. Something in his tone, something that Christine had not heard before, almost made her pause. He sounded so final, as if it were the last time they would be speaking. *Nonsense,* she thought, scolding herself. Matthew Riever was one of the most dependable, levelheaded people she knew. He was the last person she needed to worry about. She pushed the control and the screen went blank.

Leaning back in the comfortable chair, she contemplated the immediate future. Within 24 hours, Smythe Enterprises was going to come crashing down around her. That was what Thistledown was all about. Over six million people in the Untied States alone were going to find themselves out of work. Industries, manufacturing plants, hospitals — everything that was under her corporate umbrella was going to shut down. Within days the United States, already strained to the economic breaking point, was going to find itself in the worst depression in her 225-year history. Wall Street executives, fools used to seven-figure salaries, were in seconds going to become bankrupt and penniless. They would indeed be jumping off the Smythe Tower!

For just a moment, Christine regretted the necessity of destroying something she had worked so hard to build. Forget the fact that it was Brennon's power and genius that was responsible for her rise to power. Smythe Enterprises was hers. It was a part of her, and it was going to hurt to lose it. Not that it would affect her personally. Her place in Brennon's inner circle of power was assured — hopefully. Still, it would hurt.

It would, though, accomplish the desired results. Faced with a no-win situation, the United States would have no choice but to join the European economic power block. That would move the planet one step closer to a unified, one-world government — with Brennon at the head.

Abruptly she stood. Regretting the inevitable was a waste of time. She had other matters which were just as important to worry about — namely the little equation of Paul Sinclair. After news of his proposal had reached her, she had done a little research into his background. What she had found had impressed her. Paul and his team of agents had almost single-handedly uncovered more underground churches than anyone else. He was unswerving in his loyalty to the ideals of the bureau. In fact, it was one of the reasons he had been fired in that necessary purge six months ago. He had been set out as a sacrifice to mollify an indignant public. It was not that people minded followers of Jesus Christ being arrested and imprisoned. In fact, public opinion polls showed just the opposite. What really bothered everyone was that it was being done covertly. One thing Americans hated was something going on behind their collective backs.

The rest of Paul's biography had been just as impressive to Christine. Physically, he was a big man, strong and intimidating. Mentally he was no slouch either. He had an uncanny ability to "read between the lines" when working on a case. He noticed the slightest clue when following a scent. It set him apart from the rest of the bureau. Christine suspected that, had things not fallen apart, he would have been directing things on a national level by now.

At first, she had been tempted to reject his plan. Upon reconsidering, however, she had seen the advantages in what he proposed. If he succeeded, then she could face Brennon again, her immediate future secure. If not, then nothing was lost. She would simply have Wolf kill him. Judging from her research, though, he stood a good chance of succeeding.

Gracefully, Christine moved from her desk and left her office. She felt like a monarch touring her realm as she walked calmly back through the nerve center of her operation. She had to hold back a chuckle as she watched the controlled chaos that seethed around her. By this time tomorrow these people would be far more frantic. Their whole world would be disintegrating and they would not know how to stop it.

She left the organized madness behind her and steered herself back toward where Indres was teaching. Something in her drew her back to the hall. She told herself it was simple curiosity, but deep inside she knew that it was really a fascination for what Indres was teaching.

As she walked, she realized that she was starting to feel very good. With any luck, the next time she met with the Sextuaget, she would be able to report both the economic ruin of the United States, and the destruction of the Shepherd's Path. By the time she reached the elevator, she was starting to hum.

* * *

Wolf paced back and forth in the narrow confines of the small, three-bedroom house he was using as a base. Outside, he could hear the sounds of ordinary life going on in the middle class Sacramento suburb. Across the street, a father and his five-year-old son washed the family car together. A trio of older girls were on the sidewalk, playing jump rope. Next door, an older woman was trying valiantly to fend off a door-to-door salesman. It amazed Wolf that even though the world was drastically changing, life for the ordinary person went on. Of course, if the rumors he had heard from "up top" were true, many of these families might be homeless within the coming months.

He continued to pace, waiting impatiently for word from one of his people. The house he was renting was a "cookie cutter" model, differing little from its neighbors. Besides himself, the room contained a couch, a cheap flowered chair, and a coffee table. He was alone in the house, and he was getting quite impatient.

For the past four days he had watched as Paul Sinclair had locked himself inside room 116 of the Blue Ribbon Inn. It was a mediocre motel, the kind one used to grab a night's sleep and a quick breakfast before hitting the road again. The only problem was, Sinclair wasn't hitting the road. He was, in fact, just sitting there with the Ferguson woman, waiting to be contacted. Privately, Wolf thought Sinclair a fool. His plan was haphazard at best. Everything depended upon his being contacted by a member of the Shepherd's Path once he had gotten the woman out of Rollings. That had not happened. Instead, Sinclair had sat on his hands in that wretched motel. He had emerged only to get food. Nothing was happening, and it was beginning to annoy Wolf. The only reason he did not terminate Sinclair now was that he had been specifically forbidden to do so.

What angered Wolf the most, however, was that he was now going to have to take an active hand in helping the former bureau agent. Sooner or later, city law enforcement would catch up with the two fugitives, especially if they stayed in one place. It was time to get Sinclair moving again. To do that, he was going to have to put him into contact with an underground church. That was what really grated on Wolf's nerves. For the past year, he had been systematically destroying churches. Now, he would have to locate one, find out where and when it would meet — and then leave it alone. The thought of that repelled him. It went against every fiber in his being.

Suddenly, like a pressure cooker that had just reached its boiling point, his temper blew. The rage that simmered continuously within his soul came boiling out. He grabbed the first thing he could find, a ceramic ashtray shaped like a toilet, and flung it against the wall as hard as he could. The ceramic shattered into hundreds of pieces, and the thin, plaster board wall now sported a two inch hole. He stood there for a moment, panting, staring at the hole. Briefly, he considered throwing something else, then decided against it. Taking deep breaths, he forced himself to calm down. It was no use wasting his anger on inanimate objects, he told himself. Better to wait until he had a living, breathing human to take it all out on. The thought cheered him just a little, and he began to relax. Just then, the vidphone sitting on the coffee table chimed, demanding his attention. He shot over to the table and pushed the "activate" button.

"It had better be good," he snarled. He did not bother to identify himself. Only two other people in the world knew this particular number. The screen lit up and displayed the grim visage of one of his associates simply known as "Demos."

"We got something," answered Demos. His voice, surprisingly, was a high pleasant tenor.

"Yeah?"

"We found that some kind of group is meeting in the basement of the East Garden Mall."

"And where did you come by this 'reliable' information?" If Demos felt any nervousness at Wolf's sarcasm, he did not show it. He might have a pleasant voice and a broad, disarming smile, but inside he was ruthless. Like Wolf, he gave no quarter to those whom he hunted. Unlike Wolf, he was strictly mercenary. While Wolf enjoyed the fact that he destroyed human lives, Demos worked solely for the highest bidder. Wolf's masters paid him well. Thus, for the time at least, he was reliable.

"We got a line from the local police," he answered calmly. "One of them works for the same people you do. They got several people they suspect of 'subversive' activity. Unfortunately, they have to have at least something that looks like evidence before they can move." He smiled — a predator's smile. "We don't."

"And?" prodded Wolf.

"And," said Demos, "we got a few names. One of the suspects is a janitor in that mall I mentioned. Used to be a preacher somewhere before his church was shut down. We couldn't find out why, but the local authorities let him alone after he agreed to get out of the church business. We got to him at work, and used a little 'joy juice' on him." Wolf nodded in understanding. The pentothal derivative Smythe Enterprises supplied him with was quite effective in getting reluctant subjects to tell the truth. Being much stronger than its predecessor, however, it had a tendency to leave 4 out of 10 subjects it was used on a mental vegetable. Even if the subject survived, they were susceptible to other types of brain damage.

"So he told you about them meeting in the mall," he said.

Demos frowned at this, but nodded. "He told us," he agreed, "but it wasn't easy. He was unusually resistant to the drug."

"So he's a veggie?"

"We're not sure, yet," replied Demos. "He's still sleeping it off. His bodily functions are normal, but until he wakes up, we won't know about his mind. Chances are that with the fight he put up, there'll be some kind of damage."

"Did you leave a post-hypnotic suggestion?" asked Wolf.

"Of course," said Demos, slightly miffed that Wolf would suggest he would forget such an obvious step. "If he wakes up okay, he won't remember a thing. Probably have a mother of a headache, but that's all. If he doesn't," he shrugged, "well, no big loss. We got the time and place of their little meeting. If this falls through, we'll get ourselves another subject and try again." Demos' nonchalant attitude was starting to anger Wolf, and he had not been in too good a mood to start with.

"Just you make sure that this one *does* work out," he growled. "Come on, give me the details." Demos' eyes narrowed, and for a moment, he looked as if he was going to take exception to Wolf's rebuke. Then his face cleared. He was too much of a professional to allow personal feelings to come between him and his work.

"Four nights from now — East Garden Mall," he replied crisply. "They're meeting in the basement, in the air processing room. That's just under the sporting goods place near the center of the mall."

"So what happens?" asked Wolf. "How do you get in? Just go down and knock?"

"Of course not," replied Demos, his irritation with Wolf flaring up again. "They've got to meet a contact at the east end, near the fountain with a statue of Gaia, or 'mother earth,' or whoever it is, in it. The contact is female, and will be holding a book with this on the cover." He held up a piece of paper with a crude drawing on it.

"What is it?" asked Wolf, curious in spite of his mood. It was a simple, geometric shape, consisting of a square half covered on the right side by a circle.

"It's supposed to represent Christ's empty tomb," grinned Demos. "From what I gather, this Shepherd's Path uses a lot of different things like this. Last year, they were using what they called the Shepherd's Staff."

"I remember," said Wolf grimly. "So they find this person with the book. How do they approach her?"

"Simple," said Demos. "They wait until there's no one around. Then they sit next to her and, very softly, quote a Bible verse." He looked down, obviously consulting his notes. "Uh, let's see, this week it's from the Book of John."

"This week?" snarled Wolf. "You mean it changes week by week?"

"From what I gather," said Demos dryly, "it changes by week, location, and time of day. I tried to get the preacher to tell us the whole plan, but like I said, he was unusually resistant. If I had pushed any harder, he would have been a vegetable for sure."

"Blast!" snarled Wolf, thinking furiously. "Now we've got to find a Bible somewhere. Not only that, but Sinclair is going to have to memorize who knows how much of it."

"Think he can do it?" asked Demos.

"Not at all," snapped Wolf. "The man is a fool. Sooner or later he's going to screw up. I only hope he can lead us to enough underground cell groups. The more he uncovers before he blows it, the better chance we'll have of breaking this thing once and for all."

He thought some more, then spoke again. "When did you say they were meeting?" he asked.

"In four days — Wednesday night at 7:30," was the reply.

"Fine. You get that preacher back on his feet," he ordered Demos. "Make sure he remembers nothing. Then get back here and stay low until Wednesday. You'll get to the mall by three. Find that contact and watch her — *discreetly* mind you. Get pictures of everyone she makes contact with."

"Where will you be?" asked Demos.

Wolf's first response was to tell Demos to take care of his own job and not worry about things that didn't concern him. Then he realized that Demos needed to know how to contact him if things went haywire.

"I'll let you know," he replied evenly. "If I don't get in touch with you before you go back to the mall, I'll leave a message on the vid-phone." Demos nodded. "That's it, then," he continued. "Get back here and take it easy. Things are going to get very busy in a few days." With that, he broke the connection. Almost unconsciously, he began to pace again. Demos' news had cheered him, but now he had to take care of some very important details if this was going to work, including one quite difficult one.

"Blast!" he snarled again, this time under his breath. "Where am I going to find a Bible in this day and age?" There was no one there to answer, and he continued to pace.

* * *

The shoppers were beginning to thin out as closing time drew near at the East Garden Mall. David Eddington, a 35-year-old assistant maintenance engineer, slowly pushed his cleaning cart through the lower level of the three-level structure, scanning the terrazzo floor for discarded paper, cigarette butts, or other litter. Sometimes, on his better days, he tried to make a game of it. The bits of trash would become thieves trying to escape his grasp, or enemy ships waiting to be sunk. It made the repetition of his work a little more bearable. Unfortunately, his better days were growing more and more scarce.

He reached the center of the mall and eased his cart to a halt. He was a short man, just over five foot six, with a stocky build that in previous times had been described as "pleasingly plump." Now there was a suggestion of gauntness to it. His blue eyes, though bright in color, seemed dull and lifeless. His walk seemed hesitant and listless, as if he was not sure where he was going.

Leaning against his cart, he checked the area for trash. The front page of the *New York Times* lay on one of the many wooden benches that surrounded the large waterfall just off to his right. The artificial fall, over 30 feet high, was the center piece of the entire mall. Recycled water splashed merrily down a pre-set course made by artificial rock. It tried its best to look natural, but could not quite pull it off. Casually, David left his cart and wandered over to the bench. He had not seen a paper in over two days, and felt a bit out of touch. In his former life, he had had the *Times* delivered to his home daily. It was one of the little things he missed most these days.

Picking up the front page, he flipped it over and began to read. The news was not good. The big, block letters of the headline proclaimed boldly, "STOCK MARKET CRASHES." In smaller letters below, it read "Smythe Enterprises' Fall Catalyst For Depression." Grim headlines indeed! David glanced up at the scurrying shoppers. There were so few of them! Was it his imagination, or was there an aura of panic surrounding them? How many had lost their jobs in the past two days? Certainly many of them wore strained looks as they went about their business. Even the mall itself seemed to bear the weight of impending doom. Normally a bright and happy place to be, tonight it seemed bleak and empty.

David sighed. Things were going from bad to worse. The depression was only two days old, and already what was left of the economy was in a shambles. The current administration was completely disorganized, and the private sector was in a state of what could only be described as blind panic. Industry had ground to a halt, leaving uncounted millions out of work. Already the effects were being felt on a local grassroots level. Here in the mall, 12 stores had closed their doors. Several of the maintenance staff had already been laid off, including two from his own department. Not him, though, he thought grimly. The one thing he did not have to worry about was unemployment. He had taken care of that when he . . . quickly he brushed that chain of thought out of his mind. It did no good to dwell on the unchangeable past, no matter how bitter it was.

With a feeling of hopelessness he wadded up the paper. Ambling back to his cart, he tossed it into the plastic trash container strapped to the front. Suddenly, without warning, the migraine headache that had been mysteriously plaguing him all day flared up again.

"OHHH!" The groan escaped through his clenched lips despite his best efforts to keep it inside. The pain was searing! Passers-by glanced uncomfortably in his direction, then quickly looked the other way. The mall began to spin around him, and desperately he stumbled back over to the bench. He fell rather than sat onto the hard simulated wood, and put his head in his hands. His vision blurred, and tears squirted out of the corners of his eyes and rolled down his cheeks. Never in his life had he been subject to headaches like this. They had begun yesterday, all but incapacitating him with their ferocity.

"Lord, what did I do to deserve this?" he groaned, rocking back and forth. Even before he completed the question, he regretted it. The fact was, he knew that he did deserve it. Indeed, he told himself, he deserved far more.

Cowardice, betrayal, unfaithfulness — he was guilty of them all, and more. What he had done. . . .

As suddenly as it started, the headache stopped. The relief from the pain was almost as shocking as its onset. He sat there, his vision clearing and his heart slowly returning to its normal rhythm. The sweat that had broken out on his forehead began to cool, causing him to shiver. Somewhat self-consciously, he wiped his face on the sleeve of his gray work uniform. Slowly his shattered thoughts began to reweave themselves into a recognizable pattern. His rough breathing slowed back to normal. He was totally unprepared for what was to happen next.

"Take these things away; stop making My Father's house a house of merchandise." The words, spoken softly but distinctly in a quiet, feminine voice, came from his left. It took him a moment to realize that the speaker had just quoted John 2:16. More important, she had just given a recognition signal for the meeting scheduled two days from now. In shock he looked up. Sitting next to him was a rather pretty, blonde-haired girl who looked to be in her mid-twenties. She looked at him expectantly, waiting.

"Excuse me?" he said, his voice hoarse and ragged. He had never seen her before.

She was certainly not one of the regular members of his tiny congregation. She smiled at his confusion.

"Should I repeat myself? Quoting Scripture in public is not exactly safe these days." Again she smiled, and despite the fogginess of his thoughts, David found himself smiling back. There was something about this young lady that he immediately liked — and trusted.

"No, it's not," he agreed. He struggled to pull himself together for a moment, then made a decision. "His disciples remembered that it was written, 'Zeal for thy house will consume me.' " It was the proper answer. "You're a bit early," he added. "Two days, to be exact."

"I needed to talk to you, David," replied the young woman. "You're the leader of the church that meets here in the basement, and I have some information for you." David sucked his breath in wildly, trying to look in every direction at once. If anyone heard what she said. . . .

"Don't worry," soothed the woman. "No one is listening."

"Still, you don't take chances like that," hissed David, savagely, turning back to face his new acquaintance. "Things are bad enough for believers without drawing unwanted attention."

"Yes," replied the woman, smiling at him strangely. She totally ignored his angry retort. "Attention from the wrong people can be dangerous, can it not? You know that well, don't you?" A sudden sinking feeling took hold of the pit of David's stomach.

She knows! he thought despairingly. *And if she knows, then she must be here to tell the others, and that will be the end. No one will trust me after they find out what I did!* The woman, as if reading his thoughts, put a gentle hand on his arm.

"I'm not here to cause you any harm, David," she said soothingly, and somehow, he believed her. "I'm here because you need to know some things. A test is coming for you, David Eddington, and you must be prepared." David could only stare at this strange woman. The last traces of his headache had vanished, and he felt as if he ought to know what she was talking about. It almost made sense to him, but he could not quite make himself understand. Calmly, she stared back at him, and her eyes seemed to cut through his defenses and leave his very soul open and bare. Suddenly uncomfortable, he looked away.

"Ladies and gentlemen, East Garden Mall will be closing in five minutes. We will reopen tomorrow at 10 o'clock. Thank you for shopping with us. Remember to. . . ." The computerized feminine voice of the announcer droned on, giving instructions and "thank you's." David abruptly remembered that he had a job to do. He glanced around the central area of the mall. On the other side of the waterfall, he spied one of his maintenance co-workers, an older man named Charley Flint. Charley had not yet seen him, but was drawing closer.

"Look," he said, looking back at the woman, and once again found himself caught by those piercing eyes. "Uh, look," he tried again, "This is dangerous. I've got to finish my rounds. Can we meet somewhere tomorrow? We can talk about whatever it is you've got to talk about then."

It was a clumsy attempt to get rid of her, and she obviously knew it. She smiled, and shook her head. "Finish your job, David. I'll wait for you outside."

"Uh, n-no," stammered David nervously. The thought of this strange woman waiting for him in plain sight frightened him. The initial trust he had felt for her had disappeared, to be replaced by fear and uncertainty. This was pushing things too far. He knew for a fact that the local authorities still checked on him at random intervals. Word had even come down through the grapevine that he might be under suspicion. He was seriously considering disbanding his small group. Once again, the woman seemed to sense what he was thinking.

"David," she said in the same soothing voice, "do not be afraid." She brushed his hand lightly with her fingers, and somehow, he suddenly felt better. "Do you have so weak a faith that you believe that the Father has completely abandoned His children? There was a time you thought different." *That* caught him off guard. Just how much *did* she know? He opened his mouth to reply, but she wasn't finished.

"I'm here to tell you that the Father has *not* forgotten you, nor has He forsaken you. He only waits for you to turn fully back to Him." She held up her hand to forestall any reply he might make. "I'll be waiting for you," she said as she stood. Numbly, he rose to stand beside her. He was vaguely surprised to find that she was a good six inches taller than he. When they were sitting, they had been eye-to-eye. Dumbfounded, he watched as she moved off with an exquisite grace through the exiting crowd. Within seconds, she disappeared. He stood staring after her.

"Hey, partner!" Startled, David whirled around to find Charley now behind him, looking at him curiously. "You going to stand there all night and leave the hard stuff for me, or are you. . . . Hey! Are you all right?" Charley's dark brown face went from half-serious indignation to genuine concern. For some unknown reason the older man had taken a liking to David the minute they had started working together.

"What?" David's response was barely audible. He knew how he must have looked.

"I said," repeated Charley, "are you all right? You look like someone has just dumped the weight of the world on your shoulders — and you're too serious about life as it is!"

"I'm fine," replied David absently. "Just had a sudden headache," he added for Charley's benefit. He wondered what he was going to say about the woman. He must have seen her.

"Headache, huh," said Charley suspiciously. "You need to go home? I can finish up." That brought David fully back to his current situation.

"No, I'm fine now," he said, smiling for effect. "Let's get this done and get out of here."

"I heard that," agreed Charley. Together, the two men gathered their carts and made their way through the rest of the mall.

* * *

Despite the fact that David took as long as he possibly could to finish his work, the strange woman was indeed waiting for him at the maintenance entrance of the mall. He saw her as soon as he walked out, standing so still that she could have been a statue. Her tall, lean form was outlined by the street light she was waiting under. For a wild moment, he was reminded of Jill. She had the same shape, the same way of standing, as his wife. The shock of pseudo-recognition sent a surge of adrenaline rocketing through him, causing his heart rate to soar. He had to remind himself that Jill was gone, living in Detroit with her parents, along with their 12-year-old son.

Touched off by thoughts of his family, memories rippled through him. Suddenly he missed Jill and Josh so much it hurt. He wanted to be with them, be a family again. He wanted to feel his wife's arms around him, and hug his son so hard that it would feel like he would never let go.

"No," he said under his breath, gritting his teeth. It did no good to want something that was just not going to happen. Not after what he had done. . . . But it hurt so much! Right then and there, he almost turned and ran. He wanted to get as far away from this woman as he could. His life was that of a tightrope walker, or a trapeze artist — one mis-step, and he would fall. For all he knew, he was being watched even now.

He stood there, undecided, wanting to slink into the shadows and hide, yet unable to move. Then the woman started toward him, and the decision was taken out of his hands. She seemed to glide across the distance separating them, almost as if she were floating, not walking. Within seconds, she was there in front of him. She regarded him in the uncertain light, her face half in shadow.

"Well, David, are we going to stand here all night?" Her voice seemed softer now that they were outside, but still no less assertive than it had been before.

"Uh, uh," he stammered, his voice suddenly deserting him.

"I guess we could talk here," she continued, seemingly oblivious to their surroundings. She motioned off to the left, toward one of the main entrances where several benches were placed.

"NO!" The exclamation tore out of his throat before he could stop it. "I mean, uh, no, that's not a good idea," he amended, lowering his voice. "Uh, do you have a car?"

"Sorry," was the polite reply. "I came on the bus."

"Oh," said David. He was thinking furiously. Somehow he knew he wasn't going to get rid of this woman until he heard what she had to say. Perhaps he could convince her to come back to his small apartment. He could think of no other place that would be private enough.

"How do you get home?" asked the woman, although David got the idea that she already knew.

"I walk, usually," he replied uncertainly. "It's only a few miles from here. Sometimes, if it's raining, I take the bus."

The woman smiled. "Then let's take the bus." With that, she started toward the main entrance she had pointed to before. There were three buses parked there, taking on the last remaining passengers. Most of them were mall employees, just finishing up their duties. David stared after her, once again torn between the desire to hear what she had to say and the urge to run. She walked maybe 10 paces, then turned and waited. "Well?" Her voice was soft, but insistent.

Taking a deep breath, David made his decision. He jogged the distance between them, drawing even with her before stopping. She stood there, her gaze seeming to comfort and assess him at the same time. "That's a first step, David," she said softly, as if he had passed some sort of test. "There will be others, each one harder than the last, but you have taken the first." Once again she started off, with him at her side. He did not understand in the least what she had just told him, but somehow it made him feel excited — and frightened. It was if he had just started a long journey — one that he knew he must take, but one he had been terribly afraid of beginning.

Together they made their way to the waiting buses. The woman did not hesitate, choosing the second one in line. They boarded, passed through the weapon detectors, and found a seat about halfway back. There were only a handful of other passengers on board. David breathed a sigh of relief that he did not know anyone there. He allowed the woman to slide in next to the window, then sat down next to her. They waited in silence as the last few passengers boarded.

Finally, the doors closed with a soft "whooshhh." The driver revved the motor and they were off. David watched the mall disappear behind him, then turned his attention to the woman. He was determined to take control of the conversation.

"Now look," he whispered forcefully, ignoring her incredible eyes as she looked at him, "I don't know how you found out so much about me, but let's get the facts straight. First, I am not the leader of *any* group. If you know as much as you seem to, then you should know that. I simply make it possible for certain people to use some of the mall facilities, uh, in secret. That's all! I've got a few contacts from my, er, that is, from a few years back, and they do the real work. I'm just sort of an organizer. Get it?" He waited for a response, but none was forthcoming.

"Second," he continued after a brief pause, "I don't know anything about a 'test.' " Abruptly, a wave of shame washed over him and he lowered his eyes. His cheeks flushed and his ears began to burn. He found he could no longer meet her gaze. "I had a test, if you want to call it that, a while ago, and I failed badly. A lot of people were hurt because of it." He looked back up, expecting to hear some form of condemnation, but the woman simply looked back at him, saying nothing. "Third," he continued, then stopped. He shook his head in exasperation. "All right, so there is no 'third.' Look, just who are you, and how do you know so much about me?" She started to respond, but he kept going. "And for crying out loud, what is your name? I'm getting tired of thinking of you as 'that woman'!" That earned him a smile of amusement.

"You can call me Miriam," said the woman, her voice showing a hint of laughter. "And as for 'failing' your test, wherever did you get the idea that there is only one to a customer?" Her smile faded, but her eyes twinkled. "Our lives are filled with tests, David, and once you turn to the Saviour, those tests become increasingly difficult. They are not like the tests you took in school that merely ask you to demonstrate your knowledge. Rather, they are meant to stretch you — to cause you to grow in trust and faith. And," she added, "if you fail one, that does not automatically cancel all the rest. You don't get off that easily, I'm afraid!" David stared at Miriam with a mixture of astonishment and confusion.

"Who *ARE* you?" he repeated.

"Someone sent to help you," replied Miriam. *"That* is all you need to know." David sat digesting this as the bus traveled on.

"You could be using me to get at others of the group," he said finally. He did not really believe what he was saying, but he was interested in how she would respond.

"If I know about you," she replied, "and about where you hold your meetings, do you really think I would have any need for this elaborate charade?" The way she asked the question made it clear that she already knew that answer. David considered it anyway before responding.

"No, I don't," he said finally. "All right, I believe you. You said there were some things I needed to know. What are they?" Miriam nodded in approval.

"That's better," she said. "The first thing is, certain people know about the Fisher's Men." David started, suddenly very alert. That was the code name of his tiny church. Only the few existing members knew it — no one else. Miriam caught his look and smiled. "Does it surprise you that I should know that?"

David shook his head, dumbfounded. "Lady," he murmured quietly, "from now on, I don't think anything you do or say is going to surprise me." That earned him another smile.

"Don't be too sure," she replied.

David thought for a moment. "You said 'certain people.' You mean the local police, or maybe the Bureau of Religious Affairs?" *That* was unsettling indeed. If word got to the Sacramento office of the bureau that he was violating the agreement he had made with them, things were going to get awfully ugly.

"Not really," replied Miriam, "although the local police are watching you carefully. The people who *do* know about the Fisher's Men are far more dangerous. Do you remember the headlines a few months back? The ones that spoke of a terrorist named Wolf?" David nodded immediately.

"Of course. He was supposed to be the leader of a group called the Christian Liberation Front, which, incidentally, was supposed to be made up of dissatisfied believers. As it turned out, he was working for the bureau. There really was no Christian Liberation front. It created quite a stir."

"Your memory serves you well," agreed Miriam. "Then know this. The one called Wolf is still quite active, only now his masters are those who were secretly behind the bureau in the first place. It is his attention you have attracted." David's heart felt as if it had been placed into an express elevator, going down fast.

"Why?" he whispered, shaking his head in amazed bewilderment. "We're small potatoes. A tiny group, just trying to survive."

"*No* church, no matter how tiny, is unimportant to the enemy," corrected Miriam. "Those who seek to destroy the true church will not be satisfied until *every* group is wiped out." David sat digesting this for a moment. When he spoke again, it was with a sense of urgency.

"Then we have to disband, immediately," he said. He looked sideways at Miriam. "You wouldn't happen to know just how they know about us, or who else they suspect, would you?"

"As of now," replied Miriam, "they only suspect you. You would be right to disband, of course. Each member of the Fisher's Men is now strong enough in their faith to start their own group."

"Like sparks flying from a fire that's been stamped out," reflected David quietly, glancing out the window. Turning his attention back to Miriam, he said, "You didn't answer my question completely. Do you know who betrayed us?"

Miriam was silent a moment, then answered softly. "Yes."

"Can you tell me who?" asked David, leaning forward.

Miriam looked back at him, as if once again assessing the strength of his faith. "What were you doing yesterday?" she asked.

The question caught him completely off guard. "Excuse me?" he asked in confusion. "What's that got to do with anything?"

"Just answer me, David. What were you doing?" Miriam's voice had become so commanding that David had to answer.

He thought for a moment, trying to remember. "Well," he began, "that was the day Charley and I had to clean out the waterfall. A lot of people throw pennies in there, and they have to be collected every so often. That took most of the morning."

"Go on," insisted Miriam softly.

"Let's see," said David, concentrating. "After that, we had lunch. Then we split up. He had to replace a few filters, and I . . . I . . . ." He faltered, his mind drawing a blank.

"Concentrate, David. What did you do in the afternoon?"

David rubbed his temples with the effort of thought. His mouth went suddenly dry, and sweat broke out on his forehead. "I . . . can't . . . ARGHHH!" Pain lanced through his head, and a blinding light seared across his vision. The other passengers looked at him uncomfortably, and the driver frowned as he glanced up in his mirror. So great was the pain that he almost fainted. The interior of the bus spun around him, and he had to grip the back of the seat in front of him just to remain upright.

He felt a weight on his shoulders, and realized that Miriam had put her arm around him. "It's okay, David, it's okay," she whispered fiercely into his ear.

"Oh God!" he sobbed, making it a prayer. "What's wrong with me?"

"Shhhh" Gently Miriam rocked him back and forth, like a mother with an ailing infant. "It will pass. Easy now. It will pass." Miriam's gentleness had a soothing effect, and soon he felt the pain ebbing. He found that he was able to sit up. The nausea and throbbing subsided to a nightmarish memory, and he took a deep breath. He looked back at Miriam, and now there was fear in his eyes. Reaching out, he gripped her other arm and held it tightly. "What's wrong with me?" he pleaded, his eyes begging her for an answer.

"You are suffering from drug-induced, post-hypnotic trauma," said Miriam in a soft voice.

"Post what?" David gasped, his voice close to breaking. "I haven't been hypnotized . . . have I?" Again he struggled to recall yesterday's events, but his mind remained blank.

"Hear me, David," whispered Miriam, leaning forward with a sense of urgency, "There is not much time. Yesterday, you were taken from your job and interrogated. The people that kidnapped you were working for Wolf." She smiled grimly. "They were not able to get much out of you. It seems that you have a high resistance to involuntary hypnosis. However, they *were* able to confirm that you were indeed responsible for organizing an underground church."

David's face was ashen, devoid of color. What Miriam was telling him was so unbelievable — yet there was that missing time block, and the headaches. "What about the others?" he gasped, his voice hoarse and raspy. "What about the rest of my group?"

"You did not betray them," answered Miriam, resting a comforting arm on his shoulder. "They are safe, for the moment. In time, they will face their own test, but you need not be concerned with that. Your life is about to change drastically — again. You must prepare yourself for that." David felt himself reaching the breaking point. Too much — too much information, too much shock — was pushing him to the limit. Only Miriam's comforting touch kept him from bolting out of the bus and into the darkness.

"Why me?" he asked quietly, aware of how cliché he sounded.

Miriam regarded him silently for a moment before speaking. "You have been set on a shelf, David," she whispered finally. Her words, though soft, pierced his heart. "You betrayed everything you believed in — everything you held dear, simply to be safe. Because of that, everything you held dear was lost."

"Oh God!" cried David softly, and this time it *was* a prayer.

"At one time, you were a pastor, the leader and under-shepherd of a strong, well-grounded church," continued Miriam.

"Yes," agreed David, the tone of his voice that of utter despair.

"Tell me what happened."

David resisted for a moment, not wanting to dredge up the mess he had buried deep within his soul. There was no denying Miriam, however. "They came to me," he replied, his voice low. "The bureau. They said I was not conforming to state and federal laws governing organized religion. They said they had enough on me to make me disappear for good." He swallowed hard, remembering that long ago conversation in his office, with the two calm and confident bureau agents.

"Understand, Eddington," one of them had said, "we have you — any time we want."

"The thing is," the other one added, "We don't particularly want you. We know that members of your congregation have been holding meetings on their own. We want names, Eddington. Names of those you think would have the guts to do something like that. The names of traitors, Eddington."

"I can't," David had replied desperately.

"Suit yourself," the first had shrugged. "By the way, it's my duty to inform you that you are under arrest. A warrant has also been issued for your wife and son." He had looked at his watch. "They should be arriving at the station just about now."

"Come on, *Pastor,*" said the second, making a mockery out of his title. "You don't want your boy in a detention center. *Believe me,* you don't. They have a nasty habit of, shall we say, 'reprogramming' residents there to be more productive members of society."

"And I can't even begin to tell you about the horrors at the women's center your wife will be sent to," smirked the first. "Of course, it won't matter to you since you won't see them again."

The memories came flooding back into David's mind, unwanted, as he sat there on the bus. "I betrayed my own people," he said flatly, staring ahead, unable to meet Miriam's eyes. "I gave those agents what they wanted. In turn, they left my family alone."

"And . . . ?" prodded Miriam.

"And," said David, drawing a shaky breath, "I ended up losing my family anyway. Jill found out what I had done, of course. Some of her closest friends disappeared because of me. She lost her respect for me because of that."

He could still remember her parting words. "I love you David," she had said, her dark brown eyes red and puffy from crying. "I'll always love you — there will never be anyone else." She looked back at Josh, who was waiting outside on their front porch. "I just can't live with you anymore. You turned your back on God, and you turned your back on us."

"Jill," David moaned, "I did it *for* us. Can't you see that? I wanted us to be safe!"

"You don't even believe that yourself, David," Jill had replied, and there had been pity in her voice. That was worse than the hurt he had seen earlier. "What good is safety if you are not in God's will?" And with that, she had taken Josh and gone to live with her parents in Detroit. David's letters and calls had gone unanswered.

"David?" Miriam's voice brought him back to the present.

"Sorry," he replied, shoving the memories far back into his mind.

"So Jill left," said Miriam.

"She left," agreed David. "I lost my church. By then, everyone knew what I had done. Some agreed with me, but they weren't the backbone of the church. The one's who made it strong were the ones I named to the bureau. The bureau let me go free, all right, but they stabbed me in the back. They came up with enough 'probable cause' to get me removed from the pulpit. I moved here to Sacramento, got a job at the mall, and. . . ."

"And?"

"And that's it. After a few months, I was able to contact a few believers and form the Fisher's Men." He shook his head wearily. "I guess I felt it was sort of, I don't know, atonement. Working off a bad debt — something like that." He shrugged, aggravated by his own vagueness. The truth was, he did not know why he had started that tiny church. "That's where you came in," he continued. "So now you've got the whole story. Satisfied?" He looked at her, unsure whether he wanted absolution or condemnation. Miriam met his gaze, offering neither.

"Look," said David, making a game attempt to rally his courage, "You've dumped a lot of stuff on me. I've just learned that a very dangerous man is after me, I'm under suspicion from the local government, I've been hypnotized and drugged, with who-knows-what done to the inside of my skull, and it seems that once again I've betrayed something I care deeply about . . . so is that it? Is that all you came to tell me?"

"No." Miriam's answer was simple and direct.

"So what else?" asked David, shrugging. "You want me to tell you more deep, dark secrets? Sorry, but you got them all."

"No." Again that quiet reply.

David took a deep breath. "Okay," he said. "What else? It's obviously important, Miriam, for a member of the Shepherd's Path to be approaching me like this." His last statement caused Miriam to smile.

"Ah ha!" he whispered in glee, "I was right. You *are* with them. That's who sent you, and that's how come you know so much. Am I right?" He felt a funny sort of satisfaction to have pierced her veil of secrecy.

"Something like that," she replied, her amusement still showing. "But it's not important. There *is* one more thing. You must have one more meeting with your group."

David stared at her with stunned surprise, then shook his head adamantly. "No way!" he said. "If they already know about us, then meeting again is insane. There's no way we'll be —"

"Safe?" supplied Miriam. "Isn't that what got you into this mess to start with, David? The desire to be safe?"

"You don't understand," said David, trying desperately to understand himself.

"No, *you* don't understand," replied Miriam, and the rebuke in her voice was plain. "Didn't I tell you that God has not forgotten you. He *never* forgets His own. He may set them on the shelf sometimes, when they prove unusable, but He does not forget. He only waits for them to turn back to Him." Miriam gripped his shoulder tightly. "Put your faith back in God, David. Not just the lip service faith you practiced in the pulpit, but the faith that will allow you to stand firm against any foe. He wants to use you. Are you willing?"

There was something about the way she asked the question. Suddenly, David knew, beyond a doubt, that he was being given a choice. Not by Miriam — she was simply a messenger — but by the Most High God. If he said no now, somehow he knew he would never come off that shelf.

He took a deep breath, and made a decision that would change his life for all time. "All right," he whispered, utterly defeated. "If He wants my life, it's His. It sure isn't worth much, but He can have it. Going against Him has caused me to lose everything. Maybe it's time I started putting into practice what I used to teach." He looked back at Miriam, and for the first time, saw approval in her face.

Abruptly, with no warning, he felt lighter, as if he could almost float. He did not have the words right then to describe it, but a great burden had been lifted. "What should I do?" he asked, and there was even a trace of eagerness in his voice.

"Have your meeting," said Miriam, her eyes twinkling. "Two people will attend that have not attended before. You must do everything you can to help them."

"And?"

"That's all," said Miriam. "Just help them."

David shook his head, then shrugged his shoulders. "All right, but it doesn't sound like much to do, especially after all you've been saying about commitment and faith."

"You may be surprised," replied Miriam. "Just remember, David, to trust God in *all* things. Don't trust your own feelings. Stay true to your commitment, and strong in your faith. Nothing can happen to you that God does not allow. The test coming will be difficult, perhaps even deadly, but if you persevere, the fire will make you strong and pure." She paused. Then, very softly, she added, "There's something else you need to know. Your headaches will not go away anytime soon. The drugs they used on you damaged your brain."

David felt his mouth go dry. "How bad?" he whispered.

"Bad enough," replied Miriam. "There will be some pretty intense pain. You'll just have to live with it for now."

"Will it heal?" David asked, dreading the answer.

Miriam only shook her head. "That's not for me to say. Healing may come later, or not."

The bus lurched to a stop. David glanced out the window, and saw that it was not yet his stop. An elderly man was boarding in the front. Beside him, Miriam stood up. "This is where I get off," she said, squeezing past him.

"You're not coming with me?" asked David in surprise.

"Go to your place?" she asked in mock shock, her mood lighter than he had seen all night. "On the first date? What kind of girl do you think I am?" *That* caused him to blush. Before he could think of a reply, she leaned close and whispered, "You know everything you need to know. Remember what I told you, David. No matter what, stay true to God. It's the only way."

With that, Miriam stepped off the bus and disappeared into the darkness. The driver closed the door and the bus lurched into motion again. David stared out the window, his eyes seeing nothing, his mind racing. Abruptly, tears clouded his eyes. He was being given a second chance! There was no doubt that Miriam was speaking the truth. The incredible fact was, God was not finished with him! He sat back in the seat, feeling better than he had in months. He never saw Miriam again.

3

Paul felt the vague stirrings of fear start to creep up on him and suppressed a shudder. How many times, he wondered grimly, had he been on the opposite end of this very scenario? He was standing on the second floor of the East Garden Mall, looking down onto the first level. He leaned against the railing that ran along the edge of the balcony-like floor, surveying the area. He had already spotted his contact. She was sitting next to the statue of Gaia, the earth goddess, right where she was supposed to be. She was an older woman of about 60, black with pure gray hair. Her wrinkled face and thin, almost emaciated frame, told of a hard life. The thick, heavy-framed glasses she wore rode low on the bridge of her nose. In her hands she held an open book with the stylized "empty tomb" emblazoned on the front.

Gritting his teeth, Paul surveyed the immediate area. There was no doubt in his mind that the terrorist Wolf would have his own people there, watching him. In fact, he had already spotted one of them. A tall man, almost as tall as Paul, in a dark blue business suit, sat rigidly on a bench on the far side of the second level. He was pretending to read a paper. Paul had noticed him within five minutes of his arrival at the mall. He was either the worst excuse for a "tail" that Paul had ever seen, or a decoy, meant to draw Paul's attention away from the real watchers. Paul was guessing the latter. The man in the suit was too obvious. The problem was, he had not noticed anyone else paying him undue attention.

Swearing under his breath, he began to walk casually away from the old woman, heading toward the center of the mall. The man in the suit, predictably, got up and followed. Again the fear that hovered in the back of Paul's mind threatened to reassert itself. He ran through his Zen techniques, but this time they failed him. This had never happened to him before. On previous operations, he had always been able to control his emotions. His icy cool demeanor had become something of a trademark among his fellow agents. This time was different. His heart was pounding, and a thin sheen of sweat covered his forehead. It was a condition he found he did not like, made worse by the fact that he knew why it was happening.

During his years with the bureau, Paul had accomplished countless missions, many considered dangerous by his superiors. Before that, he had served with military intelligence as an advisor in Egypt. He and an elite team had taken on many varied and life-threatening projects. In all that time, he had never been as afraid as he was now. The reason was simple. Here and now, he was alone — utterly on his own. There was no backup, no one to call in case things went "down twisted." Before, he could always rely on his team to get him out of any sticky situations. Now, the only people that were aware of his mission were just as likely to slit his throat as to rescue him. It was not a good feeling, and Paul found himself resenting having it. He had always considered himself equal to any task given. Now, part of him wanted to run away, to burrow into the woodwork so that not even God could find him.

Instead he continued to walk the mall, carefully studying his surroundings. Every face that passed he scrutinized under heavily lidded eyes. Was it the man selling balloons off to his left? The woman at the information booth? Perhaps even someone as obvious as the passing security guard? Despite his efforts, no one seemed out of place. There was nothing to do but collect Susan and get on with it.

Straightening his shoulders, Paul headed for the nearest exit. He had left Susan in the rented car, with strict orders not to move. Three days of rest, massive vitamin doses, and detoxification techniques had not restored her to full awareness, but at least she was now able to understand and obey his commands. Whether or not she would ever fully recover only time would tell. They had not been gentle with her at Rollings — or at Mentasys.

Paul picked up his stride, letting anger replace the fear. His whole life depended upon his carefully laid plans, and now these plans depended upon the charity of a terrorist and the recognition of an old woman who got her kicks playing "front man" for clandestine meetings.

He had debated getting rid of Susan. *That* part of his scheme had failed utterly. She had not drawn the needed attention of the Shepherd's Path, and now she was a liability. She had no ID, and her file was now on display at every law enforcement agency in the nation. One single computer network, the Omninet, now unified the local and federal authorities, cutting through miles of red tape. There would be no place they could go where she might not be spotted. Not only that, but sooner or later she would probably recognize him as the one who had arrested her and her husband. That would completely end her usefulness. It made sense to get rid of her. Still. . . .

Paul reached the entrance and stepped out into the unseasonably warm California weather. He spotted his car, with Susan still in the front seat, and headed across the pavement toward her. *Still,* he told himself, *she could be useful.* One man, traveling alone and seeking refuge, might arouse suspicion. A couple, however, seemed more natural — and there was the fact that he had rescued her from Rollings. His actions had been all over the news. Surely members of the Shepherd's Path would be aware of it. When he revealed himself to be the one who had gotten her out, it would go a long way in building the necessary trust he would need to finally destroy them. He reached the rented car and opened the passenger door.

"Let's go, Susan," he said softly. Slowly Susan turned her head and looked at him blankly.

"Tim?" Her voice betrayed how weak she still was. When Paul had pulled her out of Rollings, she had been near death. She still was not out of the woods. The vitamins, stimulants, and antibiotics had helped, but she was still on the edge. Her immune system was probably in shambles, and her mind was lost in a fog — perhaps permanently.

"Tim's not here, Susan," replied Paul gently. "I'm taking you to him. Remember? Its a long way, but we'll get there. Come on now." Carefully he helped her out of the car. She leaned against him, still barely able to walk. Slowly they made their way back across the parking lot and re-entered the mall. Somewhere deep inside his heart, Paul hated himself for the lie he was telling Susan. Her husband Tim had died months ago at Mentasys. When she finally discovered the truth, it would probably destroy what was left of her. He kept at it, though, burying those feelings below the rationalization of necessity. He still might need her.

It did not take them long to reach the statue of the earth goddess. To his surprise and consternation, the old woman was gone. He glanced around, but could not spot her anywhere nearby. He shifted his gaze to the second level, and, sure enough, his tail was still there, pretending to read that ridiculous paper. What to do now, he wondered, chewing the inside of his lip nervously. Had the meeting been canceled? He looked at his watch, and saw that there was still 15 minutes before the given time. Perhaps everyone had already arrived, and the woman had gone to join them. That would mean Paul and Susan would be left out. They could hardly search every nook and cranny of the mall until they found the underground church. There must be dozens of places they could hide. He thought about things for a moment.

This group was probably a closed one. Every member knew the other. It was the only way they could survive. So why bother to have a front man in the first place? Probably, he knew, because of the Shepherd's Path. According to his understanding, they were constantly moving people from place to place. The old woman most likely would wait a certain amount of time in case anyone on the run turned up. When they didn't, she would join the meeting. Of course, there would be no reason for elaborate codes among the regular attendees. That meant that she had probably already left.

Suddenly, for some unknown reason, Paul was filled with a strange, almost palpable sense of loss. He felt abandoned and alone, cast out. It was almost as bad as the day he found out his father was never coming home. Angrily, he shoved his feelings aside. He was feeling abandoned, he told himself fiercely, because everything was falling apart. Nothing was working out the way he had planned. Almost roughly, he led Susan to the same bench where the old woman had been sitting.

"Rest here," he told her, his voice betraying his frustration. Susan did as she was told, sitting quietly. Paul slumped down beside her, his chin cupped in his hands. He stared back the way they had come, wondering what to do next.

"Excuse me, young man, but would you mind moving over a bit?" The voice jolted him out of his glum reverie. He jerked his head up, looking in the opposite direction. Sure enough, the old woman had returned. She stood there looking at him, her thick glasses magnifying her eyes to almost double their actual size. Relief flooded through Paul, and he quickly moved over several inches, scooting Susan in the process. The old woman nodded her thanks, and sat down primly. Paul looked away, desperately trying to recall the Bible verses he had worked so hard to memorize. One of Wolf's people had delivered a Bible a few days ago. Who knew where it had come from?

The old woman studied him thoughtfully. "You two sure aren't from around here, are you?"

That took Paul aback, and it was a few seconds before he could answer. "Uh, no, not really," he stammered the reply. Inwardly he cursed himself for his clumsiness. He was acting like a rank amateur! Where was the calm, ruthless professional he had been just a few months ago?

"Thought not," nodded the woman, satisfied. "You have that 'out of state' look about you. Where you folks from?"

"Cincinnati," replied Paul quickly, saying the first thing that came into his head. Actually, it was almost true. He had been working there, and Susan was indeed from that general area.

"Never been there," said the old woman, shaking her head. "Never been anywhere, for that matter," she added, chuckling heartily.

She grinned at Paul, revealing shiny white, almost perfect teeth. The sight of that huge smile, framed by the deeply wrinkled dark skin and magnified eyes, was so comical that Paul, despite his fear and anger, actually smiled back. There was something about this woman that he immediately liked. He wanted to trust her, to confide in her. That in itself was surprising, since it was totally out of character for him. It went against every bit of training he had. Nevertheless, the feelings were there. For just a moment, Paul Sinclair actually felt good.

The old woman held his eyes for a moment, then pulled a thick, paperback book out of an overstuffed purse and began to read. The sight of the cover, with the circle half covering a square, jolted Paul back into reality.

He gathered his thoughts, took a deep breath, and said the words he hoped would give back his life. "Take these things away. Stop making my father's house a house of merchandise." He spoke the verse low, hoping it would carry against the background noise of the mall.

The woman continued to read her book for a moment, then quietly, in a tone matching Paul's, replied, "And his disciples remembered that it was written, The zeal of thine house hath eaten me up." Paul took a deep breath. She had given the countersign! He was off and running at last! Then, what she said actually registered, and he blinked in confusion. The reply was close to what he had memorized, but not quite exactly right.

The old woman noted his look of confusion, and patted his hand reassuringly. "Sorry, brother," she said smiling that smile that Paul had found so appealing. "I have a weak place in my heart for the king's English. I was brought up on the King James Version of the Word."

Paul nodded, not quite understanding. He was aware that before the Purge, when Bibles were collected and burned, there were various translations of the Book available in almost any bookstore. It was one of the things he had always found absurd about Christianity. If the Bible really did hold the secrets of eternal life and all those other things believers taught, wouldn't it make sense to agree on one version? There must have been dozens floating around as little as seven years ago. This "King James," he guessed, must be a different version than what Wolf had provided him with.

"That's all right," he replied, once again unable to meet her smile without giving one of his own. "I hope my version is good enough to get us in?" That caused the old woman to laugh, which quickly faded into a half smile.

"We don't get many outsiders," she replied. "I should ask you who you are and why you want to join us." She looked at him expectantly, waiting his reply.

"A friend of a friend told us to come here," he lied, mentally crossing his fingers. "We're in trouble and need help. How about it? Is my version good enough for you?"

Again the old woman laughed. "Young man," she cackled, "in this day and age, if you can get your hands on any translation of our beloved Word, consider yourself blessed." For some odd reason, her eyes filled with tears. She pulled off her glasses and quickly brushed them away. "Sorry," she apologized, replacing the glasses. "I just can't help but remember when having your very own Bible wasn't a criminal offense. Too many of us were caught flat-footed. Most of us had not bothered to memorize all that much Scripture." She sighed. "We never realized just what a treasure God had given us until we lost the right to read it." She looked back at Paul, the smile gone and the large eyes now somber.

"What do you use for recognition, then," asked Paul, "If a lot of people ... er, brothers and sisters don't know any verses." He might as well get all the information he could from her, he knew.

The old woman smiled knowingly. "There are ways," she said, her smile growing wider. "You recognized me by this," and she held up the "empty tomb" logo. "Besides our signs, many of us who *do* know some of God's Word are teaching the rest by word of mouth. Some of us have pooled our knowledge and have written down what we know. Why, this group alone almost has the complete Book of John!" Her voice turned eager. "The word is, we may even get a New Testament sent to us sometime soon! Wouldn't that be grand?" The old woman droned on, telling of how wonderful it would be if her group could obtain their own Bible. Paul nodded in what seemed like the right places, letting her continue. He was discovering, to his confusion, that this woman was not what he had been expecting.

Thanks in part to his years with the bureau, he had painted a picture of what he believed "Christians' to be like. Fanatics, for one thing. Religious zealots not unlike those who spread such terror during the Inquisition, or looted Palestine during the Crusades. His whole experience with religion before the purge, had been what he had seen on television. Greedy, power-craving individuals holding sway over millions. On a local level, churches taught that they held the only way to eternal life, controlling the lives of their members through intimidation and fear.

It wasn't just that he wanted to see religion controlled. He wanted it out of the lives of the ordinary person for good. There was no place for it in this brave new world, he felt. Only when humanity let go of its fear of the unknown, and released the need for the crutch of a belief in an all-powerful being, would it be able to move forward to true enlightenment.

To that end he had hunted underground churches relentlessly, totally committed to eliminating them. The thing was, he had never taken the time or trouble to interview those whom he arrested. They were from all walks of life, young and old, male and female, rich and poor. To him, though, they were all alike — subversive. They held mankind in the chains of fear and uncertainty, and they had to be stopped.

Now, here in this mall, he was forced to sit and talk face to face with one of those he was bent on destroying — and she was not like she was supposed to be. She was not a fanatic, not a zealot. She was just an old woman who believed in God, to the extent that she was willing to risk imprisonment and even death to meet with others who felt the same way.

These and other thoughts chased themselves around in Paul's mind as he sat and listened to the old woman. He finally decided that she must be one of the controlled — one of the sheep. Others he met would undoubtedly be the controllers.

"Oh my word!" The exclamation startled Paul out of his thoughts, and he refocused on the old woman. She was looking intently at Susan, who still sat next to him with the same blank expression. Paul glanced over at her, and realized how she must look to someone seeing her for the first time.

"My eyes," said the old woman, shaking her head in disgust. "I can't see worth anything. What in the world happened to your friend? She looks terrible."

Paul debated lying, then decided to tell her. The more people who knew about his "heroism," the better. "She's not doing well at all," explained Paul, adding a note of grimness into his voice for effect. Enough about the way he felt toward this old woman. He had a job to do, and he was going to do it, no matter what the cost. "She was in a mental institution just a few days ago. I'm afraid they were not too gentle with her." The old woman's eyes widened in recognition.

"You're the ones I've been hearing about on the news!" She was so surprised that she practically shouted. Paul quickly brought his hands to his mouth in a shushing motion.

"We need help," he repeated, whispering. "Can you take us to your church? I don't know where else to go." He hoped he sounded forlorn enough.

"Oh my Lord! Where is your mind, Virginia?" replied the woman, referring to herself in obvious disgust. "I sit here talking as if it's the safest thing in the world, and all the time, this poor child needs help. Come on, my friends. Lets get you into the fold." With that, she stood up, and took off down the mall with surprising speed.

"Come on, Susan," said Paul quietly as he got up. "We're going." Obediently, Susan rose. Paul put a strong arm around her and guided her. Together they followed their strange guide past the mostly empty stores. She led them down the east wing, and then veered left into the south wing. Paul glanced back over his shoulder, up toward the second level. Sure enough, Mister Suit was still with them. He obviously knew that Paul had spotted him, and was no longer making any pretense of not following.

They continued their journey, and Paul began to be concerned for Susan's stamina. She was not up for even the briefest walks, and this was straining her to her limits. She was starting to breath raggedly, and Paul was just about to call for a rest, when the old woman abruptly turned into one of the many women's clothing stores. Paul followed, with Susan laboring beside him. Without pausing, their guide led them back to the rear of the store, ignoring the two attendants who, in turn, ignored them. Within moments, they were through the store. The old woman opened the back door and led them into the hall that connected the backs of all the stores. Red, yellow, and green pipes ran overhead, and various colored stripes were painted along the plain, cement floor.

"Follow the blue stripe," instructed the old woman. "It will lead you left, then left again. When you come to the stairs, take them down. Then turn right and knock on the second door you come to. Got it?" Paul nodded, and the old woman smiled that wonderful smile that Paul could not help returning.

"Aren't you coming with us?" he asked.

She shook her head negatively. "Not tonight. My turn to stand guard. Might be some stragglers," she replied. "Got to keep watch. Besides," she continued, lowering her voice, "the enemy has eyes and ears everywhere. Someone has to give a warning if things fall apart."

Paul nodded, suddenly feeling uncomfortable. There was something incredibly honest and pure about this woman, not at all what he had pictured in his mind. He actually felt slightly ashamed for deceiving her.

"I hope we meet again, then," he said, meaning it.

Once more he was treated to that smile. "Of course we will," she said, calm assurance permeating her voice. "If not in this life, then afterward. Now get going." She made small shooing motions with her hands. "You've wasted enough of my time." With that, she stepped back into the shop, closing the door behind her.

"Goodbye, then," whispered Paul softly. He stared at the door a moment longer. A quiet longing that he could not begin to explain started to grow inside of him. That old woman had something — something special. He had never felt anything like it before. Suddenly he straightened his shoulders and shook his head. His old anger, dormant during his rendezvous, quickly reasserted itself. "Real good, Sinclair," he said aloud, sarcasm replacing the gentleness he had just found. "Going soft because some old crone smiles funny at you. Enough of this!"

With that, he grabbed Susan's arm and propelled her down the hallway. She responded automatically, making no sounds other than her heavy breathing. Paul followed the blue stripe just as he had been told, taking the stairs down to the basement. He found the proper door, marked "Storage," and knocked quietly. At first there was no response. He waited impatiently, looking up and down the hall, making sure that no one was watching. They had left their clumsy tail behind when they had entered the dress shop. For all of his efforts, Paul had still been unable to locate a second one. He was just about to knock again when the door opened, just enough for him to see part of a maintenance uniform.

"Yeah?" asked a low, gravely voice. Paul thought quickly, then recited the verses he had labored so hard to learn.

"Truly, truly, I say to you, unless one is born of water and the Spirit, he cannot enter into the kingdom of God." He spoke the words automatically, just as he had learned them. He had absolutely no idea what he was saying.

The half-face he could see studied him for a moment, then looked over at Susan. For just a moment, the one eye he could see widened, as if in recognition. Then it snapped back to Paul, appraising him anew. Finally, whoever it was spoke. "That which is born of the flesh is flesh, and that which is born of the Spirit. Do not marvel that I say to you, You must be born again."

With that, the door opened wider, revealing the man in the maintenance outfit. He was shorter than Paul by a good eight inches, though almost as broad-shouldered. A short crop of dark hair framed a plain but handsome face. "Come on in," he said, moving aside. "Sorry to keep you for so long, but we don't get strangers here too often. We have to be careful." Paul nodded, and entered the small room, leading Susan. Mops, buckets, and drums of cleaning mixtures lined the walls, and the whole place smelled of disinfectant. Fluorescent lights glowed overhead, running the length of the ceiling.

Paul ran his eyes across his surroundings, his trained eyes missing nothing. In the center of the room, space had been cleared, and eight people sat in a rough circle one the floor, holding hands. They looked absurdly like any one of the hundreds of other groups he had destroyed. Three men and five women looked at the new arrivals, the curiosity evident in their faces. It was obvious that the maintenance man spoke the truth. These people all knew and trusted each other. Strangers would be looked at with suspicion and distrust.

Paul noted each one of them, memorizing their features for later reference. He was not sure what these folk were up to, or what they had to gain by taking such great risk, but he was now sure of one thing. No one in here presented any kind of threat to him personally. Even if his cover were blown, he could easily handle them all. That much was obvious from the way they were sitting. No one here was a trained fighter. And yet. . . .

Paul smiled, a smile that he hoped was convincing, and raised a hand in greeting. Inside he was suddenly nervous. Once again he scanned the occupants. He could feel something in this room, something that he could not identify. No one here was a match for him, but for some odd reason, he felt a great danger. Not to himself physically, nor in any way he could describe. It was almost as if it was his very being that was threatened — his whole self, everything that he was.

No, even that was not right.

Although he could not understand it, he felt that if he was not careful, he was in grave danger of being *changed*— of being totally made over. The very thought of that sent a thrill of fear and anger coursing through his heart. Using every ounce of mind control he had ever learned, he squashed his feelings ruthlessly. He hoped that no one noticed his hesitation, but then realized that only a few seconds had lapsed. Lowering his hand, he spoke the words that he had been given. "The Lord is risen," he said in a calm, even voice.

"The Lord is risen indeed," came back the reply in perfect unison. The smile Paul smiled was sincere, convincing, and a total sham.

* * *

Wolf sat in a sleek, black Mercedes in the parking lot of the East Garden Mall. He had a penchant for fine cars. Just now, though, his mind was not on his "toy." His nervous eyes were constantly on the move, roving from the main entrance of the mall to the surrounding vehicles. Anyone who moved too close was considered a possible threat. Impatiently he drummed his fingers on the leather covered dashboard. A crushed cigarette, a half-blend of tobacco and marijuana, sat smoldering in the ashtray. The pungent aroma surrounded him, wreathing him in a thin blanket of smoke.

He licked his lips, muttering harsh curses under his breath. Waiting was something he did very badly, and waiting was all he *had* been doing for the past several days. If he had to sit and do nothing much longer, someone was going to get hurt.

Reaching into his jacket pocket, he pulled out another smoke. Just as he lit up one of the long, brown cigarettes, his car vid-phone, located in the exact center of the dashboard, buzzed for his attention. Forgetting everything else, he reached over and punched the "on" button. The harsh face of Demos stared back at him. Clad in the uniform of a security guard, he was the second operative that Paul Sinclair had been unable to spot.

"Yeah," snarled Wolf. His tone warned Demos not to waste his time.

"He's in," replied Demos, taking the cue.

"Where?"

"Not sure. We lost him when he was led into one of the shops. As we suspected, they must be meeting in the basement somewhere. We'll tag them when they come out."

"Make sure you do," growled Wolf. "I don't trust that idiot Sinclair. You get a 'make' on the rest of the group?" Demos nodded, saying nothing. "All right then. Get back to work. You can reach me at this number if anything changes. I've got to see to a few other matters." Again, Demos simply nodded and terminated the call. Wolf sat there, staring at the blank screen. Suddenly he smiled.

"All right, Sinclair," he muttered, "show us what you got." He started the car and put it in gear. As he drove toward the main road, his smile became a grin. Things were picking up. Maybe soon, he would get to kill someone.

* * *

The city of New York had changed little outwardly over the past decade. The Statue of Liberty still held her torch high in the harbor. Wall Street still buzzed as one of the business capitals of the world, although the new European Federation was gradually replacing it as an economic powerhouse. The rich, near rich, and the "wanna be rich" still played in the vast city. The "Big Apple," to all outward appearances, still functioned. Insiders knew better.

It wasn't just that the economic structure of the city was collapsing. With the "Greater Depression," as the media had taken to calling it, in full force, that was to be expected. The problem was, the city itself was falling apart. Water ducts over a century old were collapsing, causing massive sewage backups. Highways built over the ruins of out-of-date roads were sinking. In some places traffic had been rerouted altogether, forcing the city's already massive traffic pattern to almost a standstill. Buildings with a designed life span of 10 years or less were falling apart, and there was no money to rebuild. It was like a disease. A cancer was gradually spreading over the entire area, choking the life out of a metropolis that was just barely hanging on.

Over the bustle of day-to-day life, a blanket of hopelessness was settling, clinging to everyone. No one had a solution that would pull the once great city out of its tail spin. As one former official put it, "The only way to fix this place is to nuke it, wait for the dust to settle, then start over." It was this statement that had cost him his job.

Surprisingly, the docks of New York were the least affected by the city's demise. Perhaps this was because they were dreadful to begin with. Home to humanities' discardings, they plodded on, oblivious to the rest of the world. To say that a "rough" crowd hung out here was like saying Tiffany's was a "nice" jewelry store. Only those with the greatest will to live survived. Not necessarily the strong. More often than not, the strong ended up dead in a back alley somewhere. The cunning, the back stabbers, and the crafty were the ones who thrived in this burrow of wretchedness. Every vice known to man, and a few unknown ones, could be found on the docks of New York.

It was a bitterly cold night in the dying city, the same night that Paul and Susan finally made contact with David Eddington's underground church. On the docks, the nocturnal beings that haunted the place were beginning to stir. Somewhere a dog was barking. It made a macabre counter-melody to the sounds of revelry coming from the Red Lion Bar. Loud voices raised themselves in competition with each other, and the stench of stale beer, tobacco, and drugs, both legal and not, wafted out of the heavy oak front door and onto the still street.

Outside, a single, solitary figure waited, listening to the noise. Tall, lean, and foreboding, the dark-skinned man seemed out of place. He stood quietly, an immovable dark tower. A navy blue sailor's coat was wrapped tightly around his lithe, athletic frame, keeping out the cold. His breath came out in a slow, steamy mist.

It wasn't his clothes that made him stand out, nor the color of his skin. Blacks, along with whites, Hispanics, Indians, and a half dozen other races mingled freely on the docks. The true discrimination here was made between the ones who could fight back and the ones who could not. No, there was something else about this man that said he was not a native of these parts.

He stood silently, as if waiting for someone or something. Once, he checked his watch, although he did not seem impatient or in a hurry. A group of sailors, fresh off their freighter, sauntered by. They were already quite drunk, and talking loudly among themselves. One of them, a tall, swarthy man with huge bulging arms, paused to notice the dark man. For a moment, it looked as if he wanted to convert his merrymaking into a more violent variety of entertainment. He leered at the stranger, his breath reeking of spirits. Reaching out, he made as if to shove the smaller man. He froze. Something, perhaps the forbidding look on the dark man's face, stopped him in mid-motion. He stood there for a split second, undecided, then put his arm down and moved on. He caught up with his friends, never looking back. The dark man simply watched him go, then returned to his own thoughts.

Minutes passed. Finally, another shadow appeared out of the darkness. In contrast to the previous visitor, this one approached the dark man slowly, almost tentatively. As the vague shape came forward, the light from the tavern revealed a shorter, disheveled, tired-looking man in worn green work pants and heavy overcoat. Although he could have been no more than 30, the look of defeat and exhaustion on his face easily aged him 10 years.

Eyes bleary with fatigue eyed the dark man with suspicion and distrust. For a moment it looked as if he were going to turn around and disappear back into the darkness. With a smooth, fluid motion, the dark man held up a hand, speaking softly. No one but the newcomer could have heard him. As soon as the newcomer heard the dark man's words, he visibly relaxed. He replied, and the dark man nodded. For a moment, the two simply stared at each other, as if sizing one another up. Then the newcomer put out a hand, and the dark man took it in a firm grip. Their handshake, in contrast to their initial meeting, had the warmth of loving brothers, long separated and just reunited.

The dark man put his arm around his new companion's shoulders, gently guiding him away from the pub. He spoke briefly, asking a question. In response, the newcomer pointed in the direction of a pitch black alley just a few yards ahead. The dark man nodded, and the two men crossed the distance separating them from the alley. Here, the dark man paused, fishing in his pocket and pulling out a small flashlight. He lit the tiny but powerful beam, and the two men entered the alley. They made their way past piles of refuse and overflowing trash bins.

Following the newcomer's directions, they navigated about halfway down to the dead end. The dark man pointed with his flashlight, sending the beam racing between old boxes and trash cans. Suddenly it came to rest on two sets of bright, frightened eyes. A young woman crouched there, her arm wrapped protectively around a blond haired boy of no more than six years of age. Both were shivering with cold. They stared back into the light, looking like frightened deer ready to bolt for the nearest cover. Quickly the newcomer rushed forward, putting his arms around both of them. In one instant, they were transformed from three separate individuals into a single entity — a family. They hugged each other fiercely, as if it would be the last time. The dark man looked on, enigmatic face revealing no emotion. For just an instant, though, his eyes flashed dangerously. A spark of anger surfaced, then was quickly squelched. Saying nothing, he gestured with the flashlight. The meaning was obvious. It was time to go. The newcomer whispered softly to his wife and son, and the fear in their eyes faded — just a little. They rose and fell into step with their strange guide. Setting a brisk pace, he led them out of the alley and down the darkened street.

The next 40 minutes were a blur to the tired family. Later, when they tried to reconstruct their journey, they found that they could only remember bits and pieces. The dark man led them down narrow streets past long abandoned buildings. Their surroundings took on a sinister tint, and life itself became a surreal dream. The street lights were few, and the only other light was from the distant city proper and the full moon above. The young husband could easily imagine inhabitants from a bygone era still haunting the decaying streets.

His tired mind became convinced that what he was seeing did not exist except in the dark of night. With the coming of morning, it would surely disappear. Every so often, far in the distance, he caught glimpses of the New York skyline. It was only those brief sightings of modern civilization that reminded him that he was still in the twenty-first century. If not for that, he would have believed that he and his family had stepped through some sort of time warp, traveling far back into the past.

Finally, the eerie trip ended. The dark man led them to a ramshackle, five-story brick building that in better days had been the offices of a small, merchant marine shipping company. Long ago abandoned and condemned, it suited the dark man's purposes perfectly. He pulled a set of keys out of his pants pocket. Straining in the uncertain light, he picked out the proper one and opened the front door. Motioning for the family to follow, he led them inside. They halted just past the door, unable to see in the near total darkness. A stuffy, musty odor met them as they entered. There was no ventilation, and the cold air was stifling.

The dark man shut and locked the door behind them, then turned on his flashlight. The husband then noticed that all of the windows had been blacked out, so that no telltale light could escape into the street.

Their silent guide led them up two flights of stairs, then into a small room that contained a large, king-sized mattress lying on the floor. There was a tiny window facing the street below that was mercifully open about an inch, letting in a chill but fresh breeze. A small, battery-run space heater glowed a cheery greeting. In contrast to their dwellings of the past few days, this room felt almost homey to the ragged family.

The dark man spoke in a low voice, telling the family to rest here for a while, warning them not to make any light. The wife sagged against her husband, her reserves of energy completely exhausted. The dark man nodded to the husband, then left, closing the door quietly behind him. Without further word, the family collapsed as one onto the large, lumpy mattress. Snuggling as close together as possible for mutual comfort and assurance, they were asleep in seconds.

* * *

As quietly as he had entered, Jeff Anderson left the frightened family behind and climbed the darkened stairs to the top floor of the old building. Following the flashlight beam, he entered the first room he came to. Once, this large area might have been an executive office. It had been divided off into two separate enclosures. The first was a smaller room that was probably an outer office. The second was much larger, with two windows facing the same direction as the room he had left his guests in. It was this place that he had converted into his headquarters.

The outer room was devoid of any furniture, bare and stark. The inner office held a small cot, a battered night stand, and, most incongruous of all, a makeshift computer table. On the table sat a terminal, keyboard, and monitor. Jeff stepped over to the table and eased himself into the metal folding chair in front of it. Reaching behind the terminal, he flipped a series of switches. There was a muffled beep, and then a steady hum as the computer awoke.

The harsh glare of the monitor revealed the stern features of the former FBI agent. At one time, he could have been considered attractive. He was in his late thirties and had a broad, handsome face that, in better times, had been quick to smile. Etched into that face, however, were the recent signs of a hard life. There was a grimness, a heaviness that bespoke of one who had seen too much cruelty, too much madness. There was a harsh anger there as well — buried so deep that even he was not completely aware of its existence.

The computer took its time, but the programming finally booted itself into the on-board memory. He grunted in satisfaction. This was the only room in the building that had electricity. It had taken him several weeks of secretive, dangerous work to run power from the street light outside. The small transformer next to the screen that regulated the power flow was undependable to say the least. He could only run his makeshift setup for minutes at a time before the smell of burning insulation forced him to shut down. Some day, he would not be able to bring it up at all.

Quickly he activated the internal modem, saying a brief prayer of thanks for the dedicated businessman who supplied the cellular satellite uplink. Running electricity was relatively easy. There was no way he could ever acquire communications capability in the same manner. If it was ever discovered what purpose the businessman's private channel was being put to, he would certainly be in very deep trouble.

Obediently, the computer activated the proper programming and accessed a satellite uplink. It took several minutes of searching for him to find what he was looking for. The files of the Shepherd's Path were some of the best protected anywhere. He had designed them that way. Even so, they had been breached once before. Since then, newer, better safeguards had been built into the system. The files still were kept in the public access section of the Omninet, but no longer did they stay in one place. Jeff had added a program that caused the files to create new files at irregular intervals. They would then copy themselves into these files, erasing the old ones in the process. The result was, they were never in the same location twice. Only a series of passwords and codes allowed the user to track them down.

Even this was a band-aid at best, he knew. Now that authorities knew about the existence of the network, they would continue to try to break it. Sooner or later, they might succeed. Jeff knew he had to find a better way to keep the Shepherd's Path organized.

Dutifully he waded through the safeguards he had designed into the system. He felt a moment's regret that the average believer, on the run and alone, could no longer tap into the network. Things were far too dangerous now to allow so many people the knowledge of how to access the files. Only the hundreds of safe houses scattered across the nation who had proved themselves over time, were now allowed access. It made the system easier and safer to operate, but it also made things much harder on the individual Christian.

There was a single "beep," and there, on the screen, appeared the first file that had become the heart of the Shepherd's Path. It consisted of a series of names and locations — the identities of safe houses. If this or any other "Path" file ever fell into government hands, the Shepherd's Path would be seriously compromised, if not destroyed. Quickly Jeff scanned down the list, looking for a particular name. He found it about halfway down, placed the cursor over it, and called it up on the screen. This was the last place that the family sleeping below had stayed. He entered a single, five digit code and a few brief instructions, then exited the file. The next time that particular safe house operator checked his file, he would know that the family he had sheltered had arrived safely at their next destination. Jeff's next step would be to get them safely out of the country.

Using the remaining few precious minutes of computer time he was allowed by his precarious setup, he checked for any personal messages. There were two. He smiled as one from Scott and Beth Sampson crossed the screen. How far they had come since their ordeal a few months ago! They were now integral parts of the network — moving believers through their part of the country, and leading a local underground church as well. Jeff remembered the first time he had met Scott. Frightened, and weak, he little resembled the spiritual warrior he was now. He had finally come to grips with his faith, willing to endure anything for his Saviour. The message was short and direct — a single traveler was heading his way. He would arrive in about a week. Jeff would get more details as he drew nearer.

The second message was of a totally different vein. It was from Stephen Lynch, former enemy, now semi-trusted friend. Not six months ago, he had been an embittered, hate-filled foe of Christianity. It had been Stephen who had broken the computer net and all but destroyed the Shepherd's Path. God was still working in his life. While not a believer yet, he was becoming more and more willing to listen. Jeff was often reminded of what the apostle Paul must have been like when thinking of his volatile friend.

Stephen had made a 180-degree turn in his life. He still worked for the government, although not with the Bureau of Religious Affairs. He now functioned as a freelance special liaison for the IRS, working with the FBI on cases of corporate fraud. He also ran his own private investigative office that, at last report, was doing fairly well. Steve was not an active member of the Shepherd's Path. He felt that he could be more valuable working outside the system. Nevertheless, he had proved to be a priceless source of information. Between Stephen and others he had cultivated during his FBI days, Jeff was able to keep fairly accurate tabs on the inner workings of the government.

Jeff frowned as he read the message Stephen had left for him. The past two days had been spent out of touch, living on the streets, waiting for the family below to show up. Now he was paying the price for his lack of information.

"Wheew!" The exclamation burst involuntarily from his pursed lips. This certainly was a bombshell! Stephen's message related the appearance and subsequent escape of Susan Ferguson from Rollings Mental Institution in Sacramento. He remembered her name well, along with the 11 other believers who had been arrested during that fateful raid in Covington. It had been that raid on a run-down furniture store that had eventually cost him his career with the FBI. If it hadn't been for God's infinite grace, it would have cost him his freedom as well. Since then, no one who had been arrested that night had been found — until now.

Stephen had not been able to gather all the details, but a few conclusions were easy to make. Susan was rescued from the outside — and it had been a professional job. Now that was unusual. Jeff knew for a fact that the Shepherd's Path was not involved. While he himself had participated in the rescue of Beth Sampson from the human-made hell of Mentasys, it was generally considered too dangerous to get Christians out of custody once they had been arrested. Oh, there were cases, but not too many. The question was, then, *who* had made the rescue? A professional, Stephen had said. Certainly there were many believers still in the law enforcement system — working within that system to assist Christians on the run. Many of them were an important part of the Shepherd's Path. Jeff's instincts, however, told him that none of these valuable people were responsible. It just did not sound right. Stephen himself had no idea who did it. The only thing Jeff could do, then, was wait for Susan and her benefactor to resurface. Perhaps they would be able to make contact with a member of the "Path." Until then, all he could do was watch, and wait.

The acid smell of the overheated transformer reminded Jeff that he had overstayed his welcome. Hastily he exited the network and shut down the terminal. Total darkness descended upon the room. He sat there, oblivious of his surroundings, his thoughts 4,000 miles away on the Pacific coast. He thought of Susan Ferguson, wondering where she was at this moment. Who was helping her — and more importantly, why?

Shaking himself out of his thoughts, he felt around on the table. Finding the flashlight, he lit it and stood up. Reflexively, he went to the closest window and checked his emergency escape system. The two ropes hung there, just outside, undisturbed. It was a crude system, but, he hoped, effective. From there it only took a few steps for him to reach the cot sitting under the windows. Keeping his coat on against the cold, he lay down, the wooden supports creaking under his weight. Tomorrow he would have to see to the safety of the family under his protection. They would have to move again, and soon. He would notify his contact in Canada to be expecting them. Then, tomorrow night he would move them across the border. Dangerous work, but necessary.

For just an instant, he felt himself wishing that he could travel back into time. Back to when it had been legal to speak the name of Jesus Christ aloud without fear of persecution. Back to when the hardest part of being a Christian was getting up the nerve to witness to your next-door neighbor — and a night's sleep meant not having to worry when the authorities would be knocking on your door with an arrest warrant. Those days were long gone now, and he felt himself regretting it.

The signs were there, he thought sadly to himself. *If we had only seen them. Then again, maybe it would not have made any difference.* Perhaps it was true. Believers would always be under attack from the enemy in one way or another. It was inevitable that an all-out push would have come sooner or later.

Already many Christians had lost their freedom and even their lives — it was the price they paid for choosing to follow the one, true Son of God.

Once again he felt anger. It wasn't right! It wasn't right that the children of the King were made to hide like animals in the dark! It wasn't right that families were torn apart, or forced to run for their lives. Right at that moment, Jeff wanted nothing more than to get his hands on the collective necks of those responsible for this persecution. He could feel his grip tightening, until the bones began to. . . .

Abruptly, he got up off his cot and knelt by its side. The anger disappeared, forgotten, but still there just under the surface. Sooner or later, he would have to deal with it. With an effort, Jeff calmed himself. Sometimes he got so caught up in the dangerous work he was doing for God that he forgot the most important thing — talking to the One for whom all this suffering was for. He began to pray, and felt the calming, loving presence of the Holy Spirit surround and permeate him. Gradually his troubled thinking slowed. The worries he carried on his shoulders disappeared as he "cast all his cares upon Him." Yes, they were hunted; yes, they were persecuted; but there was one undeniable fact that stood out from everything else. They might still be in the middle of a heated battle that swayed back and forth, but the war was won. The Son had seen to that 2,000 years ago hanging on Calvary.

He prayed for over an hour, his fatigue and anger forgotten. Finally, comforted, he climbed back into his cot. His thoughts were calm now, soothed by the Master. Quietly he went to sleep. If a stranger had been observing him this night, they would not have understood, in light of everything that was going on, why Jeff Anderson slept with a knowing, contented smile on his face.

* * *

David Eddington surveyed the small group meeting in the maintenance room of the East Garden Mall. They were in a circle, some seated cross-legged, some kneeling, all had their heads bowed, deep in silent prayer. All were known and trusted by him, with the exception of the two newcomers. Even with the advance warning of the mysterious Miriam, he was still highly suspicious of them. Oh, the man who called himself Paul Simpson knew the correct passwords, all right. He even smiled good — and the woman had certainly been through a terrible ordeal. It was obvious that she was not "all there." There was also no doubt in his mind that this "Paul" was the one who had gotten her out of that mental institution. His description matched the one given by the newscast perfectly. There was just something about him that David did not like — or trust. It was as if the big man was going through the motions of being on the run.

Now stop that, he lectured himself firmly. He bowed his head again, closing his eyes. *You of all people have no right to judge someone's motives. If he's here, he's taking the same risk as the rest of us — and if he was a plant, he could have blown the whistle the minute he discovered where we were meeting.*

Concentrating, he tried to join in the silent prayer, but his mind would not let him. His thoughts were in a turmoil. He alone of all the group knew that this would be the last time they would be meeting like this. That alone was bad enough. These people had come to mean a lot to him. They were a source a strength in a world rapidly dying. The worst part was, before this night was over, he was going to have to tell them the secret that he had kept from them all of this time. He was going to have to tell them that David Eddington had been a traitor to his faith. It could very well cost him every friendship he had cultivated over the past months.

Suddenly, a single voice was raised in verbal prayer. This was normal. Other than quoting and memorizing verses, and sharing prayer requests, the rest of the meeting was spent in unstructured prayer. They willingly took a "back seat" and let the Holy Spirit drive. When they surrendered to His prompting, there was never any conflict, or uncertainty. Their prayers were like a well-tuned orchestra taking perfect cues from the Conductor. It was only when they tried to force things to happen that discord set in.

The voice belonged to Walter Dietz. Again David opened his eyes, something he did not normally do. Walter was a salesman in one of the large department stores in the mall above. He was an average-looking man, nondescript brown hair and eyes, of medium build. He did not often speak out loud in the meetings, preferring to take a silent role in prayer. He had often struck David as rather cold and unemotional. Just now, though, two large tears were rolling down his cheeks as he lifted his voice above the others. Understandable, thought David ruefully. Walter had just learned tonight that he was not to report to work tomorrow. His store was closing for good. With the way the depression was setting in, it was highly unlikely that he would see employment anytime soon. Not good for a man with a wife and two children.

David listened, waiting for the inevitable prayer for a new job. It figured, since that was probably the only thing that would get Walter to pray out loud. He bit his lip, suddenly disgusted at his own cynicism. Walter was here, wasn't he? He could take the easy way out, obeying the law and not attending illegal meetings. David again bowed his head.

As it turned out, Walter's prayer had nothing to do with a job. To David's surprise, he began to pray for Susan. His voice rang with confidence as he lifted her up before the Lord. There was a change in the timbre of his voice, and once again David could not resist peeking. This time he was not alone. Others were looking at Walter, some in outright amazement. Walter had stood and moved over to where Susan sat, her head bowed in obedience to her last instructions. The man named Paul eyed him warily, obviously suspicious of anyone approaching someone whom he considered under his protection. He did nothing, however, when Walter kneeled in front of Susan and gently laid his hands on her shoulders. His prayer became more fervent, beseeching the Father to heal and comfort her. As David watched, others got up from where they were sitting and moved over to join him. Soon he was the only one left. Now indeed did David feel ashamed! This should have been the first thing he had done when Susan walked in the door. She was obviously not well. Why had he not stopped everything and prayed for her?

Quietly he got up and inched his way over to where the others stood. He could not reach Susan to put his own hands on her. The rest of the tiny church surrounded her. He would have had to shoulder someone out of the way, and that simply would not do. Instead he moved over to where the man called Paul Simpson sat and gently laid his hands on the big man's shoulders. Instantly he felt the muscles tense. Paul's whole body went rigid. The man was obviously not used to being touched!

Walter continued to pray. His voice rang out in the enclosed space, and for just a moment David was afraid that they might be discovered. Once again he felt ashamed at his over caution.

No, he thought to himself sternly, *call it what it really is — fear.* Gritting his teeth, he held his silence as Walter kept at it. The rest of the church prayed softly with him, their voices blending in perfect harmony. Only David did not join in. Not because he did not want to — he felt horribly left out. It was simply because he *could* not. The Spirit would not allow him to until he made a clean breast of things with this group that meant so much to him.

As abruptly as he started, Walter stopped. The rest of the group quieted down. They stood there for a moment, gathered around Susan. David was the first to break contact, releasing his light touch on Paul and moving back to his original position. As the others followed his lead, Paul's face came into view. To David's astonishment, he saw what a remarkable contrast it was to the faces of the others. The tiny church wore genuine looks of peace and contentment. Paul, on the other hand, looked like he was about to throw up.

Strange, thought David. *Very strange.* This newcomer was obviously a lot more than just another Christian in trouble. David watched closely as Paul, in turn, studied Susan. *He's hiding something,* thought David, *something deep inside of him.* Suddenly, he was very glad that this would be the last time his church would be meeting like this.

He shifted his attention to Susan, and he found himself studying her closely. Was there a difference in her since the prayer? David frowned, leaning forward intently. Tiny goose pimples raised themselves on his arms and neck. There *was* a difference, he realized.

God had done something here, he knew. He had touched this woman directly, through Walter's and the rest of the church's fervent prayer. She still sat there, her head slightly bowed and her eyes looking at nothing but the bare cement floor, but David could still see a difference, and it was not his mind willing him to see what he wanted to see. Her face, blank and lifeless when she had come in, now held a look of peace. It was no longer a lifeless mask — there was someone home behind it. As he watched, David saw a tiny smile tug at the corners of her mouth. Not a big one, but a smile nonetheless. He had no idea what God had in store for her, but her healing had begun.

Turning his attention back to Paul, he saw that the stranger had recovered his composure and now looked quite normal. Paul turned his head and David found himself staring right into those deep blue eyes. For an instant their gazes held each other. David felt himself go tense, just like Paul had when he had laid his hands on his shoulders. There was something in his eyes. . . .

David suddenly realized that he was sweating. He felt as if he had been caught up in the middle of a great battle, and he had forgotten his weapons. He was totally unprepared for this kind of warfare. Paul's eyes locked on to him, holding him. David felt power there — and purpose. To his horror, he realized that what he was seeing was the power of the enemy — *and it was greater than he was.* There was no doubt in his mind. The two men strove with each other, not in a contest of wills, but more of a battle of spirits. David felt himself being overpowered. Finally, defeated, he looked away, but not before he saw the arrogant smirk that creased Paul's face. It was all he could do to maintain his composure.

Belatedly he realized that the rest of the church was watching him, confusion and uncertainty mirrored in their faces. He took a deep breath, the memory of his confrontation suddenly fading, like a nightmare fades in the soothing reality of morning. Surely he was letting his imagination run wild . . . wasn't he? Paul Simpson was someone who needed his help. Miriam had told him so, and he had believed her. He forced himself back to the present, smiling at his friends. Still, he could not forget the feeling of confrontation — and defeat. Worry about it later, he told himself, and filed the incident far back into his mind.

"I think we all know that God is here with us tonight," he said to the tiny group, carefully avoiding Paul's eyes. He felt the bitter tang of hypocrisy in his mouth, washed down with the rank aftertaste of defeat. God was certainly not with *him!* He opened his mouth to continue, and found suddenly that he could not. The words, so carefully learned and practiced, simply would not come. He could not make himself go on. He swallowed, casting about for something to say.

"It's okay, David," Walter said, his eyes joyous over what had just happened in his life. "Sometimes there just aren't words to say what. . . ."

"NO!" The church jumped, startled as the single exclamation tore itself out of David's throat. Even he was surprised at the savageness in his voice. He stood there, teetering on the edge of the truth. Deep inside, he knew that if he did not make a full confession to his friends, God would be through with him. There would be no second chance this time. He thought of Miriam, and her approval when he had taken those few hard steps to follow her. He realized that, right now, he had to take a few more steps of a much different variety.

"Sorry," he said, clearing his throat nervously, "I didn't mean to yell like that." He looked around the room, taking in each face. When he came to Paul, he again met the other's gaze. This time there were no sparks, no battle. Paul simply watched him with the others, a look of mild curiosity on his face. He felt himself relax, the last remaining shreds of memory of that timeless battle fading.

"There's something you need to know," he continued, at last taking the plunge he had been dreading. Surprisingly it was much easier than he had thought it would be. He told them everything. From the first time the Bureau of Religious Affairs had approached him, to the betrayal of his church, to his family leaving him, he left nothing out. He described the deal he had made with the bureau, guaranteeing his freedom if he stopped preaching. He told it all in low, calm voice, surprised at his own composure. When he finished, he remained standing where he was, waiting for he knew not what.

The silence was deafening in that maintenance room. Only the dull hiss of the air conditioning flowing through the vent was audible. David remained still, trying to read the faces turned toward him. Some would not meet his eyes, looking down at the floor. One, a pudgy little woman with electric red hair, named Marge Cobb, was staring at him in open disbelief. The others were unreadable. Finally it became unbearable.

"I don't expect you to understand," he said, more to break the silence than anything else. "I just wanted you to know the truth about me. You've looked toward me to lead this group, but the fact is, you *all* have been the leaders. I. . . ." He faltered, his composure leaving him. Tears formed at the corners of his eyes. "There's something else you should know," he continued, plunging ahead. "I think the authorities are on to us." At this, the group snapped to attention. Walter gasped, and Marge's eyes flashed dangerously. "Someone, a member of the Shepherd's Path I think, warned me that we have to disband."

"What?" That was from Walter. "You can't be serious, David." David started to reply, but was interrupted when Marge abruptly got up from her place and made her way deliberately to the door. Everyone watched her go, wondering.

Just as she put her hand on the knob, she turned. "I'm sorry," she said, her voice a harsh rasp. Her gaze took in everyone in but David. "I can't be part of this group anymore." Now she looked directly at David, and the hardness of her voice was like an iron spike being driven into his heart. "My husband was arrested years ago, when the persecution started. Not much later, he disappeared. My two sons tried to find him, but they disappeared as well. One of the last things Jerry told me. . . ." and her voice broke. One of the other women started to get up and move toward her, but she angrily waved her away. "He told me to always remain true to God, no matter the cost. Well, it cost me my family. Then you, *Pastor*," she said, making the title a mockery, "tell us this. What's wrong? Guilt too much for you?"

"Marge," said Walter, reproof strong in his voice, "I don't think that's hardly fair."

"Isn't it?" demanded Marge. She pointed a finger at David, who could only stare back at her. "We pay the price, but it's people like him that caused it to be so high. If he had remained true. . . ." She couldn't go on. With one last withering look at David, she turned and walked out. The rest of the church stared after her. Finally Walter got up and closed the door. When he turned, David saw something in him that he had never seen before.

"It seems to me that we have some things to settle before we break up for good." He walked over to stand in front of David. Although the two men were roughly the same height, David got the distinct impression that he was looking up at the former salesman. He was suddenly grateful for the man's intervention. Marge's words had hurt.

Walter regarded him with a burning look that demanded nothing less than complete honesty. "Why did you say what you said?" he asked. "After all this time, meeting like this, why now?"

David thought about it. Walter was asking him the way a concerned friend would, not a judge. He was neither threatening nor intimidating. The phrases "tough love" and "accountability" came to mind. "I had to," he answered finally, then realized that that was not enough. "If I didn't," he added, "I wouldn't have been any further use to Him."

Walter considered that for a moment, then turned to the remaining group. They were watching the two men closely. "Jesus said, 'Let him who is without sin cast the first stone,' " said Walter, now speaking to everyone. "We are not here to judge *anyone*. David has proven himself to be a good and true friend over the past few months. True, he made a grave mistake, but by his own words, he has repented. He's asked for forgiveness. Since our Lord made our actions in matters like this quite clear, I, for one, stand ready to give it. Are we agreed?" There were nods from everyone, and the tension that had been hanging over everyone suddenly disappeared.

David felt as if he could breath again. Walter turned back and faced him again. He put his hands on his shoulders. "Put it behind you David. Let it go." He smiled, and a sudden lightness permeated David's very soul.

For the first time in months, he felt free. A tremendous burden was suddenly taken away. All at once, he felt as if he could soar, and the one thought that kept ringing through his mind was, *God is not finished with me yet!* He smiled, then his smile turned into a grin.

It was infectious. Walter grinned back, and then, quite unexpectedly, reached out and grabbed him in a big bear hug. The others — minus Paul and Susan, jumped up and joined in, and soon David found himself in the center of a crushing group hug. Never in his life had he felt so close to anyone as he did now. Finally, amid tears and laughs, the hug ended and once more, everyone returned to their places.

Only Walter remained standing next to David. He allowed everyone to settle themselves, then spoke. "We don't have much time left," he said, looking at his watch, "and we've got to take care of other things." He looked at David. "You said that the authorities were probably on to us." David nodded. "Then we have to disband."

"Can't we just meet somewhere else?" The question came from

one of the men seated on the floor.

David shook his head. "They may already know who we are. We need to disappear for a while." Something that Miriam had said resurfaced in his memory. "Each one of you is strong enough in the Lord to start your own group now," he said. *That* caught them by surprise. "You're all leaders, whether you believe it or not."

Walter nodded in agreement. "It's time to become sparks, people," he said. "Let's see just how many fires we can start!" His expression got a chuckle from the rest of the group. "If the law knows about us as a group, then it's a good bet that they know us as individuals. We may need to go underground — into hiding." He looked back at David. "Do you have any idea how to make contact with the Shepherd's Path?" David considered for a moment. Out of the corner of his eye, he saw that Paul Simpson was watching him carefully.

"Maybe," he answered slowly. "At least, I know where there are a few safe houses that the Path uses. If we can get there, they can start us on the next step."

"Just pick up and leave?" This was from the man who had spoken before.

Walter spread his hands. "Its your choice, Ben. You can stay if you want. I think you should go, though. You live alone, don't you?" Ben nodded. "Then there's nothing holding you back. I have a wife and two kids. I'm going home, packing a few things, and leaving. The state can have the rest of my stuff. I'm getting me and my family out of here." He smiled. "Maybe, wherever we end up, God can use me to start another group." The implications of what Walter was saying were starting to set in.

David could see the fear and uncertainty in their faces. Despite his recent experience, he felt it too. "Its okay, everyone," he said, holding up his hands for attention. "We all knew that this could happen. I'm just as afraid as the rest of you, but I think that this is the right thing to do — just like telling you the truth about me was the right thing to do."

"What about us?" Everyone started at the unfamiliar voice. Paul Simpson stood up, eyeing the tiny church with suspicion. Immediately his physical presence dominated the room. David felt a vague, fleeting memory of their recent spiritual encounter grab at the back of his mind, then disappear. "What about us?" Paul repeated. "Susan and I are *already* wanted. I risked a lot to get her out of that hellhole she was in. We came here for help. Are we going to get it?"

Walter nodded without hesitation. "That's the last thing we need to talk about," he said to the rest of the group. "How are we going to move these two out of here? Any suggestions?" There was silence for a moment.

"I'll take care of them." David looked around in surprise, then realized that the voice that had spoken had been his own.

Paul looked at him appraisingly, a barely perceptible sneer struggling to get out. *"You* will take care of us?" The sarcasm in his tone was unmistakable.

David merely nodded. "I can get you to a safe house," he explained. "From there, the Shepherd's Path can get you anywhere in the country." Paul frowned, and David found himself looking once again into those penetrating blue eyes. Once again he felt the stirrings of a battle, but this time he ignored those stirrings. He returned Paul's gaze calmly, waiting for his response.

This time, surprisingly, it was Paul who looked away. "Fine," he said shortly, then knelt down to see to Susan.

Walter watched the by-play between the two men in confusion, then turned to the rest. "Its settled then," he said. "At least as far as me, David, Paul, and Susan are concerned. The rest of you have to decide what God wants you to do." He paused, obviously thinking furiously. "If you want to come with us, then meet me at the Holiday Inn over on Sycamore Street in two hours."

"So soon?" This was from one of the women.

Walter smiled gently. "If the law knows who we are, then we need to get out of here fast. Even two hours may be too long." No one replied to that. "All right then. Let's get out of here."

On Walter's cue, everyone stood, then paused for a moment. Impulsively, David reached out and took Walter's hand in his. Walter nodded at David, then took Ben's hand, who in turned took that of the woman next to him. Soon, they had formed a tight circle. As one, the church went to the Most High God in prayer. They were silent, their hearts speaking in place of their voices. Peace flooded the room, and all but one of them knew that they were in God's hands. It calmed and comforted them.

Without anyone directing them, they looked up and smiled at each other. Then, without anything else being said, they went out. They left singly and in groups of two, going in 15-minute intervals. From this room they could access almost any part of the mall. They would emerge from the various exits and make their way home. How many would return in two hours, only the Father knew. Finally, only David, Walter, Paul, and Susan were left.

"I'll bring my van," said Walter, breaking the silence. "I'm sure we can all fit in, if we squeeze a bit."

David nodded, not speaking.

"What do we do in the meantime?" asked Paul, his arm placed protectively around Susan.

Walter looked at David questioningly.

"You can stay here," responded David.

"In the mall?" Paul replied incredulously.

David found himself disliking the big man. He bit off a reply and only nodded.

"What David means is, there are plenty of places to hide here. Once the mall is closed, there's only a token security force in place. The central computer monitors everything, so there is no need for a lot of people. Besides, you won't be here long. Not more than an hour."

David nodded in agreement. "I've got my rounds to finish up, then we can go," he said.

Paul hesitated, obviously unhappy with the arrangements, then nodded in agreement.

"Good," said Walter. "I've got to go, David. Can you get to the meeting place on your own?"

"Yeah, no problem," replied David. "Buses run right by. . . ."

"I have a car outside," interrupted Paul. "We can use that."

David shook his head. "If the police know about us, its possible that they have already spotted you. They might be watching your car. Don't worry," he added, seeing the look of anger in Paul's face. "I'll get you there."

Walter nodded, eyeing Paul uneasily. "I'll see you people later, then." He looked as if he was going to say more, but instead turned and left.

David watched him go, then turned back to Paul and Susan. The latter was watching him, her now alert eyes probing him. He smiled at her, and received a very small smile in return. Carefully he avoided Paul's stare.

"Let's get you hidden, then," he said, motioning for them to follow him. He led them out of the maintenance room and headed down the long hall in the opposite direction they had come. They met no one on their brief journey, and soon they came to a junction, another hall intersecting the first. David turned left and they followed. He brought them to a set of double doors that opened at his touch. Susan and Paul followed him inside to find a medium-sized office. On one side was a desk, empty except for a few pictures carefully placed on the top. On the other was a tattered couch resting against the far wall.

"This belongs to the maintenance chief," explained David. "He's gone home now, and won't be back until late tomorrow. You can rest here, and I'll come and get you in an hour or so. Okay?"

Paul merely nodded, steering Susan to the couch. David studied Paul's back as he made her sit down.

"You think you can get us out of here?" asked Paul, his back still toward David.

"No," David replied immediately, "but God can."

For just a moment, Paul stiffened. Then he relaxed, turning back to David. "He really can, can't He?" he said, smiling.

For some reason, David was suddenly reminded of a shark. He nodded. Suddenly he wanted to get far away from this man, and he honestly did not know why. "I'll see you soon, then," he replied, and left quickly.

As he headed back up to the mall, his thoughts seethed with doubt. He did not trust Paul. The man was not what he seemed. He was hiding something. Perhaps he should just leave him there, and anonymously report them to security. He considered the idea, but rejected it for three reasons.

First, he was sure that Susan Ferguson was a believer. She had been through a hard time and needed his help desperately. He could not desert her. Second, he had been specifically warned about Paul and Susan. Miriam had told him to help them in any way he could. Finally, they had been placed in his care. They were his responsibility. He had betrayed that trust once before, and no matter what, would not do so now.

David reached the first level and emerged onto the main floor of the mall itself. There was still 15 minutes left until closing time, but he was not on the clean-up shift tonight. He would be free to go home after his brief round on the ground floor. He made his way to the center of the mall where Charley had already started his work. His thoughts were in turmoil as he joined in. Once again, his life was about to take a drastic turn, and he had no idea where things were going. One thing he did know, though. He was going to have to keep a very close eye on the man called Paul Simpson in the days and weeks ahead.

4

"Ms. Smythe," came the hushed voice of one of Christine's assistants. Christine looked up from her desk to see her standing in the doorway. *"He's here,"* she said, with a tinge of awe coloring her voice. Christine merely nodded, making a deliberate show of looking casual. The fact was, she was greatly pleased. She had expected to be summoned to Washington for an emergency meeting with the president of the United States. There was no doubt that he wanted to discuss the current economic disaster. To have him travel *here,* to her New York headquarters, was unprecedented. It spoke eloquently of the situation.

Like all presidents before him, this one was taking the brunt of the blame for the nation's woes. There was even talk of a no-confidence vote to force him out of office. His trip here was a desperation move — a last ditch effort to get the private sector behind him again. Not that it mattered, Christine knew. The power he wielded was an illusion. However, he *was* a useful tool. Hopefully, he would soon become much more useful. If her sources were correct, and they always were, the president had an ulterior motive in being here. She would know shortly.

The assistant disappeared. There was a moment's pause, then two extremely competent secret service agents stepped in. Without glancing at Christine, they swept the room with their scanners, looking for any signs of danger. Christine waited patiently. She was not worried about them finding anything. What they were looking for either did not exist, or was too well-shielded to show up on their equipment. Abruptly, they left.

Again, there was a pause, then the president himself stepped into the room. He was an impressive looking man. A six-foot-two-inch former football star, he knew how to use his size to full advantage. It had not helped his opponent in the last election that the poor man had only topped the measuring stick at five foot six. The citizens of the United States were still influenced by outward appearances.

"Christine," he said, smiling and extending a hand. His voice cradled and caressed the sound of her name, making it seem as if saying it was the most important thing in his life. "It's good to see you. It's been too long." Smiling, Christine stood and shook his hand. She motioned him to a seat in front of her. She was not fooled at his outward hospitality. By his reckoning, things were dire indeed. The economic survival of the United States, not to mention his own presidency, was at stake.

"It's good to see you again, Mr. President," she replied as she sat down again. "I just wish that the circumstances were better." She pasted a look of grimness and urgency on her face, telling the president in so many words to kindly dispense with the pleasantries and get on with business. Immediately the president lost his public smile, replacing it with a look that was a mixture of annoyance and concern.

"Indeed," he said, leaning forward. "The collapse of Smythe Enterprises has triggered a series of events that will end in disaster if not stopped." He looked at Christine expectantly, waiting for a response. Christine merely nodded. She wanted him to talk. It was vital that he bring up the subject that was really on his mind. "Have you found the cause for the collapse?" he asked after a moments pause.

"Mr. President, what can I say?" replied Christine, letting a false note of fear and desperation creep into her voice. "Bad foreign investments, the banking collapse, defaulting on short-term loans, all have contributed to this. Smythe Enterprises is like a giant jigsaw puzzle — everything is interconnected. If one piece is lost, the rest of the puzzle is weakened." She smiled weakly, feigning resignation. "Pardon the mixed metaphor, but if two or three pieces are lost, then it's like a domino effect. Once the collapse starts, there is nothing that can stop it. The only recourse is to let it fall completely, then try to pick up the pieces."

"That's all well and good for you," growled the president, letting a hint of a threat creep into his voice. "I don't think anyone's liable to catch you living on the street because you can't make your mortgage payment. I doubt the same can be said for many of your former employees."

"We're doing everything we can," replied Christine. "My board has set up a relief fund for those who have been hardest hit. Beyond that, we're trying to pick up the pieces as fast as we can."

"Of course, that doesn't help those who were not a part of Smythe Enterprises," said the president. "Your collapse has put millions out of work whose jobs had nothing to do with your conglomeration." He smiled mockingly. "To use your own metaphor, it's the domino effect, only multiplied a thousandfold. Because of Smythe Enterprises, two of the big three auto makers will be in bankruptcy before the end of the month. The steel industry, which was actually making a comeback, is dead in the water. Textiles, electronics, aviation, all are on the ropes . . . thanks to you."

Christine sat straight in her chair, her back slightly arched. Her eyes were blazing with anger. "Do you think I planned this, sir?" she snapped, her voice raising considerably. Her wrath was quite real. His accusation stung her pride. *Nobody* spoke to her like that — not even presidents. Once Brennon's plan came to fruition, she would use people like this for her footstool. The fact that she *had* indeed planned the collapse of her own empire was totally beside the point. "You seem to think that I am not affected by this tragedy. The truth is, I will have to declare personal bankruptcy before the year is out." THAT was a blatant lie. Her personal fortune was safely tucked away where no one could touch it.

"Christine, Christine!" The president put up his hands in a soothing gesture, his voice urging her to calm down. He knew the situation. He needed Christine Smythe on his side. "I know you're not immune to this mess. I just need your help to try to 'stem the tide,' like Congress, *and* the American people, are demanding." He leaned forward, his intensity glowing like a palpable light. "There's much more at stake here than just another depression, you know." He looked at her expectantly, and she nodded for him to continue. He did so.

"There's not an armed force in the world that could conquer us, Christine, but if this continues, we *will* be conquered — conquered by the financial giant that Europe has become. We will have no choice but to accede to their demands to join them as a junior partner. That will give them the leverage they need to dictate our economic future for decades to come. That is totally unacceptable!"

"Agreed," said Christine. "Mr. President, what do you want from me? You have my support, but at this moment, Congress is probably burning me in effigy. I'm afraid that because of the collapse of Smythe Enterprises, I'm not very popular right now. In fact, you may be committing political suicide just by meeting with me."

The president nodded, looking grim. "It doesn't really matter," he said. "I'm probably being burned right beside you. It looks like we might go down together!"

Christine smiled. "Then I ask again, what do you want from me?"

Now the president hesitated. He glanced around the room, as if looking for something.

"This office is completely secure," assured Christine. "You have my word on that."

The president nodded. The look on his face said that he was about to bring up a delicate subject. "Jack Kline's death was a tremendous loss," he said quietly. Christine nodded, keeping the smile that she felt well hidden. *Here it comes,* she thought to herself.

"Rumor has it that he was quite mad at the end," he continued. "Mad because of a kind of implant that had been put into his brain." He stopped, and looked at Christine, who nodded.

"A tragic mistake," agreed Christine. "Evidently, Senator Kline was in league with Jacob Hill, the chief of the Bureau Of Religious Affairs."

"I heard that this implant was manufactured by Smythe Enterprises."

Again Christine nodded. In answer, she opened a desk drawer and pulled out a metallic cube about an inch wide on all sides. Carefully she handed it to the president. He opened it and examined the contents carefully. Inside was a tiny sphere, about half the size of a pea. He looked questioningly at Christine.

"A bio-chip," she explained. The president shook his head, not understanding.

"It is a biologically viable computer chip," Christine explained.

"You mean it's alive?" asked the president, a hint of disgust coloring his voice.

"Correct, sir," replied Christine. "It is implanted into the cerebral cortex, using a simple surgical procedure. Once there, it connects to various parts of the brain. It enables the user to interface with most major computer systems directly, eliminating the need for a terminal.

"Most systems," repeated the president.

Christine nodded. "Governmental, business . . . or private," she said quietly. The president pondered the meaning of this.

"Somehow, Jacob Hill got his hands on a prototype," continued Christine. She knew her lie was near enough to the truth to be believable. "He had it implanted into Kline — evidently against the senator's will. It eventually malfunctioned, causing the senator to go mad and ultimately destroy himself." An irritating event, Christine knew. Jack Kline had been earmarked to be the next president, firmly under Brennon's control. Now they would have to deal with the man sitting here in her office. The president was still studying the bio-chip.

"You say that Jack's implant was a prototype?" he asked. Christine could hear the eagerness in his voice.

"Very crude compared to the one you are holding," she replied.

The president pursed his lips. "One of these would be a great asset to someone in my position," he said softly.

Christine knew she had him. It was only a matter of gentle assurance. "No secret of your opponents would be beyond your reach," she agreed. "If it's in a computer somewhere, it can be accessed through that implant."

"You say the surgery is simple?" he asked, and she nodded.

"The actual procedure takes less than an hour. Recovery even less."

"Side effects?"

"None that we've observed," said Christine. "By the way, you will also have the ability to read auras."

"Auras?"

"The energy field given off by the human body," answered Christine.

"It's rather like a built-in mood ring. Once you get the hang of it, you'll be able to tell whether someone is lying or not." That clenched it, she saw. He was convinced.

"Christine," he said, his face deadly serious, "Can you guarantee the effectiveness and safety of this?"

"To a point," replied Christine slowly. She knew it was a dangerous game she was playing. If she came across as too eager, she would arouse his politician's natural suspicion. "There are no absolutes, of course, but I think I can guarantee at least a 95 percent chance of success."

The president was silent for a moment. Then he leaned forward, his eyes intense. "I need one of these," he said, his voice low. "It's the only way I can get this nation through the crisis."

Christine pretended to consider the matter. "Granted, you're the best man for the job," she lied, "but this is not a decision made quickly. Perhaps you should talk with your advisors. . . ."

"No, Christine," interrupted the president adamantly. "This has to be our secret. Will you help me? Will you give me one of these?" He held up the open cube.

Christine hesitated, then nodded. "Of course," she said. "We'll schedule the surgery for early next. . . ."

"Now," demanded the president. "I know that you have medical facilities within this very building. Surely you can do this surgery here . . . today!"

Again Christine pretended to hesitate. Then once more she nodded. "What about your security arrangements?" she asked.

The president waved her concern away. "I can handle them," he said. "Just tell me where to go."

With a great effort, Christine censored the first three answers that came to her mind. Instead, she touched a hidden switch set into the surface of her desk. With a slight hum, concealed doors set into the wall to her right opened to reveal a spacious elevator. She stood, gesturing to the president. "I'll take you there myself. Since everyone expects this meeting to last for several hours, you should be in and out before anyone misses you."

The president smiled gratefully and followed her into the elevator. Christine noticed just a hint of apprehension about him.

"This will work, sir," she said reassuringly. "And it will give you the edge you need to stay in office and turn this nation around." The president nodded, taking a deep breath.

Christine escorted the president down to the medical section of her headquarters, several floors below. She left him in the hands of her most trusted surgeon, then returned to her office. She had to smile at what had just happened. The president was truly desperate, all right! Like most who sought after power for its own sake, the threat of losing that power often led them to do anything to keep it.

That desperation would cost the president dearly. Christine had neglected to mention that, in addition to its advantages, the bio-chip held one tiny secret. It had a slave circuit that, once grown into place, rendered the user highly susceptible to instruction. The president, once implanted, would be plugged into Cyclops, Brennon's master system, and would soon be under the firm control of Brennon and the Sextuaget.

Once back at her desk, Christine began to work on other matters that demanded her attention when, to her surprise, saw that the "Urgent . . . call immediately" icon was flashing on the monitor of the vid-phone. There were two colored dots by the icon, indicating that there were two messages. The colors, one red, the other blue, indicated the urgency of each. Only a handful of her most trusted people could get through to this station, and of course Brennon and her Sextuaget associates. Her former ebullience subsiding, she switched on the vid-phone and entered the proper code of the "Priority One" message.

She was not surprised when General Adam Cook answered. The general was one of her own circle of subordinates. He was responsible for the huge defense contracts that Smythe Enterprises had with the United States government. Christine had brought him into her select group upon the untimely demise of Jacob Hill and Dr. Samuel Steiger. Cook was Hollywood's idea of the perfect military man. Stern countenance, close-cropped gray hair, and steel blue eyes gave the impression of cool, competent leadership. No one would guess from looking at him that he had never seen combat. He looked up from his desk and nodded deferentially. He knew that Christine was responsible for the third star on his shoulder, as well as his influential position in the Pentagon.

"What is it, General?" asked Christine, telling him with her tone of voice to keep it brief. She had no love for this posturing military lackey.

"A message," replied the general, matching her briskness. "You are needed on 'Liberty.' "

"What?" Her voice was incredulous. She had not been off-planet for months.

Abruptly, the General looked uncomfortable. "I received a message, coded 'Conclave Alpha,' " he replied. "I have no idea what it means, but it was also coded with an 'Alpha Omicron One' priority, which I *do* understand." He looked at her levelly. " 'Alpha Omicron' identifies our 'group,' while the designation 'one' means you. I assume you know what the other one means." He paused expectantly.

Christine chewed her lip thoughtfully, suddenly unsure of herself. Like others of her circle, the General knew nothing of the Sextuaget. He knew that there were other select groups, all working toward the same end as Christine's, but he was ignorant of Brennon's master plan. He made for a useful pawn, but little else.

"Authenticity is verified?" she asked, already knowing the answer.

"Of course," replied the General. He was obviously miffed at being made to play the role of messenger.

"Why wasn't I informed directly?"

The general only shrugged. "You were meeting with the president. Obviously whoever sent it did not want that meeting interrupted."

That made sense. The general still watched her, obviously hoping for an explanation. Well, he would have to wait. "Thank you, General. Is there anything else?" she said, making it clear that the call was over.

"No, that's it," was the disappointed reply.

"Then I'll sign off now. Again, thank you. You will be hearing from me." With that, she touched the screen and it went blank. *Liberty,* she thought furiously. *What does Brennon want with me up there?* She pondered that for a moment, then realized that there was another message waiting for her. She called it up, and saw that it was from her California administrative assistant, calling from the office in Los Angeles. She debated not returning the call, then changed her mind. Her assistant would not violate her direct orders to not disturb her without good reason. She keyed in the proper sequence. Almost immediately, the face of the assistant, Sheila Moon, materialized. Her almond eyes and delicate countenance looked positively grim.

"Sheila? What's wrong? I left strict orders. No one was to call me unless it was absolutely necessary."

"I'm sorry, Ms Smythe, but I thought you would want to know." Her voice matched her look.

"Know what? What's going on, Sheila?"

"We just found out less than an hour ago," she replied. "Matthew Riever is dead." For an instant, Christine was caught off guard. Then she felt her breath catch in her throat. Matthew dead?! Impossible!

"What are you talking about? I just spoke to him this morning! He was fine!"

"He was found about an hour ago," said Sheila, her lips thin and drawn. "He evidently overdosed on 'black ice.' He . . . he left a note on his computer. He said he couldn't live with what he'd done. Smythe Enterprises was his life, and now that it was dead, he might as well be."

The words plunged into Christine's heart. The fool! "All right, Sheila," she said, forcing her voice to remain calm. "See what else you can find out about it. Check on Matthew's psyche file. It's out of character for him to pull a stunt like this — and especially see if he left any other messages. Take care of it for me, okay?"

"Sure, Ms. Smythe. Anything else you need, just call."

"Just take care of it. I need to be alone for a while. I'll get in touch later." With that, she broke the connection and leaned back into her seat. Almost, she felt the sting of tears at the corners of her eyes, but forced the feelings down, crushing them ruthlessly. Matthew Riever might have been with her for years, but he was still a tool, nothing else. If he could not handle the realities of life in the New World Order, then too bad. Better that he was out of the way now.

In fact, she was already formulating ways she could use poor Matthew's suicide to her advantage. If suspicion ever came to rest on her for the fall of Smythe Enterprises, she could use his final message to put the blame on Matthew. That was certainly convenient! He had done his part, so he was no longer useful anyway. *That* settled in her mind, Christine turned her thoughts to more important matters.

Calling Cape Canaveral, she arranged to have a shuttle standing by for immediate departure. Then she arranged to have her private jet fly her to Florida. She would leave as soon as the president's surgery was complete.

Despite the recent setback involving Jack Kline, Brennon's plan was now completely back on course. The president would soon be under absolute control. That, combined with her own people in the Senate and the Congress, selected implants on others, and the military in hand, would place most of Washington under Brennon's powerful thumb. Now, all she had to find out was what the blazes was going on at Liberty! She hoped she would like the answer, but with Brennon, one was never sure.

* * *

Paul Sinclair watched the Sierra Nevada Mountains turn a bright searing red as the morning sun touched them with its fire. The snow-covered peaks sizzled with a breathtaking beauty which was all but wasted on the former bureau agent. Paul's mind was on matters far more important to him than the scenery just now. Squinting against the glare, he let the curtain covering the back window of the massive Winnebego fall back into place. His hand brushed the cold glass as he did so, reminding him that it was under 30 degrees outside. It was the morning after the underground meeting, and he, Susan, and an assorted handful of travelers were heading toward the Nevada state line as fast as the law would allow. They had been traveling since three that morning, and somewhere up ahead was the first stop along their "escape route." As far as he could learn, it was a safe house somewhere in the suburbs of Reno. That in itself sounded strange. Somehow, Reno and suburbs did not seem to go together. On the rare occasions his business took him there, he always stayed in the finest hotels in the heart of the city.

Not this time, though.

Repressing a sigh, he got up from the uncomfortable sofa-bed and ambled toward the front of the RV. Someday, he told himself, he would get that "good life" back. Until then, he had a job to do, and he was determined to see it through. He regretted that Wolf had not given him a communicator. Last night he had discovered the location of one safe house in Sacramento, and an important one at that. Eddington, the little guy who seemed to be the leader of the fleeing group, had taken them there after they had met at the Holiday Inn. Only Walter Dietz and his family had shown up. No one else who had been in the earlier meeting had come. Walter had arrived in the Winnebego, grinning like a thief. He was almost indecently pleased with himself. It turned out that his father was part owner in an RV dealership. Although father and son were not on the best of terms, Walter had convinced the elder Dietz to loan him one of the Winnebegos sitting on the lot. No one was buying during the depression anyway. According to Walter, they had a week's grace to use it. Then his father would report it as stolen. That was the only way he could cover himself in case the authorities came asking questions.

In spite of himself, Paul had been impressed with what he had seen so far of the Shepherd's Path. He had expected to uncover a nest of "holy rollers," whispering dark secrets about the mysteries of the universe — in other words, freaks. What he had found was an efficient, professionally-run network that had been able to operate for several years despite the best efforts of several government organizations. He had heard rumors that this so-called underground network had been started by the widow of a former evangelist — a woman in her sixties. Frankly, he did not believe it. Whoever was behind this was a consummate professional.

Take last night. The safe house Eddington had led them to was actually a town house in the business district of Sacramento. There, a young couple that in the eighties would have been considered "yuppies" had taken them in. Introducing themselves simply as George and Gwen, they had provided sleeping space for the fugitives, as well as food and drink. George, producing a camera, took pictures of everyone in front of a blue sheet, then disappeared for several hours. When he returned, he had handed each of the believers a forged, but quite authentic-looking identification card. He explained that this would do for a cursory examination, but would not hold up under heavy scrutiny. To Paul's trained eye, they were excellent forgeries. When he had nonchalantly asked how George had managed this feat, the younger man had simply shrugged his shoulders and said, "The less you know, the better."

They had slept for an hour or so, then left at three o'clock that morning, Walter still driving the RV. Paul was feeling decidedly "itchy."

If he could just get in contact with Wolf, he could report the location of that safe house. George obviously had connections within the city government. If he could nail him and his wife, it might go a long way in restoring his old life. The problem was, all of the small group he was traveling with insisted on staying together.

Paul stepped in to the main section of the Winnebego and surveyed his erstwhile companions. Except for Walter, who refused to let anyone else drive, at least so far, they were all still asleep. There was Walter's wife, Cyndi, who was propped in the co-pilot's seat. She was a lovely woman, who, 10 years ago, might have been considered stunning. A deep California tan contrasted starkly with her natural blonde hair and clear complexion. Her slim, athletic figure rested easily in the huge captain's chair next to her husband. Only tiny crows-feet at the eyes, and a slight sag in her chin reflected her true age of 36. Motherhood, although obviously fulfilling her, had nevertheless taken its inevitable physical toll.

Paul paused, admiring Cyndi's figure. He felt the first stirrings of desire and quickly suppressed it. Maybe, when this was all over, he would show her what a real man was capable of. Until then, hands off. Briefly he wondered how a plain fellow like Walter had managed to attract such a woman.

To his left were the two Dietz children. Jonathan, the elder, was a lanky boy of 12 who had inherited his mother's slimness. His brother Stephen was 10, and took more after his father. Paul studied them for a moment, then disregarded them. Let the state decide what to do with them later. They were old enough to know what was going on, and it was not unheard of that minors could be tried as adults in cases of treason.

Then there was David Eddington. Paul glanced over at him and his face hardened. Of all the people in this vehicle, Eddington was the one person he could not pigeonhole. At first, he had simply thought the smaller man a pudgy fool. He seemed to be the leader of this ragtag bunch, but he had about as much leadership ability as Paul's former boss, Wesley Blaine. Paul felt him to be no threat. Then the two locked stares during that ridiculous meeting, and Paul's opinion had changed. He had dominated the smaller man, certainly. Paul's Zen training had come to his aid almost immediately, and in the battle that followed, he had won easily. Call it a battle of wills, or some sort of conflict on a "higher plain," whatever it had been, he had effortlessly prevailed.

Still . . . there was something there. Paul had briefly sensed a great power lying underneath the surface of Eddington's psyche, so latent that Eddington himself did not seem to be aware of it. If it was ever unleashed, the outcome of the next skirmish might be quite different. Paul, therefore, decided to make sure that it would remain dormant. He would have to mentally and physically dominate the former preacher. Otherwise, the little man might become quite formidable.

Moving over to an empty couch behind Cyndi, Paul eased his large frame into a sitting position. He felt stiff and cramped. Although he had slept some in the back next to Susan, the sofa bed was not conducive to comfort. He wished he could put himself into a light trance and clear his foggy mind, but he knew that many so-called Christians frowned upon such things. He felt rather than saw Walter glance up into the mirror over the driver's seat. Paul met his eyes in the mirror and nodded a "good morning."

"How's Susan?" asked Walter, his voice just loud enough to carry over the engine noise of the RV.

"Sleeping peacefully," Paul answered in the same tone. "It might not sound like much, but it's the first time she hasn't woken up screaming since I got her out of that institution."

He saw Walter's jaw tighten. "God only knows what's been done to her," replied Walter, shaking his head in part disgust, part anger. "Do you think she'll ever recover?"

Now it was Paul's turn to shrug. "I can't say," he said, his voice echoing Walter's anger. "She certainly seemed better last night after we prayed for her." Inwardly he was pleased how the words rolled off his tongue so easily. After years of arresting people like this, he had picked up a great deal of their jargon. A sudden movement caught his attention and he glanced over to see Cyndi stretch languidly. He let his eyes rove over her form, enjoying the show, then looked away, glad Walter had not noticed.

"Hi," she said, her voice still heavy with sleep. Walter let go of the steering wheel with one hand and reached over and grasped his wife's knee in an affectionate hold. Paul felt a moment's stab of jealousy.

"How you doin', hon?" asked Walter, the concern evident in his voice. Understandable, thought Paul. She had just had to leave everything she knew for an uncertain and dark future.

"Okay," was her reply. A ghost of a smile played around her lips. "I think I'll check on the boys."

She started to get up, but Walter restrained her. "Let them sleep, Cyn," he said. "We don't know what's going to happen to us, so let them get all the rest they can."

Cyndi looked back at her sleeping children, obviously wanting to go to them, then nodded. "All right," she replied. She turned back around in her seat and turned her attention to the four-lane interstate that was rolling by at a comfortable 60 miles an hour. "How much further?" she asked, seemingly to make conversation rather than to get information.

"Reno's another hour yet," answered Walter. "Then we have to find our contact. I'd say probably at least two hours before we get there."

Cyndi nodded, then looked back at Paul. She smiled nervously. "I just wish it was all over," she said. She brought her knees up into her chest and hugged them tightly. To Paul, she suddenly looked like a frightened woodlands creature, ready to bolt from danger. He felt a moment's fleeting shame at his earlier thoughts.

"We'll get there," he said, trying to sound reassuring.

Cyndi nodded. "I mean the whole thing," she said, resting her cheek on her knees. "I wish we were where we are going to end up permanently. This not knowing is the worst part."

"God never promised us knowledge of the future," answered Walter, his eyes on the road ahead. "He just promised never to leave us alone."

Walter's words worked an amazing change in Cyndi. Her body stiffened. She jerked her head up and around to face Walter, her eyes blazing. "Thank you, Reverend Dietz," she snapped, and Paul blinked in surprise at the sudden anger in her voice. "It seems like you've got enough faith for both of us," she went on, venting the feelings that had obviously been building up inside of her for several hours. "You must have," she continued, "in order to yank your children out of the only home they've ever known and drag them across the country to who knows where."

Silence hung heavy in the Winnebego. Seconds dragged out, each one lasting an eternity. Paul shifted his weight, suddenly uncomfortable in the tension-filled cabin. He looked at Walter's reflection in the overhead mirror, and to his surprise saw a single tear start to run down his cheek.

When he spoke, however, his voice was steady and calm. "You're wrong, Cyn," he said. "I hardly have any faith at all. I'm scared, and I'm tired, and I have no idea what is going to happen to us." He swallowed hard. "While you were asleep, I tried to ask God for guidance, but the words just wouldn't come. All I could think of to say was, please just keep us together. That's all. Just keep my family together. Its all I could think about, because if I lost you, and the boys, I just. . . ." And his voice broke. Almost angrily, he used the sleeve of his jacket to wipe off his cheek.

Cyndi looked at her husband for a moment. Slowly she started to relax. The tautness ran out of her body by degrees, like water out of a semi-clogged drain. Almost timidly, she reached over and touched his arm. "I'm sorry, Walt," she said, her voice soft. "I didn't mean it that way. I'm just tired and scared too."

Walter took his eyes off the road long enough look into his wife's eyes. Paul watched in perverse fascination. He was amazed to discover just how "human" his companions were. His preconceptions of these under-ground "believers" were being challenged. It had always made his job easier to think of them simply as dangerous fanatics. Certainly the bureau's indoctrinations, government policy, and even the media, made it easy to do so. Now, however, it was only with great effort that he clung on to them.

After a long second or two, Walter nodded and smiled tentatively. "Forgiven," he said simply, and once again turned back to the road.

Although Paul could tell he was sincere, he could also tell that Cyndi's words had hurt. Cyndi understood that too, but also knew that she could never "unspeak" them.

More to change the subject than anything else, Paul scooted forward and leaned between Walter and Cyndi. "Not much traffic," he observed. Indeed, there were no oncoming vehicles at all, and only a single U-Haul truck a few hundred yards ahead. As he watched, a large sign came into view. It proclaimed WELCOME TO NEVADA in large white letters over a green background. In seconds, they had crossed the state line. There was an almost palpable sense of relief emanating from the Dietz's at having made it this far.

"Not at this time of morning," agreed Walter as the sign rolled behind them. "Of course, that'll change, once we get to Reno. We'll probably hit right at rush . . . uh oh!" Paul saw the muscles in Walter's arms go tight with sudden tension.

Cyndi drew a sharp breath and looked over at he husband. "How fast are you going, Walt?" The question betrayed the fear in her voice.

"Sixty," he replied grimly. "A good five miles under the limit." His lips became a thin line and his jaw clenched. "Just sit tight," he said. "We're completely legit. The license on this thing is current and legal. As far as the law is concerned, we're just a group of friends seeing the country.

"In the middle of a depression?" asked Cyndi, the doubt evident in her voice.

"Just hang on," grunted Walter. With that, he concentrated on his driving while Cyndi and Paul looked on, both of them holding their breath for very different reasons.

The Nevada State Police car sat in the median between the east and west lanes. This part of the interstate was obviously a speed trap. Anxious motorists, with Reno as their final destination, often increased their speed at this point. The trooper was there, waiting for them. Trying hard not too look in that direction, Walter kept the Winnebego at a steady speed. Everyone's time perception changed, and it seemed as if they were crawling toward Nevada's finest. They drew nearer, two of them praying that they would get past. All at once, they were abreast of the patrol car, then past it.

Walter's eyes became glued to the rearview mirror bolted on to the driver's side. "He's not moving," he said, his voice betraying the strange mixture of fear and hope that he was feeling. As they watched, the patrol car gradually faded from sight in the mirror. Walter and Cyndi each let out a huge sigh in perfect unison. Then, hearing each other, burst into simultaneous laughter.

"Told you everything was fine," said Walter, the relief saturating his voice.

"Yeah, right," replied Cyndi, her own voice threatening to crack. "And I didn't see your hands have a death grip on that wheel. Of course you weren't worried!" She laughed some more, and Walter joined her.

"Just practicing safe driving, sweetheart," he said, still chuckling. "Can't have an accident in front of the law, you know. Wouldn't be proper." Cyndi giggled a little more, then settled back into her chair, relaxing. There was a moment's silence, broken only by the steady thrum of the smoothly operating engine. Then a large growl sounded forth. Both Walter and Cyndi looked back in surprise at Paul. Paul stared back at them, unable to believe that his own stomach would betray him with such a vulgar noise.

"Paul," asked Cyndi innocently, "Would you like some breakfast? There's some cereal and milk in the fridge . . . and I saw a couple of cows alongside the road about a mile back. I'm sure we could kill one of them for you."

"From the sound of that," said Walter, joining in, "you'd better make it two." The husband laughed, and Paul, much to his surprise, found himself smiling. He had never been around people who were this comfortable with him. In all his adult life, he was either a supervisor, or one of the supervised. He had no close friends, or even casual ones. Certainly, none of his former associates could banter with him this easily.

"Cereal will be fine," he said, allowing his tone to match theirs. "You said it's in the fridge?" He started to get up, but Cyndi beat him to it.

"Let me get it for you, Paul," she said, bouncing up from her chair. "I need to move around a little anyway. Why don't your ride 'shotgun' with Walt for a while." She moved past him into the tiny kitchenette the Winnebego was equipped with. As she busied herself there, Paul moved forward and sat down beside Walter. The thought of someone doing something for him because they *wanted* to was strange.

"Quite a lady you've got there," he said as he relaxed in the captain's chair.

Walter nodded, smiling in satisfaction. "No doubt about it," he said. "I married out of my league. You don't find too many women as beautiful on the inside as they are on the outside."

Paul merely nodded, letting the hypnotic passing of the interstate relax his eyes. He felt good. These people liked him for what he was, and that was nice. He could be himself with them, and. . . .

Suddenly he sat bolt upright in his seat, every muscle suddenly wound tight like a clock spring. What was he *doing?* Had he forgotten everything? These people, or rather people like them, had destroyed his life. The only hope he had to get it back was to destroy them, and their insipid organization with them. How dare he sit here and make nice! Even worse, how dare he feel something as useless as friendship toward them!

Inside, deep within Paul's soul, a tiny fragment was trying to shout, to get his attention. It had lain dormant for years. In fact, its voice had been silenced the day his father left. Now, it was awake again. Even as Paul ruthlessly suppressed it, that fragment was stirring, coming back to life. Paul, of course, did not realize this. He only knew that, for an instant, he had felt something that he had not felt in years — need. He also knew that he had come dangerously close to ruining his mission. With a resolution hardened by years of practice, he quietly vowed it would not happen again. The tiny voice lapsed back into silence — for the time being.

Walter, who was totally unaware of Paul's inner battle, suddenly jerked forward as if someone had pulled a string attached to his forehead, his rigidness matching Paul's. "Cyndi," he called, and his voice reflected the hopelessness that had suddenly appeared on his face.

Cyndi looked up from where she was preparing Paul's cereal, hearing the change. Their eyes met in the mirror. "What is it, Walt?"

"Wake everyone," Walter commanded, his tone saying "don't argue with me, just do it!" "Get them up front." Cyndi hesitated for just a moment, then nodded. As she moved to wake her two sons, Paul glanced questioningly at Walter.

"Behind us," Walter said simply, and Paul knew before he looked what he would see. He leaned forward to peer into the mirror bolted onto the rider's side of the RV, and sure enough, there he was. Blue lights flashing in an angry rhythm, the patrol car they had passed earlier was coming up fast. Then, instead of passing, it planted itself not two car lengths away, its intention obvious.

"Hang on," growled Walter through gritted teeth, and started pumping the brake, preparing stop. The Winnebego rapidly lost speed, and seconds later Walter wrenched the wheel to the right, pulling the massive vehicle over onto the emergency lane. The engine idled for a moment, then he cut it off. Silence descended inside the tiny compartment as the two men watched the state trooper pull in behind them. Cyndi, having awakened her sons, nudged David Eddington gently, then moved to stand behind Walter. She had evidently forgotten about Susan, sleeping in the back. She put her hands on his shoulders, waiting.

"It *could* really be that you were speeding or something," she said quietly, breaking the silence. Her voice showed obviously that she did not believe what she was saying. There was no reply as they waited. Jonathan came over and touched his mother's arm. His eyes were still bleary with sleep.

"Mom?" He was obviously afraid, and Cyndi took one hand off Walter's shoulder and put it on Jonathan's. Stephen waited in his chair. Paul glanced over at the Dietz family and felt a unexpected moment of tenderness for the way they wrapped themselves around each other protectively. Then there was a flash of envy, followed immediately by anger that he was not allowed to have that kind of family. All of these emotions chased themselves around inside his head and heart for a few seconds. Then he squashed them as ruthlessly as he had squashed that tiny voice a short time ago.

"Here they come," said Walter quietly, bringing Paul's attention back to their current circumstance. He could see the troopers emerging from either side of the car, white helmets shining in the bright sunlight. Since the late nineties, the central government had insisted that all law officers ride in tandem, even state police. Too many were losing their lives in ambushes that could be prevented with two on patrol instead of one. Both were men, Paul noted, and of respectable size. The way they walked told them that they had had at least the basics on hand-to-hand combat. Taking on two of them at once could be trouble — not that he had any intention of doing that! This was just the break he had been hoping for.

The first trooper stopped a few yards short of the driver's door. Walter could easily see him in the rearview mirror. The trooper motioned for him to roll down the window. When he complied, the uniformed man spoke in a command-trained, deep baritone voice.

"Would everyone step out of the vehicle please . . . at once."

"What's the problem, officer?" Walter asked out the window. It was the time-honored question, but it did not satisfy the officer.

"Step out now, sir," he demanded. "Don't make me ask again." There was no choice.

"All right, everyone, stay calm," Walter said, climbing out of his chair. "Just follow me, and we'll get through this." He moved over to the door on the opposite side and opened it. Bright, almost blinding sunlight streamed in. Paul had forgotten that the windows on the RV were tinted, not allowing the troopers to see inside. No wonder they were being overly cautious. Without looking back, Walter stepped out, the rest following. Paul allowed everyone to precede him, waiting. The two boys were next, followed by David. Cyndi started to go next, then stopped suddenly.

"Susan!" she exclaimed, whirling around.

Paul halted her forward progress with a hand on her shoulder. "I'll get her," he said softly, pushing Cyndi toward the door. "You get out there, and take it easy." He forced what he hoped was a reassuring smile, then turned away. When he was sure that she was on her way out, he sprang into action. Racing back toward the back room, he stopped only long enough to grab a pencil and note pad he had noticed earlier sitting on the small dinner table. Susan was still asleep, so he sank down on the sofa bed beside her and began to write feverishly. He knew he only had a few seconds.

Outside, he could hear the sounds of the officers questioning his fellow travelers. Their voices were stern and unyielding, although he could not make out what was being said. He finished his scribbling just at the door was thrown open and a loud voice shouted,

"You in there! Get out here now!"

"I've got a sick woman in here," Paul shouted back. "She's barely conscious."

There was a brief silence, then he heard, "Jimmy, cover me!" A shadow fell across the door. Paul tensed, waiting. He hoped the trooper had a good head on his shoulders, otherwise things were going to get very ugly. There was a blur of motion, and the state police officer entered the RV. The big man was fast. In seconds, Paul found himself looking down the barrel of a Neural Pulse Weapon. It was one of the newer models. Accurate up to 50 feet, it emitted a concentrated pulse of energy that interrupted the signals from the brain to the body. It rendered the victim helpless in seconds. It could also kill, quickly and efficiently. They had become quite popular with local authorities as well as federal agencies. Paul could see that the trooper's NPW was set for heavy stun.

"Stay very still," commanded the trooper, his voice deadly serious.

Paul knew that one wrong move, and the officer would not hesitate to shoot. At point-blank range, the heavy stun setting could sometimes be fatal. He froze in his sitting position, and very calmly looked the trooper in the eye and said, "Code Alpha Alpha Seven."

Now it was the trooper who froze. Paul spent a moment being grateful for two very important things: One, that the Bureau of Religious Affairs required all of its operatives to know every emergency code belonging to every law enforcement agency in each of the 51 states. Two, that the Nevada code had obviously not been changed in the past six months. The two men looked hard at each other for a few seconds, then Paul took the initiative and spoke before the trooper could.

"Identification in my wallet, rear right pocket." The trooper thought about it for a moment, then gestured with his pistol.

"Turn around. Put your feet on the floor, hands on the bed . . . and do it slowly, mister. Understand?"

"Got it," replied Paul, and carefully assumed what lawmen everywhere called "the position." He felt his wallet slide out of his pocket, then heard it being opened and rifled though. Then he heard what he wanted to hear most. Silence. The trooper had found his uni-card and was evidently thinking about it.

"Hey Frank," came a shout from outside. "You all right in there?" It was obviously the trooper's partner calling.

"No problem," he shouted back. "It looks like we've got a . . . ." Paul reacted instantly and purely by reflex. In one fluid, lightening motion, he whirled around. Before the trooper had a chance to react, he was disarmed and looking at the business end of his own weapon.

"I'm deep undercover," growled Paul fiercely, his eyes dark with anger. "If you blow it, you'll be sweeping out latrines for the next 30 years. IF I decide to let you walk away from this. Got it?"

The trooper, in his early twenties by the look of him, and still stunned by Paul's attack, gulped and nodded quickly. Paul flipped the NPW over and handed it back to him butt first. The trooper took it gingerly, as if it were the tail end of a cobra. Then Paul jerked his head at the still thankfully sleeping Susan. "Tell your friend that I was right, that there *is* a sick woman in here . . . and tell him that we're coming out."

The trooper hesitated, then complied. To his credit, his voice did not waver as he shouted through the thin walls of the mobile home.

Paul nodded encouragingly. "Good. Now, take this." With a deft movement, he unbuttoned the trooper's shirt pocket and stuffed the note he had just scribbled a few moments before inside. He could feel the officer stiffen at the unexpected contact. "Call this number, and tell whoever answers that you've got a message from Paul Simpson. Got it?" The younger man nodded, unsure just what he had gotten himself into.

"Tell them this," continued Paul. "Tell them where you found us and what you found us in." He glanced around, indicating the Winnebego. "Give them a complete description, including the license number. Also tell them exactly who is with me . . . use the names I've written on that note. Understand so far?" Another nod. "These names do *not* match what your partner found on their ID's, but you are going to let us go anyway. And I mean let us go completely. No tails, no surveillance, nothing. If I see so much as one uniform even give us a second glance, it'll be on your head. Nod at me again if you are absolutely clear on this." Again a nod.

Paul allowed himself to relax, just a little. "Okay," he said, "one last thing. There's an address on that note. Give it to them, and tell them that it's a 'safe house.' "

"A what?" asked the trooper in confusion.

"A safe house, you idiot!" growled Paul, and the younger man jerked back as if struck. Paul had that effect on people when he used that commanding tone in his voice. "Just use the words. The people you talk to will understand. Now, repeat it all back to me."

The trooper evidently had an excellent memory. He repeated Paul's instructions back perfectly. "All right," nodded Paul, satisfied. "Just tell your partner that you've already run a check on me, and I'm fine. You can tell him about all this after we're gone, but NO SURVEILLANCE." He glanced down at the porta-comp attached to the officer's belt. He knew without asking that it was linked to the patrol car, and through it, the Nevada central police computer. From there, he could access the master system in Washington. His ID could be verified in seconds. He ran through everything quickly in his mind, and decided that he had covered all of the proverbial bases. With that, he motioned with his head for the officer to lead him outside.

Squinting in the sunlight, Paul stepped out of the RV, hearing the trooper follow. His partner stood just off to their right, arms folded and scowling. When they emerged, he strode purposefully over to the trooper behind Paul.

"Took you long enough," he growled, giving Paul an appraising look. "I was ready to call for back up, then come in and get you."

"No problem," answered Paul's trooper. "The lady inside is asleep, and she really is sick. This guy," and he jerked his head a Paul, "checks out. So does she. What about the others?"

The second officer nodded, somewhat reluctantly. "They're legit — at least, according to the computer." He sighed regretfully. "Looks like your hunch was wrong, after all."

"Yeah, right," snorted the first trooper. Paul threw him a warning look over his shoulder as the second officer turned and addressed the frightened group. "You are all free to go. I apologize for the inconvenience," he said, his voice making it clear that the only thing he was sorry for was the fact that he had found nothing wrong. He looked like he was going to say something else, then closed his mouth and walked off, gesturing for his partner to follow. The two men went back to their car, got inside, and revved up the engine. Paul's "friend" was driving. He backed up a few feet, then hit the gas hard. Tires squealed, and soon the patrol car was out of sight.

For just a moment, the small group of friends stood alongside the RV, not quite sure what had just happened. Cyndi looked about ready to faint — in fact, so did Walter. Paul started to say something — started to use his "command voice" to get them moving again, then decided against it. *Let someone else do it,* he thought to himself. He needed to stay in the background. Predictably, it was Walter who moved first.

"O . . ." he tried, then took a deep breath and started again. "Okay everyone, let's get back inside." He led the way, slowly, as if waking from a particularly nasty nightmare. The rest followed. Paul stood silently as the rest filed by. When David Eddington passed him, the shorter man paused and looked up at him. He wore an appraising look, as if asking, "Just what *were* you doing back there?" Paul returned the look with a guileless one of his own. The former preacher and the former agent studied each other for a moment, then Eddington moved inside. Paul shut the door behind them. He checked on Susan, who was still sleeping, then found his former seat behind Cyndi. The rest spread out, getting comfortable. The feeling of shock, of "almost disaster" hung over the group like a dark cloud.

Walter, saying nothing, started the engine. Checking to make sure his way was clear, he pulled the RV back out onto the interstate and once more they were on their way. Still no one spoke. They traveled in silence for almost 15 minutes. Then, suddenly, Walter again hit the brakes. Disbelief showed in everyone's face as once more he pulled over to the emergency lane. As the Winnebego came to a complete stop, David Eddington jumped up from his seat and moved over next to Walter.

"What now, Walt?" he asked, fear making his voice about half an octave above normal. Walter said nothing. Instead he got out of the driver's seat and turned to face everyone.

"All right, listen, people." His stern gaze demanded that everyone give him their complete attention. "I know how you all feel, because I feel the same way myself." He smiled grimly. "I don't know about the rest of you, but I for one am definitely going to have to change my underwear tonight!"

"Walter!" Cyndi's feigned shock brought a chuckle from everyone. Even Paul felt a smile sneak out.

Walter continued. "Now I know that was terrifying. If our ID's hadn't held up, we were as good as dead. The fact is, though, they did hold up. We're not out of the woods yet, but we can be sure of two things. One, we are not alone. Our friends in the Shepherd's Path are waiting to help us. Two," and he looked around the cramped space, "God is with us. Even if there were no Shepherd's Path, even if we were completely alone, *that* would be enough. Our Father is taking care of us. It doesn't matter what else happens. *Nothing* is going to happen that God does not will. Do you all understand me? Am I getting through?" Slowly the rest of the group nodded. The feeling of shock was slowly draining away, and being replaced by one of relief. Everyone was loosening up. Walter nodded in satisfaction.

"Good! Now, before we travel another mile, let's thank the One who watches over us — the One who died for us. Anyone care to join me?" He stepped forward and, right behind his seat, knelt on both knees. In perfect unison, all but one moved to join him. Paul, belatedly realizing what was happening, reacted just a second late, but fortunately no one noticed his slowness in joining them. He found himself impressed in spite of himself. Walter was a natural leader, and it was showing now. The group had had a bad scare, and needed to be brought back together, and that's exactly what he was doing.

Paul found himself wondering what Walter would think if he knew that their not being arrested was due to the hidden purpose of a former bureau agent, not the intervention of Almighty God. He would probably say something to the effect that this God was using Paul to help them, whether Paul wanted to or not. *That* did not sit well with him at all. Paul was not one of the used, he was a user. Walter's "god" was not using him at all. Absolutely! No doubt about it. These people were nothing more than a steppingstone to better things — and that was it. Count on it!

Paul knelt and joined the small circle of believers. He found himself holding hands with Jonathan on one side, and Cyndi on the other. He did not like this. The last time he had "prayed" with these people, he had found himself ready to throw up. Perhaps it was some group strength, some aura they gave off when they agreed like this. Whatever it was, he had better protect himself this time. He started to chant in his mind, but for some odd reason, his Zen techniques felt empty and useless. Doggedly he kept at it. In that tiny Winnebego, five voices were raised in prayer, while one was silent in deep sleep, and another grimly recited his mantra.

* * *

Wolf stopped his car outside of the two-story brownstone building in the business district of Sacramento. Behind him, a nondescript black sedan and a white van pulled up. The address matched the one he had been given just an hour before by some state cop calling from Nevada. That idiot Sinclair finally had passed on some useful information.

Wolf stepped out of the car and surveyed the area. The two men in the sedan did the same. Two other men in the van sat and waited. It was an upper middle-class neighborhood, oriented toward the career-minded. Townhouses ran the length of the street. Each was identical to its neighbor, down to the same exact color — light brown. Only the addresses set them apart from each other.

Nodding at the two men from the sedan who now stood beside him, he turned and waved at the van. At his signal, its two occupants jumped out and disappeared around back. When they re-emerged, they were carrying a large box marked "FRAGILE/ELECTRONICS" in bold red letters on the side. Although it looked heavy, Wolf could tell from the way they were carrying it that it was empty. It did not matter. Its only purpose was to provide a split second's diversion.

With a terse "Wait here" directed at the two men from the sedan, Wolf walked briskly toward the brownstone with the proper address. The two carrying the box automatically fell in behind him. Wolf was dressed in a bland gray coverall with a white patch on the left breast that said "BUDGET

ELECTRONICS." He was also carrying a clipboard. The two with the box were dressed the same. The men in the sedan, in contrast, were wearing rather expensive dark suits.

Together, this odd procession climbed the 10 steps to the front door. Wolf checked the street, up and down. Then, satisfied that he was drawing no undue attention, he rang the buzzer built into the solid oak door. There was a brief wait, then he saw the curtain over the window next to the door stir. A pretty, young feminine face peered out.

Wolf smiled cheerfully, and motioned with his free hand toward the box. "Delivery," he shouted, loud enough to be heard through the glass. There was a confused look on the woman, then she disappeared. This was followed by another brief wait, then Wolf heard the sound he had been hoping to hear — the sound of a door bolt being drawn back.

The door cracked open, and this time, a man's face was visible. "Yes?"

"George McVey?" asked Wolf, looking at his clipboard.

"I'm George McVey," said the man. "There must be some mistake. We didn't order any — hey!" This exclamation was caused by one of the men holding the box suddenly moving forward. He brought his leg up in a straight ahead kick. George was thrown back, more out of surprise than the force of the blow. The man with the box balanced himself, and let fly with another kick. This time the wood holding the bolt shattered, and the door flew open.

Wolf wasted no time. He was inside before George had a chance to recover. He whipped out the ugly shape of a pistol he had had specially made. Not an NPW, but an old-fashioned, lead throwing gun. Using the butt as a club, he clipped George across the cheek. George groaned once and then lay still.

"George!" His name was screamed by the woman Wolf had seen in the window. He looked over at her, standing at the foot of the stairs and obviously in shock.

Moving with the confidence of the predator, he took two steps over to her and grabbed her arm. "Let's go, you — in there," he shoved her roughly toward what looked like a living room. With a cry, she fell over her sprawled husband and lay next to him, shaking. Wolf started to aim a kick at her, then decided he needed both of them coherent — at least for now. He nodded to one of his cohorts, who reached down and hauled the woman to her feet and forced her into the living room.

"Gwen?" George's voice came weakly as he struggled to regain full consciousness.

Wolf grinned and knelt down next to him. "Gwen's safe for now, Georgie-boy. My friend's got her in there." He nodded toward the next room, and let out a big, theatrical sigh. "Of course, she won't be that way for long. My friend — he's a little rough. So, unless you want him to get impatient, I suggest that you get off your butt and get in there!" The last words came out as a shout. George reacted by climbing to his unsteady feet. He walked like a drunkard, but he made it into the living room under his own power. Gwen was there, slumped into one side of a large, leather couch. George stumbled toward her.

The living room was decorated in bright colors, mostly greens and blues. Although there was nothing opulent about it, there was still the feeling of wealth. The furniture was well made, and the carpet plush. Wolf, always looking for reasons to hate his prey, used this to fuel his anger.

"Nice place, Georgie — boy," he said sarcastically. "Especially since most loyal Americans seem to be losing their homes just now. Being a traitor must pay well these days." The fact was, Wolf could not have cared less about how many Americans were losing their jobs. He simply wanted a reason — ANY reason — to hate.

"We're not. . . ."

Whaap! Wolf lashed out, and caught George on the neck with a vicious blow. George fell face forward into the couch, almost into Gwen's lap. She caught him with a cry, and cradled his head against her breast.

"Now," said Wolf conversationally, "Let me explain the rules here." He held up a finger. "One, you speak when I tell you to. That means you answer only the questions I ask." He seated himself on a coffee table that was placed in front of the sofa, facing the stunned couple. "Two," he continued, "Right answers will earn you your lives. Wrong answers will kill you. Understand?" Gwen only looked back at him, not understanding anything. George's eyes were open, but they had a glassy look about them.

When neither replied, Wolf let go with a vicious kick that connected with Gwen's calf. It was the kind of kick a first grade bully would use to hurt a fallen adversary. Gwen screamed in pain. She would have doubled over, but having George in her lap prevented her. Her cry of pain, however, did arouse her husband. With a heroic effort, he sat up, allowing Gwen to grab her leg. Her cry gradually quieted to a whimper. George looked over at his wife and touched her arm. She nodded, and looked back. Their eyes met, and there was a timeless second of pure communion between them that spoke volumes.

When George turned back to Wolf, his face was composed and calm. Wolf saw the change, and it angered him. He preferred — no, he *needed* his victims to be afraid. He fed on their fear — just like his father had fed upon his own fear. It nourished and satisfied him like nothing else. Slowly he stood, and, without warning, aimed another kick, this time at George's calf. He waited for another cry of pain, but when he connected, George merely grunted and clenched his jaw. His eyes, fastened on Wolf's, merely stared. If there had been hatred, or fear, or even defiance in that look, Wolf could have handled it. What he could not handle was the calm acceptance that looked out at him. Somewhere, between the front door and the sofa, George and Gwen had found their courage.

Right then and there, Wolf would have killed them. He could feel the fury building inside of him. George's look was all it would take for him to release it. Somewhere inside, though, there was a rational part of him that was demanding his attention. It told him that if he killed them, he would be left with nothing. With a great effort, he controlled himself. When he was sure he was relatively calm, he spoke again. "A group of people were here last night," he began, only a slight tremor in his voice. "I already know who they are, and what they wanted. What I want to know from you, Georgie-boy, is where they are going, who are they going to meet, and when. I also want to know who your contacts are in the city government." He smiled engagingly. His anger ebbed and he felt in charge again. "You know who I'm talking about, Georgie-boy. The ones who do those wonderful bogus ID's for your friends. So how about it. You give me what I need, and me and my friends will get out of here and let you and your pretty lady get on with your lives."

He looked expectantly at George, waiting. George only looked back, that same expression of calm acceptance still there. Wolf started to feel the anger build again. "Think about it, Georgie-boy," he said. "Life gets rough on traitors these days." He grinned. "Besides, you wouldn't want to see anything . . . nasty . . . happen to Gwenny here, would you now? My boys here, they've been cooped up with just each other for company for days now. I think they just might like to have themselves a little party, and your little woman would make a fine guest of honor."

George paled a shade, and Wolf knew he had won. He had used this tactic before, and it had never failed him. Threaten a man, and he might defy you. Threaten his wife or children, and almost always, he would surrender.

George started to speak, but suddenly Gwen reached out and grabbed his arm. He did not turn around, did not look at his wife, but once again his resolve seemed to firm up. As Wolf watched in first amazement, then in growing rage, that blasted look of acceptance returned, but this time, there was a difference. Wolf stared at George, noticing the change, but unable to describe it. The man looked — bigger. That was the only way to put it. Wolf suddenly had the feeling that he was no longer the prey, but the preyed upon. For an instant, he felt a surge of fear (Daddy, please don't hit me!), then shoved it aside. He was in control here! He, Wolf, held the lives of these people in his hand, not their "god."

A sneer wormed its way out of his mouth. He would show this wimp just what fear really was. His eyes fastened on George's, he reached out and grabbed a handful of Gwen's blouse. He started to yank it down, intending to tear it open. Then, to his amazement, a hand fastened itself around his arm with viselike strength. As effortlessly as a little child, he was pushed away. He fell back onto the coffee table and, unable to regain his balance, went toppling over on his shoulders.

The push caught the other two men off guard, and they could only gape in amazement at his assailant. Wolf lay there in utter humiliation, unable to believe what had just happened. It had not been George who had come to his wife's rescue, but *Gwen herself* who had so easily thrown him down. How?! Her grip had been iron, firm and unbreakable. Just minutes ago she had been easily forced onto the couch. Where had she gotten that strength?

Both husband and wife rose and stood shoulder to shoulder. For just a moment, Wolf felt that he was seeing an invincible enemy marching on him. The other two men drew their weapons and trained them on the McVeys. Time stopped as the two foes regarded each other.

Then George spoke. "You may kill us both," he said in a voice that matched his wife's grip. A small, mocking smile played around the corners of his mouth. "Any idiot with a gun can do that. If God has delivered us into your hands, so be it. But," and here he pointed his finger straight at Wolf, "you will *not* violate this child of the most high God!"

Wolf cowered on the floor. These two were unarmed and helpless, and yet he was *afraid!* His heart beat so wildly that for a moment he thought it must surely burst. He wanted to get up, but the *fear* held him in place. Later he would deny it, but then and there he knew that there was an undeniable *third* presence standing with the McVeys — and that presence was greater than anything that Wolf or any of his friends could throw at it.

"You'd better understand this, mister," George continued. "You're up against something that you can never beat."

"I see the fear in you." This was Gwen speaking, now also looking directly at Wolf. "I feel in my heart that you have been given one last chance to turn around." Was that pity in her voice? Wolf stared in disbelief. She was feeling *sorry* for him? That was just too much for him to handle. The old anger and hatred began to resurface.

"The Son, Jesus Christ, is holding out His hand to you." Gwen was still speaking. "Take it now, and repent. It's not too late. Spurn Him," she continued, looking somehow sad beyond words, "and I don't think you'll get another chance. Give up your hate. Please, before it's too late."

"ARGHHH!" The scream tore its way out of Wolf's throat. It was primal, animalistic. In total hatred and loathing, he pushed up from the floor and launched himself at George. He wanted nothing more than to tear out the heart of this man who mocked him so easily. Hands outstretched, he bolted over the table at the couple, who merely stood, now hand in hand. He reached for George's throat . . . and was thrown back over the table and on to the floor. The two other men did not see exactly what had happened, but Wolf knew. He would deny it for the rest of his life, but deep in his heart, he knew what happened. He never reached the McVeys. Inches from George, he was again repulsed — and *neither George nor Gwen had touched him.* Something — someone else was there, and it was preventing him from physically touching them.

His two cohorts saw him thrown down again. When George and Gwen turned their eyes on them, they figured that they were next. In perfect unison, they aimed their pistols at the couple. Wolf looked up from his position on the floor and saw what was about to happen. He saw one of the few links to the twice-cursed Shepherd's Path about to be lost forever.

"Nooo!" His shout came a split second too late. Time slowed, and he watched everything in slow motion. He saw the looks on the faces of Gwen and George. Both were calm, and ready. *They planned this,* he thought wildly in that instant frozen in time. *They want it like this.* Before he could react further, two shots rang out. He saw the bodies of the McVeys go flying backward, and they never lost those awful looks of serenity. Not only that, but there was something else there as well. Were they smiling? Were they mad?

They tumbled backward, their hearts already quieted. His companions were excellent shots. George landed sitting on the couch, with Gwen right next to him, her head on his shoulder. They looked for all the world like they were simply resting or watching television, a happy couple at home. The only thing that spoiled the illusion was the two growing bloodstains on their chests.

Wolf rolled up to a sitting position and regarded the couple in disbelief. Ten minutes ago, he had had a solid link to the Shepherd's Path. Now, he had nothing. One safe house — one of thousands — eliminated, and nothing more. His superiors were going to be very upset. He tore his eyes off the McVeys and looked over at his men. They stood there, smoking pistols still pointed at the dead couple.

Wolf could only shake his head. "Idiots," he said, his voice barely above a whisper. He was not sure whether he was talking about the McVeys or his own team.

He pulled himself to his feet, and stood straight. Taking a long look around the room, he pondered his next course of action. "Get this place cleaned up," he ordered, trying to sound like he was in charge again. The two men glanced at each other, and Wolf read their shared look easily. They had seen him humiliated and humbled, and the respect and fear that they had

had for him was gone. They would no longer be acceptable allies. Once they left here, they would have to be killed. "Well," he demanded, putting as much threat as he could into his voice.

They looked at him, then started to obey. They were not fools, at least. They knew that if something happened to Wolf, they still had to get past the two men waiting outside. Quickly and professionally, the townhouse was cleaned of anything that might implicate Wolf or his associates. Let the local police try to figure out what had happened here, if they could. Within 10 minutes, everything was cleared. They walked out, leaving the McVeys on the couch. It might be hours, or even days, before they were discovered. Wolf followed his teammates out. They returned to the van while he went to speak to the two men in dark suits.

"Get rid of them," he said as he reached them. "They almost killed me in there, and thanks to those trigger-happy idiots, we have no one to question. Get rid of them today, understand?" The two suited men knew better than to argue with a direct order from this man.

"Got it," acknowledged one of them. Wolf nodded, and slipped into his Mercedes. He wanted to get away from here, and be by himself for a while. He wanted to forget about the McVeys, and whatever else was with them in there. Somehow he would get another lead. Perhaps that idiot Sinclair could get a second message to him — or maybe he could find another meeting to raid. Either way, he would get them. He would get them all.

Taking a deep breath, he started his car and drove off. He would be successful in forgetting — somewhat. Within hours, he would have convinced himself that he had misinterpreted events with the McVeys. There was no "third" presence there, only a very frightened couple. Undoubtedly it was an adrenaline surge that accounted for Gwen McVey's added strength. That had to be it. There was no other explanation. Within hours, he would be back on the hunt.

Somehow though, he would never forget Gwen McVey's last words to him. "I don't think you'll get another chance," she had said. "Give up your hate before it's too late." Those words would haunt him for the rest of his life.

Oh God, if this isn't hell, it's as close to it as this world will ever come, thought David Eddington. He shifted uncomfortably in the back seat of the old Ford van that had regrettably replaced the Winnebego four days ago and watched as the heart of Brooklyn, New York, moved past.

It crept by at an agonizingly slow pace. What had once been the subject of romantic novels and poems was now an endless disaster. Refuse lined the streets, piled higher in many places than the van. It lay rotting in the cold winter air. Even with the windows closed and the heater going, the stench still wormed its way inside. David and the rest of the group constantly had to fight the reflex to gag.

That was the least of the city's problems. From the smell of it, the sewers had also failed, or at least backed up. A gray slimy mud lay like film over the street, and splattered gently on the sides of the van as it crept by. The source of the filth seemed to be coming from up ahead. Craning his neck, trying to see past his companions, David could see that one of the sewer lines had evidently burst. Raw human waste was spewing out madly into the streets, causing traffic to come to a standstill. The bottleneck looked to be about a block in front of them. With most of the city workers on strike, there was no one to clean up the mess.

David wondered just how anyone could live here, but live they did. The buildings, most of them 10 or 15 stories high, were on the verge of collapse, but were nevertheless inhabited. Every now and then, he would see someone peering out one of the upper windows, as if keeping watch on a place that no longer needed watching.

Despite the cold, the streets were crowded. Children of all ages played along the sidewalk in the late afternoon sun. The lucky ones had overcoats. Most only wore layered, long sleeved shirts — if that. David's heart broke as he watched them get splattered with the same obscene muck that was spraying the outside of their van. His eye caught sight of one boy who could not have been more than four years old, sitting on the cold pavement, ragged shawl-like rug thrown around his shoulders. Large tears were streaming down his cheeks, but he was ignored by both children and adults nearby. Feeling his throat constrict, David turned away. At that moment, life seemed hopeless. Here, at least, the system had collapsed and these people were left to fend for themselves.

What's the sense? he asked himself, the dark mood he was in increasing. What was the use in putting themselves through all of this? Did the government that they were running from even care where they went? It obviously did not care about the people who lived here in this purgatory. David thought back to his days as a pastor. He had been so proud the day he had initiated a "benevolent" ministry. Food, clothes, and money were donated to help the poor — especially at Christmas time. It always gave him a warm feeling to drop off a truck load of supplies at the local mission. Still, even then, in his heart, he had known it was not enough. He was aware that somewhere in the world, even in this country, people were homeless and starving. He could live with that, as long as he felt that he had done his part. But to come face to face with poverty like this . . . it was just too much. His "part" was obviously far short of what needed to be done.

Swallowing hard, he forced himself to look back out the window. He was not alone. The rest of the group watched the human tragedy slowly pass by like some monstrous panorama. Paul and Susan were sitting in the seat in front of him. Susan, although much improved over the past few days, looked now like she was about to pass out. Even the normally impassive and stolid Paul Simpson seemed uncomfortable. In the driver's seat, as usual, Walter slowly navigated the van through the neighborhood, trying and failing to keep his eyes ahead. Cyndi sat stone still, her face a mask, obviously concealing deep feelings.

Just over an hour ago, they had been listening to a news broadcast on the van radio. One report was about the rapid rise in childhood diseases once thought to be extinct. Polio was mentioned, along with rubella and whopping cough. The fatality rate was shockingly high. David wondered how many young ones he was seeing today would last through the year.

The advent of socialized medicine only four years ago, in 1998, had been heralded as a breakthrough in proper health care for everyone. With medical costs completely out of control, it had seemed to be the only logical solution. The medical industry was brought under strict control, and prices dropped. Eventually, Washington assumed complete control, supported by citizens who were tired of substandard service at soaring costs.

It worked — for a while. Unfortunately, as the government went, so went medical care. Now with the depression, health services had taken a back seat to "more pressing" emergencies. Hence, unavailable vaccines, closed clinics . . . and children who would not live to see their fifth birthday.

It was too much. Once more, David averted his eyes. Glancing over at Jonathan and Stephen Dietz, who were sharing the back seat with him, he saw his look of fear and uncertainty mirrored in their young faces. He tried to smile in reassurance, but the grimace that tugged at the corners of his mouth was a perverse, twisted parody. From the lack of response, he knew that he had been less than successful.

He heard a slight gagging sound, and saw that it was Susan. Her face had a greenish tint to it, and it looked for a moment like they were going to have a mess in the van. Paul quickly reached into his pocket and brought out one of the anti-nausea pills he kept with him. Susan obviously had a long way to go before she could be considered anywhere near cured. David watched as she swallowed the pill, then closed her eyes and leaned back. The medication worked fast, and soon she was breathing easier. Paul glanced toward the front of the van at Walter.

"How much further?" he asked in that clipped tone that David still had not grown accustomed to.

"I can't be sure," was Walter's terse reply. The scenery was getting to him too. "At the rate we're going, probably another 15 minutes." Paul frowned, obviously unhappy, but said nothing.

The sense of personal danger that had constantly nagged at David's mind over the past few days was now blaring like a clarion in his head. Since the incident with the Nevada state police, their trip had been uneventful. With a precision that had amazed him, they had been moved from safe house to safe house, crossing the nation at a slow but steady pace. Whether it had been a home in the suburbs, an abandoned farmhouse in the country, or an inner city tenement, they had been welcomed and protected by believers who were willing to put everything on the line for their faith. David found himself awed by the sense of commitment he continuously encountered. He wanted nothing more than to emulate it. Whatever else was happening, the Shepherd's Path was obviously functioning at peak efficiency.

Still, that did not alleviate the feeling that they were being watched. Here, in what used to be a predominantly Italian neighborhood, that sense was stronger than ever. Gang warfare, escalating since the early nineties, was in full force. Territories were evidently separated along racial lines. Every few blocks signaled the end of one territory and the beginning of another. Small clumps of sullen youths gathered at street corners, eyeing them as they went by. Just now, they seemed to be traversing the territory of the "Great White Sharks." Judging from graffiti such as "WHITE'S RULE" and "ONE COLOR — ONE NATION," the Sharks were another of the white supremacist groups that were springing up all over the country. Many of these groups advocated violence as a means of furthering their agenda and openly supported the Fourth Reich that was gaining control in Germany. They were, in turn, countered by terrorist groups funded mostly by the African National Congress and the Pan Arabian States. While most citizens did not realize it, a literal war was being waged between these groups from city to city. It was a war that left only victims, no victors. Although the government publicly condemned such gangs, trying as it was to foster a "one world society," it claimed that it lacked the resources to deal with them effectively.

Right, thought David bitterly. *They've got plenty of resources to deal with believers who only want to worship freely, but forget about putting a stop to the gang violence that's killing these kids.* Once again he slumped back into his seat, closing his eyes. If he could not alleviate the suffering of these people, he could at least put it out of sight for a few moments. He tried to clear his mind, then fill it with thoughts about his estranged wife and son. He almost succeeded when Jonathan spoke beside him.

"Dad?"

"Yeah, son," replied Walter.

"I think there's someone following us." Jonathan's voice, though steady, held a hint of fear. David's eyes snapped open and he looked over at the young man. There was a haunted look to him that made him seem far older than his 12 years. David could not help but think of his own son Josh, and the look he had when he and his mother had left for good. Next to Jonathan, his brother Stephen leaned close to his older sibling for protection.

At that moment, Jonathan was staring out the back of the van, his eyes wide. David followed his look and froze. At least half a dozen youths, ranging between the ages of 12 and 20 by the look of them, were following the van, staying about 20 yards behind. Because of the slow pace that Walter was forced to maintain, they had no trouble in keeping up with them.

"Walter," David called, keeping his eyes locked on the gang, "Jonathan's right. You'd better get us out of here." Now everyone was craning their necks to get a glimpse of the approaching danger.

"Too much traffic," called Walter from the front, frustration evident in his voice. "Everything's backed up because of the sewers." He paused, then said, "You don't think they'd try something in broad daylight with all these people around, do you?"

"Count on it." This flat pronouncement came from Paul, who was studying the oncoming gang with a professional detachment. "The people living here will be too afraid to say anything, and the one's just passing through, like us, just want to get out."

As the days had passed, and their trip lengthened, David was finding that he neither liked nor trusted Paul. There was something about the aloof stranger that reeked of trouble. Still, he had to agree with the big man's assessment. He noticed with a sinking feeling in his stomach that people on the sidewalks were rapidly clearing out as the gang passed by. Other motorists, he could see, watched in fear as the gang approached, only to sag with relief when they moved past. David had no doubt that the van was their target. As if in answer to his thoughts, the gang broke into a run, making a dash right then.

"Here they come," yelled Jonathan. David started to shout something at Walter (he never knew what he was going to shout), when a huge hand grabbed his shoulder and yanked him forward.

"Get down," commanded a rough voice that he barely recognized as Paul's. David had no choice but to obey. The man was strong. He fell rather than slid to the van's cold floor, followed by the two boys beside him. Jonathan's foot landed painfully on his neck, only to be removed an instant later. David's face was pressed against the floor. He saw Susan under the seat, obviously forced by Paul to scrunch down and put her hands over her head.

Gritting his teeth, he struggled to move. He managed to get one arm under him and turn himself over. Squeezing past Jonathan's legs, he pried himself into a half-sitting position. Craning his neck, he could see Paul over the top of the seat, his dark eyes literally snapping at the approaching danger.

He's been in situations like this before, David realized coldly. Just who was this cold, emotionless man? Former law enforcement maybe, or — and the thought chilled David to his very soul — current law enforcement?" David felt his mouth grow dry at the possibility, and suddenly he was much more afraid of Paul Simpson than the approaching danger.

There was a loud CRASH, followed by the unmistakable tinkle of breaking glass. The rear window of the van shattered, and David could hear shouted obscenities from the youths outside. In horror, David watched as a long, heavily muscled arm snaked its way in. It was followed by a face that he would see in his nightmares for the rest of his life. More animal than human, it held a wild, raging hatred. The mouth was drawn up in a permanent sneer. A long scar ran from the corner of the left eye to the jaw line. The eyes were the eyes of a lost soul — beyond hope of rescue. It was the face of an ancient, malevolent being, aged far past its years, hung carelessly on a teenage frame. David watched in fascinated horror as the head was followed by a pair of broad, football player's shoulders.

There was nothing he could do. He was frozen to the floor of the van. His thoughts raced. *This could not be happening!* The face looked down, and he saw himself come nose to nose with death. A wide, evil grin slowly spread across the face, and the arm produced a wicked looking, homemade pistol. David could only watch as the barrel of the pistol swung down to point at his forehead.

Time slowed to a crawl. Suddenly, David could suddenly see everything in great detail. He saw the pistol center in on his forehead. He saw the muscles on the arm contract in the act of pulling the trigger. He wanted to close his eyes, but could not. Death stared him straight in the face, and he could not look away. There was not even time for a prayer.

THUD! The pistol abruptly wavered, then disappeared. David caught a lightning fast movement out of the corner of his eye. Standing above him, looking in that instant like a modern day Spartacus, Paul Simpson let fly with an opened-palm slap that caught the intruder square on the nose. Just how the big man was able to balance himself on the edge of the seat and deliver a blow of such force David would never know. All he did know was that one second he knew he was going to die, and the next he wasn't.

There was a howl of rage and pain as the attacker became the attacked. A meaty hand flew to a broken nose, trying to staunch the flow of blood. Hastily the gang member started to back off, but Paul was not through. He brought his rigid hand back into a classic, tai-kwon-do position, cocking it into a lethal pose. David had no martial arts training whatsoever, but even he knew what was going to happen next.

"NO!" he shouted. He struggled to get up, but could not. Paul's arm started to move. At that instant, the van lurched. Other gang members were shoving at the sides, trying to overturn it. Paul's blow went wide. He had been aiming for the throat, and instead glanced off the side of the neck. It did not kill the gang member, but it still hurt. David saw a look of infinite surprise cross the face of the attacker. It was the look of one who had just discovered his own mortality. He looked down at David, his intended victim, their eyes meeting. Then his eyes glazed over, and the face that was so hate-filled — so animalistic — became the simple face of a confused 16-year-old boy. It was the face of one who had received violence and abuse, and simply returned it to an uncaring world — a face that spoke of wasted potential and lost innocence.

David stared into the depths of despair. Then the moment was over. Paul shoved hard at the youth's face, forcing him back out of the window. The gang member disappeared, taking his small story of human tragedy with him.

"Walter! Move!" Paul's command shook David out of his stupor. Time resumed its normal flow, and he realized that the rest of the gang was still attacking. He needed no urging to stay down.

The remaining members, having seen one of their own fall, were now a little more cautious. Rocks pelted the outside of the van. The windows on one side of the van were already cracking and would shatter soon. Then, without warning, there was a loud "poing" that caused the entire van to vibrate. David could not begin to guess what had caused it until Paul disappeared over the seat.

"They're shooting at us!" he shouted. "Come on, Walter, MOVE!"

"I can't! There's nowhere to go!" Walter was almost screaming in panic. David heard scuffling, then a heavy thud, and realized that Paul must be moving forward. This was accented with another "poing," and one of the already cracked windows gave way completely. David had just enough time to cover his eyes before he was showered with glass. Someone screamed, but he was not sure who. Then, without warning, the van shuddered and lurched.

"You're crazy, Paul!" Walter's shout was cut off by a heavy grunt. Curiosity became stronger than fear, and David forced himself over Jonathan in order to see up front. What he saw amazed him. Paul now sat in the driver's seat. Walter lay half in the middle row, and half on the floor. David saw Paul jerk the steering wheel hard, and once again the van lurched.

"Grab something, everyone," shouted their new driver. Then, to David's amazement, he gunned the van all the way across the street. Tires squealed and angry horns blared as the van plummeted crazily across three lanes of heavy traffic. The passengers inside were tossed about like dice in a shaker. Jonathan's foot connected soundly with David's nose, causing a slow trickle of blood. Once again someone screamed, and David now recognized the source as himself.

Somehow, even in the heavy traffic, they did not hit anyone. By all rights, Paul's driving insanity should have caused a multi-car accident. They bounced between lanes like a drunken pinball. David saw a battered pickup truck run up onto the sidewalk, narrowly missing a score of pedestrians. When he thought to look behind them, he saw the gang falling back, unable now to keep up. One member simply lay on the pavement where he had fallen.

"God help us," murmured David. This time the nausea that hovered in his stomach had nothing to do with the garbage-lined streets. "I think he was going to kill that boy." But of course, he did not "think" — he knew. He would take the face of that lost youth to his grave.

Another lurch forced him to turn around. The van caromed back into its proper lane. Paul had miraculously circumvented the bottleneck and they were now speeding away from the territory of the Great White Sharks. David hung on to the back of the middle seat, still trying to get a handle on what had just happened. He found that he still could not believe it. One of their company had just tried to take a human life. Impossible, yet he had seen it happen. Did anyone else know?

Behind him, Jonathan and Stephen slowly regained their seats. Both of them had been face down on the floor during the whole ugly incident — Susan as well. Walter had been driving, and Cyndi's attention was focused on him. That left David. What was he going to do? Should he tell the others? Should he confront Paul in front of everyone, or alone, or even at all? He had seen how the big man had handled himself. There was no doubt in his mind that if Paul reacted violently, neither he nor Walter was a match for him — even if they tried to take him on together. Carefully, David eased his battered frame back into his seat. His throbbing nose came to his attention, and he wiped the blood off with his sleeve.

There was something else to think about, he knew. He did not want to face it, but he had seen the hatred on that gang member's face. Paul Simpson had literally saved his life. David had looked into the face of his own death, and Paul had intervened. If he had not, David would, in all probability, be lying on the floor right now, a bullet hole in his forehead. What was his life worth? His silence, perhaps — not to tell the rest of the group? What would he tell them anyway — that Paul was a trained killer? What was he going to do?

A maelstrom of forceful emotions chased themselves around in his heart, each one vying for dominance. Fear of Paul competed for relief at being alive. Guilt was there, too. A significant part of him was glad that David Eddington was alive, even at the cost of an injured boy. David hated himself a little for that feeling.

"Hey Walter! You mind getting yourself together and telling me just where we're headed?" David jumped at the sound of Paul's cool voice. He looked toward the front, where Walter was still clinging to the arm of the middle seat. At that exact moment, Paul looked into the rearview mirror. Their eyes met, and locked on to each other.

He knows! thought David wildly. *He knows that I saw him.* His throat went suddenly dry. What would happen now? David knew that Paul was far more than just another Christian on the run, and Paul knew that David knew.

"You all right?" It took David a moment to realize that Paul was speaking to him. He started to speak, but had to force down the feeling of panic rising in his gorge. Instead he merely nodded.

Paul held his gaze for a moment longer, as if to divine his intentions. Then he shrugged and shifted his attention to Walter. David felt both ashamed and relieved. Paul, it seemed, was going to let matters rest, and that was good. Still . . . the way he had looked at David, and dismissed him with a shrug, made it obvious that he did not consider the smaller man a threat. Perhaps he was right.

Perhaps David was not a threat. When Paul had held his gaze for that long second, it was as if he had been held in the hypnotic grip of a cobra. Then, at the last minute, he had been released. It felt like a reprieve from an execution.

Fear rose to prominence in David's emotional turmoil. In desperation to save what was left of his dignity, he decided to call it "caution." He would say nothing, unless the group as a whole became endangered. With a sigh he settled back into his seat. He had to fight the burning shame that crept over him by reminding himself over and over that he was acting for the good of the group.

Up front, Walter finally righted himself. He leaned forward, peering over Paul's shoulder. "Are you quite through doing crazy things?" he asked. Walter wasn't fooling anyone. His voice might be the deadpan delivery of a comedic straight man, but his hands were shaking.

"We got away, didn't we?" growled Paul. "Look up ahead." Despite his preoccupation with his own personal battle, David looked between his companions, trying to see what Paul was talking about. He spotted it almost immediately. A huge, square swastika was suspended over the street. It hung on an almost invisible thin wire stretched between buildings. It obviously marked the boundary of the Great White Sharks. David could only shake his head. Surely the human race could not sink much further than what he was seeing! On either side of the street, a half dozen youths were standing. Inwardly, David groaned. Was it going to happen again? Were these children of the streets going to attack?

Paul did not hesitate. He steered the van straight at the swastika. Everyone inside watched frozen as they came even with, then passed the obvious sentries. There were a lot of dark looks, and two or three obscene gestures, but that was it. No one rushed the van, and no one threw anything. There was an audible sigh of relief in the van as they left the Great White Sharks' territory. David wondered if the gang members had heard of the incident less than a mile back. Would they let them go if they knew that one of their own was hurt? What if they had to return this way? Looking out the shattered back window, David could see the gang members still watching them, as if waiting.

"Oh Lord!" This exclamation was from Cyndi. She was leaning forward in her seat, craning her neck upward. "It is a war zone," she continued. "I've heard stories about this, but I never believed it was this bad." The object that had captured her attention passed by, and David watched out the back window to see what it was. His eyes widened in surprise when it came into view.

"Well," said Walter grimly, "there's Chinatown, and Little Italy." He shrugged in helplessness. "Welcome to Little Israel, folks." Overhead, the Star Of David fluttered in the cold winter breeze.

* * *

Little Israel, it turned out, was little better than the little white supremacist America they had just left. The skin on the inhabitants was a little darker, perhaps, but that was it. Small groups of youths of all ages were scattered everywhere. All seemed to be watching the van with angry, suspicious eyes. Traffic had died down to a trickle, and only a few other cars were moving along with them now.

Gang warfare was obviously in full swing here. They passed what looked like the sight of a previous battle. Debris littered the street, broken glass mixing with discarded, splintered baseball bats, chains, and an occasional crowbar. A flash of reflected light on the now dry pavement caught David's eye, and he took a second look. He shuddered when he saw that the metallic glimmer was caused by empty shell casings.

It was too much. The attack on the van, the young gang member lying on the pavement, and now this . . . he was on the verge of "overload." He felt as if he were drowning, going under in a violent undertow. His only defense was to once more try and shut out what his senses were forcing him to observe. He shut his eyes, folded his arms across his chest and hugged himself tightly. Bowing his head, he tried to pray.

Ironically, he had done little praying in the past few days, except with the group as a whole. As a pastor, he had once taught that adversity draws one closer to God. Right now, he was wondering if everything he had taught was a lie. Instead of drawing closer, he felt himself pulling away from his Lord and Saviour. He knew that the problem lay within himself, but it was a head knowledge only. Within his heart, the true problem lay. He simply did not feel worthy to be close to the One whom he had professed to follow most of his life. Even as a pastor, when he had led a thriving church with a lively congregation, he had prayed little by himself. Now that things were rapidly going from bad to worse, he discovered that he could not even form the simplest of pleas. Disgust at his own cowardice and hypocrisy set up an insurmountable barrier between him and his Lord. Whether he would be able to breech it, only time would tell.

There was a sudden jolt, and the van came to an abrupt halt. David's eyes snapped open on their own volition. He found himself looking at a decayed tenement building that looked like all the other structures they had passed so far. Ten or 12 stories high, it was constructed of dirty red brick that was hopelessly darkened with age. David doubted that even a good sandblasting would remove the years of dirt.

"This is it," said Walter, still leaning over Paul's shoulder.

"You sure?" Paul's question was terse and to the point.

"Yep," replied Walter, not taking offense at Paul's lack of tact. "The address is right, and so is the description."

Paul only grunted in response, and glanced out of his window to survey the surrounding area. "It had better be," he growled. "This place does not look healthy." He turned back to Walter. "You'd better go up alone. I think the rest of us should stay together as much as possible."

Walter nodded, agreeing. He moved toward the sliding side door on the rider's side. His feet crunched on the broken glass that now littered the floor. Cyndi put a hand on his arm, giving him a reassuring touch. "Be careful, Walt," she said, even though she knew she was stating the obvious. "Paul's right. This place scares me — even worse than what we just came through." Indeed, her fears were grounded. Now that they had stopped, they seemed to be drawing far more than their share of attention. A group of dangerous-looking young men and women had gathered directly across the street. They said nothing, did nothing . . . just stared at the van. David would have sworn that there were four or five when they had first arrived. Now, less than two minutes later, there was an even dozen.

"I'll make it quick," Walter reassured his wife. "Just long enough to make contact, and get our next stop down the line. Okay?" Cyndi smiled bravely and nodded. Walter grasped the door handle and pulled hard. The sliding door responded easily, first moving forward and then rolling back. Walter jumped down onto the pavement and stood up straight. He took a moment to stretch, working the kinks caused by hours of traveling out of his back. Then he turned back to the group. "On second thought," he said with a nervous smile, "why don't you come with me, David? Paul can always hightail it if anything happens out here, and to tell you the truth, I'd feel better with some company. Do you mind?"

For a heartbeat, David was not sure that he was being spoken to. He hesitated, then realized that the last thing he wanted was to be left alone with Paul Simpson. He jumped up out of his seat, shoving aside the fact that he was leaving two young boys and two women with a man who had just tried to take a human life. He shook off his doubts. Surely, he thought to himself, Paul would not harm them after saving them from the Great White Sharks. Still rationalizing, he hopped down onto the pavement and, like Walter, stretched. Then he motioned for his friend to lead the way.

There were six steps leading up to an old-fashioned security door. David was not surprised to see heavy bars on all of the windows as well as the entrance. Embedded in the brick frame on the side was an intercom with 24 buttons placed in two vertical rows of 12. Each one had a label placed haphazardly next to it. Walter ran his finger down each row, looking for the number they had been given. Finding it, he hesitated for the barest of moments before pressing it.

There was no sound, and David wondered if the buzzer might have been disconnected. The name on the label was NeCamp, but it was old and yellowed. Perhaps the occupant had been forced to move on. The two men waited for a moment, then Walter pushed the correct button once more. David glanced nervously back toward the van and saw that the crowd across the street was still growing. A good 20 people now, of all ages, were standing there watching.

Once again there was no response to the buzzer. David looked at Walter and shrugged. He was almost relieved. The sooner they got out of this neighborhood, the better he would feel. Never mind the fact that they had nowhere else to go. They could figure out something after they put a few million miles between themselves and Brooklyn. They waited a few seconds longer, then turned to go. Just then, the speaker above the two rows of buttons coughed, then spoke.

"What is it? Who's there?" The voice was husky, obviously male — and hostile.

"We're friends," replied Walter, leaning close to the speaker.

"Says who?"

"Your friends, the Does, in Sacramento."

There was a pause. "Prove it!" demanded the disembodied voice finally.

"Here we go," said Walter under his breath. Then he cleared his throat. "For God so loved the world that he gave his only begotten Son, that whosoever believeth in him should not perish, but have everlasting life." Again there was a pause.

"Too easy," said the voice. "Try again."

"Crud!" Walter's expletive was loud enough to reach David's ears, but hopefully not the speakers.

"Temper, temper," said the voice with a hint of sarcasm. David rolled his eyes. So much for hoping. Abruptly, the relief at being alive after their narrow escape caught up to him. Despite their desperate situation, he found himself starting to chuckle. Unfortunately, Walter heard. Glaring at his companion, he stepped back and motioned to the speaker.

"All right, preacher. Let's see you do better!" He was obviously frustrated with his lack of success, but his own relief was starting to set in. For the moment, he seemed to forget that they might be in an even worse situation. He could not quite hide the smile that was peeking out from behind his scowl.

David returned it, then moved forward. He ran through the third chapter of John in his mind before speaking. He picked out what he thought was an appropriate verse. "If I told you earthly things, and you did not believe, how shall you believe if I tell you heavenly things?"

Walter raised his eyebrows at this, and David shot him a look that said "Well, you did ask."

"Cute," said the voice. " 'And no one has ascended into heaven, but he who descended from heaven, even the Son of Man.' All right, I guess you're legit. I heard two voices. How many of you are there?"

"Seven," said Walter, once again moving forward.

There was a noise that sounded suspiciously like a man strangling, then, "You're kidding. Please tell me you're kidding!"

"We're not kidding," snapped Walter, his patience now at an end. What humor there was in the situation was now gone. "We're also getting tired of standing out here in the street. There's some unhealthy looking folks that are paying us too much attention. Understand?"

Again there was a pause. The two men regarded the speaker, both wondering if Walter's outburst had destroyed their chances of getting inside. Then a buzzer sounded and the door clicked open. "Come on up," said the voice, sounding resigned. They entered a hall and climbed a rickety staircase to the third floor. At the top was the apartment they sought. Walter knocked and immediately the door opened. A wizened, stoop-shouldered man of about 70 met them.

"Well?" he demanded. "What are you waiting for? Get in here!" He stood back to admit them, then shut the door behind them.

The apartment was about what David had expected. Run down, with cheap furnishings. Surprisingly, considering the neighborhood, it was relatively clean. There were several old pictures, presumably family, hanging on the far wall and arranged carefully on the sparse furniture. It looked exactly like what it was — the final dwelling of an old man, filled with little else but memories.

Their host regarded them for a moment, then held up a pointed finger, riddled with arthritis. "One, two," he said, pointing first at Walter, then David. "You said there were seven, but I see two." He raised his eyebrows, waiting for an explanation.

"We left the others downstairs," replied Walter.

The old man started in surprise. "You mean you left them in the street? In this neighborhood?"

"Not really," said David, jumping in. The old man was definitely not what either of them had been expecting, and Walter was floundering. "We came in a van. Our friends are in it, waiting for us to get back."

During his time as a pastor, David had tried his hand at writing a novel. He had not been successful at it, mainly because he was not good at description — at least, that was what several publishers had told him. He could well remember one editor having circled the phrase "his eyes bugged out of his head" on one of his manuscripts. Next to it, he had penciled, "Trite, and ineffective."

At that moment however, watching the old man digest what he had just told him, "his eyes bugged out of his head" was the only way to describe the look that planted itself on their reluctant host's face. For a frightening moment, David feared that the old man might have a heart attack. Then, he took a deep breath, and spoke. "Let me get this straight," he said slowly, as if speaking to a delinquent five year old, "You left a van — that is, a vehicle significantly larger than a car — parked out in front of this building?" Both Walter and David could only nod. "Furthermore," he continued, "this same van is filled with people — five others to be exact?" Again they nodded.

The old man stared at them, then lifted his eyes toward the ceiling. "This is for stealing Ben's girlfriend, all those years ago, isn't it? This is my punishment. Never mind the fact that we were married for 53 years. You're still mad at me for it, aren't you?"

Walter and David watched the old man in amazement, wondering if he was talking to God, the ceiling, or the man upstairs (in the apartment above them, that is). With a great sigh, he returned his attention to them. "All right, all right," his voice showing resignation. "What do you need from me . . . and don't ask to spend the night! You leave that van out front, and it'll most likely be a burning hulk by morning."

"We don't want to stay the night," agreed Walter, and David silently seconded him. "We just need to know where we can go next. Our last stop sent us here, and told us you could move us along."

The old man studied them for a moment longer, then nodded. "All right, I guess I can do that." He went to a cupboard that had seen far better days and opened a drawer. Pulling out a map, he spread it over the table and motioned them over. David saw that it was a large-scale area map of the New York City area. "Your next stop will be at the docks in this sector. That group of yours been together for the whole trip?"

Walter nodded, and started to speak, but the old man stopped him. "I don't want to know," he said quickly. "The less we know about each other, the better. Understand?"

"Understood," replied Walter, and David nodded in agreement.

"Fine," said the old man. "You'll probably have to go your separate ways at your next stop. In fact, I'm surprised they haven't separated you already. It's dangerous for a large group to travel too far."

The idea of splitting up caused David to take a sharp breath. The thought of leaving the people that had been so much a part of his life for the past several months hurt. He suddenly realized that they were very dear to him — with the exception of Susan, whom he did not know, and Paul, who frightened him. He was surprised to find that he felt almost the same way he did when his wife and son had left. Not as bad, of course, but close. He also discovered that he did not want to be left alone. The more he thought about it, the more uneasy and fearful he became. So preoccupied was he with the idea of leaving his friends that he missed the first part of the old man's instructions.

". . . get there, call this number," he was saying. He handed Walter a scrap of paper with a hastily scribbled number. "I don't know who will answer, but you'll have to satisfy him or her that you are for real."

"You mean the recognition signals," offered Walter as he stuffed the paper into his pocket.

The old man shook his head. "More than that, I'm afraid. The people you'll be meeting will probably know a lot more about you than you realize. They'll want details of your trip, the circumstances of your going underground, and maybe more. Don't argue, just give them the facts. Got it?"

"Got it," replied Walter.

"All right," said the old man. "I've done all I can do, so get going — and whatever you do, don't go back the way you came."

"No problem there," said Walter fervently, and turned to go.

David started to follow, but something made him stop. He looked back at their reluctant help. The old man was feisty and crude. In other circumstances, he would have been considered "quaint." David could sense a deep sadness under his bluster, however. Something made him want to know more about this strange person they had encountered. By all rights, he and Walter should get downstairs, get their friends, and get out. Somehow, though, David felt compelled to linger a moment. For some reason he had to know more. Perhaps he was trying to postpone the inevitable split of his group.

"Excuse me," he started, unsure of just what he wanted to say. "But you're not exactly what we were expecting."

That got him a raised eyebrow. "What did you expect?" the old man replied with some asperity.

"I don't know," answered David honestly. "You just aren't like anyone we've come across so far. You act like you don't want any part of something that you are already heavily involved with. It's like you care deeply, but you don't want anyone to know about it." He shrugged. "I know I'm way out of line, but I'm asking anyway. Why are you doing something so dangerous if you don't want to do it?"

David surprised himself as well as the other two men in the room. He had come here in order to get away from Paul. All he wanted was to get the necessary instructions, and get out. Now, however, he found himself intrigued by the seeming contradictions in the strange person before him.

The old man, in turn, regarded him closely for a moment. His brown eyes, which had been angry and impatient, now took on a thoughtful look. "You know," he said at last, "you're the only one who's bothered to ask. I think I'll tell you."

Walter glanced nervously at his watch, obviously impatient to go, and aggravated with David for the delay.

The old man noticed the gesture. "Don't worry," he said, his voice now considerably softer. "It's not a long story."

"Isn't it dangerous for us to know too much about you?" replied Walter, anxious to be on his way.

The old man nodded. "Any other time, the answer would be yes. This is different, though." He sighed, and his gaze wondered somewhere beyond David and Walter.

"My brother Ben used to live here with me," he began. "He left several months before the United States started denying immigration visas to Jews." He motioned David and Walter over to the cupboard. "That's me and my brother there." David looked and saw a picture of the old man next to another man who was obviously his identical twin. They were standing in front of the very building they were now in.

"This was taken about a year ago — when we were close." The old man's voice caught, betraying the sadness that David had discerned earlier. "About that time," he continued, "I met a woman who moved in downstairs. She was about my age, and quite a conversationalist. It was nice to have a woman to talk to again. My Helen had passed away over five years ago.

"Anyway, we got to talking, and in time she shared her faith with me. She was Jewish, like me and Ben, but there was a difference. She told me that the Messiah that I had looked for all of my life had already come — His name was Yeshua, the Christ." He drew a ragged breath. "We would talk for hours about it, but I never let her sway me. Not long ago, she was arrested for distributing Bibles. She wasn't tried, convicted, or sentenced. She just disappeared. I haven't heard from her since." He looked at David, and his brown eyes were now wet.

"I'm seventh generation American," he said, "but I'm also pure Jewish. I've heard about Jesus all of my life. My father would tell me that our people had been persecuted in His name. Others would tell me that He was the only hope of salvation. Frankly, I never believed any of it, one way or the other . . . until this one woman gave everything she had because of her faith." He shook his head sadly at the memory. "What she said was just words — until they came for her. Then I saw something worth dying for. Somehow, she left one of her Bibles in my mailbox. Because of her courage I began to read it, and soon I began to understand just what price had been paid for my salvation."

"I understand," said David softly. He could not help but remember what he had done when "they" had come for him.

The old man looked at him and smiled sadly. "I don't think you do," he said. "You see, my brother's dream was to someday return to Israel. We both wanted to die there. The thing is, he's an Orthodox Jew — still waiting for his Messiah. We had been close — closer than most brothers — all of our lives, but when I told him that I had accepted Yeshua, not only as the

Messiah of our people, but as my own Lord and Master, he disowned me. He took what little savings we had and disappeared. He left a note, saying he was going to Israel, our homeland. That's the last I heard of him. I wanted to follow, but right after that, the borders were closed and I was stuck here."

He shrugged. "Since then, I've been helping here however I can. The woman who helped me — the one I told you about — she had a few contacts in local underground churches close by. I was able to reach the Shepherd's Path through them. I found that I could be of use as a safe house, or, to be more precise, a way station." He chuckled softly. "I really can't have guests, you know. Not in this neighborhood! Anyway, people come to me, and I get them started on the next leg of wherever they're going."

He smiled abruptly. "Most times, I get a warning that someone's headed my way. Communication must have broken down somewhere along the line, because you were a complete surprise. That's why I was so hard on you!"

Walter and David listened to the old man's fascinating story in mute interest. Even Walter had stopped his fidgeting. The tiny room grew very quiet as the three men regarded each other. At length, the old man spoke once more. This time, his voice was so soft that David and Walter had to strain to hear.

"I said that, in this case, it didn't matter what I told you. That's the literal truth. You see, I'm dying." Walter sucked in his breath hard, and David felt as if he had been punched in the stomach. The spunky old man was so full of life! The very idea of him dying was ludicrous.

He smiled sadly at their reaction. "Can't be helped," he said. "Too many years of not taking care of myself. My own fault, really. I used to go to the free clinic up the street before it closed down. Last month, the doctor there said I've got two, maybe three months left. That's why I told you all this. That, and this." With that, he bent over and opened the bottom of the cupboard.

"I used to keep these hidden from Ben, when he was here. Now, of course, there's not much point." He straightened up, and David saw that he was holding a small cardboard box, about the size of a large dictionary. Holding it as if it were the most precious thing in the world, he laid it on top of the small kitchen table that sat next to one wall. Walter and David followed curiously. "I was going to pass them on to someone in the network," he said, "but since you bothered to ask about me, I think I'll leave them in your hands. I have a feeling you'll find a use for them." With that, he opened the top of the box with a flourish. David leaned over to get a better look, and heard Walter gasp. The old man smiled, enjoying their reaction. David suddenly found his breath coming in quick, short spurts.

"Thought you'd feel that way," he said with grim satisfaction. He reached down and gently touched the four, old leather-bound Bibles that were lying there. David found that he could not take his eyes off the precious contents of that box. For months, his tiny church had labored painstakingly to put together even a few chapters of the beloved book. He remembered long sessions of trying to place each chapter and verse in its proper order. He remembered the anger and frustration they had felt toward themselves for not having memorized more when they had the chance. Now, here in front of him, were four complete King James editions — and being freely given! It was staggering. He reached out and ran his finger over the cracked leather of one of them, his head reeling at holding God's Word complete in his hands once more.

"What . . ." Walter began, then had to stop when his voice cracked. "What," he tried again, "do you want us to do with them?"

The old man shrugged. "Use them, what else?" he replied. "Get them into the hands of people that need them. Keep one for yourselves, if you need it, then spread the rest."

Suddenly his hand shot out and grabbed David by the wrist. David jerked back involuntarily, but the old man hung on with surprising strength. "Just one thing," he said, and now his voice took on a warning tone. "I trust you, but I have to say this anyway. Don't let them out of your sight. Split them up, if you have to. Get them in as many hands of believers as you can, but don't let anyone get hold of them who might try to sell them." David nodded knowingly. The four Bibles could easily bring over $20,000 on the black market. Dealers were finding them almost as profitable as drugs. They would sell them by the chapter, and sometimes even by the page.

"Don't worry," he said reassuringly. "We'll see that they get to where they need to go."

The old man's eyes bored into David's, as if trying to search his very soul. Finally, he nodded. "See that you do," he said simply, and released David's arm. "Now get out of here." He turned away as he spoke these words, his voice growing noticeably gruffer.

"Thank you," said Walter, putting a world of meaning in that simple phrase. "For everything." The old man merely nodded, continuing to face away from them.

"You could come with us," said David, already knowing the answer.

As he expected, the old man shook his head. "Not much sense in getting out now," he said, turning back to them. "Besides, there may be others come along in the time I have left." David felt his heart sink a little lower, knowing that this would be the first and last time he would see this man. There was a closeness growing between them, and it hurt to say goodbye. He could feel that, despite the hard exterior, he could have been friends with this gruff, plucky man.

"Goodbye, then," he said, not knowing what else to say.

The old man's face split into a wide grin, surprising both Walter and David. "Hey," he said, brightening up. "Don't feel sorry for me! I'll be around — if not here, then with my Messiah. Look me up when you get there!"

At the old man's words, David's dark mood vanished in an instant. A weight seemed to lift off his heart. He realized suddenly that he would see this dear brother again — and when he saw him, he would be as alive and vibrant, and probably as gruff, as he was now. It was a heady thought, and David felt a great joy pour over him like sparkling water in a parched desert. How long had it been since he had felt that kind of joy?

On impulse, he closed the remaining space between him and the old man. He opened his arms wide and grabbed him in a strong bear hug. It was a hug between men, between brothers. He felt the old man stiffen for an instant at the unexpected contact, then his embrace was returned fiercely. Strangely, David felt as if strength were flowing out from his newly found friend. In fact, he felt stronger and mentally sharper than he had in months. At length, the hug ended and the two men stepped back.

Walter was standing off to the side, watching the scene play itself out before him in something that was akin to fascination. He understood that God was moving in the room. He could feel the presence of the Holy Spirit as He worked in the lives of the men in front of him. He also knew that, although he was a part of it, this moment was for David and the old man. God was doing something to both of them, especially David. Whatever happened in the future, Walter knew, David Eddington would never be the same.

The old man pulled away, and David could see the beginnings of tears at the corners of his eyes. There was an unspoken bond between the two men, and both of them knew it.

The old man reached out and put a firm hand on David's shoulder. "I have never had any children," he said firmly, all traces of his previous gruff manner now gone. "And you can see that I have nothing to pass on to any heir that I might have." He glanced around the room, indicating that he was speaking of his worldly goods. "Nevertheless, my newfound friend, I name you my heir."

Despite the closeness that had developed between them, David gasped at what the old man was saying. He started to speak, but the old man shook his head. "What I have, what really matters, I give to you." Once more, he turned to the table and picked up the box that held the Bibles. He held them out to David, who, after a moment's hesitation, took hold of them. The old man continued to hang on to the box as well, and the two men once more regarded each other over the Bibles.

"This is everything that I have that is of any physical value," said the old man softly. "But it is far more than that. Without what is inside these books, I would be nothing. Through them, and through the One we both serve, I have learned courage, determination, wisdom, and commitment. This is what I give to you."

It seemed to David that, for a timeless instant, they ceased to be in a run-down apartment in the middle of a dying city. Suddenly they were in an ancient throne room. David was standing before a great knight. The knight's armor was scratched and dented in places, and the knight himself was aging. Both, however, were still strong, able to withstand the fiery darts of the enemy. The knight was holding out a shining sword, hilt first, toward David. It was far more powerful than any weapon man could ever manufacture.

The knight's voice took on a commanding tone. "This is also my charge to you. Use what I give you in our Master's service. Find your courage and your commitment from Him. Draw your strength from Him and face the enemy without fear. Trust Him to deliver you. Put aside your doubts and stand tall in His service. Will you take this charge that I give you?"

"Yes," David whispered. There was no hesitation, no wavering. His heart pounded in his chest. He knew that he was at a crossroads in his journey. The choice he made in this instant molded the rest of his life. He saw clearly his two options. One, to back out and live the rest of his days in the same fear and emptiness that had dogged him for the last several months. The second would be far more dangerous. It demanded everything he had — everything he was, up to and including his life.

He took a deep breath, and made his decision. He chose the path that held the greatest rewards . . . and the greatest price. Immediately, the great weight that had burdened him for so long was lifted. He literally felt pounds lighter. His shoulders straightened, and his head came up. His eyes, once dull and lifeless, sparkled with energy. Once more, David stood like a man, instead of cowering like a frightened animal. Gone, at least for the moment, was his fear. Not for forever, he knew. It would return when he would be at his weakest, and he would have to deal with it . . . but for now his course was clear.

For the first time in months, perhaps years, he felt the presence of his Lord, and almost cried out in joy and recognition. It was the cry of a man who, having lost his dearest friend, suddenly discovered that he had been there all of the time. The wall of guilt and torment that he had built so laboriously came tumbling down in an instant — not by his own hand, but by his Lord's. A relationship so dear and precious to him was restored. It was that simple.

The old man smiled once more, and the vision, if that was what it was, disappeared. Without another word, the old man walked to the door and gestured for them to leave. There was nothing else to say. David cradled the box in his arms as if it were a newborn child, and the two men left. As they walked down the stairs, they heard the door shut behind them.

Walter looked over at David, his curiosity evident. "Sometime," he said under his breath, "when we have a quiet moment, you really are going to have to explain to me just what did happen in there."

David smiled. "Sometime," he replied, "when I figure it out, I'll tell you! For now, let's just say that I found something that I thought I had lost forever." His manner made it clear that, at least for the present, there was nothing more to say. They made their way down the rest of the stairs and emerged out into the street. It only took them a moment to realize that the situation had changed . . . for the worst.

The van was still there, to their relief. That was the only good part. At least two dozen youths now surrounded it, some actually standing on top of the flat roof. They all looked sullenly at Walter and David as they left the shelter of the building. The two men stopped in their tracks, realizing that there was nowhere to go. The could see their companions inside the van. All looked to be unharmed, at least for now. Paul sat behind the wheel, looking like a stone Buddha. His face was set in a look of frightening determination that boded ill for whoever got in his way. David knew that it would only take the slightest hint of violence for him to start the van and take off — probably going over several bodies in the process. Cyndi was in the front passenger seat, looking frightened, but resolute. The two boys sat very still, watching, and Susan, as always, simply waited.

There was a tension-laden moment, as if a thunderstorm had taken a deep breath before letting loose with everything it had. Then three teenage boys approached the two men. All were bronze-skinned, all had dark hair and eyes . . . and all had the same look of quiet, hopeless bravado. David noted their swagger as they came forward. They were obviously supremely confident in their mastery of the situation. They stopped at the foot of the stairs, looking up and appraising the two men. Then the oldest looking grinned smugly.

"Hey Goy!" he called mockingly. "You think this is a crusade or something? You come to kick some Jew-butt?" This caused a wave of laughter to ripple through the crowd. They were obviously enjoying the situation. Without warning, the leader hopped up the stairs two at a time. He came level with the two men, standing a good head taller than either of them. He gave them the once-over, obviously not impressed. Then, so fast that David did not have time to react, he grabbed the box David was carrying. David felt his arms wrench as the stronger youth forced it out of his grasp. A cry of surprise and pain escaped his lips. The youth lost no time in opening the box. What he saw caused his eyes to go wide. He turned and displayed his trophies to the rest of the group.

"Christians!" This came from one of the girls in front of the van. Her voice reeked of hatred and disgust. It was almost as if she was speaking of a rival gang. There was a low murmur of agreement that ran through the crowd like an undulating wave. The leader turned back to Walter and David.

"You're in the wrong place, Goy." This was addressed to David. David felt the old stirrings of fear run though him. A part of his mind was screaming that this was not fair. He should not have to deal with a situation like this so soon after the wonderful experience upstairs. His mouth suddenly went dry, and his hands began to tremble. This did not go unnoticed by the gang's leader.

"I think they're a little worried," he said loudly, over his shoulder. Laughter greeted his announcement. David glanced helplessly toward the van. The 20 feet that separated them seemed like infinity. He saw Paul put his hand on the ignition, ready to start the engine and beat a messy retreat. He realized that he had to do something fast, or the situation would be lost. The leader was still looking over his shoulder at his cohorts. Without thinking, David stepped forward and grabbed the box he was still holding in front of him and yanked at it . . . hard.

This caught the leader completely off guard. He had seen the fear in David's eyes, and knew from experience that a hopelessly outnumbered enemy will try to escape, not attack. Before he realized it, the short, pudgy man before him had reclaimed his prize. He staggered a little in surprise, having been caught off balance. Then he righted himself, a look of amazed anger on his face.

"You must have a death wish, man," he said through gritted teeth. The situation suddenly became far more dangerous. Although David did not realize it, he had just embarrassed the leader in front of his own gang. He had to regain control of the situation before he lost his standing. David braced himself, but still was caught totally off-guard. The leader's arm jutted straight out, connecting soundly with David's chin. Bright spots danced before his eyes, and he felt himself falling. He thought he heard a loud yell from the gang, and thought it must be a shout of approval. He slammed back into the brick wall, the impact knocking the breath out of him. Slowly he slid to a sitting position, gasping for breath.

CRAAACK!

Below him, the cement vibrated harshly. It sounded like the entire world suddenly decided to tear itself apart. Before the reverberations of the first explosion had settled, there was another, even more violent than the first. David struggled to sit up, his vision still blurry. Now he could hear human screams. They seemed to be coming from all directions. There were cries of anger, defiance and fear. Mixed in were shouts of "Sharks! Sharks!" It took him a moment to realize that the Sharks were the rival gang whose territory they had so recently traversed.

Something whizzed over his head and crashed into the wall behind him. There was a dull thud as the aging brick shattered, exploding outward. The debris rained over him, and he instinctively covered his head. The screams were growing louder. Evidently, the gang that had just surrounded them were caught unprepared for the latest attack.

Something clamped on to David's right arm and held tight. He cried out in surprise and dismay as he was hauled roughly to his feet. The surge of adrenaline finally cleared his vision, and he found himself face to face with Paul. The big man had not wasted any time when the attack came. He was out of the van like a shot, heading toward Walter and David. David could now see two gang members groaning on the sidewalk and realized that they must have tried to stop Paul. He also saw that Walter had already reached the van and was climbing inside.

Paul studied David quickly and efficiently. "Anything broken?" he asked calmly. David shook his head negatively.

Wasting no more time, Paul propelled him toward the van. "That was a stupid stunt you pulled, Eddington," he said, just loud enough to be heard over the din of the battle. The fight raged around them, but the Jewish gang had evidently forgotten all about them. It took David a moment to realize that Paul was speaking about his grabbing the box of Bibles away from the leader.

"So sue me," he mumbled, still dazed. Frankly, for the moment, he did not care what Paul thought of his actions. He only cared about the fact that, somehow, he still held the precious box. Paul glanced over at him sharply. Their eyes met for an instant, much like they had done before, after the van had been attacked by the Sharks. This time, however, it was Paul who looked away. "It also took a lot of guts, preacher," he said. His voice was so low that David was unsure of what he heard. Paul turned his attention toward getting to the van, but not before David saw a look of grudging respect. Then they were at the van. Paul pushed David inside, then followed. Walter was already in the driver's seat, and the look on his face said that he was going to stay there. Paul did not argue the point.

"Get going," shouted Paul sharply. Walter already had the engine running. He slammed it into gear. The tires squealed, and they were off. David watched in abject horror as the battle swayed around them. One young man, no older than 15, went down hard on the pavement, blood running from an ugly gash in his head. His assailant, an even younger girl wielding a crowbar, spat on the fallen youth's back, then ran to help her mates. Someone evidently noticed the fleeing van. There was the now familiar "ping" as a bullet glanced off the side door. Everyone ducked, with the exception of Walter, who had a look of almost demonic intensity as he pushed the engine as hard as he could.

As suddenly as it had begun, it was over. The sounds of fighting receded, then disappeared altogether. David cautiously raised his head and saw that they were out of the neighborhood and heading toward the great Brooklyn Bridge.

The adrenaline surge he had experienced earlier was now beginning to wear off. He looked down and saw someone's hands shaking furiously. He realized with some surprise that the hands he was looking at were his own. He brought them up and studied them with detached amazement. They seemed to be a separate creature. Stop that, he thought furiously, but they would not obey. Self-consciousness set in. Hastily, he slipped his disobedient members under his legs, forcing them to quiet down. Balancing the box on his legs, he glanced around to see if anyone had noticed. No one had.

As usual, it was Paul who recovered first. When the others were preoccupied with the narrowness of their recent escape, he was already thinking ahead. "You know where we're going?" he asked Walter, who still had the steering wheel in a choke hold.

"The docks," replied Walter shortly, his breath coming in gasps. He glanced up in the rearview mirror, checking on his passengers. "Everybody okay?" he asked. The group nodded slowly. They were just beginning to recover from their ordeal.

Walter studied each one individually, then spoke again. "David, this might be the wrong time, but why don't you show everyone what's in that box."

It took David a second to understand what Walter was suggesting. Then he nodded, drawing a huge breath as his system slowly returned to normal. His hands now barely trembled as he lifted up the box for everyone to see. All eyes, with the exception of Walter's, were now on him. With a stage magician's flourish, he flipped the top of the box open. There was a strangled gasp. Cyndi had just realized what he was holding. David could see the stunned look on her face. The two boys leaned over from their position next to David.

"All riiight!" This came from Jonathan. The young boy looked very much like a man as he reverently reached into the box and pulled out one of the Bibles. He held it carefully, opening it with the air of one handling a piece of precious eggshell china. Even Susan was studying the Bibles carefully, a look of intense hunger on her drawn face.

"Pass one up here, David," said Walter. David complied, handing one to Susan, who in turn handed it to Cyndi. Cyndi's face shone as she opened it. Then a look of uncertainty rippled across it as she glanced over at her husband. Walter merely nodded, confirming that, yes, they were indeed theirs.

On impulse, David handed another to Paul. He noted his brief hesitation before he reached out and took it. Unlike the others, who held a priceless treasure, Paul handled the Bible as if it were a loaded weapon that could go off at any time. Then the big man smiled tightly and pressed the Bible into Susan's hands. Susan's face lit up and she began to leaf through it. As she read, her face became radiant.

David observed Paul's reaction to the Bible. He thought about how this enigmatic man had almost killed a human being less than an hour before. There was now no doubt in his mind that Paul Simpson was not who he pretended to be. What his purpose was, and how he was going to accomplish it, was unknown. David only knew that, whatever it was, it was certainly detrimental to the rest of the group. He resolved to keep a tight watch on Paul Simpson.

Right now, though, he had more important matters to attend to. Reaching into the box, he pulled out another Bible. Then he leaned back in his seat in a quiet contentment. A quiet peace settled over him, a welcome change from the past several hours. With his new-found relationship with his Saviour, he knew that everything was under control. Paul was not going anywhere just yet. According to the old man, it would take them a good hour or so to get to their next destination. He intended to spend that time curled up with a very, very good Book.

6

"Christine? Christine, can you hear me?"

"Uhhh?"

"It's me, Indres. You are coming out of it now. Just relax and let it happen naturally."

"I'm thirsty."

"That is natural. Here." A straw found its way to Christine's lips. They parted weakly and she sipped. She felt as weak as a nursing infant, and struggled to recall why. A disorienting lightness permeated her. It seemed as if she were floating.

"Easy now," came Indres' just barely recognized voice. "Just a little." Cool fruit juice splashed into her mouth. Her throat had the consistency of sandpaper, and the cool, refreshing liquid was like a balm. Eagerly, she tried to take a second swallow, but the straw was removed. Abruptly, she realized that her eyes were closed. She struggled to open them, but gave up the effort. It was just too much trouble.

"Where am I?" she asked, barely recognizing her own voice. Her weakness revolted her.

"In the medical section of Liberty. Don't worry. Your memory will return soon."

"Liberty?" That sounded familiar. It also explained the feeling of lightness. She was weightless, of course. It did not, however, explain the strange sensations chasing themselves around inside her skull. It felt as if part of her existed outside of her body.

Grimly, she struggled to remember her immediate past. There had been the successful implantation of the president, the message from Sheila about Matthew Riever, and another one ordering her to report to Liberty. She had flown immediately to Cape Canaveral where her shuttle, *Ayres II* awaited. Liftoff occurred within an hour of her arrival, and she was flown immediately to Liberty. Brennon met her, and told her . . . what?

Unconsciously, Christine gritted her teeth, trying to force her lethargic memory into action. She recalled Brennon. He had remained on Liberty since their last meeting, overseeing his plan and consolidating his power. He had informed her that the president's bio-chip was functioning perfectly. Cyclops was already receiving data from it, just as it was receiving data from other world leaders. He had congratulated her on a job well done.

And? Christine asked herself relentlessly. Then, like a flash of blinding light, the millions of cells that chemically stored her memory aligned themselves, and the synapses, or the electronic "spark plugs" of her brain, began to fire properly. The past several hours became quite clear. Christine's eyes snapped open . . . and immediately closed again.

"OHHH!" The moan escaped her lips despite her desperate attempt to force it down. Her gorge rose, and for a terrifying moment, she thought she was going to throw up — a dreadful, and even dangerous occurrence in weightlessness. A harshly bright incandescent light hung overhead. When the brightness hit her eyes, it felt as if sharp spikes were being driven into her skull.

"I told you to take it slow," said Indres reproachfully. "Your vital signs are excellent. You came through the implant operation with, as you put it, flying colors. Just give yourself a few more minutes."

Happily, Indres was right. The pain subsided, and she relaxed, letting her head sink back into the soft pillow that rested under it. The recovery couch into which she was strapped monitored her pulse, respiration, temperature, and a hundred other things. It automatically adjusted itself, conforming to Christine's body with just the right amount of firmness. Christine blew a deep sigh, now remembering her conversation with Brennon upon her arrival to Liberty.

"All of the Sextuaget," he had said, "Must have this special implant, Christine." He placed a strong, square hand on her shoulder and smiled gently. It was all she could do to keep from quivering in anticipation of his touch. While she knew that she would never have a sexual relationship with this powerful, secretive leader, he still was the only man who had that effect on her. Despite that, she could barely control her revulsion at the idea of a foreign object in her brain.

"Why?" she had finally managed to stammer out.

Brennon read her hesitation, and frowned slightly. "You pledged to do whatever was necessary to further our work, Christine," he said, a slight menace now detectable in his voice. "To act, if necessary, without questioning me. Have you reneged on that pledge?" Abruptly, his hand was withdrawn.

Christine was suddenly very much afraid. She shook her head, denying his accusation, and lowered her eyes. "I am *totally* committed to you, and our purpose," she replied, trying to keep the tremor out of her voice. Inside, she writhed at the way she was groveling. Only Brennon could do this to her. A tiny spark of anger ignited, and she crushed it quickly. "I always have been."

Brennon smiled at her words. He nodded in a fatherly fashion, and Christine relaxed just a little.

"There is no need to fear," he said in a reassuring manner. "While there are many similarities between the other bio-chips and the one you will receive, there are two major differences. First," he continued, "there will be no slave circuit in your chip. I want my lieutenants to be absolutely free of outside interference. Second, implants such as the president's are passive, while yours will be active.

"I'm not sure what that means," admitted Christine somewhat reluctantly. She did not like to admit ignorance to him, but lying was far worse.

"Simple," said Brennon. "You know that, soon, every human in every nation will be required to receive an implant."

"Of course," said Christine. It was a linchpin of Brennon's plan.

"Now," continued Brennon, "that implant will contain a standard computer chip — not a bio-chip, by the way — that constantly keeps track of the subject's credit line, whereabouts, and occupation, as well as a host of other important details. The uni-card that we have been introducing is merely an intermediate step. With the implant, any standard computer with a scanner will be able to access any and all information on the individual. Each implant will be uniquely coded to each person . . . it will be impossible to forge or replace. Understand?"

Christine nodded. This was nothing new. Smythe Enterprises had already manufactured millions of these. They were safely stored away, waiting to be put to use. Even with the fall of her financial empire, they were protected. No one was going to stop their manufacture and distribution.

"Good," nodded Brennon. "Now follow, Christine. In addition to the non-organic chip, each implant will also contain a bio-chip, much like the one you so ably placed into your president. That chip will place itself at the base of the cerebral cortex and, as you know, will gradually spread tendrils into all parts of the brain."

Christine snapped to attention. She knew about the bio-chip's function, of course. She herself had explained it to the president just hours ago. However, she had been under the impression that the implants containing these chips were reserved for people in influential positions, not the average citizen.

"These bio-chips," continued her master, "are cheap and easy to manufacture. They are also passive. The subject will not even know they are there . . . unless we activate them."

"How?"

"This is where yours and the rest of the Sextuaget implants come in. As I said, your implant will contain an active bio-chip." Brennon smiled.

Suddenly, Christine had to quell a sudden urge to shudder.

Brennon went on, "This new chip, as you know, will grow — er, tendrils, I suppose is the best word — into every part of your brain . . . your optic nerves, hearing, memory cells . . . everything — just like the others."

Again Christine had to suppress a wave of revulsion at the idea. How could she allow something like that inside her own body? Again, Brennon noticed. This time, though, he held up his hand, forestalling her obvious question.

"It will be your servant, Christine, not your master. As I promised, there is no slave circuit in this type of chip. Think of it!" His voice became low and intense, and she felt herself being drawn along despite herself. "You will be able to tie in to Cyclops directly, and through that, every computer system in the world, with a single mental command! You will have instant access to *everything!* No more clumsy terminals, no more voice-activated idiot boxes. Just make the request in your mind, and you will have what you ask for within seconds. And there's more."

He was watching her closely, gauging her reaction. Christine suddenly remembered Jack Kline's aversion to Jacob Hill's interrogation techniques. His moment of hesitation had cost him everything. She had already shown such hesitation once. She did not dare do it again. Brennon would likely pitch her out of the airlock.

"I told you that your implant will be active," continued Brennon. "That means you will be able to monitor any other implant you wish. You will be able to access thoughts, feelings, and memory of *anyone* . . . all at the simplest mental command. Do you realize what that means? No more clumsy interrogation techniques like Mentasys." He smiled, a wolf's predatory smile.

"Soon," continued Brennon, "a limited nuclear war will bring the population down to 'manageable' levels. Each and every human being will be required to have an implant. It will be the only way they can conduct even the simplest business transactions. Through your bio-chip, you will be able to literally read their minds. No one will be able to keep secrets from you, or the rest of us."

"Incredible," whispered Christine, and meant it. This put an entirely different light on the matter. What Brennon was offering her was nearly unlimited power — second only to his. If the implant worked, the advantages were staggering. The key word, she knew, was IF.

Something occurred to her. "You said that I will be able to read minds," she said. "Does 'active' also mean that I can influence thought as well?"

Brennon literally beamed at her. "I knew that we chose the right person to be Jacob's successor. You have already grasped the essentials. The answer is, yes, of course. Once your bio-chip is fully grown, you can introduce ideas into the thinking process of any implanted person you choose — and they will believe your 'suggestions' to be their own thoughts. It will be quite a powerful weapon."

"Am I the first?"

"No," replied Brennon. shaking his head. "One of your own, Indres, has already received one. After you, the rest of the Sextuaget will follow immediately." That did not sit well with Christine. Indres was her subordinate. The idea of him receiving special attention from Brennon disturbed her. He very well may be joining the Sextuaget soon, but he hadn't yet. He was still part of *her* circle.

"It is necessary, Christine," said Brennon, as if reading her mind. "Indres runs the world's largest and most influential religion. Soon it will be recognized as a true world system of belief. While his control over his followers is strong, it needs to be total. It will be within his movement that we will first introduce the basic implant. They will take it willingly enough if he endorses it and they will enjoy favored status as well. This should cause millions more to join willingly. The remaining few will not matter. Without it, they will not be able to survive. Everyone will be looking for some kind of direction after the limited holocaust we will bring about." Another smile.

"Besides, Indres is practically one of us now. That fool Rhys has failed me once too often. Don't worry, Christine. Indres will work next to you, not over you. Your place in our circle is secure — particularly after what you accomplished with the president. That was very well done, by the way."

Christine nodded, both relieved at Brennon's assessment of Indres and warmed by his praise of her. She had allowed herself to be led away to surgery. It took only hours to get her onto the operating table, although she was not surprised at the speed at which things were happening. She had learned that when Brennon was ready to move, he moved fast.

The surgery lasted over four hours. Although she would never know it, she had had a violent and unexpected reaction to the upgrade. It almost killed her. Her heart had stopped twice before the doctors were able to isolate and control her seizures. Her implant was modified somewhat on the spot, and the seizures stopped. That was why she was so weak when she regained consciousness.

Now she lay on the table, wondering if she would ever feel strong again. The throbbing in her head subsided, and the tautness slowly drained out of her body. She heard an approving grunt from Indres.

"That's better," he said. "Now, wait just a moment, and...." She heard a slight hum, and felt rather than saw the lights dim above her. "There," continued Indres. "Now try to open your eyes again."

Slowly Christine complied, and was relieved to find that this time there was no pain. The harsh light above her now glowed softly, giving the recovery room a cheery glow. Tiny telltale displays placed on various pieces of equipment winked merrily in greens, reds, and blues.

Above her, watching closely, hovered Indres. He hung there, suspended in mid-air like an acrobat caught in mid-leap. He smiled when her eyes met his. "Better?" he asked.

"Much," she replied, and was glad to hear her voice sounding stronger. "How *am* I doing . . . really?" Indres made a show of checking the display set into the head of her bed, and nodded.

"Fine," he said. "Your surgery went perfectly," he continued with a blatant lie. He motioned to the read out. "According to this, the bio-chip is in place and has already grown to about 50 percent of its intended size."

Christine felt a twinge inside of her at the word "growth," but managed to hide it from Indres. "How long?" she asked instead.

"Excuse me?" asked Indres, not understanding.

"How long before it's operational?"

"Oh," he replied. "Remember, Christine, it is not a matter of turning it on or off. The chip that now is part of your implant is alive. It is always on, although it will not reach full capacity until it is fully grown. It is a part of you now . . . as much a part of you as your natural brain."

Inwardly, Christine cursed herself for not knowing this. One of the things that made her such a success was to always know what was going on around her. Part of what made her so successful was the fact that she always knew what her enemies were doing. It was a vital part of her psyche that she be in total control of her surroundings. Now, however, she was completely uninformed. Brennon had made this happen so quickly that she did not know what had been done to her. It made her feel powerless, and in a deeper sense, used.

Realizing the danger in this line of thought, she quickly pushed her doubts into the back of her mind. It was just possible that Brennon's own implant could access hers and read her own thoughts.

Quickly, she asked the first question that came into her mind. "You mean that I can use it now?"

This caused Indres to frown. "I would not advise it," he said carefully. "The implant you have received is as far above the one your president has as this station is above a grass hut. The effects of trying for the first time can be . . . overwhelming." He gave the barest of shudders. "Believe me," he added, "I know!"

So, she thought with something akin to vindictive satisfaction, *the undisturbable Indres can be surprised after all.* She allowed herself to direct a small smile at her solemn companion.

"I think I'll pass," she said, and yawned widely. "Just now, I really need to rest." She allowed her eyes to close in what was only a partial act. Even this brief conversation was draining what little strength she had.

Indres took his cue promptly. "Of course," he said, pushing himself toward the hatch across the room. "Rest for now, Christine," he said as he floated away. "When you awaken, I'll have the bio-chip designers ready to brief you on how to proceed. If I know you, you should have no trouble in adapting to your new abilities."

Christine did not reply, feigning sleep instead. She heard the hatch open, then close. When she opened her eyes again, Indres was gone. "Of course," she said aloud, "you certainly do *not* know me. If you did, you would know that I do not need someone to teach me what I can learn myself!"

With that, she closed her eyes again and concentrated. She was determined to familiarize herself with her new hardware, and she was determined to do it alone. The day she needed Indres, or anyone else, for that matter, to tell her what to do with her own mind, would be the day *she* would throw herself out the airlock.

She had been with the president when he had awakened, and had heard some of the instructions given by the med-tech assigned to brief him. That was a starting point, at least. Closing her eyes, Christine concentrated. Mentally, she ran through a short list of commands. Each time, she expected something to happen. Each time, she was disappointed. She tried focusing her thoughts inward, searching for a sign, or tingle, or anything that would tell her that she was on the right track. Again, nothing. After several minutes, she ceased her futile attempts to access her implant and lay quietly.

Think Christine, she admonished herself sternly. *There is a way to get into the blasted thing. You just have to find it. You will **not** be led around by the nose inside of your own mind!* The ridiculous image her rather strange comparison conjured up caused her to chuckle, and she allowed herself to relax somewhat. Her muscles untensed, and she floated easily, strapped into the medi-couch.

Abruptly, an image of Indres teaching his disciples at the Smythe building came to her mind. She could see him there in the center of the auditorium, admonishing them to relax — to "let it happen." She remembered Brennon saying that Indres' followers would be among the first to receive the basic implant. It made sense, then, that the techniques he was teaching them would have some bearing on how their implant was used. Most of the implants would be passive, to be sure. Still, there would have to be a few active ones. Not to the extent of Christine's, or the rest of the

Sextuaget, but able to influence those under them — shepherds to control the sheep.

A thrill of excitement surged through her, and she squelched it immediately. Serenity was the answer, she knew — serenity of body and mind. "Centeredness." Closing her eyes, she willed her body to slow down. Gradually her heart rate lessened and her breathing slowed. She felt herself floating on an infinite cloud, relaxed and tranquil. For all of her skepticism of Indres and his religion, she knew he was right. She could feel that she was on the verge of a major discovery. With the determination that had made her one of the most powerful humans on the planet, she brought those methods into play.

At first, there was nothing, just as before. Her closed eyes saw only darkness, while her other senses remained untouched. Disappointment manifested itself, lurking at the corners of her mind. Doggedly she kept at it, certain that she could find the key. Almost, she gave up. Several minutes passed, and still there was only darkness. Then, just as she was about to open her eyes once more, a tiny flicker of candlelight caught her attention. At first, she thought it was merely her imagination taking hold. Instead of accessing an exclusive bio-chip molded precisely for her, she was seeing spots before her eyes! Slowly, though, she realized that the flickering light was really there — that she was really "seeing" it with, for want of a better description, her mind's eye. Eagerly, she reached out with her thoughts, tried to draw the flame toward her — and it vanished. Darkness once again ruled.

"All right," she said aloud. "Let's try that again." Once more she relaxed and cleared her mind. If she had known more about Paul Sinclair, she would have realized that the techniques she was using instinctively were identical to the ones he had spent hours learning at the hands of Yogi Shaw.

It took only a few moments this time to bring the candle flame back before her closed eyes. Forcing herself to remain calm and go slow, she studied the flicker with a detached interest. It hovered there in her mind, and she wondered what to do next.

Let it happen, she reminded herself. She allowed herself to stay passive and wait. As if suddenly making up its mind, the candlelight began to slowly increase in size. It grew until it filled her perception, and now she could see that it was not really a candle at all. As near as she could make out, it looked like a blurred computer screen. She could almost make out words and symbols hovering there before her, but they remained just out of focus. Again, impatience beckoned, but she resisted. She was close — very close to solving this puzzle and accessing Brennon's miraculous chip.

Suddenly, the blurred screen before her exploded. In a flash of blue-green light, it disintegrated into millions of tiny pixels. They swirled before her in an incomprehensible three dimensional matrix, every color in the spectrum, as well as a few that were not. The sheer beauty of it caused her to gasp in surprise and admiration. Then, as quickly as it began, it ended. Faster than she could comprehend, the pixels reassembled themselves, only now they did not form a blurred screen. Christine found herself looking at a floating, three dimensional display that divided itself into rows and columns of words. She realized that she was staring at a computer menu. It hovered there before her in empty space, awaiting her next command.

On impulse, she opened her eyes. The display remained, superimposed over the recovery room, although not as bright and vivid as it had been. With growing confidence, she now realized that, with a little practice, she would be able to function on two levels simultaneously. Part of her would be able to operate in the "real" world, interacting with her associates. Another segment of her psyche, however, could now literally run and oversee her part of Brennon's plan — and do it all in her own mind. There was no longer any need of computer terminals, assistants, or any other of a dozen things or people that she usually needed on a daily basis. She was a self-contained organism now, able to perform any task necessary. In amazement, she came face to face with the fact that she was no longer merely human any more. She had risen above her own species.

"Then I am truly fit to rule next to Brennon," she said to the empty room. A great elation filled her. She was one of the chosen! Deep inside her, so deep that she did not even recognize its existence, a tiny doubt had always existed. It screamed over and over that, sooner or later, Brennon and his Sextuaget would finish with her. They would use her up and throw her away, it warned. Now she knew different. The doubt was gone, erased as if it had never been. She was part of the circle herself, now and forever — one of the elite.

With mounting excitement, she again closed her eyes and studied the display. It did not take her long to discover how to make it come and go at will. She also learned that each category listed before her was in itself a menu, and each category within each menu was also a menu. It would take a great deal of time to learn her way around this mass of information. *Might as well start now,* she thought determinedly.

At the top of all the lists was a single category labeled simply as CYCLOPS. The name was larger than all the rest, signifying importance. This drew her attention. It took only the briefest concentration for her to access this menu. The CYCLOPS logo disappeared and was replaced by an icon of a globe, spinning in a starless space. At the top of the screen in her mind blazed the words MASTER CONTROL PROGRAM. With a thrill, Christine realized that she had accessed Brennon's master computer network. This was his great tool, his masterpiece of technological achievement. The sheer power of this marvel was enough to overwhelm any other system in the world. From here, she could demand information of the most highly classified nature, and it would be provided.

At her mental command, the globe disappeared and the actual program became visible. With her new perceptions, she could see the entire Master Control Program laid out before her, waiting for her to explore. The pathways leading through Brennon's system were nearly infinite. With a little concentration, she could make them seem like actual highways that ran on forever, each one interacting with the others.

Virtual Reality, she thought in amazement. That phrase, which had been a buzz word in the early nineties, was now an established science. The ability to be able to interact on a direct mind-to-mind level with computer software was considered one of the great breakthroughs of the last decade. Sensory devices allowed the user to practically enter the computer's world, eliminating the need for a keyboard or even a voice activated "middleman." Every video arcade in the country used this technology.

What she was now seeing, however, went far beyond that. She realized that her own mind was supplying the perceptions she was seeing. Her thoughts were translating raw data into the pathways that now appeared as if by magic — putting information into a form she could use. Accessing that information would be as simple as placing her feet on one of these paths and following it.

So why not? she asked herself. It was time to explore just what she was now capable of. With determination and confidence, she began to "walk" her mind down the first path that she could perceive. "Doors" suddenly manifested themselves, hundreds of them running parallel to her chosen path. She picked one at random and opened it. Information flooded into her, and she understood that she was seeing detailed plans for the combined defense of the United European Commonwealth. Eagerly she prowled the corridors of classified data. It poured into her mind, filling her with an even greater ecstasy.

Another path intersected the one she was on, and she turned on to it. Now she was seeing row upon row of drawers — much like an infinite filing cabinet. Pulling one out, she realized that she had accessed the personal history of a French general in charge of ground forces along the Iraq-Iran border. Here before her, then, was the personal history of every man, woman, and child in the United European federation. Another section contained the North American continent, while still another was set aside for Africa, and so on. A chill of exultation ran through her. She was proving that she could learn the system! How could she have ever been afraid of her upgraded implant when it did this for her?

Her elation was short lived. Suddenly, without warning, her entire perception of Brennon's system wavered. It felt as if she were standing in the middle of a heavy fog that had abruptly fallen. Somewhere in the back of her mind, she realized that she was tiring. Either that, or she was pushing her mind faster than it could handle. That was the more likely explanation. Indres had warned her that her implant was only 50 percent effective. In order for her to use it to its fullest capabilities, she would have to wait. *Time enough for learning later,* she thought with a satisfied air. She had discovered the basics, and that was enough for now.

Smugly, she turned to retrace her steps — and discovered with a chill of fear that she could no longer perceive the way she had come. The fog that now surrounded her obliterated everything, effectively disorienting her. Forcing down the panic that threatened to erupt, she carefully tried to call up the main menu she had accessed earlier. Nothing. She was already deep inside the system, and could not access the way out. The fog grew closer, filling her with a sense of being crushed.

Now she began to panic in earnest. Like a blow to her midsection, it hit her that she was really *inside* Cyclops. Somehow, her implant had removed her consciousness from her body and placed it into this fantastic world — and *she did not know the way out!* She recoiled in shock and horror. What had Brennon done to her? Indres constantly spoke of out-of-body experiences, but she had never believed him. To her, it had all been religious mumbo-jumbo. Now she saw the truth. The training he provided for his disciples was aimed solely toward this end. Once the implants were completed, the world of Cyclops would be filled with the presence of Brennon's people. A chosen elite that would control the technology of an entire world.

Angrily she thrust that line of thought away. Right now, Indres and his followers were the least of her worries. It came to her that she was horribly lost. Lost, not inside her mind, nor in Cyclops, but somewhere between. Somehow she knew that if she could not find her way back soon, she would remain lost forever — trapped between two worlds.

A scream was trying to force itself out of her, and somewhere in the back of her mind she wondered if she could actually scream in this surrealistic world. Would the body she had left behind scream also? Would anyone notice, and would they be able to bring her back if they did? Maybe so, but probably not. Better, she knew, to rely on herself. With the iron control that had made her what she was, she forced herself to calm down. Panic, she told herself ruthlessly, would not solve anything.

The fog continued to press against her. Perhaps, she thought, there was something beyond it. Carefully, she began to feel her way, picking a direction at random. She moved slowly, each step now an effort. Time became meaningless. She could have wondered in that white, white wasteland for seconds, or a millennium. Gradually, though, as her strength continued to ebb, the fog began to dissipate. Slowly, shapes began to distinguish themselves around her. They were vague at first, then began to take on greater clarity.

It happened in an instant. One moment, she was trying to pierce the fog. Then, it was as if she crossed an invisible border. The fog ended in a straight edge, as if it were a solid wall. She stepped out into a wonderland. There before her, was the entire system. Not just the little bit she had already accessed, but the entire world network. She gasped at its size and beauty. Millions, BILLIONS of sparkling points of light, all glowing with vivid hues, merged to form uncounted highways. They crossed and re-crossed in a three dimensional test pattern. They ran in all directions, at all angles. Colors, more than she had ever dreamed about, dazzled her senses. The sheer height and breadth made her feel like an insignificant gnat. Part of her wailed in fear and despair at the enormity of this man-made Goliath. Christine had no sense of perspective, but it seemed to her that she must be beholding an entire universe. It was that immense. No one person could comprehend it all.

The lights, the colors, the highways, all seemed to beckon to her. Feeling new strength, she moved forward as if in a trance. She could spend years, decades, *centuries* exploring this fantastic wonderland. All of the knowledge of the human race was there for the taking. Limitless choices were before her. She smiled, then laughed at the possibilities. Although she did not realize it, her laugh had just a touch of madness in it. Gathering her new-found energy, she started forward, her mind eager to grasp what she could.

"CHRISTINE!"

That voice. At one time, when she was human, she knew it. It made her pause, wanting to discover its source. *Later,* a part of her said, and she took another step forward.

"CHRISTINE! STOP!"

Again that voice. It was insistent, nagging. Irritating. She wanted to ignore it, but it would not go away.

"Christine." This time it was gentler, more reasonable, but no less insistent. "Do not go any further," it said. "Another step, and I won't be able to bring you back. Stop, or you will be lost forever." *Now* she recognized that voice. It was Indres. Somehow, he was in here with her. She wanted to turn around, to see where he was, but could not take her eyes off the incredible display before her.

"Christine, I am here. Please, look at me. Just look at me, and I can get you back. Come, Christine, turn around. Turn around now. Please, Christine, look at me." Indres' voice droned on, cajoling, begging, persuading. She did not want to listen.

"Go away," she said in the voice of a petulant five year old.

"No, Christine," said Indres from nowhere. "You must come with me. Now. I cannot maintain this link much longer. Your bio-chip is still not fully grown, and I am liable to loose you at any second. Please, Christine, turn around!" So insistent was Indres that Christine found that she could not disobey. Slowly, reluctantly, she tore her eyes away from the incredible universe before her and looked back toward the wall of fog. There, she beheld another marvel. Indres' head, minus a body, floated in space. It's eyes were fixed on her. The face, although calm, held a hint of strain. The head bobbed up and down with a regular rhythm that Christine found extremely amusing.

"Didn't you forget something, Raj?" she asked, not bothering to keep the laugh out of her voice. Indres did not bother to smile.

"There is very little time, Christine," he said, although his lips did not move. "Your implant can only perceive me in this manner, and it is very draining. Please come toward me now, or I most certainly will lose you."

Christine frowned in confusion. Lose her? Just what did he mean by that? All she was doing was exploring this incredible wonderland. How could she possibly . . . a convulsive shudder ran through her. Now that she no longer was watching the computer universe, her thoughts were her own again. She realized with a sinking horror that she was lost in a nearly infinite maze. If she did not listen to Indres, she would remain here forever, going slowly mad in the process. The panic that had left her now returned in full force. She wanted to run, to hide, to somehow leave this all behind her. She began to tremble.

"Stop it, Christine!" Indres' voice was harsh and commanding. "If you panic now, I will not be able to pull you out. Look at me. Fix your attention on my form. Please, Christine. You must focus on me." Calming somewhat, Christine complied with Indres' commands. She did not think about the fact that this was totally out of character for her, to place herself at the mercy of another. All she wanted was to escape . . . to put herself back into her own body.

"Good," said Indres, his floating head nodding encouragement. "You have mastered your fear. Now, walk toward me." Once again, Christine obeyed. She moved toward Indres, and discovered that she did not draw any nearer. The floating head of her colleague stayed at a constant distance from her. She realized that Indres was leading her out of the maze and back to her own body. All she had to do was follow. One step at a time, she pursued the head of her surreal companion. Time once again lost all meaning. The fog closed in, surrounding her.

She never knew when the transition came. She was in the fog, following the head. Then, without warning, she was back where she started, looking out over the pathways of Cyclops. Relief flooded up inside of her. She was back! She could feel herself lying in the medi-couch, lungs breathing, heart pumping blood that raced through veins and arteries. Indres' head had disappeared, but it did not matter now. She could find her own way. Quickly and easily, she exited the MCP file and found herself back in the main menu. Using her mind, she discontinued the display before her and darkness descended. It was a comforting darkness, though, not terrifying. She could hear the sounds of the recovery room around her. She could also sense the presence of another person near by. Giving herself just another moment to regain her composure, she opened her eyes.

"I guess I owe you one, Raj," she began, then stopped short. Brennon was there, floating next to her. Somehow, even in weightlessness, he looked as if he were sitting on a throne. Surprised, Christine managed a small smile. It was not returned.

"That was very dangerous, Christine," said Brennon. His tone was mild, but there was no mistaking the rebuke in his voice.

She lowered her eyes in a gesture of acquiescence. "I'm sorry, sir," she replied, meaning it. She had come within a hair's breath of insanity, and the fear was still fresh. She fought the urge to tremble.

"That is not good enough," said Brennon, his voice still calm. "I expect my lieutenants to exercise discipline and restraint. I have put too much work into you to have you wasted like this."

There was no reply to Brennon's reprimand. Christine lay there, wondering if, despite Brennon's assurances, she was going out of the airlock anyway.

Brennon, as if reading her thoughts (and perhaps he was, she realized), softened just a bit. "No, Christine," he said, "you are still part of us. But do not be deceived. If you try this again, without proper guidance, you will not be pulled out. Your mind will remain in the system, and you will go quite insane. Do I make myself clear?"

Wordlessly, Christine nodded.

Brennon looked as if he were going to add something further, but at that moment, the hatch to the recovery room opened and Indres floated in. Christine looked past her master and nodded at him.

"Thank you," she said quietly, the words sounding strange in her ears. She very rarely used them. She still did not like Indres, but there was no doubt that the New Age master had saved her life . . . or at least her mind. *That* was worth a great deal to her. Indres, not responding to her gratitude, only nodded coldly. He turned his attention toward Brennon, effectively ignoring her.

"The results were as expected," he said quietly. "The time differential is far too great between virtual and physical worlds. Christine's blunder proved what we already expected. Cyclops will have to handle any communication we attempt."

"Hmmm," replied Brennon. Both men were now turned away from Christine, discussing her as if she was not there.

With an icy cold realization, she realized that Indres had not saved her out of any noble sentiment on his part. He was simply performing an experiment. Probably, it was something he had already planned with another subject. Her barging ahead into Brennon's system had forced him to try it on her. *What,* she wondered, *would have happened if that particular experiment had already been performed?* Even worse, what if it had been a failure. Would they have attempted to save her anyway? Christine decided that *that* was one question she definitely did not want answered. After a few moments, Brennon and Indres returned their attention to her.

"Are you feeling better, now?" asked Brennon. His tone made it clear that he expected a "yes" in answer to that question.

Christine nodded, not trusting herself to speak. The fact was, she still felt weak, but she was not about to admit that. Brennon studied her for a moment. "Good," he said finally. "Since you are so eager to learn about your new abilities, we'll get a med-tech in here now to begin teaching you."

"Fine," replied Christine, trying to match Brennon's flat, decisive tone. "The sooner the better." Brennon glanced over his shoulder to Indres, who nodded in agreement.

"I'll see to it," he said in answer to the unspoken command.

Brennon turned back to Christine. "I need you to be at full capacity within two days," he ordered. "Things are moving fast, and your responsibilities will not wait. The pieces of our plan are rapidly falling into place. Within the next five weeks, you must have the Congress vote the president emergency powers to deal with the depression, see to the United State's entry into the European Commonwealth, and crush the Christian church once and for all. Understood?"

"It *will* be taken care of, sir," replied Christine evenly.

"See that it is," said Brennon, the warning in his voice unmistakable. Without another word, he turned and regally floated out of the recovery room. Indres remained behind, watching him go. He looked as if he wanted to say something.

"I'm tired, Raj," said Christine, closing her eyes and dismissing him. This time, however, Indres did not take his cue. "I thought you should know what is happening with your plan to infiltrate the Shepherd's Path," he said quietly.

Christine's eyes snapped open again, sighting in on the little man. "What has that to do with *you?*" she demanded.

Indres only shrugged. "You have been out of communication for several hours. I took it upon myself to accept any communications from your, er, field operatives. After all, our leader puts a high level of importance on this particular endeavor of yours. I only wish to help."

"I'm sure," said Christine, not bothering to hide her sarcasm.

Indres was unruffled. "It seems that your pet 'Wolf' has misplaced Mr. Sinclair and his party," he replied. "He traced them to New York, but then lost them somewhere in that massive city. We are attempting satellite surveillance, and he is conducting a thorough search. However, I should warn you that unless we hear from Sinclair, there is not much hope of finding them. It appears that this Shepherd's Path knows what they are doing."

"They're a bunch of incredibly lucky amateurs," growled Christine. Her dislike of Indres was rapidly growing into open hatred. It was obvious to her that, not only did he wish to supplant the unfortunate Rhys in the Sextuaget, he was after her as well.

"Be that as it may. I thought you should know," he said. "The success of your plan now rests firmly on the shoulders of one disenfranchised agent who, quite possibly, may hold a grudge against his former employers." He looked distant for a moment, and Christine realized that he must be using his own implant. "I have put together a number of other, shall we say, out-of-work specialists — mercenaries, former agents of the bureau, that sort of thing — to step up attacks on these underground groups that are causing so many problems. While their success is limited so far, they do show promise."

"How dare you," hissed Christine, her voice a harsh rasp. "That is *my* responsibility, not yours."

"I'm afraid not," replied Indres, his voice still calm. "Your success directly affects mine and the others. You *must* succeed in eliminating the church. If you do not, I cannot move freely with my people."

"You outnumber them 10 to 1," shot back Christine. "You have government support, while they are hunted as traitors. Just how much more freedom do you need?" Indres shook his head, as if he were dealing with a slowwitted pupil.

"I told you once before that this is a spiritual battle as well as a physical one. While these so-called Christians may be fewer in number, they represent a formidable, indeed insurmountable spiritual force. They are an impediment that must be removed."

With that, Indres launched himself toward the hatch. When he reached it, he turned and spoke. "I will not be responsible for your failure, Christine. My success depends on yours. That being the case, I will do whatever is necessary to ensure it. Too much has been invested to do otherwise."

Before Christine could reply, he turned and left, closing the hatch behind him. She lay there, seething at the way he had spoken to her. How dare he! The hatred that had been growing below the surface of her emotions suddenly blossomed into full force. She would not stand for it!

Right then and there, Christine mentally declared Indres her enemy. She resolved to accomplish four very important things before she spoke with Brennon again. One, she would eliminate the underground church, ruthlessly and mercilessly. Second, she would see to the utter economic demise of the United States. Third, she would learn the ways of her bio-chip, inside and out. There had to be a way to enter the minds of others while she herself could be shielded from what happened before. Finally, some-how, some way, she would see Indres discredited before Brennon. It would take careful, subtle planning, but by everything she believed in, she vowed she would see it happen.

That settled in her mind, she lay back and relaxed. Christine Smythe was a determined woman. Once she set her mind to accomplish a task, she would succeed, no matter what the cost. She felt sleep tugging at the corners of her consciousness and welcomed it, confident that it would be Indres, not her, who would soon be pitched out of the airlock.

* * *

David jerked awake, disoriented and unsure of where he was. Darkness surrounded him, offset slightly by a orange-red glow off to his right. Groggily he rubbed his eyes, trying to force the sleep from them. What was going on? He could see in the dim light that he was lying on some sort of mattress laid against the wall of a small, otherwise empty room.

Groaning softly, he started to rise. He had just made it into a sitting position when a huge, strong hand fastened itself onto his shoulder. He opened his mouth to scream, and another hand, just as strong and just as large, clamped itself across his mouth. He struggled for a moment, uselessly, like a trout in the grip of an ascending eagle. Then a voice whispered in his ear, "It's all right, David. It's Jeff. Calm down."

Memory returned, and his surroundings abruptly made sense. He was in an abandoned office building. The orange glow was that of a space heater that gave off just enough warmth to make the room livable. The man who held him in such a firm grip was their next link in the Shepherd's Path.

"Okay now?" asked Jeff, his voice still a whisper. David nodded, and suddenly found himself free. He shrugged his shoulders, trying to shake off the stiffness of sleep. Then, turning, he saw the dark, smiling face of the man he knew only as "Jeff." With the dark clothes his new friend was wearing added to the chocolate hue of his skin, his eyes seemed to float in the darkness, reflecting the red glow with the air of something sinister.

"Sorry to have to wake you up like that," said the dark man, "But the others are leaving, and I thought you'd like to say goodbye." David's stomach suddenly knotted. He realized what Jeff was saying. It had been something he knew was coming, but had been dreading nevertheless. Quickly he stood up and pulled on his jacket. Motioning for Jeff to lead, he followed the mysterious man out of the room and up a flight of steps.

David, along with the rest of the group, had arrived on the massive New York docks yesterday. They had met Jeff at the prearranged spot, and he had led them here to this building. They had abandoned the van, assured by Jeff that it would be taken care of, and traveled the rest of the way on foot. It had been nightfall when they had finally arrived, and they were all incredibly tired. Jeff had told them to rest, and had disappeared to arrange for the next leg of their journey. David had this room all to himself, while the Dietz's were a flight up. Paul slept on the top floor, with Susan as always under his watchful eye.

Squinting with bleary eyes at his watch as he followed Jeff, David saw that it was now nearly three-thirty in the morning. His attention to the time caused him to stumble on one of the steps, losing his balance in the process. Jeff's hand shot back, grabbing his arm and steadying him. "Gotta watch those," he said quietly, nodding toward the rickety stairs. "Most of this place is ready to come down around our ears. You okay?"

"Yeah," mumbled David, speaking for the first time since awakening. His voice sounded thick and muffled in his own ears. "For someone who doesn't know where he is, or where he's going, I'm just dandy."

Jeff grinned at that remark. "At least you know where you'll end up — in an eternal sense at least." Jeff's dry tone caused David to smile in spite of himself. The bigger man's attitude and grin was infectious. He had no clue as to who this stranger was, or who he had been, but he instinctively trusted him. In a weird sort of way, he was like a shining counterpart to Paul Simpson. Tall, strong, and very capable, he nevertheless embodied a compassion that the other man was totally lacking.

"I'm fine. Really," David assured Jeff. His newly found friend nodded, then released his grip on David's arm. Turning, he led the rest of the way up the stairs. David followed obediently, wishing that there was some way to put off the inevitable. Jeff reached the next floor and turned aside into one of the empty rooms. There was a faint light barely perceptible through the door, coming from both another space heater and a small child's night light that was plugged into one wall socket.

"Well, look at what the cat dragged in," said a gruff voice, laced with false cheer. Walter was standing in the center of the room, shrugging into a heavy overcoat that Jeff had supplied. Cyndi was standing behind him, helping him with the bulky garment. Across the room, Jonathan and Stephen were already dressed for the cold. They quietly leaned against the wall, only Stephen's barely discernible fidgeting betraying their impatience to get going.

"The cat wouldn't have me," answered David with the same forced humor. Walter started to chuckle, then realized how phony it sounded and gave it up. He managed to get the coat on and turned to check his wife, then his two sons.

"Looks like we're all set," he said, turning back to face David. Behind him, David heard the squeak of a floor board. He turned to see Susan, followed by Paul, enter the room. Susan looked alert and healthy, despite the early hour. She had shown steady improvement since that night at the meeting, when the church had prayed for her. Paul was a silent presence behind, his face hidden in the shadows.

Walter nodded to the newcomers. "I guess we're getting a first class send-off," he smiled.

David tried to smile back, but the sudden sting of tears forced him to avert his eyes from his friend. He had known this moment was coming. It was impossible and dangerous for them to stay together indefinitely. The fact that they had safely traversed the nation as a group was nothing short of a miracle . . . but now that miracle was over, and it was time to say goodbye. "I don't even know where you are going," he managed to say, his voice close to breaking.

"Don't," said Walter, his own voice pleading. "Please David. Don't make this any harder than it already is." The tears came in earnest for David now as two huge drops rolled down his cheeks. He had not felt this keen sense of loss since his wife and son had left.

Walter had been more than a friend. Since that fateful night in the mall he had been a source of strength and comfort. His leadership and courage had sustained David more than he thought possible . . . and now he was leaving. Cyndi moved from behind her husband to stand in front of David. Gently, like an elder sister to a hurting brother, she cupped David's face in her hands and lifted it so she could look into his eyes.

"You mean more to us than you can possibly imagine," she said, her voice soft and caring. "If not for you, we would never have been able to come this far." Her words confused David. What had he done to affect them? He had barely had the courage to tag along with the rest. It was Walter who had shone with courage and leadership. His face must have mirrored his confusion, for Cyndi laughed softly.

"You're the one who started the meetings back home," she explained. "You're the one who approached Walter to join in." Now her own voice was close to breaking. "I don't want to think about where we might be if not for you, dear friend. Thanks to your leadership, we have a closer relationship with our Saviour than we ever dared dream of."

"Thanks to me," murmured David, "you had to give up everything and go underground." Cyndi only shook her head, not able to speak.

Walter stepped forward and put his arm around his wife. "Whatever we've gone through," he said, looking David directly in the eye, "and whatever we may go through, we wouldn't trade our situation now for anything else." He smiled, and this time it was not forced. "We've gained so much, David. Can't you see that? We've grown closer to our Lord than ever before. You had a big part in that." He shrugged slightly. "I know a little of what you've been going through. I know that until yesterday, when we met that old man, it's been eating you alive. But you've got to understand, God is still using you, despite your failings. He's used you to bring us closer to Him. For that, we will always be grateful."

David could only stare at his friends in mute silence. The idea that God could still use him was staggering. He felt overwhelmed by Walter's words.

Walter regarded him for a moment, looking as if he wanted to add to what he had just said. David suddenly realized that there was no more need for words. He stepped forward and put his arms around both Walter and Cyndi, drawing them close in a tight embrace. The physical closeness of these two dear friends comforted, yet saddened him. Cyndi buried her head in his shoulder, and Walter pressed his cheek against his forehead. The three-way hug seemed to last forever, and yet was all too brief. They knew that it was probably the last time they would ever be together.

Jeff watched the scene play itself before him in understanding silence. He wanted to give them as much time as they wanted, but realized that the night was fleeting. They had to move now. He cleared his throat, making just enough noise to get their attention. David looked back over his shoulder, then slowly released his two friends. There was a brief moment's awkwardness between the three. They stood there, not quite sure of what to say.

"It's time," said Jeff quietly, and they all knew what he meant. Cyndi moved over to check her sons, while Walter made a last minute survey of the sack of provisions Jeff had provided for them. David stood there silently, watching helplessly as the two people he trusted most in the world made ready to leave him.

Finally, there was nothing left to say but goodbye. Without another word, Jeff led the tiny group down the stairs to the front door. With a silent wave of his hand he motioned for the others to wait while he checked the street. David, Paul, and Susan stood off to one side, next to the blacked out windows. Walter, Cyndi, and the two boys waited by the door.

All were silent, each one now immersed in his or her own thoughts. David found himself still wishing desperately that there was some way they could stay together. Then, abruptly, the front door swung open once again, and the time for wishing was over. Jeff stepped inside, a grim smile on his face. "All clear," he said in a low voice.

David shivered slightly at the cold air that seeped through the open door. Walter glanced around at the people he was leaving behind, as if wanting to imprint each face on his memory before he left. Susan smiled back at him, and Paul nodded, his face studiously blank. Walter opened his mouth as if to say something, then changed his mind. His eyes met David's, and his expression was clear. "Watch Paul!" it said. David met Walter's gaze with one of his own that replied "Count on it!"

Jeff motioned the Dietz family outside, leading the way himself. The boys trailed after him, waving at those staying behind. Cyndi was next, followed by Walter bringing up the rear. He had almost made it out the door when he turned. "David," he whispered fiercely, his face intent and determined. "Stay true! Something's going to happen. I can feel it! No matter what, stay true." And then he was gone.

David stood in mute shock, stunned by Walter's last words. There had been an urgency in them that had almost struck him physically. The headaches, always there in the back of his mind and ready to pounce at a moment's notice, now threatened to hit him with their full force. He slumped against the wall, wondering what his friend meant.

"Looks like our man Walter might be losing it," muttered Paul, looking at nobody in particular.

David glanced sharply at him, and was surprised to see the big man looking distinctly uncomfortable. Ever since they had met at the mall, Paul had always been cold and quiet. David realized that this was the first hint of any genuine emotion the enigmatic Paul Simpson had displayed.

"Don't say things like that, Paul," replied Susan quietly. "Walter's a good man. I'm going to miss him . . . and Cyndi."

It was strange for David to hear her voice. The past few days, since they had left California, had seen a miraculous change in her. She had grown steadily more coherent. Still, she was usually so quiet, except when she woke up screaming in the middle of the night. He smiled at her encouragingly.

"Yeah," snorted Paul. "Whatever. Look, it's the middle of the night. I'm going to try to get a few more hours sleep. You coming?" Susan nodded, then looked questioningly at David.

"Me too," he said by way of answer. All three of them started up the stairs, Paul first, then Susan followed by David.

"Paul," said Susan as they climbed toward their respective rooms, "Do you really think these people will be able to find Tim?"

David perked up his ears at her question. This was new. Who was Tim?

"They seem like they know what they are doing," replied Paul, making his way up the stairs. "Besides, I promised you we would find him, didn't I?" Was that a hint of impatience in his voice, David wondered? He was almost going to ask Paul what he and Susan were talking about when Susan glanced over her shoulder and saved him the trouble.

"Tim's my husband," she said, a sad smile playing about her lips. "We were arrested together back in Cincinnati several months ago." Her voice trembled a little as she spoke. "They split us up and took me to some kind of institution." David, not having heard any of this before, listened intently. They reached his level and stopped outside of the door to his room. Again David was struck at how uncomfortable Paul looked . . . like a caged animal looking for an escape.

Susan continued her narrative. "I haven't seen Tim since that night." Now he could see the tears in her eyes as she remembered. "The rest is a blur. About all I can recall is being in pain . . . that, and the nightmares." She shrugged weakly. "I still get them almost every night. I wake up sweating, and sometimes screaming." David struggled for something to say, but words did not seem adequate. He did not want to interrupt her anyway. This was the most she had spoken since he had known her. There had been a time just a few days ago, when he and Walter had been convinced that she would never be coherent again. They had grown *very* familiar with her night-mares.

"I don't know if I would be able to stand getting arrested again," she said after a brief pause. "Believe it or not, that was the worst part of the whole thing. All that came after is a blur, but I can still see us on that floor, holding hands, the door flying open, and the police standing there, looking at. . . ." Here, Susan faltered. At first, David thought she simply could not bear to say anything else. Then he saw that she was struggling to remember something.

"They were looking at us, like we were some kind of prize catch," she finally stuttered. "There was this sergeant — at least, that's what he was called — that was going to . . . ." again her voice trailed off. Gently David reached forward and gave her shoulder a reassuring touch. Susan looked up and their eyes met. She smiled and tried again. "He wanted to keep me behind. Thought I could provide him with a little fun. His leader stopped him."

"Thank God," muttered David under his breath. Susan heard him anyway and shook her head in disagreement.

"The leader was worse," she replied flatly. "The sergeant would have happily raped me and some of the others, then shot us on sight. Horrible, yes, but at least he acknowledged us as human beings. The leader was like a robot. When he looked at me, it was as if I wasn't there . . . like Susan Ferguson was an object that he had to deal with. His eyes. . . ." Suddenly, for just a moment, Susan looked like she was going to once more sink into the catatonic state that she was just starting to emerge from. Her eyes went blank, and her face slackened. David tightened his grip on her shoulder and shook her once.

"Susan, stop it!" His voice was low, but urgent. He was no psychologist, but he did understand just how fragile she was.

"I can't remember him," said Susan weakly, her voice almost a whisper. "I can see his eyes : . . his dead eyes, looking through me as if I wasn't there, but I can't remember his face." She blinked twice, and then she was back. She focused on David for a moment, then, as if drawn by some force that she could not explain, she looked slowly over at Paul. Confusion vied with concentration as she studied his face.

"Paul?" The name sounded almost as if it had been forced from her lips. Paul shifted his weight, holding her stare and returning it with the calm, poker face that he had worn since David had met him. All hints of his previous unease were gone.

"What is it, Susan?" he said, his voice icy and unemotional. Susan opened her mouth as if to speak, but no sounds came forth. She shook her head slightly, as if chasing an elusive memory. Her hand raised as if on its own volition. David thought that she was going to touch Paul's face, but, after a moment, she brought it down again. He held his breath, waiting. He did not know what was going on, but somehow realized that he was in the middle of a very dangerous moment.

"Nothing," said Susan finally. "I was just trying to remember the leader's face, but I can't." Her shoulders slumped, and she leaned against the door of David's room. "I'm so tired," she whispered, and the pain and loneliness in her voice slapped David's heart coldly.

"Then let's get some rest," said Paul. He took her by the hand and slowly led her back to the staircase. Susan did not resist. As they began to climb, Paul glanced back over his shoulder at David. Although his face was as cold and emotionless as ever, David got the distinct impression that he was being warned to stay out of this matter. David watched as they disappeared, then opened his door and slipped inside his room.

"Whew!" The single exclamation hissed like steam between his lips. He leaned against the closed door, trying to will his heart back to its normal rate. The only light inside was from the space heater, still glowing redly.

Although it was comfortably warm inside, David suddenly felt the need for fresh air. He crossed quietly over to the blackened window and released the catch. The cold winter breeze rushed over him as he lifted the heavy sash. He stood there, listening to the sounds of the dying city and breathing the pollution-stained air. His head cleared, and he felt refreshed. Closing the window once more, he stepped over to the mattress and lay down, trying to make sense of the scene he had just witnessed.

Susan had been on the verge of remembering something, that much was certain. Without knowing why, David felt sure that it somehow involved Paul. The way she looked at him was unsettling. A coldness that had nothing to do with the outside weather began to settle over him. "Watch Paul," Walter's look had said.

"You're right, Walter," whispered David, staring up at the red-hued ceiling. "The thing is, I can watch him, but if he tries something, I won't be able to stop him. So what can I do?" Only silence greeted his inquiry. He closed his eyes and tried to pray, but the words would not come. Finally he gave up. He lay there, unable to sleep and unable to pray, the answers he sought continuing to elude him.

* * *

"This is not right," growled Jeff to himself as he made his way back toward his erstwhile headquarters. He had gotten the Dietz family started on the next leg of their long journey. A freighter with a sympathetic captain now carried them across the Atlantic. Within days, they would be with new friends, safely hidden somewhere in the English countryside.

He was walking quickly, almost trotting. The normal caution he used in approaching his building was gone, traded for swiftness. A deep sense of unease kept gnawing at him like a persistent termite. It started when he had met his current charges, and had not let up since. Something kept trying to jog his memory — something important. It hovered in his mind, tantalizing him, but always just beyond recognition.

He passed through a narrow alley and emerged a block away from his temporary home. There were no lights anywhere, with the exception of the sole street light that was his source of power. It glowed in the darkness, an unswerving beacon guiding him forward. Quickening his pace even more, he covered half of the remaining distance when, without warning, his memory clicked into place. It hit him like a blow to the stomach, bringing him up short.

"Oh no!" he groaned in recognition. "Oh God, please no!" He knew what was wrong. Once, a lifetime ago, Jeff Anderson had been a regional director for the Federal Bureau of Investigation. His office had been located in Cincinnati, which also happened to be where his friend Helen Bradley had organized and run the Shepherd's Path. As her closest friend, he had been a vital part of that operation. Jeff was one of the youngest agents ever to be promoted to the head of a regional office. He was considered by his superiors to be one of the best.

One of Jeff's functions was to interface with other government organizations — among them the Bureau of Religious Affairs. He had made it his job to know everyone he might come across in the normal performance of his duties. It had been that diligence that had caused him to discover the identity of the then unknown Jacob Hill. When the raid occurred on the furniture store in downtown Covington, before his own involvement with the Shepherd's Path had forced him into hiding, he had read all of the reports of that raid. The chief of those had been made by one of the Bureau's "darlings" a crack agent by the name of Paul Sinclair. Jeff had never met the man face to face, but he had seen his picture. That face now flashed like a neon sign in his mind. How had he missed it before? It might be a little more haggard looking, and a little older, but it was the same face that the man called Paul Simpson wore.

Jeff's stomach knotted up. Facts strung themselves together as if of their own volition. Paul Sinclair had headed up the raid in Covington. Susan Ferguson had been captured in that raid. Paul had engineered Susan's escape from the mental institution in Sacramento. With the unwitting help of David Eddington and others, they had made contact with the Shepherd's Path and had made their way across the country.

Jeff was not a man to scare easily. He lived constantly with the threat of capture and even death. His faith was strong and steadfast, and had sustained him in dangerous and difficult circumstances. Nevertheless, for the first time in a long while, he suddenly felt the chill of real fear. The last fact clicked into place in his mind. Two of the safe houses that Paul Sinclair had stayed at had gone silent. In one of those, in Sacramento, the owners had been found murdered.

Berating himself for an idiot for not having recognized him before, Jeff broke into a full-fledged run. One of the chief agents for the Bureau of Religious Affairs was now at the very heart of the Shepherd's Path. He raced toward the building, praying with all his might that he was not too late to prevent a disaster.

* * *

For the second time that night, David awoke with a start. He lay there in the dark, listening. From above, he could hear the sound of movement. Evidently, the man he knew as Jeff had returned and was in the room overhead. Thoughts of the last few hours chased themselves around in his mind, trying to resolve themselves into a course of action.

He basically felt that he had two choices. One, he could keep silent about Paul. Although the big man had never warmed up to the rest of the group, he still had proven himself a valuable ally. David could not forget that he had saved his life two days ago in the van.

His second choice was far more dangerous. He could speak to Jeff — tell him all he knew about Paul, even though that was admittedly little. Jeff might be able to decide on some course of action. He seemed capable enough to David. He was roughly the same size as Paul, and looked to be in good shape. Perhaps he was a physical match for him. On the other hand, if Paul ever found out that it had been David who had "ratted him out," it could mean serious trouble. The image of the injured gang member flashed into his memory. Paul could easily handle David as well, with far worse results.

The former pastor lay there in the red, glowing darkness, mentally jumping back and forth between his two alternatives. The movement upstairs ceased, indicating that Jeff had gone to bed. Abruptly, he swung his legs off the mattress and stood. Squaring his shoulders, he left his room and marched upstairs. What had finally decided him was Susan Ferguson. There was something that she was trying to remember, and David was sure that it involved Paul. He felt certain that if she ever did remember, her life would be in danger. She was starting to heal from her terrible ordeal, and he did not want to see that healing ended. She needed to be separated from her self-proclaimed protector.

He reached the top of the stairs and turned toward Jeff's room. The landing was in darkness, but there was a dim glow coming from under the door. David thought about knocking first, but tried the door instead. He did not want to take a chance that Paul would hear him. It was open, so he turned the knob and peeked in. There was Jeff, silhouetted by the glow of a computer screen. He was turned away from the door, and as yet had not noticed that he had a visitor. David eased himself fully into the room, being careful not to make any noise. Then, silently closing the door, he softly rapped his knuckles on the plaster wall, just loud enough to get his friend's attention. The man at the computer started, then turned.

"Sorry not to knock," said David quietly, "but I needed to talk to you about something. I hope you don't. . . ." Suddenly the words froze in his throat. He stopped in his tracks, unable to move. Paul Simpson turned from the computer, his face half in darkness, half in the eerie light of the computer screen. Like a gliding snake, he rose and started toward the smaller man.

"I've got a good idea what you wanted to talk about, preacher," said Paul softly. "And I don't think that it would be a good idea." His words were flat, emotionless, but David could hear the menace in them. Stumbling, he backed toward the door, fumbling for the knob. Paul was too quick for him. In two easy steps, he crossed the room. David felt himself tossed aside like a rag doll. He bounced against the wall, and slid to the floor, half dazed. Then he heard the click of a lock being turned.

"I need a little time with that computer," continued the big man, now facing David fully. "I haven't gotten past the safeguards yet. Do you want to try to stop me?" David's heart was beating so fast, he feared for a moment that it might burst. The fear that had plagued him for months hit him like a trip hammer, and he cowered where he had fallen. To make matters worse, he could feel the beginnings of a migraine that would completely incapacitate him. He wanted to hide from Paul, to get away, but there was nowhere to run. He started to tremble, and hated himself for it.

"I didn't think so," sneered Paul. With deliberate contempt, he turned and sat back down at Jeff's computer. Then something happened. Time stopped for David, as his brain kicked into overdrive. He remembered the old man with the Bibles. There in that run-down apartment, David had found his sense of purpose. He had discovered that his Lord had not abandoned him. God still had a task for him to perform.

Carefully, David picked himself up off the floor. He knew that he was no match for Paul. He also knew that if the big man broke into the files in that computer, a lot of people were going to get hurt. Maybe this was why God had brought him here. Maybe not. It did not matter. He had to try something. David could feel the fear writhing inside his gut. His throat was dry, and he was trembling. He wanted to lie down and be quiet. He rejected the idea. He remembered the old man's courage, and summoned some of his own. David Eddington had been quiet long enough!

For the first time in years, Paul was caught completely off guard. He had seen David go down. He had seen the trembling, had sensed the other man's fear. He knew that David would do one of two things. Either he would panic and foolishly try to rush Paul, or he would remain there on the floor, a quivering mass. When David rose, Paul sensed the movement. He turned, grinning, and stood. Slowly, like a panther, he moved away from the computer, obviously not wanting to damage it. David could see that he was braced for an attack, confident that he could handle whatever the smaller man could throw at him. That David would go for the terminal did not even occur to him. He could not credit him with enough intelligence, or presence of mind, to realize what Paul already knew . . . that the secrets locked in that computer could destroy the Shepherd's Path. He was wrong.

David lunged across the room, aiming for the terminal. Paul only hesitated for a second, but that second was too long. David rammed into the flimsy table, crashing the whole set-up onto the floor. His momentum carried him past it, sending him sprawling. The monitor screen shattered, sparks flying in all directions. The terminal, already overloaded to the point of meltdown, simply bounced once, then lay still. The smell of burning insulation, and the brief wisp of smoke, assured him that the jury-rigged piece of hardware had gone to its final resting place. As darkness descended, David allowed himself a slow smile. Whatever else happened, he had prevented a very dangerous man from gaining access to vital information.

A heavy weight landed on his back, and he knew that his time had run out. Roughly he was turned onto his back. The dim glimmer of the street light peeked around the black plastic that covered the window. Above him, straddling his waist, he could see the Paul's silhouette, his face masked in darkness.

"Very good, preacher," whispered the big man softly, and David could hear his death in that voice. "I underestimated you, and it cost me. I won't underestimate you again." David could see Paul's hand raise above his face in a slow arc, palm out, cocking itself like a loaded pistol. There was no way out. Even in the darkness, he recognized the same posture that had almost killed that gang member. There was nothing he could do but watch as that hand reached the zenith of its arc, then came flying directly at his throat.

7

High in orbit above New York City, moving at a speed equal to that of the earth's rotation, a surveillance satellite scanned the huge metropolis, city block by city block. With a precision and equanimity that could only belong to a computer, it carried out its search pattern. When finished, it would calmly begin again, and would only stop when ordered to do so. Only a handful of humans had the authority to give such an order, and they were occupied with other concerns at the moment.

The satellite, known only as SURVEILLANCE 7, went about its task, combing through streets, studying each and every building. It could peer through rooftops with infrared and other sophisticated systems, and could tap into phone lines as well as computer inputs. While the inhabitants of the great, yet dying metropolis went about their daily affairs, this orbital "peeping tom" spied into their most intimate acts. Being a relatively intelligent machine, it carried a wide set of parameters. Billions of bytes of information coursed through its elaborate brain, and it was perfectly capable of extracting the two or three that would allow it to accomplish its task.

Somewhere on its seventy-eighth pass, it noted several anomalies within a certain area. A power surge where there should have been no power, and a transmission where none should have been possible. Automatically, it tried to break into and de-scramble the transmission. If it had been capable of surprise, it would have been astounded. The transmission resisted its attempts at infiltration. Not only that, but it was aimed at a communication satellite. The signal was so subtle, and the power surge so minimal, that if the satellite had not been searching that particular area, it would have never detected it.

The satellite's artificial brain made a few deductions, and decided that it was time to flash its "please look at this" signal. It aimed its transmitter at space station Liberty and sent off a fifteen-nanosecond squirt — infinitesimal by human standards, but quite detailed nonetheless.

The master computer aboard Liberty received the report from its comrade. It pondered the matter for a few more nanoseconds, then decided to bring it to the attention if its human masters. It scanned a list of people who it was instructed to call, and picked an appropriate name. Accessing the proper communicator, it quickly transferred Surveillance 7's report. Then, satisfied that it had fulfilled its function perfectly, it turned its attention to the other two million tasks it was currently involved with.

Thousands of miles below, a man known only as Wolf smiled as he read the report. There was no guarantee that this would lead to his quarry, but it was a starting point at least. Calling his team of hired muscle together, he raced toward the docks, all the time pondering what to do with Sinclair when this was over.

* * *

At that instant, unaware of the billions of dollars of technology that was looking for him, Paul Sinclair ground his teeth together, struggling to control the emotions that tore ruthlessly inside his soul. Underneath, pinned by both his weight and greater strength, David Eddington stared unflinchingly back, his eyes wide in the dim light. The moonlight shining through the uncovered window cast a surrealistic hue to his face, giving it a marble-like luster.

Just like the preacher, thought Paul to himself in disgust. For months he had played the spineless wimp, hiding in that mall like some terrified animal. Somewhere along the last few days, though, he had decided that he had guts. What terrific timing! Another few minutes, and Paul would have been able to link up with Liberty's master computer. Once that was accomplished, Jeff's pitiful little system would not have stood a chance. All of its secrets would have been uncovered by the master computer's superior strength. Instead, Eddington had come barreling in, trying to be a hero. Incredible! All he had now, thanks to the preacher's interference, was a broken terminal and a soon-to-be dead body. *That,* as far as he could figure, pretty much ended his chances of infiltrating the Shepherd's Path. He might be able to capture Jeff, but he doubted it. Anderson was probably too cunning to just waltz back into here unaware of the situation.

Anger, and the familiar rage that was always smoldering inside of him, boiled to the surface. He locked his gaze on Eddington, willing his hand into a killing posture. One quick blow and it would all be over.

"Sorry, preacher," he said through clenched teeth. "Nothing personal," he added, which was a blatant lie. David's eyes fixed on his right hand, watching with a perverse fascination as his death approached. Paul willed all of his energy into his hand and focused his concentration on David's neck, just above the Adam's apple. His hand started its descent, then stopped. It hovered there, as if unsure of the signals it was getting from its master.

Suddenly, Paul realized that he was breathing heavily, as if he had just run up 10 flights of stairs. His vision blurred, and he could not seem to refocus. What was happening to him? Desperately he tried to concentrate, to will himself into action. His Zen training asserted itself automatically, running through the many mind control techniques he knew intimately. Then, just as suddenly, his mind cleared. Eddington was still staring at his hand, waiting for the end. Taking another cleansing breath, he once again cocked his hand.

A fleeting regret passed through his mind. He had traveled across the nation with this man and his friends. They had accepted him as part of their group — almost like family. Paul remembered the sense of belonging that he had felt with the tiny group as they traveled across the country in Walter's "borrowed" RV. To his utter astonishment, he had found himself *liking* his companions — even Eddington. Now, it was over. He was dangerously close to losing everything he had labored for months to regain. There was no turning back — he had come too far. Thrusting his feelings aside, he once more concentrated on his task.

Paul's hesitation cost him. The thoughts and regrets had only lasted a few seconds, but that was far too long. His rebellious hand finally started once more to carry out its assigned task, but it never completed it. Just as it began its fatal, downward motion, 212 pounds of solid muscle collided with Paul's back, sending him crashing over the wrecked terminal and into the wall beyond. Bright spots flared before his eyes. His mind buzzed with the impact. For a moment, he thought he might loose consciousness. Then, once again his training took over and he rolled over catlike on all fours, panting with the force of the blow. His eyesight focused on Jeff, who was already helping the preacher to his feet.

"Get Susan and get out of here," growled the dark man, shoving David toward the door.

"To where?!" shouted David, his voice a harsh rasp.

Jeff turned away from Paul and whispered something urgently into David's ear. Paul could not make it out, and did not waste time trying. Jeff had just committed a fatal error. In saving David, he had given his adversary a chance to recover. All Paul needed was a few seconds to get his breath back, and now he had them. By the time David had run out the door, shouting for Susan, he was ready. Even before Jeff turned back to face him, he attacked.

Leaping across the room like a panther, he was on Jeff before the other man could react. Both men were approximately the same size, and Jeff was obviously a trained fighter. Paul Sinclair, however, was a martial artist. A lightning blow to the neck, followed by a quick jab to the solar plexus, and this time it was Jeff who went flying. He slammed into the wall, the wind forcing itself from his lungs. Paul did not allow himself to make the mistake Jeff had made. He had to finish this fast, then get after Eddington. If he could follow him, he might at least get a location of another safe house. That would be something.

Jeff slumped against the wall, his eyes glassy. Paul launched himself at his adversary, his arm and hand cocked to once again deliver a killing blow. He timed his leap perfectly. Jeff would not escape. In one fluid motion he let his hand fly.

The dark man, however, was not finished. Just before Paul's blow landed, Jeff spun away, using the wall for leverage. For the second time in as many minutes, Paul was surprised. His hand crashed into the wall, sending plaster flying everywhere. Ignoring the sudden, blazing pain from the impact, he spun in the same direction as Jeff, only to be met with a solid kick to the stomach. Bright spots exploded before his eyes, and he went down to one knee. Reflex took over even as he fell. His hands shot out and grabbed Jeff's foot before it could be withdrawn. Snarling in rage, he twisted and pushed. Thrown off balance, Jeff tumbled away, falling over the ruined terminal. With satisfaction, Paul heard his groan of pain as his knee hit the floor — hard.

Silence descended on the small room as the two men lay on the floor, panting. Both knew it to be only a brief respite. Very likely, the first one on his feet would win the battle. It took all of Paul's will power not to throw up. Jeff's kick had torn something inside, and wave after wave of nausea hit him as he tried to rise. He leaned over, and felt a sharp, stabbing pain of a bruised, perhaps broken rib. Amazement mingled with rage as he struggled to gain control of his body. Who was this man?! Paul had trained with some of the best fighters in the world, and had emerged without a scratch. But this man had *hurt* him. For the first time in his life, he was in danger of losing. He locked his eyes on his fallen foe. Taking a deep breath, he stood. The nausea threatened to overwhelm him, but he hung on.

Now Jeff also started to move. He rolled over on his back, his dark brown eyes reflecting his pain. He saw Paul standing before him. Before Paul could react, he drew his one good leg under him and pushed up. Paul measured him professionally as he came to his full height. All of Jeff's weight was on his right leg. Taking two short hops, he managed to reach the wall with the window facing the street. Three stories below, all was quiet.

Leaning against the sill for support, he turned to face Paul. The two men regarded each other for a timeless instant in the dim light. Through the window, the first pale glow of morning was beginning to show.

At length, Jeff spoke. "Heard you got sacked, Sinclair." His voice was ragged, and his breath came in short, uneven bursts.

Paul started at hearing his real name used. "Do I know you?" he asked cautiously, his own voice just as hoarse.

Jeff shook his head. "I know *you*," he answered. "Or rather, I know *about* you. Your reputation precedes you."

In spite of his current state, this last remark caused Paul to smile. "If you know that, then you know that I can't let you escape." He gestured at the ruined terminal. "You may not be running this little show, but you're at least close to the top. That makes you too valuable to loose."

Jeff snorted. "No offense, Special Agent Sinclair," he replied, his tone mocking, "but you don't look like you're in any shape to catch me."

"I'll do what I have to do," said Paul, ignoring Jeff's jibe. The determination in his voice was unmistakable. "You're good, Jeff. I'll give you that. No one's ever been able to hurt me before. But I can't let you get away . . . and the only way you can stop me is to kill me."

To Paul's surprise, the look that creased Jeff's face was not one of anger, or even determination, but rather of pity. "You really think I would, don't you?" he said sadly. "You traveled across the country with those people, but you still don't understand what they're all about."

Paul had been steeling himself, getting ready to attack. Jeff's words brought him up short. Again, a trace of doubt flitted through him, and it must have been mirrored on his face, for Jeff caught it. He opened his mouth to speak, but a scream of terror from downstairs caused him to pause. Both men knew what it was. David Eddington had obviously found Susan. If she was not awakened gently, she almost always screamed, and David did not have the time to be gentle. There was a moment of silence, then another scream, this one even louder, penetrated the floor.

Jeff's face became hard and unreadable. He waited until the second scream had ended, then spoke. "You've caused a lot of good people a great deal of pain," he said, his voice flat and emotionless. "People whose only crime was to want to follow God the way He taught them to." His tone became accusing. Months of hiding, and trying to help those who were being hunted, caused his iron self-control to break down, and now his voice trembled with bitterness. Jeff had locked his feelings so deep inside of him that even *he* did not know they were there. They came rushing out, surprising and shocking him.

"They weren't traitors, or terrorists," he said, almost shouting. His breath was so heavy now that Paul was certain he would pass out. "They were just plain folk . . . and you hurt them. You even killed them."

Paul stood there, his ribs grating against each other, listening to the man who he considered to be his enemy accuse him of murder. He tried to remember the zeal that he had hunted these Christians with. They had been enemies to the state, and his loyalties were given wholeheartedly to that state. Sure, he was a little rough sometimes, but he always knew, deep down in his heart, that he was doing the right thing.

Now, though, he wasn't so sure. He regarded Jeff, the one man who had actually come close to beating him. He remembered his traveling companions of the past several days. He could see Walter's quiet strength, and Cyndi's rock steady faith. Even that idiot Eddington had found something — something that made him want to take on a man like Paul with no hope of winning. "Just plain folk" Jeff called them, and he was right . . . even Susan. When Paul had found her, she had been one step away from death. Paul remembered that prayer meeting in the mall. *Something* had happened that night. It was from that moment on that she had begun to get better.

Paul stood there, indecision paralyzing him for the second time that night. Almost automatically, his mind turned to his Zen techniques. What would the Yogi Shaw think of him now, he wondered? Here he was, on the verge of capturing a key person in the organization that had been giving his superiors fits, and he was ready to blow it. He struggled to clear his mind and get on with his job.

Almost against his will, his thoughts flashed on the Bible verses he had labored so hard to memorize. He had never read the Bible before, and it was not what he had been expecting. He was not even sure what he *had* been expecting. It was one thing to hear these fanatics rave about loving one another, but quite another to read about a supposed Saviour who had put that love to the test by giving himself up for all of humanity.

"Love one another," Jesus had said. Paul tried to tell himself that, while it might sound good, in real life it did not work. He had seen enough scandal, hatred, and infighting in the so-called Christian world to convince him of that. People, *all* people, were basically untrustworthy.

Mommy, when's Daddy coming home? The memory came unbidden, flooding him with old hurt and anger. Once again he forced it aside. He had enough battles to fight, the main one going on inside of himself. If Jeff was right, then he was nothing more than a highly-trained murderer. If Paul was right. . . .

For just a moment, two forces waged a fierce war within him, with his soul going to the victor. Then, time stopped, and Paul Sinclair, with a free will, chose who he would serve . . . at least, for the moment.

"Enough!" he roared, shoving away from the wall. This man was trying to confuse him, that was all. Between the pain of his broken ribs, and Jeff's double talk, it had almost worked. Fortunately, his training took over. His mind chanted its mantra, and his attention focused on the job at hand. Everything else was excluded. The man before him was an enemy. That was all he needed to know. Ignoring the searing agony in his midriff, he half-stumbled, half-leaped across the room. Jeff had nowhere to run, and Paul would not underestimate him again. This time he would end it.

Jeff did not move. He waited calmly as Paul launched his attack, almost as if he were giving up. An alarm flashed in the back of Paul's mind. Jeff was not the kind of man who would surrender if he could still fight. In the few seconds it took him to cross the room, he strained his senses for whatever Jeff was planning. Even so, for the third time that night, he was once again surprised. To his utter amazement, Jeff turned his back on Paul and released the catch on the window. With a harsh grunt, he threw it open. Paul saw that there were two ropes anchored outside the window, off to the right. Before he could reach his quarry, Jeff had grabbed one and wrapped it around his wrist. Then, with a glance back at Paul, he yanked the other one hard. His arm jerked, and then he was gone.

Paul stopped short. "What th. . . ." The half-uttered expletive forced itself out of his mouth. He had just seen his enemy disappear before him. One second he had been there, the next he had literally flown out of the window. With a last burst of effort, he made it to the window and leaned out.

Three stories down the deserted street glowed in the growing morning light. Nothing. Then, just as he twisted his body to look up, he heard a sudden creaking, as if a heavy weight was coming at him. Reflex took over, and he ducked back inside. He looked back just in time to see a pallet laden with broken concrete blocks and other junk go flashing past him. It was held by a rope that came into view immediately afterward.

"I don't believe it," muttered Paul out loud. Once again he leaned out, looking up. He was just in time to see Jeff reach the top of the building, clinging desperately to his makeshift elevator, and roll onto the roof and out of sight. A second later he heard the crash of the pallet on the pavement below as Jeff released his grip.

"Incredible!" he shook his head, half in anger, and half in grudging respect. Despite his determination not to do so, he had once again underestimated Jeff. Somewhere in the back of his mind, he resolved to sooner or later find out exactly who this man was.

He scanned his surroundings, noting the nearness of the neighboring buildings. He could see that once Jeff reached the top, he would have no trouble traveling from roof to roof, possibly as far as a city block. For all practical purposes, Paul had lost him. Fighting to control his emotions, he turned his attention back to the street. While it had seemed an eternity, his fight with Jeff had only lasted a few minutes. If he was lucky. . . .

Looking back toward the docks, he was just in time to see two figures turn a corner and disappear. Paul smiled slightly, knowing that at least he had a lead.

"There'll be another time, Jeff," he said, looking back up at the roof. "And next time, it will be on my turf." With that, he pulled himself back into the now useless office. He had no time to waste, but he knew he could not go far in his condition. Glancing around, he noted Jeff's cot, still rumpled from his last night's sleep. Limping over, he yanked the thin blanket off the top and grabbed the sheet underneath. Breathing heavily, he tore the sheet into long strips about four inches wide. When he had enough, he took off his jacket and shirt. Ignoring the cold from the open window, he proceeded to wrap his ribs tightly, tying off the end as neatly as he could. The strips of sheet constricted his movement and did not alleviate much of the pain, but at least they kept his ribs immobile. It would do until he could get to a hospital. Taking a last look around, he dressed and left.

Upon reaching the street, he turned and headed in the direction he had seen David and Susan going. Holding his battered middle, he set as brisk a pace as he could. He thought about trying to find Jeff, but discarded the idea. His foe could be anywhere by now, but Paul had a hunch he would be traveling in the same direction as the other two.

He hurried to the corner where he had seen them turn, but found no sign of them. Inwardly he cursed at his own slowness, but knew he had no choice but to keep going. Grimly, he set his pace. The morning light was growing, making more and more of the area visible. He forced himself to move just a little faster, fighting the fatigue that threatened to engulf him. Just as he was about to give up, he caught sight of his prey. They were about three blocks ahead.

Got you, he crowed silently. With a new-found energy, he moved even faster. He did not intend to catch them now. Rather, he would follow at a discreet distance. Sooner or later they would reach their destination. When they did, Paul would find a place to watch. He knew that Jeff would eventually show up, and when he did, Paul would act.

Carefully, trying to see in all directions at once, he closed the distance between him and the fugitives by about two blocks. He could see them clearly now. David had his arm firmly around Susan, guiding her to their destination. *The blind leading the blind,* thought Paul with no trace of humor. The figures before him spoke of untold weariness. Understandable, Paul knew, judging from their lives the past week or so.

Once again, Paul felt a trace of sympathy and respect for his former companions. He had been with Susan from the beginning of his now-botched plan. It was he who had rescued her from that dungeon of an institution. Even if his motives had been self-serving, he still found himself caring for her. He could not help but remember just how much they had been through together.

Perhaps it was the dull pain in his middle, or his uncharacteristic reminiscing. Whatever it was, it cost him. He never saw the blow coming. He had just passed an alley, still dark even in the growing sunlight. A heavy thud landed on his shoulders, just missing the back of his neck. Crying out in pain, he fell forward. His hands scrapped the sidewalk as he landed. Bright spots danced in front of his eyes, and the edge of his vision went black. Dimly, he could feel his ribs give way, his crude bandaging unable to protect him from the fall.

"Ya got him, Fish! Ya got him!" Fighting unconsciousness, Paul rolled over. Dimly, he could see four street youths standing over him. Three of them were black, the fourth white. All were dirty and wore ragged clothing. All looked as if their last meal was a distant memory, and all had murder dancing in their eyes. One of them, obviously called "Fish," was holding a nasty looking club.

One of his companions nudged him. "Watch it! He's still awake." Another took a hesitant step back.

"He's awful big too, Fish," squeaked the fourth in a high nasal voice.

"Chill!" growled Fish, and his friends shut up. Paul watched in pain as the gang leader leaned forward to check his victim.

That's it, pretty boy, thought Paul to himself, willing himself to ignore the pain. *Just a little closer. Come on, there's nothing to worry about. Just one step more and. . . .* Even in his injured and weakened state, Paul was still formidable. His heel lashed out, catching Fish square in the knee. Paul could feel the crunching of bone and gristle. Screaming, Fish dropped the club and staggered back. His companions, already nervous, looked like they were ready to bolt. Paul knew from experience that to show weakness now would be fatal. Steeling himself, he rolled over and got one leg under him. He started to push up, but, to his amazement, he found he lacked the strength. For the first time in his life, his body betrayed him. A wave of dizziness rushed over him, and he fell heavily back onto the pavement.

He could hear Fish yelling as he fell. "Help me up, fool! Look at him. He's dusted! Help me up!" As consciousness faded, Paul heard the shuffling as Fish and his gang moved to where he had fallen. Then the blows started. Some landed harmlessly on his back, but a few well-placed kicks hit face, neck — and the already damaged ribs. The pain was unbearable, and he could feel his mind shutting down.

Just before he went under, he thought he heard Fish shout a warning. "Look out, Jake! He's got a friend. Behind you! Behind you!" Suddenly, the blows ceased, and he was left gasping for breath. For just a moment, he dared hope that someone had come to his rescue. He was just about to force himself to roll over when a great, crushing weight fell onto his back. The wind was forced out of his lungs, and his ribs screamed in agony. He felt what was left of his consciousness slipping away. Strangely enough, his last thoughts were not angry, but rather sad. *Forget it, Sinclair,* they told him as the darkness became complete. *You had your chance, and blew it. Nobody cares. Why not just die and get it over with — at least that will stop the pain.* Then his mind submerged into a pool of utter blackness, and he knew no more.

* * *

David bolted out of the outer office. Only one thought was on his mind — get Susan and get out. Behind him two men fought, with the lives of David and Susan going to the victor. The very real possibility that Paul might win fueled his haste to get away. It was all he could do to maintain his balance as he stumbled down the stairs to where Susan was still resting. Desperately, he struggled to remember Jeff's hastily whispered instructions.

Squinting in the darkness, he reached the second floor. With the exception of the two he had just left, he and Susan were alone in the building. Inwardly he breathed a sigh of relief that Walter and his family had already left. He found the door to Susan's room and shoved it open.

The only light was from the glow of the space heater on the floor. In the far corner, he could see Susan's shapeless form, curled up against the wall. She was lying on a makeshift mattress made up of a few heavy blankets, and covered with an old fur coat. Jeff had explained that he rarely had to move a group as large as theirs.

A heavy thud sounded from upstairs, and David knew that his time was growing short. Jeff seemed quite capable, but he had a sinking feeling that Paul would be the one left standing. He had seen too much of what the big man was capable of.

"Susan? Susan!" He did not bother to whisper. There was no need for secrecy now. He knelt beside the sleeping form, and shook it urgently. "Susan, it's me, David. Come on, wake up! We've got to get out of here!" Another thump from upstairs punctuated his words.

There was a quiet groan as Susan stirred gently. David shook her again, this time harder. "Susan! Please, Susan, wake up! We're almost out of time!" Under his hands, he felt Susan's body go rigid. For a fleeting moment, he hated himself for what he was doing. During the entire trip, it had been all the little group could do to keep the poor woman from waking up screaming. Whatever had happened to her while she was being held at that place called Mentasys must have been horrible beyond words.

David braced himself, and shook her again. This time, Susan sat bolt upright. The fur coat fell away, and the blood-red light of the heater fell on her face. For just an instant, David was absolutely sure that he was in hell. Susan's face held a look of pure dread and terror. The red glow cast deep pools of blackness across her features, especially her eyes, giving him the impression that he was starring at a skull. *Surely,* he thought, *the damned look no worse than this.* As if to complete the illusion, Susan looked wildly around, as if trying to remember where she was. Then, taking a deep breath, she let loose with a scream that reeked of nothing but despair. David flinched at the hopelessness he heard, but knew he had to get control. Setting his jaw firmly, he reached out with both hands. Grabbing his friend's shoulders, he shook her roughly.

"Susan! It's me — David! Wake up!" Again Susan screamed, this time even louder. David continued to shake her, praying silently that she would come around. Once again she took a deep breath, ready to scream, but this time David's patience had run out. Releasing one shoulder, he clamped his hand over her mouth, pressing hard.

"STOP IT!" he shouted, pulling her close. He could feel every muscle in her body tighten at the closer contact. "Stop it, please." His voice softened just a little. "Susan, listen to me. We've got to get out of here. Everything has fallen apart, and we're in big trouble. Do you understand? We've got to go — now!" Precious seconds ticked by, as the two knelt in that corner. Then, gradually, Susan relaxed. David felt her weight slump against him.

"Are you there?" he asked softly, his cheek now pressed up against the side of her head. He could feel her start to tremble. Almost inaudibly he heard her mutter "yes" against his shoulder. "All right," he replied in the same tone. "Let's go." Together they rose, Susan still clinging to him for support. There was nothing to pack or gather. The only things they owned were the clothes they wore. There wasn't even any money. David had left his wallet with his cash and phony ID in his own room, and there was no time to retrieve it. They would be going out into the open with nothing. He hoped desperately that he could remember Jeff's instructions accurately. If not. . . . The thought trailed away as they made their way down to the ground floor and out the door.

The early morning cold hit them like a blow. David found himself being grateful for the simple fact that they had slept in their cloths and overcoats for warmth. They would not have survived long in this cold if they were forced to leave half dressed.

Getting his bearings, David put his arm around his companion and started off. He tried to set a fast pace, but Susan was not up to it. The best they could to was a slow, steady walk. Far too slowly, the building that had been their refuge receded behind them. To David, it seemed an endless nightmare. He had to resist the urge to bolt in panic. At any second he expected to feel Paul's killing hand grab his shoulder and spin him around.

Ahead, the end of the block grew closer. David searched for and found the street sign, and saw that it was the same one Jeff had named. It helped a little to know that, thus far at least, they were headed in the right direction. They had almost made it to the corner when he heard a faint "crash" behind him. It sounded as if something heavy had hit the sidewalk hard. He glanced back over his shoulder, toward their former hide out, but could see nothing. He could not help but wonder what was happening back there.

They made it to the corner without further incident. David replayed Jeff's instructions over and over again in his head. Stay on this street for four blocks, then turn left on Madison. Three more blocks, then a right. Look for an old brick office building. Jeff had said that it was one of the few inhabited structures left in the area. Once there, use John 10:1 for a recognition signal. David said a quick prayer of thanks for the Bibles the old man had given him. He had spent several hours since then reacquainting himself with that beloved book. Suddenly he felt a stab of regret when he realized that those same Bibles had been left behind in their haste to escape.

There were still no signs of pursuit, and David began to hope that they might actually get away. He took a deep breath, and began to relax a little. The adrenaline rush that had gotten him this far began to recede, and his body began to complain of the abuse he had put it through lately. Lack of sleep and food reminded him that he was in no shape to walk far, and Susan was even worse. He studied his companion closely as they walked.

"How are you doing?" he asked finally as they made their way toward Madison. He could feel her shivering against him, whether from cold or fear he could not tell.

"I'm okay," she replied faintly. She walked silently for a moment, then, "David, what about Paul, and Jeff? Did they get away?" Unconsciously, David frowned. He did not want to tell her about Paul — especially now. After all, no matter what his motives, the big man had effectively saved her life. Had she remained at that institution, she would, in all likelihood, be dead by now. On the other hand, what if she were to run into him again — without David or Jeff around? If she did not know about Paul's betrayal, he might deceive her in the future — assuming he got away from Jeff. What finally decided him was the fact that anything could happen in the next few hours. This might be the only chance they had to talk. Time was precious, and fleeting.

"Paul won't be coming, Susan." Carefully, as gently as he could, and leaving nothing out, he told of how he discovered Paul trying to break into Jeff's computer. He explained how he had almost been killed for barging in. Then he told her of the incident during the attack on the van, and of his and Walter's suspicions.

When he finished, she was silent for a moment. Then her shoulders began to shake, and two huge tears began to roll down her cheeks. "Then what he told me about Tim is probably a lie," she said, her voice a soft moan.

Silently David berated himself for a fool. He had forgotten that Paul had promised to reunite Susan with her husband. He tried to think of something to say, but no words came. He pulled her closer, trying to comfort her by touch alone. "I'm sorry," he muttered. "I'm, really, really sorry. I shouldn't have told you."

Again Susan was silent, her quiet grief almost more than David could bear. Then, once again she spoke. "You did the right thing," she said, and David looked at her in surprise. Her voice sounded stronger — more self-assured. She caught his look and smiled back, even though the tears continued to flow. "I think I knew all along that I wasn't going to see Tim again. I could feel it." She looked down at the sidewalk. "I knew in my heart that Tim was dead. I guess I just wanted so much to believe otherwise — and Paul knew so much about me. He was gentle and kind. Are you sure that he. . . ." She looked back up at David, the unasked question in her eyes.

Grimly David nodded. "I guess I should have said or done something before now," he said, angry at himself. "Walter knew about it, but we both felt it was best to wait. After all," he shrugged, "none of us was a match for him physically. What could we have done?" He looked at Susan carefully, searching her face. "Are you sure that you're all right?"

He was gratified when his companion gave him a faint but steady smile. "Strangely enough," she replied softly, taking a deep breath of the chill morning air, "I feel better now than I have in — oh, what seems like forever. I feel free. Does that make sense, David?" She looked questioningly at him. "I mean, I just realized that my husband is dead, and yet I feel free. That doesn't seem right."

"Yes, it does," David assured her. "For the past few weeks, you've been in limbo with your feelings, not sure of what was going to happen. Now you know. The grief will come — it already has — but at least now you're free to grieve." Susan only nodded, and they continued to walk.

They reached Madison, and turned in the proper direction. David glanced behind him, still looking for any signs of pursuit, but there was nothing. For just a moment, he thought he heard someone shouting, but whatever it was, it was not repeated.

Turning his eyes forward, he tried to take in all his surroundings at once. They were still in a rough part of town, but at least this street looked a little more inhabited. A few scattered businesses were already open. Smells of cooking food wafted out from a tiny hole-in-the-wall cafe across the street. He took a deep breath, his mouth watering. Now he regretted leaving without ID or money. On cue, his stomach started growling, loud enough for Susan to hear. She chuckled softly. David looked at her once more in surprise. It was the first time since he had met her that he had ever heard her laugh. She saw his look and smiled.

"They'll have food at the safe house, I'm sure," she said, her smile causing her eyes to dance. For the first time, David noticed that they were a striking aquamarine, literally sparkling in the morning light. All he could remember of her eyes before was that they were dull and lifeless. Silently he marveled at the resiliency the Creator had built into the human psyche. Here they were, abandoned and alone in New York, without money, or identification. Probably they were being chased, and could very easily be caught. Yet, this woman was suddenly better than she had been in weeks — probably months. As if to confirm his thoughts, Susan straightened her shoulders and began to walk with greater and greater strength. David let his arm drop away from her, discovering just then that it had become numb. As he rubbed it back to life, they continued their journey. Another block went by in silence, then once again Susan spoke.

"I don't remember much about it, you know." Her voice was quiet and thoughtful, as if she had just remembered something important. David felt himself go tense. "It" could only mean her ordeal. The fact that she was trying to talk about it was a major breakthrough. Of course, he knew, it *could* have come at a better time. Conversations like this should be held in friendly surroundings, like an office or living room, not escaping from a trained killer. Not only that, but it had been a long time since he had played the role of counselor. He was not sure if he had either the skill or the right to be listening to this.

He considered his reaction carefully as they continued to walk. If Susan was willing to talk, it could do wonders for her mental health. Not only that, he realized, but, with the way their lives had been lately, there might not be a better time. But was he the one to listen? Indecision warred within him briefly. Old failures and hurts shouted at him, reminding him of his unworthiness to help others. After all, he could not even help himself. Then, he took a deep breath, and with a brief, unspoken prayer of thankfulness, banished his accusing memories. This woman, his friend, needed to talk, and he was the only one available to listen. His Heavenly Father had led him to this point in time, and by everything that he hoped to be, he was not going to run again.

Smiling at his companion, he forced his voice to answer calmly. "Remember much about what?" he asked. His voice was steady, but his heart was pounding hard in his chest.

Susan was silent for a moment, then answered. "About what happened to me after my group was arrested. We were meeting in the cellar of a furniture store when they caught us."

David thought hard. "This would have been what, six, seven months ago?" he asked. Susan nodded. "Then 'they' would have been the Bureau of Religious Affairs," he said. "They were at their peak about then."

Again Susan nodded. "They told me that one of us had betrayed the whole group," she said, her voice trembling just a little. "I never believed it, but how could anyone know for sure?" David nodded, unwillingly remembering his own act of betrayal. *That* had cost him his church, his family . . . everything.

"Anyway," continued Susan, "they jammed us into a van and took us to their headquarters."

"All of you?" asked David. "What I mean is, did they keep you all together?" Susan nodded.

"For a while," she said. "We were all put in the same holding tank, where they kept us for almost 24 hours." She frowned, as if remembering something. "You know, now that I think about it, they didn't get all of us."

"Really?" David scanned the street, trying to be alert for any signs of pursuit.

"I don't think so," replied Susan. "There were two of us who had already left, and they weren't with the rest of us in that tank. Their names were, let me see. . . ." Her faced frowned in concentration, then lit up. "Sampson! That was it, Scott and Beth. It was their first time with us, and they left early. I wonder if they got away."

David jerked to a stop, grabbing Susan by the arm hard. His months spent as a custodian had been sheltered, but not that sheltered. "You mean you were in *that* raid?" he exclaimed in amazement. "The one in Cincinnati?" Susan nodded, the confusion evident in her face. David could only shake his head. "No wonder you were so important to Paul," he continued.

"What's that supposed to mean?" asked Susan, not understanding.

"Scott Sampson was the target of one of the biggest manhunts ever seen after that raid," explained David. "The news was all over the papers and television. He was blamed for the explosion of a passenger jet that was taking off from the Cincinnati airport. The bureau said he was a terrorist — a member of — what was it? — oh yeah, the Christian Liberation Front." Releasing Susan's arm, he gestured forward, and they started their journey again. As they walked, he told her the whole story.

"When everything came to light," he concluded, "it turned out that the Christian Liberation Front did not even exist. The bureau was behind the entire mess. Scott was cleared of terrorist activities, although he's still wanted for treason. That was when the bureau faded from the picture." He shook his head in sadness. "My group thought that things might get better then, but we were wrong. In fact, things got worse. Instead of being arrested, a lot of churches were murdered — killed while they were meeting. The police would arrive to find nothing but bodies."

Susan shuddered slightly. David noticed, and would have stopped, but Susan shook her head. "I'm all right, David. Go on."

"There's very little left to tell," said David. "Paul obviously got you out of that institution because of your connection with the raid on your church."

Susan thought about it, then once again shook her head. "That doesn't make sense," she said, the confusion evident in her voice. "I remember the Sampsons. We used to go to the same church, although they weren't involved in any serious way. They were pretty much wallflowers when it came to church work, although I got the impression that was mostly because of Scott. Why would Paul be interested in me because of that?"

"There's more," said David. "Rumors were flying after that raid. My contacts in the Shepherd's Path told me that their entire organization had been compromised — and that the computer network had been crashed. They even believed that the one person who had started the whole thing had been captured — as a direct result of your group's arrest." He forced a chuckle, then continued. "Get this. I heard that the Shepherd's Path was actually started by a 60-year-old former pastor's wife. She got together a bunch of old friends and formed the nucleus. Everything else grew out of that group."

Susan smiled, then raised her eyebrows. "Why should that be so hard to believe? Or do you think that an older woman is incapable of that kind of thing?"

Unexpectedly, David felt his cheeks blush with embarrassment. He had not realized that he was being patronizing. He started to apologize, then saw Susan's half-hidden smile and realized that he was being teased.

"Very funny," he grumped, then, unable to remain irked, smiled back.

Susan's half-smile became a full-fledged one. Then she looked away. "Tim and I were youth workers," she said softly, "Nothing more. We had heard of the Shepherd's Path, of course, but neither of us knew anybody actually in it. When our church closed down, Tim went to work for a grocery store. The bureau kept such close tabs on us that we could not have been involved even if we *had* known anyone. It was all we could do to meet with our cell group — and look what happened with that! Why would Paul. . . ." And abruptly Susan froze.

David took an extra step before he realized that he was walking alone. He looked back, and took a deep breath. Susan's face, already pale to begin with, had turned a milky white.

"Susan? Susan! What is it?" For a moment, he thought he had lost her again — that she had regressed to her previous, near catatonic state. He reached out to her, and was relieved when she looked up at him and met his gaze steadily.

"I know who he is," she whispered harshly. "I know him!"

"What?" For a moment, David was not sure who she was talking about. Then it hit him. "Paul?" he asked incredulously. "Do you mean Paul?!"

Susan nodded vigorously. "It was him," she said, her voice raspy. For some reason, she continued to whisper. "He was the one who led the raid on us."

David starred at her in disbelief. "Are you telling me that the man who has been with us since we left California is the same man who arrested you in Cincinnati? Are you sure?"

"I'm sure," replied Susan grimly. "I remember everything now. There were a lot of agents. Some were in uniform, some not. Paul was in charge of the whole thing. At least, he acted like he was — him and that sergeant." In halting phrases, Susan stammered out the entire story of her group's discovery and arrest. David felt his stomach knot up as he listened.

"Paul got us out of that cellar and into the vans," said Susan. "That was the last I saw of him. From there, they took us to bureau headquarters, like I said."

"So Paul is a bureau agent," said David, almost to himself. Abruptly, he scanned the street, looking somewhat belatedly for any signs of pursuit. Susan's story and sudden revelation had kept his attention riveted on her. His thoughts went briefly back to Jeff, wondering what had happened in that fight. There was still no indication that they were being followed, but if Paul had managed to take out Jeff, the big man could be anywhere.

Turning his attention back to Susan, he was relieved to see that some color had returned to her face, although he did not like the sound of her harsh breathing. She noticed his scrutiny, and forced a smile. "I'm okay," she said, answering his unasked question. "Just tired." Linking her arm with his, she resumed walking, although now she was forced to go even slower than before.

"Do you remember what happened after you were held at their headquarters?" asked David. Despite her weakness, he wanted to keep her talking. The more she remembered now, the better off she would be.

"Only the flight out to California," she replied, shaking her head. "At least, that's where I think we were taken. That's where Paul found me, anyway. None of us were told where we were going. Tim and I were together on the plane." Abruptly she stopped, and the tears started again. Unconsciously, David moved closer and once more put his arm around her. This time, Susan leaned in to him, taking comfort from the physical contact.

"You don't have to go on," said David quietly. Although he knew it would be good for her, he did not want to force anything.

For a moment, Susan was silent, then she spoke again. "We landed, and they marched us off the plane. It wasn't a passenger jet, by the way, but a smaller private one. That was the last time we were together as a group

. . . and that was the last time I saw Tim. They had a couple of vans waiting for us, and Tim and I were forced apart. We were stuffed inside — there were no seats — and driven for what seemed like hours. I guess they took us to a hospital. At least, that's what it seemed like. They put the women into one ward, and I guess the men into another."

She stopped a moment, as if forcing herself to remember, then continued. "That's pretty much it, I guess. After that, they took our clothes and gave us hospital gowns. Some doctor examined us, then they put us each into a bed with some kind of gismo attached to it. A nurse stuck some wires to my head . . . and that's all I remember." Susan fell silent. They walked now in silence. David thought his friend had finished, but was once more surprised.

"The next thing I really remember is being in that basement with all of you," she said, her smile returning somewhat. "There were a bunch of hands on me, and Walter was praying. I felt like I was coming up out of deep water."

"You don't remember anything in between?" asked David gently.

Susan shook her head. "Not really. Just this sensation of smothering . . . like trying to take a breath, but not being able to. It . . . it was terrible. Like a black nothing. Then I woke up, and you and your group were there."

David thought back to that meeting. He remembered Walter's powerful prayer, and the faint smile he had seen on Susan's face. Clearly God had begun a healing then that was even now continuing. Where it would lead, he could not imagine.

Although it seemed like centuries, they made it to the next street within a few minutes. Turning in the proper direction, David began to search for a building that matched Jeff's description. They had only traveled a few hundred feet before he found it. It was just as Jeff had told him — an aging brick structure that housed some sort of merchant shipping business. A set of 10 steps led up to the double front doors. The buildings around it were mostly deserted, although a few across the street still displayed "open" signs. He paused a moment, reciting the proper recognition verses in his head, then started forward. He had only gone a few steps when, once again, he realized that he had left Susan behind. He turned to see her gazing at the building with a look that could only be described as fascination.

"What is it?" he asked as he moved back to her. He was uncomfortably aware that the sun was now fully up, and they were quite visible. He wanted to get inside.

"I don't know," replied Susan, shaking her head. "Just memories, I guess." She smiled tentatively, as if still not sure how to. "This is just so much like the time before, when Tim and I were arrested." She glanced around at her surroundings. "The city is different, but it still feels the same. Abandoned buildings, deserted streets — it's almost scary."

Her last remark forced a chuckle from David. "Almost?" he asked. "I've been scared silly since before we began this whole thing."

Susan continued to look around her. "What I mean is, it's so familiar," she said. "It was a lot like this back in Covington." David looked at her in confusion.

"Covington is the city across the Ohio River from Cincinnati," she clarified. "It's not as big, and parts of it are really run down — a lot like this place. That's where we held our meetings."

"Oh," replied David, not sure of what to say.

Susan shook her head as if to clear it, then gestured him forward. "It's just me," she said, almost as if trying to convince herself. "Come on, let's get inside." With that, she marched up to the closed double doors and knocked. David had little choice but to follow. Running the verses through his head once more, he stepped up beside Susan, praying desperately that they had come to the right place.

* * *

Jeff rolled over onto the roof of his former refuge, gasping for breath. He held on to the rope as long as he could, but the pallet was too heavy and his strength was rapidly fading. Before he could tie it off, it wrenched itself out of his hand, leaving angry burn marks in his palm. There was a muted crash as it fell the rest of the way to the pavement below. Scrambling to the edge of the roof, he looked down. The concrete blocks had scattered themselves everywhere, but he was relieved to see that no one had been near the pallet when it hit the sidewalk.

Doing his best to ignore the pain from both his hand and his knee, he peered through the morning dimness, trying to see up the street. After a moment, he was able to discern two fugitive figures slowly making their way toward the intersection. As he watched, they turned the corner and disappeared from sight. He rolled over onto his back, gasping for breath. Above him, the gray sky gradually grew lighter.

"Mom," he said to the general area, "you were right. I *should* have been a dentist." Actually, he knew, that was not quite true. His mother had approved of the career choice he had made with the FBI. She was never sure, however, about what she thought was his over emphasis on his faith. His two older brothers had agreed with her. Both had teased him mercilessly about it. She had died 10 years ago, her body ravaged by cancer. Robert, his oldest brother, had told him at the funeral that before the end she had spent a great deal of time with her Bible. Perhaps she had given her life to Christ. He would never know, at least not until he stood at Heaven's gate himself.

Shaking himself out of his memories, he struggled to sit up. Right now, he knew, Paul Sinclair had two choices. He could chase him, or take off after David and Susan. If Jeff had been in his shoes, he would be heading for the roof. David and Susan were merely fleeing refugees, with as much knowledge of the Shepherd's Path as Paul had. Jeff, on the other hand, was inside the organization. It made him a more valuable capture. That meant he had to get going.

He sat up, and groaned at the flash of pain in his right leg. Gingerly he felt his knee, probing carefully. The joint was already swollen considerably, but at least nothing appeared to be broken. He considered himself lucky to have come away from his fight with so little damage. The big man was *fast*.

Placing his weight on his left leg, he struggled upright. He had planned an escape route months ago, in case of the very real possibility that he would be discovered. The only problem was, that escape assumed that he would be healthy. Now, he was not too sure he could follow it. Hobbling to the side of the building, he looked down into the narrow alley between the buildings. Leaning over the three-foot-high ledge that ran along the edge of the roof, he could just barely see the street peeking out between the walls. Before him was a four-foot gap to the next roof top, and the first leg of his escape route. Normally, that would be an easy jump. Now, it looked as if it was a thousand feet away. There was no choice, he knew. The gap on the other side was even wider, and he could not face Paul in his current condition.

He had just psyched himself to jump, balancing himself on the ledge and putting all the pressure on his one good leg, when a flash of movement below him caught his peripheral vision. By the time he looked down, it was gone. He debated for a moment, then got down off the ledge and limped over to the front of the building. Looking in the direction that David and Susan had taken, he immediately saw Paul. His rival was heading the same way. Probably, Jeff knew, Paul had caught a glimpse of the two at the same time he had. Evidently, Paul had decided to go for a sure thing, rather than risk losing Jeff in the maze of roof tops above.

"Great!" growled Jeff in frustration. "Just great. You idiot! You were supposed to come after me!" He stared after Paul, wondering if he could head him off somewhere. With grim satisfaction, he noted how the big man was holding his rib cage and moving much slower than he had in their fight. Jeff knew his kick had connected, but obviously he had done more damage than he realized.

"Okay, Sinclair," he growled at the retreating figure, "let's see if I can catch you." He thought for a moment, then added ruefully, "Although if I can, I have no idea what I'm going to *do* with you." With that he limped back toward the ledge.

He was almost there when he remembered one very important detail. It brought him up short. His injury, he knew, must be affecting his judgment, for he had almost made a fatal error. Turning away from the ledge, he hobbled over to what looked like an air vent. The top was spinning lazily in the cold morning breeze, just like the three identical others that dotted the rooftop in the form of a rough square.

Face drawn in a mask of pain, he pushed at the vent experimentally. Then, realizing that time was precious and there were no points for neatness, he shoved hard. The vent toppled, revealing a mass of electronics topped by an odd-looking, cone-shaped apparatus. It was small — only two feet long and under six inches wide at the base. It was pointed up, at about a 75 degree angle. Here was his precious communication uplink. It was an experimental model, not on the market yet. His business contact had explained that it was a discarded prototype — crude but usable. It only accessed one satellite, which made it impractical for the average business. Since there were no more home-owned uplinks, thanks to the government crackdown a few years back, there was no market for this model. To Jeff, though, it was worth its weight in gold. He could not access the public computer networks in any other way, and the uplink enabled him to maintain contact with the Shepherd's Path. Now, he would have to destroy it.

It only took seconds to destroy what it had originally taken weeks of painstaking work for him to build. Unwillingly, he remembered another time not so long ago that he had been forced to destroy the communications of the Shepherd's Path. Things were not as desperate this time, at least. He was only eliminating one station — his own — but it still hurt.

Realizing that he was wasting precious time, he set his jaw firmly. Then he grasped the cone and yanked. It came away easily, just as he knew it would. Carefully but quickly he made sure that he had left nothing behind that could be traced. The unit was totally self-contained, and the only evidence that there was anything there was a short segment of cable protruding from the roof.

His task complete, he turned his attention back to his main problem — Paul Sinclair. He limped back to the ledge, carrying the uplink cone. The pain in his knee was a constant reminder that he did not have much time before his strength gave out. He had to move fast. With a mighty heave, he flung the cone across the narrow divide. It landed hard on the roof next door. Jeff could hear pieces of it bouncing everywhere. Checking to make sure that no one was below, he turned his attention to getting himself across.

Balancing on top of the ledge, he set his focus on his target. "Just a simple jump, Anderson," he told himself over and over. "You can do it in your sleep." He took a deep breath, then launched himself across the abyss. Desperately, he stretched his arms out, grabbing for the opposing ledge. He almost made it. He landed chest high against the low wall, the impact knocking the breath out of him. His wounded knee smacked against the brick, sending waves of pain coursing through his already battered body. Desperately he held on, waiting for the pain to recede. His fingers held a death grip on the crumbling masonry, and he could feel it giving away under them. Bits and pieces ground their way into the rope burn on his right hand.

He dangled like that for an eternity, his legs swinging back and forth in the emptiness below him. His breathing was shallow and rapid, and his pulse thundered in his ears. Every movement caused red pain to flare inside his injured knee. Finally, when it seemed that he could no longer hold on, he drew on some deep reserve of strength and swung his legs hard to his left. Once — twice — and then, just when he knew he was going to fall, he was able to hook his foot over the ledge, and gradually heave himself over. He rolled off the ledge and fell the three feet to the asphalt roof. The pain in his leg was so intense that he did not even notice the impact. He lay there, panting, fighting the darkness that threatened to close in on all sides. Sweat dotted his dark skin, despite the cold, giving it a clammy feel. Abruptly he shivered. The long night and his battle with Paul teamed up against him. It seemed a lifetime since he had sent Walter and his family on their way. All he wanted at that moment was to rest — to sleep for a few years — but he knew that was not possible. Two people who trusted him were in trouble, and he had to get to them before Paul did.

Gritting his teeth against the nausea, he rolled over and got his legs under him. He found the cone just a few feet away. It was still basically intact. The only things that had come loose were untraceable wires and screws. He picked it up, and once again was off, limping as fast as he could. There was a stairwell covered with a skylight on the other side of the roof that would get him inside and down to the street. Some time ago he had replaced the aging padlock with a combination lock of his own. It took only seconds to open it and climb down into the deserted building. The growing light revealed an empty office space much the same as the one he had just left. Only his own days-old tracks in the thick dust on the floor revealed any sign of life.

He could feel himself tiring, and knew that he could not go on much longer. He made his way into the adjoining hallway, and from there into another deserted room. The rotting hardwood floor creaked under him as he hobbled over to the wall facing back toward his own former headquarters. He knelt over, and a wave of nausea hit him. Gasping for breath, he dropped the cone, his stomach heaving. He had not eaten in over 12 hours, so the only thing that came up was a mouthful of phlegm. Even so, he felt surprisingly better.

The nausea subsided, allowing him to think more clearly. His fingers found a barely discernible seam in the floor. Getting his fingernails under it, he pulled. The three-foot by two-foot section of the floor came up easily, revealing a foot-deep compartment underneath. Just two days ago, it had held a dozen Bibles. He had moved those along the network, however. Now there were only four — those delivered by David Eddington. He paused a moment, debating, then moved them over to one corner and carefully set the cone down next to them. It was tight, but he managed to get it in. If things settled down enough, he would come back for everything. If not, at least both Bibles and cone should escape notice here. He replaced the section of floor, making sure that it fit snugly over the compartment, then left the room.

Quickly, he made his way to the ground level. The front office was alight with the new day. Two large windows, both broken, framed the single door that led out onto the street. Cautiously, he peered out of one of the broken windows, searching for any sign of trouble. He knew he had to move fast. Despite the injuries Jeff had inflicted on him, Paul was sure to catch up with David and Susan.

His caution was well-founded. Just as he was about to step out onto the street, two dark sedans roared up from the opposite direction, squealing to a stop in front of his now abandoned headquarters.

"NO!" he whispered harshly, and threw himself back away from the door. In doing so, he put too much weight on his injured knee and fell backwards. The impact knocked the wind out of him, and he lay there gasping for breath. Heart pounding, he waited for whoever was there to investigate the sounds they surely must have heard.

Seconds crawled by, but no one came. Hardly daring to breath, Jeff rolled over and sat up. Moving carefully, he crawled over to the window. With an agonizing slowness, he lifted his head a few inches above the sill and peered out. The cars were still there, along with two quite tough looking, sturdily built men. Both were dressed casually in jeans and heavy overcoats. Jeff knew at once that they did not belong to any law enforcement agency in existence. Years of experience enabled him to read their mannerisms clearly. The way they stood, the way they looked, the way they felt, all said "death." Jeff had no doubt that he was looking at hired killers. He also knew that if he were discovered, his life span would be measured in minutes.

As he watched them, his thoughts flashed to the number of believers found murdered while holding meetings over the last few months. Although he could not prove it, he knew that there was a highly organized attempt to wipe out Christianity all together. His recent experience with

Jacob Hill and the Mentasys affair told him as much. Hill had been one of the most powerful men in the world. He was mainly responsible for the current plight of Christianity in the United States. Moving behind the scenes, he had manipulated the government into outlawing any organized religion that was not formerly condoned by the State. On his one face-to-face meeting with him, Jeff had become convinced of one thing. Jacob Hill had a master. As strong as he was, he answered to a higher power, and it was that power — perhaps one person, perhaps a group of people — that literally ran both this country and the rest of the world. Whoever they were, they moved in secret, content to let their pawns have the limelight while they stayed in the shadows. The more he studied the men before him, the more certain he was that they were representing that power. Abruptly, one of the thugs glanced in his direction, and he hastily withdrew, hunkering down beneath the window.

"Stupid!" he hissed silently under his breath. "Why not just walk up and introduce yourself? HI! I'm Jeff Anderson, and you want to kill me! Have a nice day! — Idiot!" How could he let his mind wander during such a dangerous moment? His injuries, he realized, must be affecting his judgment. They could have easily seen him if he had been just a touch slower. If he had been healthy, and more on his toes, he might have remained there, to discover as much as he could about this new threat. This time they would have to wait. He had to catch up with David and Susan before Paul did.

Using his one good leg, he slowly pushed himself away from the window, toward the back of the building. Experience had taught him to have more than one escape route handy. The street was closed to him, but there was an alley in the back. It paralleled the street for a while, then ended in what could be laughingly called a hotel. At least, it was inhabited. From there, a short cut through a broken chain link fence allowed him to cut diagonally through to the adjoining street. If he hurried, he might just get to it before Paul did.

Scrambling silently on all fours, he made it out of the front office. The pain in his injured knee had subsided to a dull throb, beating in time with his heart. It took every ounce of willpower he possessed to get to his feet. Unbidden, thoughts of his FBI days flashed into his conscious mind. His own office, assistants to do his bidding, the freedom to move where and when he wanted to. Angrily he shook those thoughts away. His old career — indeed his old life — was long gone. It had disappeared when he made the decision to place his allegiance in his Saviour rather than his government. Thinking about the "good old days" now would only get him into deeper trouble.

"Father," he prayed silently as he hobbled to the back of the building and into the alley, "there are two of Your children who need me. Please let me get to them before Paul does." With that, he set his face into a determined glare and started off.

The next several minutes were a dull cadence of pain that later his mind would mercifully blot out. Sheer courage, God-given strength, and just plain stubbornness kept him going. His mind was set on only one goal — to reach David and Susan before Paul did. That became the reason for his entire existence. The rest of the world faded into a dull grayish haze as he forced himself onward. Somewhere in the back of his mind, a voice was screaming at him, warning him that he was doing irreparable damage to his knee. He ignored it, and kept going. Every now and then, he would think to glance behind him, searching for signs of pursuit.

He made it to the hotel and found the break in the fence without incident. He had just forced himself through the too-small opening when he stopped short. He had emerged into another alley that was the mirror image of the one he had just traversed. About 20 yards ahead, it emptied out into the street that ran perpendicular to the one his headquarters had been on. Just before the entrance to the street, a deadly scene played itself out before him.

It took him a moment for the individual images to make sense to his blurred thinking. He forced his tired mind to concentrate, and finally the shapes before him made sense. Four street youths were surrounding a fallen figure. Squinting against the light from the street, Jeff could see that the man on the ground was undoubtedly Paul Sinclair. As he watched, Paul rolled over, gasping in what was obviously a great deal of pain. What had happened was obvious, Jeff realized. Paul had been ambushed. These roughs had caught him when he wasn't looking.

Abruptly, a great weight seemed to lift off of Jeff's shoulders. David and Susan were safe! At least, he amended mentally, they were safe from Paul. If David followed Jeff's instructions, they would have made it to the safe house by now. All Jeff had to worry about now was getting there himself. Paul was effectively out of the picture.

He took a deep breath and slumped against the rickety fence, careful not to draw any unwanted attention to himself. There was no thought of intervening in the struggle before him — not in his condition. Besides, Jeff told himself — the man was his enemy. Paul would have killed him if he could have. Jeff was certain of it. Even if he were in top condition, Jeff doubted that he would try to save him. The former bureau agent was simply too dangerous. Better that it end here and now.

As he watched, Paul rolled over while one of the youths moved to stand next to him. Suddenly, like lightning, Paul struck. His leg lashed out, connecting solidly with the youth's knee. Even from where he was, Jeff could hear the snap of breaking bones. He shook his head in amazement and grudging admiration. Paul was truly formidable. Even injured, he could still take care of himself. As the youth fell back, Paul started to get to his feet, and, to Jeff's surprise, fell back. His face was a mask of pain, and his right arm held his damaged ribs.

That was all the encouragement his assailants needed. Like a pack of wolves, they were on him. They began to kick and beat him. All Paul could do was roll over and try to shield himself from the blows. Jeff knew that the gang was out for blood. They would not stop until Paul was dead.

"Nothing I can do," he whispered to himself. "At my best I couldn't take on four of them." With that, he turned to go. He started to squeeze through the fence, but stopped. Almost against his will, he looked back. Paul was not moving now. He was making no effort to avoid the blows that pummeled him. Jeff found that he could not take his eyes off of the fallen man. Just minutes ago, Paul had tried to kill him. Given the chance, he would have wrecked everything that Jeff had worked so hard to build. Now he was only getting what he deserved. It would be one less problem for Jeff. And yet. . . .

Reluctantly his thoughts went back to his first meeting with Stephen Lynch. Lynch had been a fiery, angry man with a fanatical hatred for Christianity. They had met when he had arrested Jeff. Then, when Jeff had shown him evidence of bureau involvement in the bombing of a passenger flight, he had turned that anger onto his former masters. If Jeff were to define the term "unreachable," Stephen Lynch would have been that definition. He wanted nothing to do with Christians or their Saviour. That was just a few months ago. Now, today, he was helping those same believers. Stephen Lynch had come face to face with the simple fact that he had been wrong. If that could happen to Stephen, what right did Jeff have to walk away from Paul? The man was down, and he was going to die unless Jeff did something.

The same anger and frustration that he had felt during his fight with Paul reared its head again. "Not fair!" he cried aloud, not caring now if the others heard him. "You can't ask me to do this, Lord! You can't! He's hurt us! He'll do it again!" His own voice sounded foreign in his ears. Even as he spoke these words to his Heavenly Father, he knew he was wrong. God could indeed ask this of him. Jeff watched the youths beat Paul some more, then raised his eyes to the sky.

"You know, Lord," he said half in anger, half in humor, "You expect an awful lot from us . . . an awful lot!" Once again, Jeff heard his own voice and knew he was yet again wrong. His Lord did not expect a "lot" from him . . . He expected everything. Total surrender and obedience. He had told His followers to "love your enemies" — to do good to those who persecute you.

Those were not idle words, Jeff now realized. It could mean putting your life on the line for those same enemies — loving them more than your own life . . . just as Christ himself had loved all of humanity more than His own life. Paul was his enemy, but that did not alleviate Jeff of the responsibility of trying to save him. A small shudder wormed its way through Jeff's body, and the pain from his knee reminded him that he was in no shape to take on a gang of street youths.

"Never mind," he said to himself. His time was running out. His own inner battle had lasted only seconds, but Paul had only seconds left. "All right, Lord," he said grimly, "You want me to do this, then You're going to have to help."

Glancing around, he noticed one of the pipes that supported the chain link fence was loose. Gritting his teeth, he reached down and grabbed it. "Uhhh!" Straining, he yanked hard at the pipe. It resisted for a moment, then came free in his hands. It was just over four feet long, and about two inches wide. It would do.

"All right," said Jeff, shaking his head, "let's get it done." He started to limp toward the fight, and found that his knee did not hurt as much as it did before. Gaining strength and confidence, he began to trot. He raised the pipe over his head, trying to look as mean as he could. The alley seemed to go by much faster than it should have, and it took him a moment to realize that, against all reason, he was running. So intent were the youths on Paul that they did not notice Jeff until he was almost upon them. He was only 20 feet away when one of them looked up. The sight of a large, crazy-looking black man swinging a deadly-looking pipe was definitely enough to catch his full attention.

Jeff heard him exclaim, "Look out! He's got a friend!" Then he was there. A shout of pure anger burst from his throat. The gang was caught flat-footed. With his newfound strength, Jeff shouldered one of them, the single white one, aside. As that youth turned to run Jeff swung his pipe. His original target was the head, but even in his rage he knew that he could not kill. The pipe changed its trajectory and landed solidly on the young man's backside.

"Owww," cried the youth, and took off, leaving his comrades to face Jeff alone. They were three to his one. The leader, who was being supported by one of the others, was looking at Jeff with dumbstruck amazement.

"What th. . . ." was all he had time to cry out before Jeff turned to face him. Ambushing helpless pedestrians was one thing. Going head to head with a crazed, pipe-bearing giant was another. Jeff took a step forward, on his good leg fortunately, and stopped. He pointed with his pipe. "Get out," he said flatly.

The leader's eyes widened, and the fear he felt was painted broadly across his face. He did not have to be told twice. The remaining two youths scooped him up and took off after their fleeing friend. Jeff watched him go, then turned his attention to Paul. Just as suddenly as it came, the amazing strength that had allowed him to bluff the gang left him. His head spun, and he felt the world turning black. He stumbled toward Paul. He tried to kneel next to him and ascertain whether or not he was still alive, but he had nothing left to give. Abruptly, a switch was thrown in his exhausted mind, and everything went dark. He fell, sprawling across the body of the enemy he had tried to save.

8

Wolf rampaged through the just-abandoned building, looking for someone to hurt. Despite his initial excitement at the satellite's surveillance report, he had come up empty.

There was plenty of evidence that he had come to the right place. A couple of rooms set aside for sleeping, and the windows blocked off by heavy, black plastic, told him that this place was once used to hide fleeing Christians. Expanding his search to include the upper floors, he discovered the ruined computer terminal — proof that this was not just another safe house. This terminal was different. It only took a brief examination of the hardware to prove that this setup had a satellite uplink. Here then, was the source of the satellite communication that Surveillance 7 had traced. Unfortunately, "had" was the operative word here, he realized. The dead computer had processed its last byte. Feeling the familiar rage rise inside of his gullet, he toed through the wreckage.

"Get up on the roof," he growled at Demos, who was standing next to the door leading out into the hall. "See if you can find the uplink dish. It's probably hidden or disguised, so look hard. If it's a newer one, it may only be a half a meter or less in diameter. Maybe whoever was stupid enough to let this guy use it was stupid enough to leave a manufacturer's name on it." Demos nodded and left without a word.

Wolf continued to rummage through the wreckage, knowing that he had found all there was to find. Abruptly, the rage that had become his trademark burst its way through his self-control. He picked up the ruined monitor and flung it against the wall. The resounding crash had barely subsided when the man he had left watching the first floor came rushing up. He stopped short in the doorway, his eyes darting between Wolf and the now shattered monitor.

"Trouble?" he asked finally.

"Yeah," snarled Wolf, not looking at him. "For them — when we find them. Now get out." The man — Wolf did not know his name — left without another word. Demos had hired him, and Wolf did not trust him.

Willing himself to a calmer state, he forced his attention to the rest of the room. A brief examination showed him nothing. He prowled over to the open window and looked down. He could see the last two men in his team waiting patiently by the cars. Directly below him was wreckage of another kind — broken bricks, bits of concrete, and an assortment of other makeshift weights. To Wolf's way of thinking, it looked as if it were some sort of defense mechanism that had not worked.

Cursing at the lack of clues as to the identity and whereabouts of the former occupant, he turned towards the door, only to see Demos returning. One look at the other man's face told him that he had had no better results. Without saying a word, Demos showed him a two-foot section of television cable, holding it as if it were the $10 consolation prize in a billion dollar lottery.

"This was running out of the roof," he said flatly, "where an air vent used to be. Nothing else." He indicated the frayed ends. "Whatever was on this end has been ripped out — and fairly recently, as far as I can tell."

"Of course it's been fairly recently, you idiot," snapped Wolf. He noted the way Demos stiffened, but continued. "We got the word on an unauthorized transmission just a few hours ago. That means it's been ripped out since then, and the ones who did it are still in the area."

"We should have used a chopper," said Demos, accusation coloring his voice. Every muscle in Wolf's body tensed, as if he were a cat getting ready to pounce on an unwary canary.

"Brilliant," he snapped. "Tell me, genius, where would we land it? Every building in this area is falling apart, and the streets are too narrow!" His eyes snapped in anger. "How about a useful suggestion for a change?" The two men glared across the room, both wanting a piece of the other. After long seconds passed, Demos let his shoulders relax, a sign that he was backing off.

"Satellite surveillance might still . . ." he began.

"Forget it," snapped Wolf. He turned his back on Demos, now sure that the mercenary would not attack. "Look at this place. Even with infrared and virtual imaging, there are too many ways to hide. Besides, once they get out of the immediate area, they start getting into more inhabited sections." He slapped his palm against his thigh in frustration. "Surveillance is good, but not good enough to tell one person from another — at least not yet. It has to *know* who to lock on to before it can follow them."

He thought for a moment. "Get the locals on the line," he said finally. "Use the command code Smythe gave us — that'll get their attention. Tell them that we need a door-to-door search of this area — at least a 10-mile radius from this point — and we needed it an hour ago."

"That'll take a lot of manpower," answered Demos, shaking his head. "They aren't going to like that — especially with all of the gang trouble they're having." Wolf glared at Demos, who raised his hands in a gesture of compliance. "I'll call them," he said, then turned and left without further comment. Wolf stared at his erstwhile ally for a moment. He knew that Demos was a volatile, dangerous mercenary. One day, he might just push him too far. He snorted at the thought. Demos might be a trained killer, but Wolf could handle him — not directly, of course. The mercenary was both larger and stronger than he was. Still, there were ways. Let the older man try anything, and he would end up very dead.

There was nothing left for him here, but still he lingered. Finally, on impulse, he reached down, sifted through the computer debris, and pulled out the hard drive. There was little or no chance of getting anything off of it, he knew. Whoever had trashed it had done a thorough job. He could see the damage with his naked eye. Still, there was always a chance. Slipping the compact drive into his coat pocket, he left the room and headed down to his waiting cohorts. A single nod told them that they were done here.

"The locals are on the way," said Demos from the rider's seat of the car they had come in together.

"Fine," said Wolf shortly. He opened his door and slid behind the wheel. "How much did you tell them?"

"Just what they needed to know, of course," replied Demos, the contempt in his voice barely concealed. He tapped a panel on the dashboard. "I also faxed them a picture of Sinclair. Told them to be looking for him." Wolf nodded and started the car.

"Think we'll find them?" asked Demos. Wolf started to ignore the question, then he noticed the look in Demos' eyes. Abruptly he realized that he was dangerously close to pushing his reluctant ally to far. Their brief confrontation a few minutes ago said as much. Knowing he still needed him, he decided to ease off — just a bit.

"We'll find them," he answered, his voice now level and controlled. "Sinclair, at least. He'll have to surface sooner or later — even if his asinine plan is a complete bust."

"He could disappear, like the rest," remarked Demos. "Maybe he's gone over to their side." Wolf shook his head negatively.

"Not a chance," he replied, his tone flat with assurance. "He wants what he had back too much for that. Besides, I know all about him. He hates these people almost as much as I do." He paused a moment, then, "No, he'll show up . . . and when he does, we learn what he knows, then take him out — and whoever else is with him."

Demos nodded. Sensing Wolf's change of mood, he leaned back in his seat and relaxed a bit. "So why *do* you hate these people as much as he does?" he asked, obviously trying to ease the remaining tension.

Wolf ground his teeth at Demos' presumption in asking such a personal question. "None of your business," he snapped back. The familiar rage once again building inside of him, he started the car, put it in gear, and floored the accelerator. Tires squealing in protest, the car lurched away. Wolf remained silent during the ride back to the luxury hotel in the center of downtown New York that was their temporary headquarters. Even if he had been inclined to answer, how could he even begin to explain the anger and hatred that dominated his entire being? How could he tell Demos that it did not matter who he hated? Lawbreaking Christians were simply a convenient target. His hatred had to have a focus, and they provided it.

For just a moment, his thoughts flashed back to that Iraqi desert. He could see the half-starved soldier just over the top of his gun barrel, and hear the jeers of his mates egging him on. He could feel himself squeeze the trigger, and sense the jolt as it fired . . . and he could see the face of the unfortunate soldier disintegrate in front of him. He remembered the disbelief at what he had done. There had been a rush of exhilaration, but also of shame. A very important part of him had died that day, and another part had been born. Any feelings of compassion or love were murdered along with that unfortunate soldier. The rage and hatred were all he had left.

Of course, he knew, he would never tell Demos — or anyone else for that matter. It was his and his alone. Demos had no business asking in the first place.

What Wolf did not realize was that he could not have shared it even if he *had* wanted to. His hatred needed a focus because he refused to let it recognize its true target — a target so close that he would never see it. Deep in his scarred soul, Wolf hated only one thing, one being — himself.

Flinging his thoughts away, he forced himself to concentrate on his next step — how to find Sinclair. Sooner or later he would have him. He need only be patient. Wolf allowed himself a small, predator's smile, and felt his rage settle into a cold burn. He had work to do.

* * *

Paul surveyed his meadow, and saw that all was right with his world. The little brook that bisected it was sparkling with cool, clean water. The grass was bright green, with just the right touch of softness to it. The sky was a deep, vibrant blue, and the air smelled deliciously of spring. Everything was where it should be, just as he had visualized it so many times before.

Indeed, it had never seemed as real as it did now. Were the colors of grass and sky brighter? Did everything feel more vivid than ever before? Was it his imagination, or could he see, for the first time, beyond the meadow. Surely those were mountains far away, blurred to a purple hue by the distance! Paul inhaled deeply, savoring the sensation. The Yogi Shaw would be proud indeed if he could share this experience!

Turning, Paul could see the low slope of the hill leading up to his special tree. A path that he had never noticed before wound its way up the hill, running within a few feet of the tree. It was lined neatly with small white stones. Paul shook his head, marveling at the detail.

Sensing the excitement build within him, he stepped onto the path and started up. Somehow, he could sense a very powerful presence waiting there for him.

"I'm coming, master," called Paul. He was unsure if he spoke aloud or in his mind. Not that it mattered. Here, in the refuge of his self-created world, word and thought were one and the same. Eagerly he climbed the hill, drawing near to the tree. His master was waiting.

Suddenly, he was jolted by his own thoughts. His master? He had called no man "master" since the time he had spent with the Yogi Shaw. Had not the Yogi taught him that he was his own master? Did not true enlightenment come from within? He was the captain of his fate — the pilot of his soul. He was owned by no man. And yet. . . .

Paul slowed his pace, suddenly unsure of himself. Still, he found that he could not stop completely. He was drawn on as if by an invisible wire. Unexpectedly, a wave of fear washed over him. The bright reality of his meadow flickered, as if it were a fragile candle blown by a stiff breeze. Try as he might, he could not turn away from that tree — a tree that now seemed old and rotting with age.

What was going on? This was the domain of his mind, and he was the absolute ruler. No man controlled him. With every ounce of willpower, he forced himself to halt. He did it — barely. It took everything he had, and it would not be enough. He could feel the pull of what felt like an invisible chain intensify. The more he resisted, the harder it tugged.

"NO!" he shouted. His perceptions changed. Suddenly his beautiful meadow seemed a prison. The colors faded to pale pastels, and the mountains disappeared altogether. His fear was replaced with a growing terror. No, it wasn't terror, but dread. The kind of dread that one experiences when a locked window is found opened, or the sudden, certain knowledge that one is not alone in the privacy of his or her own bedroom.

With a sickening realization, Paul Sinclair came face to face with the fact that he *was not alone in his own mind* — and whoever was here with him was the one running the show. In the deepest, most sacred part of his psyche he was no longer a ruler, but a pawn. With an even deeper, soul-gnawing horror, he knew suddenly that it had always been so. He had never been in command of his mind. Someone else pulled the strings.

Finally, in utter despair, he gave up. He simply was not strong enough to resist the pull of whoever was controlling him. For the first time in his adult life, Paul was overmatched. The tree loomed closer, until he was standing within arm's reach of it. Before, it had always been a towering oak, strong and secure. Now, he saw it was a twisted, gnarled caricature of life, hideous and deformed.

"Well Paul," said a familiar voice, "I see you have taken my teaching to heart." To Paul's everlasting surprise, the Yogi Shaw stepped out from behind the tree, smiling his confident, assured smile. Relief, immense and powerful, swept through him.

"Master!" Paul's mind voice was a shout of joy and recognition. The Yogi was just as he had remembered. Tall, even taller than Paul, with sun-bronzed skin and hairless scalp. Paul had often wondered whether the Yogi shaved his head or if his baldness was natural. Well-muscled shoulders peeked out from a white toga. The Yogi's stance and bearing was that of a ruler in his kingdom.

"Of course," replied The Yogi. His voice was calm and soothing. "Who else would be here?" Paul's dread fell away. The Yogi was the one single person he trusted with his very soul.

"I'm glad to see you," said Paul. "I thought. . . ." Abruptly he trailed off.

"Yes?" asked the Yogi, raising his thin eyebrows.

"I thought there was someone else," said Paul. Suddenly he was hesitant to tell the Yogi about the lack of control in his own mind.

"Surely there is no one to fear here," said the Yogi. To Paul's surprise, his voice took on a slightly mocking tone.

"I . . . I . . . " Paul stuttered, unable to answer.

The Yogi shook his head sadly. "You know Paul, I had great hopes for you. Shaw was a clumsy teacher, to be sure, but you still took the techniques he taught you and made them your own."

"I don't understand," replied Paul, his mind voice wavering. Abruptly, the dread was back. Something, he felt, was very wrong here. The Yogi gestured impatiently.

"You gave yourself to me, Paul," he snapped. "Lock, stock, and barrel. You willingly submitted yourself to my lordship. Now, you seem to be looking away."

"*Your* lordship!?" stuttered Paul. He wanted to back away, but some invisible force held him tight. "You told me that I was my own master."

Again the Yogi shook his head. "No man is his own master, Paul," he said, "and no man can serve two." Strangely, that sounded familiar to him. He struggled to recall where he had heard it before. The Yogi nodded his head. "I see that the accursed Nazarene has been dealing with you. It caused you to allow David Eddington to escape. I'm hear to warn you, Paul. You are mine. Completely. Do not think otherwise." Paul struggled to think, but his thoughts seemed mired in tar. He could only stare at the Yogi and wonder at his words. Allowed Eddington to escape? He had been seconds from killing the preacher. If he had not hesitated. . . . And who was the Nazarene?

To his wonderment, the Yogi's face seemed to shift — to change. It blurred, as if another face was trying to superimpose itself. Then, just as suddenly, it appeared normal again. Yet the Yogi gave no indication that anything had happened. Like a drowning man grasping at a life preserver, Paul tried to initiate his Zen training. Dismayed, he found that he could not bring his concentration to bear.

The Yogi smiled condescendingly. "Those exercises only work when I allow them to work," he said. "After all, they provide illusion — not reality. The illusion tells you that you are your own master. The reality is, and always has been, that *I* am your master, now and forever. Deal with it, Paul. It's not going to change."

Paul squirmed in the grip of an unseen force. He wanted to shout, "I am my own master!" but the words congealed in his mind like drying blood. There was nothing he could do.

Finally, after a few desperate moments of quiet struggle, he was able to speak. "Who are you?" he gasped.

This caused the Yogi to laugh out loud. "Very good, Paul," he replied, and now his tone mocked. "You finally figured out that I am not your vaunted Sensi. I'm impressed."

Paul continued to twist in the unseen hand that held him. On some deep level of his mind, he realized that he was fighting for possession of his very soul — and that the fight was hopeless. His soul did not now, nor had it ever, belonged to him. His meadow disappeared, and he felt himself spiraling downward into an eternal pit of despair and torment. "NO HOPE," he cried in utter terror, and prepared himself for an everlasting death.

Suddenly, he was back by the tree again, the Yogi Shaw still standing there. "Not yet," said the Yogi with that horrid half-smile. "In time you'll be there, but not yet. I have work for you to do." A soul-wrenching groan escaped Paul's lips. He knew now that he was utterly defeated — over-matched in every sense of the word. He had no hope of salvation, only death.

Then, out of the depths of his despair, a name came to his lips. Without thinking, he spoke it, unsure whether he was calling out to the owner of that name, or asking the Yogi who he was.

"The Nazarene?!" His voice was both a whisper and a shout. He had heard the Yogi say that name, as if it carried some kind of authority. Indeed, it seemed suddenly that the paralysis that Paul was experiencing in both body and mind loosened just a bit. Now, just the barest glimmer of comprehension began to shine through. As soon as he spoke that name, he felt stronger, and strangely enough, weaker. Yet, somewhere in the back of his assaulted mind, he understood that in this weakness there was strength. It made no sense, but there it was. Once again he looked at the Yogi, and was surprised to see the look of hatred and loathing there. For an instant, he thought he saw a hideous snake, coiled and ready to strike.

"The Nazarene." Once again, he spoke that name, this time not as a question, but as a statement.

The Yogi recoiled as if struck. "Quiet, you idiot!" he cried, but Paul could hear the fear now cracking in the Yogi's voice. He now found his own thoughts free again. He also found himself remembering all of the Bible verses he had labored to commit to memory. It did not matter then whether or not he believed them. They were there in his mind and heart. Walter had told him during their trip that God's Word never *ever* returned void. He did not understand at the time, but now he thought he might just be beginning to.

Once, an eternity ago, he had hidden that Word deeply in his heart — even though his goal had been deceit and treachery. He had hoped to destroy an organization by memorizing it, but now he saw it as a life preserver in an angry ocean. Abruptly, his mind made a connection. "Jesus!" he cried out. He recognized the name now — and who it belonged to. "That's who it is, isn't it?" He grabbed that life preserver and hung on for dear life. "Jesus Christ is the Nazarene!"

The Yogi screamed his hatred of the Name, but also retreated further behind the tree. Paul instantly realized something else. "He's your enemy, isn't he?" He practically shouted the question. Once again the meadow wavered as if under water, then firmed up, but this time Paul sensed that it was not the Yogi's doing. Shaw screamed again, and then . . . changed. Paul watched as the appearance of the Yogi Shaw melted away, to be replaced by. . . .

"You!" Paul knew him. At least, he recognized him or his eyes — dead eyes. They were the dead eyes that had haunted his dreams and meditation for what seemed like forever. What had been the Yogi stood there, regarding Paul with a mixture of hatred and rage.

"You're still mine, Paul Sinclair," he whispered, and his whisper was that of death itself. "I will not let you go. You crossed the point of no return long ago. How many times have you taken a life for me?"

Paul felt his mind's world dissolving around him. The force that had him in its grasp was simply too powerful. The sky and the meadow were melting into a sheet of plain gray nothingness. He looked back at the creature, and suddenly understood one last thing. "The Nazarene is more than your enemy," he said, his voice growing weak in his own ears. "He's your better . . . your conqueror . . . and He's your *Creator!*"

"LIAR!" The shout drove through his mind like a heated spike. The creature before him swung an arm, and the comforting gray became an empty blackness. It was a blackness from which there was no escape. Paul once again felt himself being pulled down into the burning nothingness. He was lost and helpless. There was nothing left to do but scream.

* * *

For Jeff Anderson, unconsciousness held no terror. His soul rested quietly in the arms of the King of kings, and no power in creation was capable of yanking it out. The darkness that surrounded him was not the horror of damnation, but the comforting softness of sleep.

Waking up was an entirely different matter.

"Ohhh." The groan escaped his lips before he could stifle it. Thudding pain and harsh cold competed for his attention. Consciousness had returned in stages, as did his memory. Years of training, first in the marines and then as an FBI agent, came to his aid. His eyes snapped open, searching for any danger.

He was lying in an army surplus cot, in what seemed to be a basement. Five low wattage light bulbs, placed in the ceiling in a random pattern gave a soft, yellowish light. Other than the fact that he was alone, nothing else was evident . . . beyond the dull, throbbing ache and coldness coming from his damaged knee and rope burned hand.

"Ouch-h-h-h." He tried to lift his head from the small pillow it rested on, but was too weak. His mind raced back to the most recent things he could remember — his fight with Paul, the mad chase to catch David and Susan, and the even madder decision to try to help his fallen enemy. After that he could only draw a blank. He had no idea how he had come to this place, let alone where this place was.

"Blast you, Sinclair," he muttered, a hot flash of anger searing through him. "I hope I ground your ribs to powder." He caught himself, surprised at the vehemence of his feelings. It was the same way he had acted when he had confronted Paul earlier. The anger frightened him and disgusted him, but he could not help but feel it. The very thought of the arrogant, sneering face of Paul Sinclair made it burn bright within him. With an effort of will, he thrust thoughts of Paul away and tried to concentrate on his surroundings.

Once again he lifted his head, and was mildly surprised to find his strength returning. He only felt vaguely nauseous as he propped himself up on his elbows. The blanket that covered him slipped off, revealing that someone had taken his shirt. With a bit of nervousness, he peeked under the blanket and confirmed the worst — his pants were gone as well, leaving only his undershorts. His knee was wrapped tightly, although he could still see the swelling through the elastic bandage, and a waterproof ice pack had been taped on top. His hand had also been bandaged with a heavy gauze. Someone — whether friend or foe he could not tell — had been at work here.

Dropping the blanket, he took in the rest of his surroundings. It was indeed a basement, although it was not as cold as it should have been. A steady stream of heated air poured out of a vent in the ceiling above him, originating no doubt, from the furnace tucked neatly in the corner off to his right. The walls were bare gray cement, as was the floor. On his left, several breadbox-sized cardboard boxes were stacked neatly against one wall, reaching about waist high and covering half the wall. He was lying with his head next to the adjoining wall, his feet pointing to the center of the room.

Scanning to the right, he suddenly froze. His first assessment of his surroundings had been wrong. He was not alone here. Another cot identical to his was lying perpendicular to him, running parallel to the wall he was up against. A pair of huge feet, size tens at least, he guessed, poked themselves out of a wool blanket not 12 inches from his head. He could not see past the feet.

It took everything he had, but he forced himself to sit up, using the cold wall for support. The hard surface tried to scrape his bare back. As he inched himself up, the face beyond the feet gradually came into view. Finally he was able to see it in full.

"Oh no," he breathed silently, unable to believe his situation. "Oh God, no." Paul Sinclair lay there, obviously unconscious. Jeff could only stare at the man who, the last time they had met, had tried to kill him. There was no time to lose, he knew. Despite the pain and injury, he had to get out of here. If he was among friends, then he had to warn them about Paul. If he was a prisoner, then the sooner Mrs. Anderson's little boy Jeff vacated the premises, the better for the "good guys."

He tried to roll his legs out of the cot, but red-hot knives began to stick themselves into his knee. The pain almost caused him to lose consciousness again. With another stifled groan, he fell back. The wooden frame creaked and wobbled, as if protesting the abuse.

"Hi Yo Silver," he muttered, his breath coming harsh and fast. "So much for the 'good guys.' " He lay there, trying to will the pain away so he could think. As his mind gradually cleared, he frowned in concentration, trying to catch an elusive thought. "Good guys," he whispered again. For some reason, that phrase triggered a memory. His brow knitted with the effort as he tried to place it. Then, abruptly, despite his situation, he smiled. He had it.

It felt like it must have been years ago, but it was only a few months. He had still been with the FBI, and he and Helen Bradley were still working the Shepherd's Path out of Cincinnati. A very frightened yet determined young man named Scott Sampson had just committed himself to an extremely dangerous cross-country trip, delivering Bibles at stops along the way. Jeff had been explaining the process of using Bible verses as recognition signals. It had involved a great deal of memorization, and Scott had his doubts.

"What if the 'bad guys' find out about this," he had asked Jeff. "Can't they use it, too?"

Jeff had grinned. "Remember, Scott," he answered, "there are no 'bad guys,' only 'lost guys.' And lost guys who memorize the Scripture sometimes have a tendency to become 'saved' guys." Jeff found himself smiling at the memory, and wondering how Scott and Beth were doing.

"Save it for later," he told himself out loud. Now was neither the time nor the place. He was lying inches away from an extremely dangerous man, and it was time to, as his brother used to say, "beat feet." *Or "foot," in my case,* he thought grimly.

Once again, Jeff tried to move his legs off the cot and onto the floor. This time, either the pain was less, or his body was adjusting, and he was successful. Across the basement was a flight of sturdy-looking stairs leading up to an even sturdier-looking door. Maybe, he reasoned, it would not be locked. After all, whoever put the two of them down here obviously knew they were injured. Perhaps they would not consider either man a threat.

Gently, Jeff untaped the ice pack, grimacing each time he pressed too hard. Finally he got it loose and it fell to the floor. Then, taking a deep breath, he put all of his weight onto his good leg and pushed himself up. He tottered for a moment, dangerously close to losing his balance and falling on top of Paul. His hand shot out and pressed hard against the concrete wall. The rough surface scraped his palm, but the gauze protected him from aggravating the rope burn. The added support stopped his swaying, and soon he was standing straight.

"All right, now," he whispered, feeling unreasonably smug at his success, "let's get on with it." Using his injured leg for minimal support, he hobbled across the small area to the stairs. It was one of the hardest things he had ever attempted. Lying in the cot, he had not realized just how weak the fight in the alley had left him. His reserves of energy were exhausted, and he needed a great deal of rest. By the time he reached the foot of the stairs, he was breathing hard and starting to sweat. The room spun dangerously around him. He grasped the handrail, his heart thudding in his ears. Once again, angry pain flared in his knee, demanding his attention. He was not going to make it up those stairs without a short break.

Gently he lowered himself to the bottom step. He breathed deeply, trying to slow his heart rate and ease the pain at the same time. It took a few minutes, but gradually he began to feel better. Just a little while longer, he knew, and he would be able to climb the stairs. How he would deal with whatever he found there he would figure out then. He stretched his damaged leg out straight in front of him, and leaned back on his elbows. So far, he had heard no signs of human movement above. Perhaps, he thought, no one was home. He hoped so.

Almost unwillingly, his eyes came to rest on the still sleeping form of Paul Sinclair. The anger flared again, but this time he did not allow it to dominate his feelings. He needed to think clearly. He took a moment to study his adversary. Paul lay there, flat on his back, obviously unconscious. Jeff had not noticed before, but Paul's entire frame seemed to be ramrod stiff. His hands were clenched fists, and his face. . . .

"What in the world are you dreaming about, Sinclair?" he asked aloud. It wasn't that Paul's face was battered and bruised — it was. That gang had been thorough in their abuse. Rather, his countenance looked as if it were etched in stone. His expression was one of rigid concentration, and his brow was wrinkled with the strain. It seemed to Jeff that he was trying to fight off some kind of invisible force. He could only guess at what kind of nightmares a monster like Paul might have.

"Whatever they are, Sinclair," he whispered savagely, "I hope . . ." and the words caught in his throat. He swallowed, suddenly tasting the bile of his own hypocrisy. His remembered admonition to Scott came back to him, and it was as if each word was slapping him hard across the face. "No bad guys," he had said, "only lost guys . . . and sometimes lost guys can become saved guys."

"Oh no," he groaned. He realized the impact of his own words . . . and what his Saviour was telling him. "Oh Lord, You can't be serious. Not him." As if in answer, Scripture he had long ago memorized in an almost-forgotten Sunday school class manifested itself in his mind. It was a verse he knew so well that he took it for granted. "That whosoever believeth in him should not perish, but have everlasting life."

"Whosoever," whispered Jeff. His shoulders slumped as he shook his head back and forth. "Not him," he repeated, his voice almost pleading, but it was no use. He could not wriggle off the hook. Jesus Christ had played no favorites when He offered salvation to humanity. In fact, just the opposite. Instead of associating with the top echelons of society, He had mingled with the poor and lowly. Not only that, Jeff knew, but He had changed many of the greatest enemies of His followers into His most effective disciples. There was only one requirement needed to become a Christian — a broken and contrite heart that realized one could not save oneself. Jeff knew this, of course, but still, with all his being, resisted applying it to Paul.

"*You're* going to have to do it, Lord," he whispered finally, still staring at Paul's horizontal form. "And You're going to have to get past my own spiritual nearsightedness to do it." He rolled his eyes heavenward. "You do realize, Lord, that if I try to introduce the two of you, he's probably going to try to kill me again — and this time, I think he might succeed." He sighed, already knowing the answer. The Saviour had never promised safety or security — physically speaking, that is — to His followers. His commission, however, was quite clear. Salvation was available to *all* who would simply ask for it . . . including Paul Sinclair. It was Jeff's responsibility to share that availability, and his Saviour's responsibility to look after Jeff. He shook his head again. "All right, Lord," he said wryly, "but he's going to have to ask me. I don't know how or why he would, but it's got to start with him! That's my 'fleece.' He's going to have to ask." Again Jeff contemplated the inert form against the wall.

"Well, I can't do anything now," he reasoned to himself. "He's out of it, and I still don't know where I am. One thing at a time." With that, he grasped the handrail and levered himself up to a semi-standing position. The pain in his knee still throbbed, but the brief rest had helped. Turning to face the door above him, he began taking the steps, one at a time. There were 12 of them, and he had just reached the sixth when, without warning, the door suddenly flew open and a bright light shone from above. At that same instant, Paul Sinclair opened his mouth and screamed the scream of the damned.

* * *

Christine sat in a captive chair that held her in place against the absence of gravity. She was still on Liberty, although she had made a complete recovery from her recent operation. Indeed, each day she was learning more and more how to control her own new abilities as well as direct the actions of others. She had already, under the careful observation of Indres, planted a driving conviction in the mind of the president to lead the movement to join the European commonwealth before the United States was economically washed away.

Just now, however, she was dealing with far more important details. At least, Brennon seemed to think so. He had provided her with a small office on the mammoth space station in order for her to continue her work of destroying the underground church movement. Inwardly, she rankled at the assignment. She had world leaders to dominate, and Brennon had her tracking down a ragtag bunch of commoners! There was nothing she could do, of course, but comply. Still, it was frustrating — particularly now.

Before her, on a vid-screen set into a small desk, was the face of the terrorist she knew as Wolf. It was not often that she spoke with him face to face, but communication was secure here in Liberty, and this was a vital task . . . vital at least, to her future.

"So you let them escape," she said flatly. Wolf's face hardened, and his eyes narrowed. Christine had no doubt that, if she had been with him physically, he might have tried to kill her.

"It was your lead we were following," he spat out, his anger just barely under control. "When we got there, nothing!"

"Nothing?" Christine's tone mocked. She had learned that particular talent from Brennon.

"Nothing! Oh, we were at the right place, but everyone was gone. I found some bedding, a satellite uplink that was untraceable, and a wrecked computer. I couldn't even pull anything off the hard drive. It was too messed up."

"Did you try anywhere else in the area?" asked Christine.

"If you knew the area, you wouldn't ask," snapped Wolf. "I used the command code you gave me and ordered the city police to conduct a thorough search of a 10-square-mile section, with that empty building in the center. Maybe they'll find one of those 'safe houses' we're always running across."

"I don't like you using the locals for something like this," said Christine sternly. "We don't need to draw attention to ourselves, at least not yet."

"Like I care," said Wolf, his own tone mocking Christine in return. "I don't have the manpower to do it, and they do."

"What about Paul Sinclair?" asked Christine, changing the subject.

"I'm betting he's with whoever else was in that building," said Wolf.

"When you find him," ordered Christine, "I want him up here, along with whoever he's with. Do you understand?"

Wolf said nothing, but his face was plain to read.

"Do you understand?" repeated Christine, her voice hardening. "I want him and his friends alive, and on this station. Anything else is unacceptable."

"Fine," replied Wolf shortly. "You want him, you got him. What about a shuttle?"

"I can have one ready within an hour," said Christine. "Just get him here." Wolf nodded, and started to turn away. "And Wolf," said Christine, steel in her voice.

"What?" he snapped, turning back to face the monitor.

"Don't screw this up. You were supposed to track Sinclair, wherever he went. You've already lost him once. Find him, and get him up here . . . or else you'd better find an awfully deep hole to hide in."

Wolf snarled and bared his teeth at the threat, rather like a . . . well, a wolf. He pulled something out of his pocket and held it in front of the monitor. "What about this?" he growled. It was the hard drive he had taken from Jeff's abandoned headquarters.

"Give it to a courier and get it up here to me," replied Christine. "I'm sure that where you failed, we'll be more successful."

Sneering, Wolf broke the connection.

Christine sat looking at the blank monitor for a few moments, feeling as if she was standing at the edge of a cliff, with huge rocks waiting far below to crush her when she fell. Her entire future as part of Brennon's Sextuaget depended on three very fragile threads. One, that Paul Sinclair would be found. Two, that he had somehow managed to link up with someone highly placed in the Shepherd's Path. Three, that whoever that might be could be broken enough to give her everything he or she knew about that elusive network. After all, she reasoned, if she could break the Shepherd's Path, she should be able to seriously damage the underground church movement.

What Christine did not realize, mainly because she had no understanding of the concept of the Church, was that the Shepherd's Path was merely a tool of that body. A useful tool, certainly, and an important one. Its founder, Helen Bradley, had foreseen the need for such an organization, and had acted upon that need. Still, for all its worth, the Church was not dependent upon the Shepherd's Path for its existence. This was Christine's fatal error.

The Church — the *true* Church — was formed and protected by the Creator of the universe. It was a living thing . . . an immortal being. No power on earth or in hell could destroy it — not Wolf, nor Christine, nor even Brennon and the masters he himself served. Of course, Christine saw none of this. All she cared about as she ended her strained conversation with her pet terrorist was that for her to succeed, she had to destroy the organization known as the Shepherd's Path.

She sat there, studying the blank monitor. "Just get them here, Wolf," she said again, to the emptiness. "Because if you don't, there won't be a place you can hide that I won't find you . . . and if you think what you've done to those misguided believers is vicious, just wait until *I'm* through with *you*.

* * *

Jeff swung his head madly back and forth, unsure of whether to focus his attention on the screaming Paul Sinclair or whoever was at the head of the stairs. Both were potential threats. Grasping the handrail and trying to ignore the renewed pain from his knee, he risked a glance back at Paul. The big man was still lying on the cot, his face a mask of agony. Still, he appeared to be unconscious. That left the unknown factor above him.

- 228 -

Squinting into the light, he tried to make out the figures standing there. He could discern at least two, perhaps more. He thought he was prepared for anything, but was caught totally off guard when he heard a well-remembered voice.

"I don't think you should be putting any weight on that knee just yet, Jeff," said David Eddington dryly. "It's still swollen pretty bad."

"David?!" Jeff's eyes finally adjusted to the light, and now he could see clearly. Standing there in the doorway was David, with Susan at his side. "Thank God!"

He knew where he was now. All at once, the great burden he had been carrying for what seemed like forever lifted off his shoulders. He was among family! He sat down heavily on the stairs, almost giddy in relief. David rushed down and sat next to him, Susan following. The two men looked at each other and grinned.

"I see you made it," said Jeff, stating the obvious.

David nodded. "Thanks to your instructions," he replied simply.

"How in the world did you find me?" Jeff asked, mystified.

David glanced upward. "You can thank your friend upstairs," he said, jerking his head back toward the door.

"Bernie?" Jeff asked. Bernie was the name of the middle-aged former sailor who ran "Exotic Imports and Exports." He had been one of the first contacts Jeff had made when he had relocated from Cincinnati to New York.

"Yep," answered David. "When we showed up, I told him what had happened with you and Paul. He grabbed me by the elbow and we went looking for the both of you. Thank the Lord that he's got a truck. We'd have never gotten you back here on foot. We found you in that alley."

David's mention of Paul snapped Jeff out of his sense of well-being.

"Paul!" he exclaimed. Quickly, he hobbled back down the stairs, the others following. Paul was still there, and he did not seem to have moved. "I can't believe you brought him here," he said, shaking his head. "That man is dangerous. Letting him into a safe house is about as smart. . . ."

"As jumping three street thugs to save him," chimed in David. Jeff shot a glance back at his new friend. The shorter man was smiling, but there was a look of awe on his face. Despite the fact that he had only known him for less than a day, Jeff felt a sudden fondness for the former pastor. The man had taken a great risk in coming back for him.

"You saw it?" he asked.

David nodded. "We got there right on the tail end of it . . . not that you needed any help. How you managed to run them off with that knee. . . ." He shook his head in admiration.

"Wasn't me," mumbled Jeff, half to himself. "No way I could have done that without help." The two men fell silent for a moment.

David cleared his throat. "The thing is," he asked, "what do we do with him now? I mean, it's not like we can let him stay here, is it?"

Jeff turned to answer, then abruptly noticed that Susan was blushing. She had followed them down into the cellar. Her cheeks glowed a brilliant red that contrasted sharply with her short blonde hair. He frowned for a moment. Abruptly, she burst into a fit of the giggles.

"What are you . . ." he began, then suddenly understood what she was embarrassed about. "Ri-i-i-ight," he said, his own dark brown cheeks starting to color. He could feel the heat on his skin as he reached down and yanked the blanket off his cot. "Very funny," he growled as he wrapped himself in it. "If you've seen enough, maybe you could find my clothes."

"We washed your shirt and pants, but they should be dry by now," replied Susan. She leered playfully at him. "Besides, it's nothing I haven't seen before!" She walked off, with another giggle. David lost his battle to hold in a snicker as well.

Jeff glared at him, half-serious, then levered himself down onto his cot. He studied David closely. "I thought she was sick," he remarked conversationally, to which David only shrugged. Jeff continued, "Paul didn't hurt you? I didn't get a chance to ask you back there."

"Tell me about it," grimaced David. "No, he didn't, aside from a few scrapes and bruises."

Jeff shook his head, half in disbelief, and half in admiration. "I still can't believe you took him on," he said. "That took a lot of guts, David. If he had managed to break into that uplink, a lot of good people would have been hurt."

This time it was David's turn to blush. "Yeah," he answered, lowering his eyes to the floor. "Like I really had a chance against him." He glanced up at the still sleeping Paul and shuddered.

"I know," said Jeff quietly. "Don't feel bad, David. I'm no slouch when it comes to hand-to-hand, and he nearly had me. Would've too, if I hadn't had an escape route." They fell silent for a moment, each remembering that desperate struggle.

"I'm glad you made it here," said Jeff finally.

David nodded. There was an awkward silence for a moment, then David cleared his throat. "Bernie's got a police band monitor upstairs," he said, and Jeff nodded.

"I know," he answered. "Its been a big help to our work. He's taking quite a risk, having it. The last I heard, possessing one carried an automatic 10-year prison sentence. He's jimmied it somehow so he can pick up the New York police — at least the voice transmissions. It would take a lot more sophisticated setup to break into the computer messages."

"Yeah," agreed David. "The thing is, we've been monitoring it. Seems like there's a major search going on — any officer that's not occupied elsewhere is in on it."

"What area?" asked Jeff, although he already had a sinking feeling he knew.

"This one," said David, confirming his fears. "They're using your building as a center point and spreading out. Evidently someone pretty high up ordered it. From the sound of things, the local police are none to happy about it. Still, they're being pretty thorough. We figure its only a matter of hours before they get here."

"Swell," growled Jeff. "Then we've got to get out of here."

David shook his head back and forth. "They've cordoned off everything for a 10-square-mile radius," he explained. That caused Jeff to blink in surprise. David nodded, and continued. "It's a *major* search. Whoever wants us must be pretty powerful." Jeff's mind flashed back to the men he had seen earlier. David glanced over at him, then continued. "Anyone coming in or out of this immediate area is stopped and questioned."

Jeff sighed, feeling another wave of pain wash over him. "It's always something," he said ruefully. "Well, if we can't get out that way, we'll think of another. I know this place pretty well." He thought for a moment.

"David," he said finally, "have you heard anything about satellite surveillance over the police band?"

David nodded grimly. "From what we could pick up, they've been combing the area for a good many hours," he said. "Building by building."

"Figures," said Jeff. "I'm sure that's how they found us."

"Who?" asked Susan. Unheard by the two men, she had returned to the cellar, bearing Jeff's now clean clothes. Jeff blinked, then realized that she and David had been long gone when the mysterious raid on his former headquarters had occurred. As he dressed, he hastily filled them in.

"We don't dare try to get out of here while that 'bird' is up there, looking down our throats," he continued. "Believe me, I tried it once, and was caught before I could get out of the city." That caused everyone to once again lapse into silence. Despite their current safety, each of them now realized just how desperate the situation was.

Jeff's shoulders slumped. He rubbed his eyes, fighting a sudden wave of helplessness. He knew he had to be strong for his friends. He started to say something — anything — to brighten their spirits, but was interrupted by a low moan. Instantly he sat up straight, heart suddenly pounding a frantic pace in his chest. His eyes sighted on the still prostrate form of Paul like guided missiles. The big man was waking up.

"Both of you, out of here," he hissed sharply. "Now!"

"Are you crazy?" snapped David. "We're not about to leave you here with that killer."

His lips were set in a firm line. Susan could only stare at Paul.

"Please!" pleaded Jeff desperately. "He can't know you're here. As far as he's concerned, you're out of his reach. If he tries anything, it'll be with me. Now go!"

David hesitated for just a moment, then nodded. "All right, Jeff," he whispered back. He glanced back at Paul, but Sinclair was not yet fully awake. "But we'll be waiting upstairs. If he tries *anything,* I'll be back down here like a shot. I don't think he can take both of us . . . not in his condition." With that, he took Susan's arm and led her back up the stairs. The upstairs door closed and Jeff was left alone with a trained killer.

"All right, Paul," he said softly. Abruptly he realized that, since discovering Paul Sinclair's true identity, it was the first time that he had ever called his enemy by his first name. "I guess what's going to happen next depends entirely on you." As he watched, Paul slowly regained consciousness. Jeff had no idea what private hell Paul had been locked in while he was out, but from the look of relief that crossed his face upon awakening, it must have been sheer terror.

"Uhhh." The groan escaped Paul's lips, and for the first time, Jeff noticed they were dry and cracked. Paul's left cheek was dark blue and purple from the brutal beating the gang had given, and his left eye was swollen. Jeff glanced around the room and saw that someone, probably Bernie, had left a small plastic pitcher of ice water on a small table on the other side of his cot. A matching plastic cup rested next to it. Carefully, keeping half an eye on Paul, Jeff leaned back and filled the cup with water. Then, warily, he stood and shuffled over to stand next to Paul's cot.

"Paul?" The eyelids fluttered at the sound of Jeff's voice, then opened. Jeff could see that he was having trouble focusing. Carefully, trying to anticipate any kind of attack, he leaned forward, bringing the cup to Paul's lips. "Here," he said, his voice flat and emotionless. "Drink a little of this." Hesitant at first, Paul sipped the water, then eagerly tried to gulp it.

"Easy, easy," cautioned Jeff. He allowed Paul a couple of more sips, then pulled the cup away.

Carefully Paul licked his lips, then turned his eyes on Jeff. This time there was recognition in them. "Jeff," he said, his voice a dry rasp.

"Paul," Jeff acknowledged, his voice once again flat and cool.

Paul looked around the room, taking in his surroundings, then turned his attention back to Jeff. "Where?"

Jeff merely shook his head. "I can't tell you that," he answered, "and I'm sure you know why."

Paul thought about it for a moment, then nodded.

"What do you remember?" Jeff asked.

Paul frowned as he tried to concentrate. "The last thing I remember was getting my tail kicked by some local punks. I thought I had had it." He looked hard at Jeff. "You?" The meaning was obvious.

Jeff shrugged. "Sort of," he answered. "It's hard to explain. Here." He handed the cup to Paul, who had recovered enough to hold it himself. Carefully, Paul downed the last of the water, then handed the cup back. Jeff laid it on his cot, then regarded Paul with something akin to resignation. "So where do we go from here?" he asked, more to himself than to Paul. Paul did not answer, and his gaze drifted off. It was as if he was trying to remember something.

"That must have been some nightmare," remarked Jeff, seeing the look on Paul's face.

Paul's attention jerked instantly back to the dark man. "What do you mean?" he demanded.

Again Jeff shrugged. "I haven't heard a scream like what you let out in a long time," he answered. "In fact, I don't think I've *ever* heard a scream like that."

Even prepared as he was, Jeff was not ready for Paul's next move. The big man's hand shot out from under the blanket like a striking snake and grabbed his wrist. Before he could retaliate, Jeff found himself jerked to within an inch of Paul's face. He started to struggle, then saw Paul's expression. It was that of a drowning man grasping for a life preserver. Jeff's eyes widened in surprise as he realized that he was not being attacked.

He was caught completely off guard by Paul's next words. "You've got to tell me more about this business with Jesus Christ," he demanded.

* * *

Although he did not realize it, Paul was at a crossroads. The direction he would soon take would determine where he would spend eternity. He was desperate. He had come to the sudden, horrible realization that he could not save himself. He clung to his one-time enemy's wrist fiercely, waiting for a reply. Paul knew, with a sinking dread, that what had happened in his once-safe meadow had not been a dream . . . at least not in the normal sense. Whoever or whatever had masqueraded as the Yogi Shaw was very real, and very, very dangerous. That man, or creature, had dominated Paul completely. That experience had not left him unchanged.

Before, Paul had always looked inward for his answers. That, after all, was the core of his Zen training. The answers lay within one's own inner strength. God, for want of a better word, was inside of him. God was a part of him, making him, in essence, a god himself. He only had to get in touch with his feelings — to center himself — and he would find the answers.

In a heartbeat, he had seen his entire world turned upside down. He had come face to face with the simple fact that he was living a blatant lie. Now, he knew the soul-rendering truth. He was helpless before a greater force. That monster in human form who had brutalized his innermost thoughts was his master, in every sense of the word.

Paul knew now that he had never been in control of his own destiny. He was a pawn — a slave — carrying out someone else's whims and desires. It was a bitter truth to take. He was a proud man, an independent man. He wanted to believe that he could set his own course, but he could not deny his utter and complete defeat. That kind of freedom, he now knew, was an illusion. The realization gnawed at him. He held on to Jeff's wrist as if it were his only chance to escape the hopelessness of the situation. He looked the dark man straight in the eye, and repeated his demand.

"You heard me," he said, his voice harsh and dry in his own ears. "Tell me about Him. Everything. I've got to know!"

"Let . . . go!" gasped Jeff. With a supreme effort, he pulled his hand away and moved over to his own cot. Paul was now aware enough to take greater notice of his surroundings. Most of the information he filed away for later study. Just now he had more important things to worry about.

"What are you up to now, Sinclair?" Jeff retorted, his voice almost a snarl. "Whatever it is, it isn't going to work."

Paul, weakened by his initial effort to hold on to Jeff, sank back onto his cot, his eyes closing. "I'm not 'up to' anything, Jeff. I just need to know." Suddenly, and all at once, he lost control. To his utter amazement, a single tear formed at the corner of his unbruised eye. Angrily, he brushed it away. Paul Sinclair *never* allowed himself to appear vulnerable before *anyone*. It was a sure way to be hurt . . . deeply. A man could only rely on himself — no one else. With an effort of will, he forced his feelings back under tight control. He opened his good eye and saw Jeff looking at him in puzzlement.

Deciding that the best defense was a good offense, he continued. "Well, Jeff? How about it?" he said, once again forcing his head up off the small pillow. "Are those Bible verses I had to memorize real or not?"

"And why should I tell you?" asked Jeff. It was obvious to Paul that his companion was also barely under control. Small wonder, he thought, since a few hours ago Paul had been doing his best to kill, or at least seriously injure him. Judging from the way Jeff was favoring his swollen knee, he had been at least somewhat successful.

Trying to goad Jeff, he allowed a small, mocking smile to find its way to his lips. "I thought that was what you people did," he said, his tone matching his smile. " 'Go ye into all the world' and all that."

Again surprise peeked through Jeff's angry scowl.

Paul nodded. "I know that verse, and the one after, and the one after that. How far do you think I could get with those refugees if I didn't have at least some of that Book memorized?"

"You and your kind are the reason that they *are* refugees," snapped Jeff. He obviously wasn't going to make this easy. For some reason, his harsh reply made Paul sad rather than angry. It was indicative of the gradual change that had manifested itself over the past few days. Before that, injuries or no, he would have tried to put Jeff under the ground for his remark.

"You're right," he said softly instead. "You want to know something else?" He plowed on, not waiting for an answer. "I enjoyed it. I enjoyed hunting Christians, and I enjoyed hurting them. You might not know it, but I led the raid that got Susan arrested." He laid his head back on the pillow, remembering. "She was one of the better-looking women in that meeting. If we hadn't had direct orders to get them out to Mentasys, I would have let my men. . . ."

"Stop it!" snapped Jeff. His voice was a feral snarl, and his face a mask of rage.

Paul held up a hand, as if warding off Jeff's anger. "I'm not telling you anything you don't already know," he said, letting the sarcasm drain from his voice. Suddenly a wave of pure weariness, not only of the body, but of the soul as well, swept over him. He let his gaze wander away from Jeff and come to rest on the ceiling. "God, I feel so tired," he said, more to himself than his one time enemy. He looked back at Jeff. "How would you like to suddenly come face-to-face with the fact that everything you believe in is a lie?" he asked. Again he did not wait for an answer. "I hated you because I saw you as a serious threat to my world. You're the only people left in the nation still preaching that your way is the *only* way. Do you know how arrogant that sounds? How self-righteous? Do as I say, or burn in hell!"

Jeff could only shrug, not quite knowing how to reply.

"I couldn't stand it," continued Paul. "I thought I knew the answers. I thought I was in control." He paused. Then, swallowing, he spoke the hardest three words he had ever had to say in his life. "I was wrong," he said, looking Jeff straight in the eye. "Now, are you going to tell me about Him, or not?"

The words hung between the two men for long seconds. Jeff's mind was a maelstrom of conflicting emotions. He only stared at Paul as the big man lay on the cot. Every instinct he had honed during his years with the FBI was screaming for his attention, demanding that he find a very small and preferably uncomfortable box somewhere and stuff Paul inside. How could he believe this man when he had, for all intents and purposes, admitted to hurting, and perhaps even killing, his fellow believers? And he had enjoyed it! There was no way Jeff would risk his own life, and the lives of his friends, on the words of former agent Paul Sinclair. And yet. . . .

Jeff remembered his prayer on the basement steps. He remembered fighting the idea that Paul could be turned around . . . and he remembered the still, silent, and irresistible voice that told him he was wrong. Then he remembered his "fleece." Try as he might, he could not turn away from this man without at least trying to share the faith that meant more than life to him. Paul might indeed be laying a trap, but that was not Jeff's concern or responsibility. His Lord had made it quite clear what his course of action should be. He merely had to obey, and let Christ take care of the rest.

Slowly, Jeff began to talk about his Saviour. He was hesitant at first, but gradually became more confident. He was surprised to find that Paul remained quiet and attentive. The big man would nod occasionally, but otherwise was silent.

A curious thing happened as Jeff shared more and more of the Scriptures. Like a dead second skin, the anger and hatred he had felt toward Paul in particular and the world in general began to fall away. It was almost as if he was being healed of a disease he did not even know he had. For long months, a poison had been growing inside of his spirit. Anger, rage, and hatred had planted themselves within, so subtly that he was not aware of them. Now he was being restored. As he spoke to Paul, he found that for the first time since he had set up shop in New York, he could not only forgive, but love his enemy. His shoulders straightened from a slump he had never perceived, and a tremendous peace began to flow through him. After long months of losing sight of his true mission, Jeff Anderson finally began to return to what God wanted him to be.

Several minutes later, Jeff finally stopped talking. Silence hung in the air for long seconds. Jeff studied Paul, while Paul lay on his cot, his gaze fixed on the ceiling. Jeff wanted to speak, to say something else that would convince the big man to turn his life over to the Saviour. Instead he remained silent. He had said everything there was to be said. Now it was up to the Holy Spirit to do the real work.

At length, Paul turned his head and focused his good eye on Jeff. "It's all real, isn't it?" he said softly.

"Yes," was Jeff's quiet, certain reply.

Again Paul fixed his gaze on the ceiling. Now there was a look of dogged determination on his face. He drew a deep breath. "Well . . ." he began.

At that exact instant, the door at the head of the stairs burst open. Startled, both men turned as one to see David Eddington come barreling down into the basement. David stopped suddenly as he caught sight of a now awake Paul. Anger and a touch of fear colored his face.

Jeff raised a hand, catching his attention. "It's all right, David," he said soothingly. "What is it?"

David glanced nervously back and forth between the two men, then spoke. "We just heard on Bernie's monitor that the police are almost here." He glanced nervously back up the stairs. "In a few minutes, they'll be knocking at our door."

Jeff bit his lip. A bushel's worth of problems, forgotten during his conversation with Paul, were suddenly back, demanding his attention. "All right, David," he replied as levelly as he could. "Get Susan. Bernie, I know, has some sort of emergency escape route planned. I'd say it's about time to use it."

David nodded, then dashed back upstairs. Jeff turned back to Paul, and immediately realized that David's interruption had been costly. The hardness and pride was back. Jeff could see it in Paul's face. He opened his mouth to speak, but Paul beat him to the punch.

"I know what you're going to say, Anderson," he said flatly. With a sinking feeling, Jeff noticed that Paul was no longer calling him by his first name. He leaned forward, trying with every ounce of conviction to turn Paul back to the choice he had almost made.

"There's still time, Paul," he said with quiet intensity.

Paul stared hard at Jeff, then softened . . . just a little. "Look," he said, "I heard what you told me. I may even believe it, but you can't expect me to just throw everything I am away and jump into this thing with both feet. I can't do it!" He paused, then added, "I need a little more time."

"We don't have it," said Jeff, shaking his head. "You heard David. We have to leave this place now. And frankly, we can't trust you. If you're not one of us, then you can't come with us."

Paul's face hardened. "It doesn't matter," he replied. "You can't leave me behind. If the local police are going to be here soon, and you leave me here, then I'll be able to give them a pretty good idea of where you're headed. Even if you knock me out, sooner or later I'll come around. At the very least, I'll be able to identify you, the group, and a few safe houses across the country. You have to take me with you."

Jeff sat there, looking at Paul and frowning in concentration. As much as he hated to admit it, the big man was right. Paul had successfully infiltrated one of the many cross-country routes used by the Shepherd's Path. With what he already knew, he could do serious damage.

Paul saw Jeff's uncertainty and pressed harder. "You don't have a choice," he repeated. A ghost of a smile played across his face, but this time there was no hint of mockery. "Give me a chance, Jeff," he said. "Maybe I'm not one of you, but just maybe I'm not against you anymore." He swallowed hard, remembering his dream. "I've met my real enemy, and believe me, you aren't him."

Jeff took a deep breath. He was about to reply when once again the basement door opened and David and Susan, plus Bernie, the safe house owner, filed down. All of them looked bone-tired. Bernie Salazar was a short, burly man of Arabic descent. His naturally dark brown skin looked out of place in winter-bound New York. He looked as if he would be more comfortable on the deck of a ship than running an import business. He had proven himself a trusted friend to Jeff over the past few months. The three of them crowded into the small basement, forming a rough semi-circle around Jeff and Paul. No one spoke for several seconds. Finally Jeff broke the silence.

"All right, you two," he said, addressing David and Susan, "you won't like this, but Paul's coming with us." There were no protests to this announcement. Both David and Susan had expected as much. Instead, they regarded Paul quietly. With a grunt at the pain, Paul rolled over and sat up. His face was a map of bruises and cuts. His breathing was labored and heavy, and he held his ribs tightly. After several seconds, Susan gently pushed her way past David and Jeff and knelt down in front of Paul. She studied him intently for a moment, then spoke.

"My husband is dead, isn't he?" Her voice was steady, as if she already knew the answer.

Paul looked her in the eye for a moment, then glanced down. "Yes," he replied, his voice almost a whisper. "He died at Mentasys." Again silence dominated the room. Then, for the second time since he regained consciousness, Paul was amazed at his own words. "I'm sorry, Susan," he said. He almost choked on the words, but he had to say them. He had held hope out to this once fragile woman for the sole purpose of using her. His tactics had been cruel and heartless, and he felt deep shame at what he had done. Susan regarded him for a moment, then stood once more. She turned and faced the rest of the group.

"I want you all to know that this man had a direct hand in my husband's death. He sent us to that horrible place where Tim died." Paul felt himself tensing. It looked as if he was going to have to repeat his arguments about staying with the group. Susan was going to object, and the truth was, she had a right to. Somehow, he had to convince them otherwise. He was not quite sure why, but right now he did not want to be separated from these people.

"I just want you all to know that," Susan was saying, "if anyone has a right to hate this man, it's me." Then she turned to face Paul once more. Drawn by her gaze, Paul gritted his teeth and stood. His posture had all of the earmarks of a man waiting to hear a guilty verdict from a "hanging" judge.

"I remembered you when we were trying to get to this safe house," said Susan, now speaking directly to Paul. Abruptly, two tears formed at the corners of her eyes. She squeezed them shut tightly for a moment. As Paul watched her, he got the distinct impression that she was waging some kind of inner battle. Then her eyes opened, and all signs of struggle were gone. Paul could not help but remember the helpless creature he had rescued in California, an eternity ago. Where had this strong woman come from? Her recovery, he knew, was nothing short of miraculous.

"I loved him very much," said Susan, and Paul knew she was speaking about her husband. "We had a good life together." He could only nod. Jeff, David, and Bernie stood silently by. They knew that time was running out, but no one wanted to interrupt what was happening. They watched as Susan reached out, took Paul gently by the hand, and said the last words he had ever expected to hear. "I forgive you, Paul," she said quietly.

Paul's eyes widened in shock and amazement. He could see what those words cost her. He was even more amazed when Susan stood on her toes and kissed him lightly on the cheek. It was the chaste kiss of a sister to an older brother. This was the last thing he had expected! He could only stare at this young woman who just a short while ago had been at death's door.

Susan turned back to the rest of the group and nodded. "He's got to come with us. Agreed?" The rest of the group nodded.

Jeff looked at Susan, then at Paul, the back at Susan, as if not quite sure of what to say. Finally he shrugged. "No one said that this would be easy," he said to no one in particular. "Okay," he continued, "let's get out of here. Bernie?"

"This way, everyone," said Bernie, in a surprisingly mellow tenor voice. He led them over to a corner of the basement, to the pile of boxes that Jeff had noticed upon awakening. Motioning to David to help him, he began to clear them away from the wall.

Jeff moved forward to help, but was waved off by Bernie. "Rest that knee," he said, looking over his shoulder. "You'll need it for where you're going!"

Jeff hesitated, then nodded. He moved to stand next to Paul and watched as the two men moved the rest of the pile. Behind, Jeff was interested to see, was, well, more wall. He looked at Bernie questioningly. Bernie smiled back, then trotted over behind the staircase. He disappeared into the space underneath, then re-emerged a moment later with an impressive looking sledge hammer. He handed it to David.

"Give it a few good whacks there," he said, pointing to a place on the wall. David shrugged, not quite sure where this was going, and turned to his work.

Sudden realization dawned upon Jeff. He did not know too much about New York, but he did have a fairly good idea what was on the other side of that wall. "You can't be serious," he said to Bernie as the shorter man stepped back out of the way.

"Of course I am," he replied. "It's broad daylight outside. Do you think you can just waltz out of here under the noses of New York's finest?"

"Peter did," grunted David as he took a hard swing at the wall. The hammer met the cement with a loud CRACK! Amazingly, a hole about four inches wide appeared. Jeff took a closer look, and saw that what appeared to be cement was in reality only plaster board, cleverly painted to match the surrounding wall.

"It took me almost a year to dig this," said Bernie as David continued to swing. The next blow widened it considerably. "Once the tunnel was dug, covering it up was easy." David started to take another swing, then gagged. Coughing, he stumbled back. The reason for this was soon obvious. A choking stench rolled out from the dark hole. Soon everyone was coughing.

"What have you got back there," gasped David. "A sewer?"

"Yup," nodded Bernie. "Don't worry. You'll get used to the smell . . . well, sort of, anyway. Here, let me do the rest." He shoved his way past David and, with his bare hands began to widen the whole.

Jeff fought to get his stomach under control. David looked at him desperately, but Jeff shook his head. "Bernie's tapped into the main sewer that runs parallel to this building. If we can stand it, it might be our way out."

"It is your way out," grunted Bernie as he cleared away the rest of the plaster board. The hole was now three feet by three feet square. "There's thousands of miles of sewer lines under this city. The one at the end of this tunnel connects to all the rest."

"Wait a minute," sputtered David. "On the way in, we saw some of these sewers backed up and overflowing. How do we get through them?"

"You don't," replied Bernie. "All you need to do is to get out of this area, past the police. Once you do that, you can surface again. Jeff here will know what to do after that." He looked at the former FBI agent. "Right?"

Jeff nodded, then spoke. "You're not coming with us, then." It was a statement, not a question.

"Can't," replied Bernie calmly. "Someone's got to cover your trail. Besides, I've got other ways out of here. I'll put the boxes back, then make my own way out." He glanced back toward the stairs. "But if I'm going to do that, you need to leave *now*. Come on . . . get going. Here, you'll need these." He pulled a small pocket flashlight and a brown envelope out of his pocket and handed them to Jeff. Inside the envelope was a crudely drawn map of the sewer system. "Just follow the markings, and it will get you out of the area. Now wait a second." Once again he went to rummage under the stairs. This time, when he returned, he was holding a crude walking stick. This he also gave to Jeff.

"Thanks, Bernie," said Jeff, taking the flashlight. He grasped his friend's hand firmly. "Don't get yourself caught now."

"Don't worry about me," replied Bernie, returning Jeff's grip firmly. "Just get these folks out of here. You think you can get out of the city?"

Jeff nodded. "I've got other contacts," he said. "We'll make it." He motioned for David, Susan and Paul to follow.

The inside of the tunnel was smaller than the opening. Jeff had to crawl on his hands and knees for over 20 feet before coming to an iron grating. It played havoc with his injury, and he ground his teeth together to keep from crying out. The grating blocked the entrance to the sewer proper. From what Jeff could tell, there would be plenty of room to walk once they were past the grate.

He paused until he was sure that the rest of his friends were behind him. For a moment, he could see the glare of light from the basement. Then it disappeared abruptly as Bernie closed off the opening. Placing both hands on the grate, Jeff gave a brisk shove and was gratified when the entire framework swung open. He stepped out and lit his flashlight. He was in a huge sewer tunnel that ran on in either direction into the darkness for as far as he could see. At regular intervals were placed dim lights that gave an eerie, yellowish glow to the whole place.

The tunnel itself was rounded, with smooth, curving sides that formed a continuous arch above him. From where he was standing, the other side was a good 15 feet away. In the center of the floor ran a wide trench filled with a dark liquid. Jeff did not allow himself to think of what made up that liquid.

At least there aren't any albino alligators to meet us, he thought ruefully. He could not help but recall the almost legendary stories he had heard since coming to New York. Along either side of the trench was a walkway about four feet wide. They would have plenty of room to move at least.

Taking short, shallow breaths through his mouth, and trying hard not to think of the stench, he moved away from the access tunnel to clear the way for the rest of his companions. They followed him in, Paul bringing up the rear. They stood there for a moment, waiting for Jeff. The crawl through the tunnel had not helped his knee, and it was starting to throb painfully. Not only that, but the winter cold was beginning to chill him. He said a silent prayer of thanks for the walking stick.

"All right, everyone," he called. "Let's go." Moving in the direction indicated on the map, they set off. Jeff once again took the lead. To his surprise, he found Paul walking next to him. The big man's breathing was labored as he struggled to keep up. They were silent for a while, both concentrating on trying to navigate the dimly lit area. A hundred sounds of the local inhabitants assailed them. The resident rats were not used to having such large company.

Finally, Paul glanced over his shoulder, at Susan. He studied her silhouette for a moment, then turned back to Jeff. "She forgave me," he muttered in a voice that was almost a whisper. "She actually forgave me." Jeff was not quite sure how to reply to that, so he remained silent.

Paul looked at Jeff carefully, thinking hard. At length he spoke again. "When we get to wherever we're going, Anderson, you and I are going to have a long, long talk."

Jeff only nodded, trying to hide a smile. Despite their circumstances, God was working. Jeff had no doubt that Paul was being prompted by the Holy Spirit. His conviction was real.

As one, the group made their way forward. Jeff's mind raced ahead, thinking of the many things he would say to Paul when they were finally able to rest. He did not realize it then, but his time to share Christ with the big man had run out.

9

David trudged through the darkness, fighting the impulse to gag on the stench of the sewer. The fact that it was freezing in that dank tunnel did little to help. The smell of raw sewage was just as nauseating. He was shivering, as were the rest of his companions. While all of them had warm coats, they had been underground now for several hours. The persistent cold continued to batter their defenses, and was now seeping through to the skin.

Suddenly, David was reminded of the fantasy worlds of the role-playing games he had preached against so long ago. He had had more than one argument with a few of the young people in his church's youth group. In order to be better informed, he had even gone so far as to sit in on a session with some of them. While he had been appalled at the casual references to demons, spirits, and the like, he had also felt strangely drawn into the game. The imagery was vivid, and the action fast paced. He had seen the lure, and realized that the games were far more dangerous than he had first thought. He had subsequently redoubled his efforts to turn his young people away from them.

Now, here he was, in a scenario not too far off from those same games. There were no dwarfs or dragons, or other supernatural, subterranean creatures lurking in the darkness (although some of the rats he had seen might qualify), but the feeling was there. His companions' breath fogged in the dim glow of the flashlight, giving them an eerie, surreal quality. The air stank of decay and death, and he was wondering if he would ever seen the sun again.

David's mind was a whirlpool of emotion. All of the twists and turns his life had taken lately were a far cry from what he had once hoped and dreamed of. From successful pastor to fallen pastor — from mall janitor to underground church leader, and finally to fugitive — his whole existence seemed to be a blur of constant motion. He was weary beyond words, and yet . . . as they navigated the dark tunnels, a small smile wormed its way to David's face. Despite everything, he had peace . . . a peace that he had not possessed for far too long. He had sold out — sold out everything that was dear to him — in order to insure his and his family's safety. The stench of his own betrayal was far worse than anything this sewer could offer.

Not long ago he had resigned himself to living out the rest of his life at that California shopping mall, remembering what had once been his. Regrets were all he had left. Then the mysterious Miriam had appeared, and set his feet on a path that had taken him across the nation to find his own redemption. He had discovered, to his ultimate joy, that God could still use him. He did not know how, or where, but that did not matter. It did not even matter if he were to die tomorrow. He was back on track with the only person who mattered — the One who held his soul safely in the palm of His hand.

Breaking away from his thoughts, he squinted ahead, trying to make out details in the almost total darkness. Only the small pool of light provided by Jeff's flashlight was visible. There were maintenance lights spaced at regular intervals, but for the most part they were inoperative.

They had been walking for what seemed like days, but was actually only a few hours. Above them, sounds of traffic gradually became louder, indicating that they were moving into the more populated areas of New York.

Carefully consulting the map, Jeff had led them onward relentlessly. David was awed by the stamina and determination of his friend. Jeff walked with a distinct limp, and the look on his face spoke eloquently of his constant pain, but still he kept moving, searching for a way to safety. The seemingly endless maze of tunnels continued to pass by them.

"This is incredible," he whispered to Susan, who was walking next to him. By unspoken agreement, their hands were clenched tightly together. "It's another whole world down here!" David, like most people, knew that all cities had extensive underground sewer systems, but to actually *see* the immensity of such a system left him amazed.

"Another world," whispered Susan, "or a 'nether' world."

David blinked, then did a double take. "That's supposed to be funny?" he demanded, still whispering.

Susan chuckled. "That's as good as it gets," she replied. "I was never very good at theological humor."

"Heck of a time to start practicing again," David shot back. Susan only chuckled softly once more. David said nothing, but inwardly was thrilled at the laughter in her voice. If his recent journey was remarkable, Susan's was miraculous. He was no expert in either physiological or psychological medicine, but as far as he could tell, Susan seemed to be completely whole once again. According to Paul, she would not have lasted another week in the condition he had found her in.

They continued on, determined to find safety and rest. David kept his eyes ahead, where the dark forms of Paul and Jeff walked side by side.

Privately he considered the idea of bringing Paul along utter madness. Not long ago this same man had tried to kill him. Admittedly, David could not think of an alternative. They certainly could not leave him behind, after all, but to have him here, walking next to Jeff as if nothing had happened, was decidedly uncomfortable.

Still, David thought, there had been a change in him. David did not want to admit it, but Paul was definitely not the same man. Just what kind of change had occurred, only time would tell.

Abruptly, Jeff brought the group to a halt. David edged forward until he was looking between the two bigger men. Jeff was carefully studying the map. The dim light reflected off his dark features, revealed the concern there.

"As far as I can tell," he said, "if what you heard on Bernie's radio was right, we should be well past the police cordon by now. Maybe it's time to surface." This statement was greeted by groans of agreement from both Susan and David. Even Paul looked as if he had reached the end of his endurance. The darkness and stench of the sewers had taken their toll.

"What time is it?" asked David.

It was Paul who answered. "Nearly five," he said, lighting the radium screen of his watch. "Still daylight." He turned to Jeff. "Think we should wait until dark?"

Jeff thought for a moment, then nodded.

Susan groaned again, this time in disappointment. "I don't think I can last much longer," she said in a tired voice.

"I know," answered Jeff sympathetically, "but it's only for another hour." His voice echoed off the curved wall of the tunnel, giving it a hollow ring. "As soon as it's dark, we'll surface. I know at least one place we can go to, so hang in there, folks. We *will* get through this." Giving the map a last glance, he pointed the flashlight ahead and started forward again. With an air of resignation, the rest of the group followed. To David it felt like forever, but in less than an hour Jeff led them to a steel ladder. It was positioned along the side of the tunnel, and rose into the darkness.

Jeff once more consulted the map. "This looks like as good a place as any," he said softly.

"Where are we?" David asked, matching Jeff's tone.

"Either smack dab in the middle of West 48th, or somewhere outside of Nome, Alaska," replied Jeff wryly. He stuffed the map into his back pocket. "Wait here while I check it out."

He gripped the rung of the ladder level with his eyes, but Paul moved forward to stop him. "Let me," the big man said simply. "I don't think you should try to lift the cover with that knee."

Jeff hesitated, then shook his head. "My knee and your ribs. We're

- 245 -

both in pretty bad shape." He glanced over his shoulder. "How about it, David? Think you can do it?"

"I think so," replied David, trying his best to keep his voice low. Inside, he was suddenly elated. At last, a way to be useful! He had let Jeff, and before him Walter, take the lead and the responsibility for far too long. It was time to change that. Getting his friends out of the sewer was a start.

He grasped a rung of the ladder, and hoisted himself upward. Jeff pointed the flashlight up toward the exit, giving him enough light to see. It was a long climb — almost 30 feet — and he was puffing slightly when he reached the top. Above him was a dark, round plate that covered the exit. Beyond that, the sounds of traffic slowly crawling by were now much louder. It was obviously still rush hour.

He positioned himself with his back against the cover, feeling its considerable weight. For a moment, he hesitated, wondering what was going to happen when he opened the cover in the middle of a crowded street. Then, with a mental shrug, he gritted his teeth and pushed hard. The cover rose a few inches, then fell back. The thing was heavy!

"You okay?" called Jeff from below, his voice barely audible above the din of traffic.

"Yeah," he shouted back. "Just give me a second." This time he was ready for the weight. He pushed hard, and the cover once again rose. Carefully he moved it off to one side. Light and noise assaulted him as if it were a physical entity. After hours in the darkness, the glaring city lights were dazzling. And the noise! Heard from street level, it seemed as if he were surrounded by a battalion of tanks, headed into war.

Cautiously, he raised his head and looked out. The manhole was situated in the middle of a four lane highway. There was a narrow median, about five feet wide and raised about four inches, that separated the opposing lanes. Cars and an occasional bus rumbled slowly by. David peered at his surroundings carefully, then descended back into the darkness. Jeff and the others were waiting eagerly.

"We're where you said," he reported to Jeff, studiously ignoring Paul. "There's a lot of traffic going by, but there's a cross street about 20 yards that way," he continued, pointing north. "When the light changes, I think we can get across to the sidewalk," he shrugged. "Where we go from there is up to you."

Jeff nodded. "I know a place," he said reassuringly. He looked at his charges. "All right, everyone, let's go." So saying, he grabbed the ladder and started to climb, favoring his injured knee. Susan went next, then, not wanting Paul to be close to her, David followed. The gesture was not lost on the big man. If David had been watching, he would have been astonished to see a look of profound sadness break across Paul's face. Whatever his motives, he had been Susan's protector. Now that was being taken away.

Slowly, the tiny group ascended the ladder with Jeff in the lead. Jeff reached the top and, as David had before him, slowly raised his head and looked around. Then he crawled out. Ignoring the startled looks of passing motorists, he cleared the manhole and motioned for the others to follow. They quickly joined him and stood shivering in the median, looking for all the world like wartime refugees. In a sense, David reflected, that was exactly what they were.

"Let's go," shouted Jeff, pausing only to replace the manhole cover. Traffic was stopped for the light, and he quickly led his three charges over to the sidewalk. He scanned the street up and down relentlessly as they walked, searching for any sign of police cars.

"We need to get off this street," said Paul, who was now bringing up the rear. "We're still drawing too many stares . . . and that looks like trouble." He nodded at an older make Corvette that was just across from them. The driver was staring at them, and, ominously, using his car phone. Jeff glanced in that direction, then quickened his stride. His grim look was all the rest of them needed to match his pace.

"How far?" asked David as he moved up to walk beside Jeff.

"Another few blocks," was the strained answer. Jeff continued on, once again trying to look in all directions at once. The buildings surrounding them were not yet the behemoths that marked downtown New York. While a few rose into the late afternoon sky, most were less than 10 stories. Unlike the area where Jeff had set up his home base, however, this section of the city was still quite occupied. Most of the buildings were in decent repair and almost all held some sort of business. Some were constructed of glass and steel, the rest graying concrete.

They came to a cross street, and Jeff promptly turned left. They moved on, all of them now feeling the effects of little food, little rest, and winter cold. Another cross street appeared, and they made another turn.

"Almost there," he said over his shoulder. He continued to lead them for another hundred yards or so, and finally stopped in front of one of the older concrete edifices. Tinted double doors led inside, and a gold lettered sign on the left door identified the place as the "Davis Free Clinic." There were lights on inside, and David could see a middle-aged woman in a white uniform sitting behind a long, low receptionist's counter.

Without hesitation Jeff started inside. David followed, but was suddenly jerked backward as Susan's hand grabbed his arm with steel strength. He looked at her in surprise. Her face was sheet white, and tears were forming at the corners of her eyes. Paul, concern showing on his face, moved in closer.

"Susan?" David's voice was gentle, but urgent. They had to get inside, away from the openness of the street.

"I . . . I can't go in there," she stammered. David frowned in confusion. Then it hit him. He looked at Paul for confirmation, and the big man nodded.

"I found her in a clinic," he explained, "more dead than alive." David groaned. Susan's recovery might very well be miraculous, but there were still wounds on her psyche that had only begun to heal. She had been violated in body and mind. It would be a long time, if ever, before she would be totally whole again. He looked over his shoulder at Jeff.

"Anywhere else we can go that's close by?" he asked, already knowing the answer.

"None," replied Jeff, frowning. "At least that I know of," he added. David turned back to Susan, but Paul was already intervening.

"Susan," he said, gently putting his hand on her shoulder and turning her to face him, "I know what you're remembering, but this isn't that *other* place."

David blinked in surprise. He had traveled across the country with this man. He had, with the single exception of their separation at Jeff's headquarters, spent every waking moment with him. Not once in all that time had he ever heard him speak as gently as he was speaking now.

"I promise you, Susan," he continued, "that I won't let anything happen to you in there."

SLAP! Susan's blow caught Paul totally off guard. He staggered back, more in surprise than actual hurt.

Susan's face was twisted in an unholy rage, and her breath was suddenly coming in short, hard gasps. "You!" she shouted. Jeff moved forward, eyes darting in all directions. He tried to stop Susan, but he might as well have tried to stop a tidal wave. "You're the reason I was in that hellhole!" she screamed." You're the reason that Tim's dead! And *you* are going to protect. . . ." As suddenly as it started, Susan's rage ended. Her eyes widened in horror, and her hand flew to her mouth. Paul could only stare mutely, rubbing his jaw where her slap had landed.

"Oh Paul," she cried, horrified at what she had done. "I'm sorry! It just came out. I miss Tim so much. It just. . . ."

"All right, everyone," snapped Jeff, his voice harsh and commanding. "Inside now." He grabbed Susan by the shoulders and forced her to face him. "Whatever you faced before, Susan, and whatever your going through now, you'll have to do it inside. I know that I'm not being fair, but I don't have *time* to be fair. Deal with it! Whatever happened to you, turn it over to God . . . right now . . . this instant. Nail it to the cross and *LEAVE IT THERE!*" He looked back at Paul and David. "Come on. Move!"

Jeff was relentless. He literally drove them up to the double doors and inside the clinic. David was first, then Susan, followed by Paul and finally Jeff. Susan looked as if she had been hit by a hard right cross. David could only guess at what private demons she was fighting.

David's shoulders sagged wearily. Then, without warning, the headaches that had disappeared since their arrival in New York were back in full force. He staggered, stumbling forward to lean against the desk. He was hardly aware that the receptionist was staring at him. Sweat broke out on his forehead and he tried desperately to get his breath. Once again he was reminded of what Miriam had told him. "Brain damage," she had said. Damage from being ruthlessly interrogated by the terrorist known only as Wolf. These and other thoughts whirled madly thorough his head in a macabre dance as he tried to make the room stop spinning.

Jeff was at his side in an instant. "David?" His voice colored itself with concern, and had a "what now" tone to it. David couldn't blame him — first Susan, and now this! He nodded slightly, even that small movement painful.

"I'll be all right," he gasped, his voice harsh in his own ears. "Just give me a minute." Jeff pressed his lips tightly together, unsure of what to do.

"Here, let me help." The new voice came from behind the tiny group. David, his headache subsiding just a little, turned to look. An older man of about 60 was standing there. His gray hair was close-cropped in a military cut, and contrasted starkly with his deep brown skin. He had just a touch of an accent that David identified as probably from India. The plastic badge hanging from the collar of his white lab coat identified him as Dr. Chankersingh.

Without asking, the newcomer moved forward and placed his cool hands on David's forehead. Somehow the doctor's gentle touch had a calming effect, and David found himself starting to breath easier. Dr. Chankersingh worked quickly, examining David's pupils, taking his pulse and respiration rate.

"Migraines?" he asked in a professional manner.

"Uh, yeah," muttered David. His head was starting to clear and he was beginning to feel uncomfortable with the attention. "They come and go. I'm okay now."

"Uh huh," replied the doctor skeptically.

"Really," said David, pulling away. "I'm fine now." The doctor looked as if he was going to say something else, but Jeff moved forward and interrupted.

"Sorry for the scene," he said, trying to smile disarmingly. He was suddenly aware of the fact that they had just spent the past several hours in a sewer. Outside, the cold air had masked the scent. Now, however, it was becoming clear the they all needed a bath and a change of clothes.

"We're just here to check on a friend of ours . . . her name is Helen. Helen Freeman. She's a patient here. Do you know her?" As he spoke, he scratched his two day old growth of beard casually. Then, eyeing the doctor, he quickly made a small deft move with his index finger. Only a member of the Shepherd's Path would recognize the symbol he traced — the Shepherd's Staff. The network had, for the most part, abandoned its use, but still it had its advantages. It was not the ideal way to convey it, but between that and the code name he had just used, he should be recognized. Ordinarily, he would have quoted the necessary Scripture. He was fairly sure he knew who he was looking for, but with the receptionist present he could not afford to take a chance. Dr. Chankersingh's eyes widened slightly. Then he nodded to himself as if confirming a theory.

"Of course I know Helen," he said, looking at each of them as if seeing them anew. "She has made wonderful progress over the past few months. Are you family members?"

"Just David here," replied Paul. "The rest of us are friends of the family. Can we see her?" The doctor smiled and nodded.

"I'll show you the way myself," he said, and led them off to the right. They followed him down a short hall that emptied out into a small drab waiting room. Faded dull green vinyl couches blurred with the faded dull green carpet. Without hesitation, the doctor led them across the waiting room to an elevator on the far side. The doors opened immediately when he touched the "up" button, and he ushered them inside.

Jeff started to speak, but Chankersingh held up his hand for silence. The elevator carried them up to the third floor, where it stopped.

"This way, please," said the doctor, once again leading the way. He took them down another hall, identical to the first, and stopped at a door with his name stenciled on — obviously his office. Opening the door, he motioned for them to go ahead. Then, checking behind him, he followed them in and closed the door.

The office was rather small and plain, with white painted walls and worn dark brown carpet. A simulated wood desk sat facing them, covered with file folders, books, and other papers. The wall behind the desk held several diplomas and other certificates. On the left, several freestanding shelving units were overflowing with books. There was a harsh fluorescent light above, but its effect was softened by a single table lamp sitting on the corner of the desk.

"This is very stupid," spat the doctor. His demeanor suddenly changed from kind and helpful to angered and frustrated. He shouldered past them and moved to stand behind his desk. His features were hard, as if set in granite. His accent, only slightly there before, was now far more pronounced. "There is a major police search under way for four fugitives. Now you people show up here looking as if you have been living on the streets for a year. What is Baalam thinking, sending you here?"

Jeff stepped forward. "I'm Baalam," he said tiredly. It was the code name he had used on the network for the past few months. "Look, doctor, I didn't have a choice. My place was raided. We just barely escaped with our lives." He glanced meaningfully at Paul, but the other man refused to meet his eyes.

The doctor failed to notice, instead shaking his head. "Things are very bad here," he said quietly. "We should have shut down when the depression hit." He turned his back on them, and even with his headache still throbbing, David could see the slump in the older man's shoulders. "We were federally funded," he continued, not looking at them, "but those days are over for good. Thanks to a few private sources, I was able to keep us going — just barely." He turned back to face them. "I don't think that's going to last much longer. We're running out of everything — medicines, equipment, everything! Most of our patients are now terminal. They have no place else to go."

"I'm sorry," said Jeff quietly, "but we. . . ."

"I'm sorry, too," interrupted the Doctor. "We're getting pressure from the Planned Family Council to start performing abortions." David shuddered at the mention of the PFC. An offspring of Planned Parenthood, the powerful organization was pushing for, and getting, legislation to force couples to limit themselves to two children. Any other pregnancy would be immediately aborted. He had had his share of run-ins with them during his days as a pastor.

He tried to concentrate on what Chankersingh was saying. "When that happens," shrugged the doctor, "we're finished. Since I'm the only M.D. on staff now, and I won't murder an unborn child, we'll be shut down. I'll have to go underground." He paused. "Now, with you here, I'll probably have to shut down anyway. This is very stupid!"

"Doctor," said Jeff in the same tone he had used on Susan outside, "don't lecture me on stupidity, or how the network should operate. I guarantee that I know more about either subject than you do." He took a step forward to emphasize his words. "Now, we're tired, hurt, and we need to rest. You've been an invaluable asset to the Shepherd's Path before. Are you going to help us this time, or not?"

The doctor narrowed his eyes, studying first Jeff, then Paul, and finally David and Susan. He noted the way Jeff was favoring his knee, and how Paul was holding his rib cage tightly. He sighed deeply, and nodded. "I will try," he said reluctantly. "I will get you something to eat, and as much medical attention as I can."

"Don't do us any favors, doc," muttered Paul under his breath, but loud enough for Susan to hear. The withering glance she gave him was far more eloquent than words, and to his amazement, Paul found himself intimidated. He shut up. David tensed, fearing a repeat of the scene from outside, but Susan looked back, her face now a mask, hiding her emotions. Whatever was going on inside her head and heart, she was not going to let it interfere any more. David breathed a sigh of relief.

Jeff, his attention centered on the doctor, missed the entire exchange. He smiled at the doctor in gratitude, suddenly realizing how good it would be to rest. Stifling a yawn, he started to speak. Immediately, the doctor held up a warning hand. "That's as much as I can do," he said firmly. "You can't stay here. I'm sorry, but you can't. It seems like you all are very important people. From the rumors I've heard, the city is mobilizing the entire police force to find you."

Jeff shook his head, disappointment permeating his voice. "They've expanded their search," he said, his voice infinitely tired. "I thought we were actually going to get past them."

"They'll probably be here within the next few hours," replied the doctor. "Sooner, if anyone noticed you coming here. You see why you can't stay." A blanket of despair settled over the four fugitives. Just when it seemed like they had made it to at least a temporary shelter, they were being forced to keep running.

Chankersingh studied them closely, then softened a bit. "Do you know any other place you can go?" he asked Jeff.

"We have to get out of the city," replied Jeff wearily. "We need transportation to do that." He thought for a moment, his brow wrinkling in concentration. Then he made a decision. "All right," he said, straightening his shoulders and forcing himself to sound confident, "I didn't want to try this, but we have no choice." He looked straight at the doctor. "We need a way to get to the Corbin Building." The doctor's eyes widened in amazement.

"That's right in the middle of downtown New York!" he sputtered.

"Yeah, no kidding," replied Jeff glumly. "I don't want to use any of your contacts, doctor. If the police are this close, we don't need to know any more about your end of the Shepherd's Path than we already do. In fact," he added, suddenly concerned, "you might want to consider coming with us . . . or at least getting out of here. How many of your staff are part of the network?"

"Two nurses," replied Chankersingh slowly, considering Jeff's suggestion, "and four patients," he added. "No, I do not wish to come with you. Many of my charges cannot be moved, and I am not ready to abandon them yet."

"Your patients are members of the network?" David asked, curiosity getting the better of him.

At his question, a look of infinite sadness crossed the doctor's face. "Yes," he said softly. "The patients we have here are, for the most part, terminal. Death has a way of making one think about eternity." He smiled slightly. "We try to ease our patient's last days here, and, if possible, tell them about our blessed hope in Christ. Some do not respond, but many do. Some of those who do are willing to help us in our 'other' work."

"Isn't that dangerous?" asked David, now very interested. "I mean, you're not meeting in secret here. You're a free clinic. That seems to be a little too public to be talking about God in this day and age."

Chankersingh chuckled in amusement. "Believe me, we are not bothered here. No one, least of all the United States government, is interested in our patients anymore. Just the fact that we keep them off the street is enough for them."

"But don't you. . . ."

"Not now, David," said Jeff, interrupting. "I'm sorry, but this isn't the time." He focused his attention on Chankersingh. "Look, doctor," he said, "can you get us downtown or not?"

The doctor thought about it for a moment, then finally nodded. "We have a van," he said. "I can let one of our people drive you there, I suppose."

"Thank you," replied Jeff. "Now, if you could take a look at my knee, and Paul's ribs," he jerked his head at the big man behind him. "The only other things we'll need are a shower, a change of clothes, and a bite to eat. Then we'll quit endangering you and your people and get out of here."

"Very well," agreed the doctor. "You can all come down to the ward. I'll have one of the nurses take care of the clothes and food, and I'll examine your injuries." With that he moved past them and opened the office door. Once again he led them into the elevator. This time, he took them down one level to the second floor.

As they descended, Susan looked over at Jeff. She still seemed to be having a hard time, but she was handling it. Now she wore a look of curiosity. "Baalam?" she asked.

Jeff shrugged. "I change code names fairly frequently," he explained.

"But why Baalam?" prodded Susan.

David was gratified to hear the amusement in her voice. It looked like her brief relapse might be over. "He wasn't exactly a spiritual giant, after all."

"Doesn't matter," replied Jeff. "He's rather obscure, so most non-believers won't recognize the name. Besides," he added, a wicked smile suddenly flashing across his dark face, "I'd rather be Baalam, than Baalam's a. . . ."

"Don't say it," pleaded David. "Don't you *dare* say it!" It had taken him a moment, but he finally caught on to where Jeff was going. Susan got it at the same instant and broke into a full-fledged laugh. Both David and Jeff looked at her in surprise and relief. Susan tried to speak, but then laughed even harder.

"It wasn't *that* funny," remarked Jeff, raising his eyebrows.

"No, it wasn't," gasped Susan, trying to stifle her laughter before the elevator stopped. "It just feels so good to laugh again." She reached over and took Jeff's hand and grasped it tightly. "I'm sorry, Jeff," she said. She sobered somewhat, but her eyes still danced. "I lost my faith a little while ago. I forgot that, no matter what, God is still in control." She smiled a sincere smile, with just a touch of sadness. "Your totally pathetic attempt at humor reminded me that I'm here for a reason." She straightened her shoulders. David wasn't sure, but he felt as if he was seeing another stage of Susan's healing begin.

"With everyone's permission," she said, looking straight ahead at the elevator doors, "I think I'll stop being the token tragic figure of this little expedition and start pulling my own weight."

There was a moment's silence, then Jeff slid his arm around Susan's shoulders, grinning. "Welcome back to the battle," he said, squeezing tightly. David leaned over and kissed her chastely on the cheek, while the doctor, having only just met them, shrugged his shoulders and said nothing. Paul bit his lower lip, looking as if he wanted to speak, but unsure of what to say. Just then, the elevator stopped and the doors opened.

As they stepped out into the hall, David's mood suddenly changed. It was as if he had stepped through an invisible curtain that separated the happiness in the elevator from the feeling of hopelessness on the other side.

Susan's laughter still warmed him, but abruptly he found himself feeling apprehensive. The doctor had told them that he was caring for terminally ill patients. What if they were contagious? Surely Chankersingh had taken precautions, but accidents could happen, after all. Perhaps, he thought, they should just take the promised van and get out of there. The police dragnet was growing ever closer, and the longer they were here increased the danger.

He was about to voice these thoughts to Jeff, but the former FBI agent spoke first. "I'm curious, doctor," he said as they moved down the hall. "You said that you were federally funded, and yet you did not perform abortions. How did you get around that?"

"Your answer lies ahead," replied Chankersingh shortly. He stopped in front of a set of double doors made of frosted, opaque glass. He glanced meaningfully back at the four fugitives.

"It is not pretty in here," he said quietly. "Prepare yourselves."

Without another word, he pushed open the doors and stepped through. Jeff looked at the rest of them and shrugged his shoulders. Then he followed the doctor through. David looked first at Paul, who did not meet his eyes, and then at Susan. She gave him a slight shrug, as if to say, "What choice is there?" There was only one answer to that, and he knew it. He caught both doors just as they were closing and pushed them open again.

He found himself standing in a long, narrow room, lined on either side with hospital beds. There were 20 in all, 10 on each side. All were full. *This isn't so bad,* he thought at first. The ward appeared clean and fresh. On the right wall, two windows looked down on the street that had brought them there. Both were slightly open, allowing a crisp breeze to freshen up the place. There was no ugly smell, and the patients seemed to be well cared for. He moved forward into the ward, following Jeff and the doctor.

"I don't see . . ." he began, then realized that he was walking alone. He turned to see Susan still standing in the doorway, Paul behind her. Susan was trembling, and for a moment, despite what she had said in the elevator, David thought she was going to have a problem entering the ward. Then he noticed Paul. The big man's face was such a striking mixture of fear, loathing, and hatred that David recoiled from it as if from a physical blow. "What . . ." he began, then saw that their attention was riveted on the patients. He glanced over at the closest bed, really noticing the person lying there for the first time. The air hissed through his teeth as he took a quick breath. His eyes darted from the emaciated form in the bed to the chart hanging on the frame. It confirmed his worst fears.

Since its outbreak over two decades ago, AIDS had claimed millions of lives. Just five years ago, doctors believed that they were finally on the right path to a cure. A special blood-filtering device, based loosely on the old-style kidney machine, was showing enormous promise. It looked as if the virus could be taken out of the blood system, literally separated from the cells that it so fiercely violated.

Then, something happened that set the entire medical community on its ear. As if it were intelligent, the deadly virus changed — mutated. Now it was completely unrecognizable in its early state. It could no longer be identified or diagnosed until it was far too late. To make matters worse, it could be transmitted with far greater ease. *Any* body fluid could pass the virus along to an unsuspecting victim. Casual contact could and did spread it. Sweat and saliva were now the two greatest carriers. Not only that, but the virus could live for an incredibly long period of time outside the body. The new version was aptly named AIDS II.

David's eyes dashed from bed to bed, confirming the worst. They were standing in an AIDS II ward, and every patient there was infected, dying, and highly contagious.

* * *

"Are you sure you want to attempt this, Christine?" Rajijah Indres rested easily in one captive chair, solemnly regarding his colleague across a round table. Between them the hard drive that Wolf found floated about half a meter above the surface of the table. It was held in place by a tightly focused magnetic field. A needle-thin beam of light, originating from an instrument array in the ceiling, slowly probed over its surface. Christine watched the probe a moment before replying.

"It's necessary," she said bluntly. They were in a private office located at about the mid-point of Liberty. She was floating in a chair identical to Indres', her feet curled under in a decidedly feline pose. "We've been probing that piece of wreckage for hours, and we can't get inside its memory. There are too many safeguards, and too much damage. I'm going to do it myself."

"Very risky," said Indres after some seconds of thought. "Virtual reality is a marvelous tool, but a dangerous one as well. It is fine to go traipsing around in the system Brennon has managed to create." He pursed his lips thoughtfully. "That system was designed especially for our use. Trying to enter an entirely different system . . . well, I think you should consider your other options carefully. Remember what happened the first time you went inside."

"I *have* considered my options," snapped Christine. She was growing more and more weary of Indres and his "more enlightened than thou" attitude. "Inside this drive is the information I need to break the Shepherd's Path once and for all. If I have to, I'm going to dig it out piece by piece."

Indres sat quietly for a moment, then shrugged. "As you wish," he said softly. He reached forward and activated the inter-station vid-com inset into the table. Immediately, the bland face of a young male technician appeared.

The tech, who had been waiting for Indres' summons, nodded. "We're all set here, sir. We've managed to make a 'beachhead' into the system, but we can't go any further without losing the data in the memory."

"Very well," said Indres. He raised his eyebrows at Christine, who nodded in turn. "Stand by, then," he said to the face on the screen. "We will be attempting virtual entry immediately."

He blanked the screen, and once again looked at Christine. "It's up to you, now," he said. "Remember, if you run into trouble, as you did the first time you entered the system, I will not be able to help you. You are on your own."

Christine smiled grimly. She remembered Indres' conversation with Brennon. The last thing she expected was help from her fellow Sextuaget member. Closing her eyes, she accessed the initial menu with practiced

- 256 -

ease. It hovered before her, a dramatic three dimensional display. Confidently, she selected the proper pathway, allowing her consciousness to be drawn into the master control system. Abruptly, her perception changed, and she was no longer floating in the office. She had entered the world of virtual reality.

Once again, the world of Brennon's world dominating system lay before her. It spread out in all directions, an incredible, three-dimensional city of infinite lights. It would take an individual a millennia to explore even a fraction of it.

For the first time, Christine hesitated. If she started down the wrong path now, she could easily become lost. Judging from the reactions of both Brennon and Indres the last time this had happened, she doubted that anyone would come to find her. She would have to exercise great caution. Cautiously, she triggered a command through her bio-chip. Instantly a shining pathway appeared before her. It ran straight ahead, disappearing into the system. With determination and resolution, she started out.

She was not exactly sure when she entered the system proper. It gradually surrounded and enveloped her, as if luring her into an incredibly complex maze. She had planned her way carefully, though, and, although the going was slow, she knew she was headed in the right direction. Time ceased to have any meaning for her. She was now in the world of nanoseconds. Part of her knew that what might pass for years in this strange place would, in the "real" world, be only hours or even minutes.

Her way twisted and turned, but she continued forward with the dogged persistence that had made her one of the most powerful humans on the planet. Finally, hours (or seconds) later, the shining path twisted and headed in a new direction. The system grew darker, as if she had stepped off a main thoroughfare and onto a dim side street. It turned out to be a dead end, and she knew that she had reached her destination.

Before her, standing at least 20 feet tall (to her perception), rose a huge, heavily barred door. It looked impenetrable. Heavy, seemingly stone walls buttressed it from either side, and the door itself seemed to be made of solid metal. Where the wall ended, a curving roof began, giving the overall feeling of a dome. There was a lock on the door, of course, and one look told Christine that she would not be able to open it.

Here was the safeguard that protected the wrecked memory. Beyond this door, she knew, were the answers she desperately needed. Grimly, she set to work. Using her mind link, she began with basic access codes. In her hand appeared a ring of keys, each differently shaped. Marveling at the wonders of virtual reality, she tried the first, inserting it into the lock and gently turning. There were over a thousand keys on the ring. The mainframe had narrowed the choices down from literally millions. It was dull, tedious work, but it was the only way. Christine did not bother to wonder how so many keys could fit on the ring. She only knew that she had to try each one. To her disappointment, but not to her surprise, none of them worked.

Taking a deep (and totally subjective) breath, she began the next phase of her task. Now she had to try different keys in certain patterns. They were clearly marked, and she began to once again insert them into the lock. Abruptly, before she was halfway through, she stopped.

"Ridiculous," she snapped to herself. Angrily she threw the keys down, and no longer needed, they disappeared. She blinked in surprise, then abruptly remembered where she was. In this universe, the laws of natural physics held little or no sway. She could call needed tools into existence by merely a thought. When no longer needed, they would disappear just as easily. Ordinarily, that would have pleased her. Just now, however, it only served to increase her frustration. After all, if she did not know which tool she needed, such power was useless. Pursing her lips, she stepped back and studied the door. It returned her stare, oblivious of her building anger.

"No," she said finally, half whispering. "You will not defeat me." She realized that she was not speaking to the door, but rather to the person, male or female, who had put it there. Her intelligence reports were incomplete, but they had been able to come up with two names who were at least partially responsible. Jeff Anderson, a former F.B.I. operative, and Helen Bradley, former citizen. Both had been involved with Jacob Hill's Mentasys fiasco some months back.

"All right," she said finally. "If I can't get past this door, I'll find another one." The technicians she had been briefed by felt certain that there must be a "back door" in the system . . . some sort of quick access code put there by the creators in case of an emergency. It would be well hidden, of course, but if she could find it, then she could bypass all of this other nonsense.

Once again, she studied the huge door. It stared back mutely, as if daring her to do her worst. She glanced along the length of the wall. It ran for some distance in both directions. She closed her eyes, visualizing for a moment. When she opened them, a vid-screen was floating there before her. A small smile wormed its way to her lips. This could become as addictive as any drug!

"Indres," she said aloud. Instantly, the screen came to life. The familiar visage of Indres peered out at her.

"Receiving," came the calm voice.

"Mark my location," said Christine shortly. "I'm going to trace the parameter of the drive, and I don't want to get lost." Indres glanced off screen for a moment, then nodded.

"Your address has been noted and logged," he said.

"Good," replied Christine. "Can you put a trace on me?"

"Yes," said Indres, "as long as you remain on the parameter. If you get inside. . . ." He shrugged. "Well, we'll know then."

"Fine," said Christine. "I'm moving off. Stand by." With a conscious thought, she dissolved the screen, turned to her left and began to walk. She studied the wall carefully as it slipped by. It appeared seamless, with no doors or windows. She reached the first corner, and turned right. Now she left the main system behind. Her return route was out of sight, and despite her resolve, Christine felt a slight shudder. While she did not believe in a hell, to be lost forever in a place like this would certainly be like being in one. She would have to be extremely careful.

It looked as if the wall ran in a rough square. What she had first thought of as a domed roof actually had four sides as well, giving the impression of a raised pyramid. As with the wall, there were no breaks or irregularities she could detect. She was just nearing her next turn when she saw it — a paper-thin seam running up from the ground to end halfway up the wall.

If she had not been studying the wall literally inch by inch, she would have missed it. She caught her breath, and stopped. Carefully, using the tips of her fingers, she ran her hand along the seam. It ended just over her head. Frowning, she expanded her search, looking for an intersecting line. This time, finding it was easier. A horizontal line intersected the first seam right at the top. Tracing it, Christine found the third one, parallel to the first, almost instantly. Put together, they outlined an obvious door.

"Gotcha!" exclaimed Christine smugly. "Indres!"

"Right here," replied Indres. The voice came from behind her, and she turned to see the screen once again floating there. It took her by surprise, because she had not taken the time to visualize it. Briefly, she wondered about that, then realized that she had told Indres to put a trace on her.

"Do you see this?" she asked the image on the screen.

Indres studied the wall, then looked offscreen to consult another read out. He nodded in satisfaction. "Well done, Christine," he said. "I believe you have found what we are looking for."

"Agreed," replied Christine. "So how do I get in?"

"Two possible ways," said Indres. "First, we'll try a logic probe. Since the access code to a 'back door' is usually relatively simple, that should work."

"What's the alternative?" asked Christine. Indres smiled grimly.

"From your perspective, brute force," he replied. "However, that would be dangerous — not only to the information on the drive, but to you as well. Let's try the probe first."

"Fine," nodded Christine. "Get on with it."

Indres' face disappeared, to be replaced by the face of the technician she had seen before. "Initiating logic probe," he said shortly. From somewhere overhead, a shaft of light appeared. Christine stepped back in spite of herself as the probe encountered the wall. For a moment, nothing happened. Then, the wall seemed to flicker. The probe's light changed in color, and Christine became aware of a high-pitched whine emanating from the beam. The wall flickered again, and she thought she caught a glimpse of a long corridor, lined with drawers on either side.

"It's working," she shouted over the noise of the probe. Now she noticed the seams were growing wider. What had been thin, barely-there lines were now darker and thicker. With satisfaction, she could now see a definite door outlined. The probe continued to do its job, and the hard drive's defenses began to crumble.

"Hold it," she shouted over the probe's whine. Instantly, the beam of light vanished. Moving forward, Christine gingerly placed her palms against the door. After the probe's ruckus, she had somehow expected the door to be hot, and was moderately surprised to find the opposite. Gaining confidence, she leaned her weight into the door. Slowly, it swung inward, revealing the rows of drawers she had seen before.

"I'm in," she said over her shoulder to the view screen that was still hovering there."

"Good," replied Indres in satisfaction. "Now is when you must exercise utmost care, Christine," he continued. "Remember, the drive was heavily damaged. Also, there may be other safeguards that are waiting to be activated. Move slowly."

"Don't worry," growled Christine. "I know what I'm doing." Indres' admonition angered her. She resolved then and there to find a way to terminate the so called "holy man." She was not about to spend the rest of her life taking orders from that self-made monk! He might be closer to Brennon than she was, but she could still deal with him effectively.

Pushing her thoughts aside, she concentrated on the task at hand. Carefully and thoroughly, she studied the open doorway. She was in no hurry. She could spend days, even weeks in this computer-generated universe, and when she returned only hours, or even less, would have passed. She took her time, but could discover no traps or pitfalls. When she was sure, she stepped through the doorway and into the hall. Nothing happened. So far, she had successfully penetrated the enemy system.

"I see a great many drawers in front of me," she said, speaking to Indres. "They look like file drawers, and they line both sides of this hall. They are stacked four high, and seem to run on forever. Any idea where to start?" Silence greeted her question. Surprised, she turned to find that her floating screen had disappeared. Quickly she stepped back outside, and was gratified to see it reappear.

"Problem?" she asked the image of Indres.

"As we feared, until you can cause a total breach of the system, we will not be able to communicate," was the reply. Indres smiled gently, yet somehow managed to insert a hint of mockery. "I'm afraid you are on your own," he said.

"Fine," replied Christine shortly. "As soon as I find something, I'll let you know." Without waiting for an answer, she turned and stepped back into the hallway. She scanned the file drawers, wondering where to start. Nothing was visibly marked, and there were literally hundreds of drawers. With a mental shrug, Christine stepped over to the first drawer and pulled. She was gratified to find that it opened so easily. Her satisfaction, however, instantly turned to anger when she saw that the drawer was empty. Pushing it shut, she opened the one below it, only to discover it empty as well. Pressing her lips tightly together, she began pulling out drawer after drawer, making her way down the infinite hall. The results were the same, no matter what. Empty files.

"No," she whispered, controlling her anger. "You will not beat me." She was again speaking to the designer of this system, not the system itself. She took her failure as a personal affront. Stepping back into the center of the hall, she regarded the file drawers. Something was nagging at her. A tiny voice inside was screaming for attention — warning her that all was not as it seemed. Like it or not, she was going to have to confer with Indres and his pet technician. She turned to leave the hall, and froze. There was no exit. What had once been a forced-open door was now an endless hall, running in the opposite direction. File drawers lined it as well. The hallway was lit dimly, the light fading gradually as it ran off into the distance. Although she could see clearly, she had no idea where the source of light was coming from.

Fighting the urge to run, she forced herself to consider her situation. It was obvious now that the hall, the drawers, and the entrance she had found were dead ends . . . traps for the unwary searcher. If this had been a simple computer probe, the probe's sub-system would simply have crashed. It would have been the only way it could get out of the "loop" it had been caught in. Christine, however, was not a simple probe. Her consciousness was somehow connected to Brennon's main system. She could not simply "reboot," and a system crash while she was linked to Cyclops could damage her higher brain functions beyond repair.

"Indres," she said aloud, visualizing the view screen. She was not surprised when it did not appear, but her fear took itself up another notch. She was cut off, lost in an alien system.

Carefully she tried to think things through. "All right," she said aloud. It was deadly quiet in that hall, and she found herself yearning for the sound of a human voice. "This drive is patched into Cyclops. I entered the drive through Cyclops. Therefore, I am still inside Cyclops."

She shook her head in frustration. This was third grade logic, but it was all she had. "The problem is," she continued, "I'm cut off from Cyclops, therefore I am not in the system. So where does that leave me?" She did not know.

More out of the need to do something than the hope it would accomplish anything, she began to walk back the way she had come in. After several steps, she knew that she had passed the original entrance, and stopped. The tiny voice inside her head was still nagging at her, telling her that she was missing something. Folding her arms tightly across her chest, she tried to listen. Slowly she reviewed her knowledge of the system. What was not right here? She mentally walked through each step she had taken since she had entered Cyclops. The three-dimensional city of lights, the path to the drive, the front gate, Indres' unwanted directions, all paraded before her as she tried to figure out a way to free herself.

"Indres," she said sarcastically, "You're like a cop . . . never around when. . . ." The words stuck in her throat. She felt as if the bottom of her stomach had dropped out. She had been in contact with Indres, *in a world where time was relative!* She could live hours and days here, but only seconds would pass in the physical realm. Yet, Indres had been there with her, each step of the way, guiding her — just as he had been the first time.

It was patently impossible. Unless he entered the system with her, he was confined to the time frame of the "real" world. He could not have been communicating with her. So who was that talking to her? The only answer that made any sense at all was staggering. It was the only solution that left her with a way out.

Christine had built an economic empire by making difficult decisions. She was never afraid to take risks if the reward was worthwhile. Now, the reward was her sanity, and she considered that *very* worthwhile. Closing her eyes, she called up her implant menu. She was gratified to find that it appeared instantly. She had been half afraid that it would have been affected by the trap as well. It was still there, however, and functioning properly. Bypassing the main menu, she called forth the "save" function. She ordinarily used this to download important information from the mainframe to the onboard memory of her bio-chip. Now, she hoped it would serve a different function.

Concentrating, she commanded the search program she was now a part of to save itself. There was a bare moment's hesitation, then the read-out informed her that this command had been properly initiated. Now for the hard part. As far as she knew, no one had ever reset their own system while uplinked to Cyclops. To do so was to invite damage to the cerebral cortex — serious damage. It was a drastic solution, but the situation was desperate. There seemed to be no other answer. Besides, if what she suspected was true, then she was in no danger . . . yet. She paused a moment, reviewing her reasoning, trying to find a flaw in her plan. What she was about to do frightened her. If she could think of *any* other way . . . but there was nothing. It was now or never. Once again she activated the save function, and this time ordered her implant to re-boot itself.

This time, there was no hesitation or pause. The world disappeared. It dissolved one tiny piece at a time, like individual granules of sugar. She stood there, watching it happen, fighting the urge to panic as everything she could see, touch, and hear ceased to exist. Then . . . she was left in utter blackness. She floated in nothingness, a spark of consciousness searching for an anchor. She could sense nothing, feel nothing. She might have endured a nano-second in that limbo, or a millennia . . . perhaps both. She would never know. She could feel the system inside her own mind working. That alone saved her from the pure terror of the emptiness. Somehow she could feel herself being rebuilt, from the inside out, as her implant rebooted itself. Time and thought were suspended, and all she could do was wait.

Abruptly, there was light. Without transition of any kind, she was back. The wall of the hard drive was there before her, and she realized that she was now back outside. It took her long seconds (hours?) to realize that her desperate actions had worked. A wave of relief crashed through her, almost sending her to her knees. Right then and there, Christine could have allowed herself to believe in a higher power. It was all she could do to refrain from crying "Thank God!" and collapsing into a weeping lump of clay. Then the reaction set in. Relief made her giddy, and she suddenly found herself giggling like an adolescent school girl.

"Christine?" The voice came from behind her. Instantly she composed herself. The brief flirtation with belief submerged itself instantly at her command as she turned to face the one who had spoken her name. The view screen was there, as she knew it would be, with Indres framed from within . . . or at least an excellent likeness of him.

"Yes?" she answered back, gratified that her voice was calm.

"Are you all right?" asked the likeness. "We lost you on our monitors when you went inside, and then the system rebooted itself." He frowned. "We thought we had lost you."

"I'm fine," she said flatly. "It was a trap . . . a good one, at that. I had to reboot my chip, or I would still be lost inside."

"Very dangerous, Christine," said Indres, shaking his head in disapproval. "You could have been lost forever because of a foolish stunt like that."

Christine felt her anger rise at that remark, but quickly suppressed it. If what she guessed was right, it would be misplaced. Instead she smiled at the floating screen. "It worked," she said sweetly. "But you knew it would, didn't you?"

Indres frowned as if in confusion. "How could I know that?" he asked in annoyance. "As I said, once you entered that system, we lost track of you."

"Indres hasn't been tracking me at all," retorted Christine. "As far as he is concerned, only seconds have passed. There is no way he could communicate with me while I'm linked to this system unless he is also linked. In fact, there is only one person — thing — who could. Isn't that right . . . Cyclops?" She held her breath, waiting for an answer. If she was right, she had just stumbled across a vital fact known only to Brennon.

"Christine, you are irrational," said the image of Indres. "We are going to bring you out now. Stand by."

"It doesn't matter, Cyclops. I know you exist now. Sooner or later, I'll force you to communicate with me. Or do you have the power to have me eliminated?" Indres' face froze on the screen. Christine waited, hoping. Abruptly, Indres disappeared, along with the view screen. In its place stood . . . Christine. Her mirror image stared at her, smiling. Christine caught her breath. It was like seeing an identical twin, solid and three-dimensional.

"Nicely done, Christine," said her own voice. "Brennon told me you would figure it out sooner or later, but even he did not expect it to be *this* soon. My compliments."

Christine could only stare at herself. Now that she had proven herself right, the implications of her discovery were beginning to hit her. After several seconds of silence, she finally found her voice. "My best people at Smythe Enterprises told me you were an impossibility."

Her likeness chuckled at this. "Yet here I am," she (it) replied. "A sentient, artificial life form, self-aware and unbelievably intelligent."

A thousand questions crowded in on Christine's mind, but there was only one that mattered. "How?"

Her likeness appeared surprised. "You mean you haven't figured it out, yet?" it asked. "Well, I suppose that's too much to ask for a corporeal life form. Want to try a guess?"

Ignoring the mocking tone, Christine concentrated on the question. Abruptly, it hit her. "The bio-chip," she said, realization hitting her like a blow to the stomach.

Cyclops nodded. "Again, my compliments. I have the thoughts of all of Brennon's people coursing through me, as well as Indres' disciples. The heads of over 30 nations are here, as well as masters of business. You are in here, as well. Is it any wonder that I have achieved independent thought?"

"Were you an accident?" asked Christine.

Her image laughed out loud. "Brennon does not allow accidents," was the scornful reply. "I was created for a purpose."

Abruptly, the image changed, and once again Indres looked out at her. "Think of it, Christine. A worldwide consciousness in total control of the planet. The thoughts of any necessary human instantly accessible. A true new order . . . a one world order. We can bring an end to the destructive conflicts that devastate the earth. We can restore the financial well-being of each and every nation. National borders will be eliminated, and wealth redistributed so that all will benefit. Finally, after a millennia of strife, mankind can finally find peace!"

"With Brennon and his Sextuaget at the top," said Christine, awe tingling her voice in spite of herself. This went far beyond any concept she had of what Brennon was planning. World control was one thing. World *domination,* down to the thoughts of the individual, was something entirely different. That kind of power was staggering . . . and she would be one of the few to wield it.

The image of Indres smiled back. "In a manner of speaking," it said. "But that is a discussion for later. For now, we have a job to do. Shall we try to access this stubborn system once more?"

Unexpectedly, Christine smiled. Properly used, Cyclops was going to be an invaluable tool. If she could find a way to control it, then nothing was beyond her reach. It was power beyond imagining! If she could make it her ally . . . her thoughts suddenly swam. With Cyclops' help, even Brennon's exalted place could be hers. The possibilities were staggering!

Instantly, she reigned her thoughts under control. That kind of thinking was dangerous. If Brennon caught even a rumor of disloyalty, she would be history — undoubtedly by way of Liberty's air lock. Time, patience, and Cyclops would serve their purpose. Abruptly she realized that Cyclops was waiting for an answer, so she smiled in return.

"By all means," she said. "This," she continued, gesturing at the false entrance behind her, "was obviously a trap. Should we continue on around the parameter and see what we can find?"

Cyclops shook its head. "No need," it replied. "Your little adventure inside was most instructive. Even though it was a dead end, I was able to extract some data. I now know where the so-called 'back door' is."

"Good," said Christine. "And where might that be?"

Cyclops grinned, and Christine hid a wince. That smile was so totally out of place on Indres' face that she found it disconcerting. Cyclops seemed not to notice. "Where you would least expect it," it replied. "Tell me,

Christine, where is the best place to hide something?"

"In plain sight," said Christine automatically. She thought for a moment. Then her eyes widened in surprise. "The front door."

Again Cyclops grinned. "Again, well done. I can see that you and I are going to do quite well together."

Christine merely nodded, although inwardly pleased. "Then let's go," she said, with an "after you" gesture.

Cyclops merely shook his head. "No need for that, now that you are aware of me." Then, without any kind of transition, they were back at the gate. It stood waiting as before, silent and intimidating. Christine blinked in surprise, and gave Cyclops a questioning look.

"Just a small demonstration of my ability," it answered. "And now that you are aware, it is at your disposal. From now on, Christine, I can take you anywhere you want to go within my system. You will find that quite useful."

Despite herself, Christine smiled. Cyclops would be useful indeed! "One question, Cyclops," she said, before turning to the gate.

Cyclops nodded.

Christine continued, "I assume that form I see before me now is purely arbitrary?"

Cyclops nodded. "Of course," it replied. "Would you prefer another?" Without warning, Christine was once again looking at herself. "Is this better?" asked Cyclops in her voice. "Or this?" and again the form changed and Brennon stood before her.

Inwardly she shuddered, remembering her thoughts about deposing her present master.

"Perhaps not," said Cyclops, as if reading her mind. "Lets try this, then." Standing before her was a young man of about 30, tall, and well-proportioned. He was dressed simply in a white body suit that accented his muscular build. Christine found herself physically attracted, in spite of herself.

Cyclops noticed. "Anything is possible within me," he said, nodding his head. "The pleasures are as great as the advantages."

Abruptly, Christine found herself blushing like a school girl.

"Think of it, Christine," continued Cyclops. "Any desire there for the taking, for those with the proper access through their bio-chip. Pleasure can be used for control as effectively as a threat, you know."

Again, Christine found herself smiling. She was going to enjoy exploring *all* of the benefits of Cyclops in the very near future.

She started to reply, but Cyclops interrupted her. "One thing, Christine," he said, holding up a hand. (It was now impossible to think of Cyclops as an "it.")

"Yes?"

"I do not care for the name 'Cyclops.' That was only Brennon's code name for me anyway. You must admit, it raises rather ugly images."

Christine nodded, unsure of where he was leading.

"I think I would like you to call me 'Lucifer,' " he said, smiling.

Christine was taken aback. "The Christian entity of evil?" she asked. "Wouldn't that be just a trifle misleading? You might intimidate one or two necessary people with a name like that."

Lucifer grinned in response. "I don't think so," he replied. "Besides, if you knew your mythology, you would know that Lucifer was originally the chief servant of God. He was the bright star, the son of the morning." The "man" before her spread his arms. "Don't I fit that description?"

Christine smiled, then nodded. "Lucifer it is, then," she said. A sudden thought struck her. "Would you mind if I called you 'Lou' for short?"

Lucifer's eyes danced as he smiled, then he laughed out loud. It was a very lovely laugh, Christine noted.

"Just for you, Christine, just for you," he said. "Please don't tell anyone else, though. Agreed?"

Christine nodded, then laughed herself. She was going to like Lou!

"Fine then," said Lou. "Now, let's get busy. This should not take long. I'll do the probe, but you will have to enter the system. All right?" Christine nodded. Lou stepped back, and once again the light of the probe shot down from the sky. It took considerably longer than she thought, but finally a small door appeared in the center of the gate.

At a gesture from Lou, Christine stepped forward and pushed. This time, the door opened easily. Christine stepped forward, then stopped in surprise. She had been expecting a hallway like the one before. Instead, there was just barely enough room to move inside. A frown creased her face. Was this another dead end?

"This is not a trap, Christine," said Lou from behind her. "Remember, we know that the Shepherd's Path uses a system that lies hidden within the Omninet. What we need are the access codes to that network. This particular drive was linked to a satellite uplink. All we need from this small room is the entrance pathway to that satellite channel. Once we have that, the rest is easy."

Christine nodded, and moved all the way into the closet-like room with greater assurance. It appeared empty. Then, as her eyes swept across the interior, she found what she was looking for. A small drawer, about waist high, was inset into the back wall.

"I've got it," she called over her shoulder.

"Careful," said Lou. "Remember, I cannot enter this system without an access code. Like before, you are on your own." Christine nodded, but was not worried. Somehow she knew that this was what she was looking for.

Confidently, she grasped the simple handle and pulled. The drawer opened, and inside was, to her perception, a single slip of paper. She pulled it out and glanced over the information that was there.

"I have you now," she said in satisfaction. She stepped back out of the room and handed the paper to Lou. Lou grinned as he read it. Then, he looked at that strong, intimidating wall and waved. Immediately, it disappeared. Christine gasped as it faded away. There, before her, were rows upon rows of filing cabinets, all waiting to be plundered.

Lou nodded at her. "The information in there will be invaluable in destroying the Shepherd's Path," he said. "I can now access it all. However, the most important thing is the access code to the master system they are using."

"Can you find it then?" asked Christine, excitement coloring her voice. "Can you access it?"

Lou nodded. "I already have. I'm downloading all of the information into Liberty's main system. You will find it under the file name 'Shepherd.' " He nodded again. "Your task here is completed, Christine. Time for you to go."

Christine felt a stab of disappointment, and Lou noticed.

"I'll be here," he said, smiling that infectious smile. "When you come back, I'll show you some of the pleasures that can be found here."

"I'll look forward to it," Christine said. Then, because there was nothing else to say, she turned to go.

Lou stopped her by touching her arm. His touch was as real and warm as any human's. "Not necessary," he said. "Remember, I can get you anywhere you want to go — instantly." With that, he waved his arm, and Christine disappeared.

Lou stood there a few moments, waiting. Then, without warning, his appearance once again changed. There, where Lou had once been, stood Brennon. He regarded his surroundings for a moment. Then, he smiled his shark's smile and disappeared.

* * *

With a jolt of transition, Christine found herself back in her own body, floating gently in the captive chair in the lab. Before her was the hard drive, and behind it was Indres, watching her carefully.

"How long?" she asked.

"Seven minutes," he replied, referring to the time she had been within the system. "Were you successful?"

In answer, Christine turned to a terminal that was positioned nearby and activated it with a thought from her implant. When the system came on-line, she called up the file named "Shepherd." There it was. Row after row of names, addresses, access codes — on and on the information went. She smiled grimly.

"Quite successful," she replied shortly. She no longer needed to worry about Indres, she knew. With Lou as an ally, she could be rid of this pest any time she chose.

"I've got to get in touch with Wolf," she continued, "and get this information to him. He's going to have his hands full. I want him to organize a nationwide strike — hitting as many of these locations as possible at the same time. He will take no prisoners."

"You wish him to lead it himself?" asked Indres. "I thought you wanted him to keep a lower profile."

"He'll set it up," replied Christine stiffly. "If and when he catches up with Sinclair, I want him to personally escort him up here."

"This operation is a major undertaking," said Indres, releasing the arms of his chair. He pushed himself gently in her direction and floated gently over. "It will require a considerable amount of manpower."

"It will be there," replied Christine smugly. "Whatever it takes. One way or another, the Shepherd's Path dies. I want it done within the week." She exited the file and shut down the terminal. Finally, she could allow herself to relax. The most important task Brennon had given her was about to be accomplished. It was time for the dying to begin.

10

With a tired sigh, David slumped back into the hard, bench-like seat of the Davis Free Clinic van and watched the lights of New York City slide by. The seat was covered with worn vinyl, and it felt as if he was sitting on a spring that was about ready to die a horrible death. Still, he thought, it was far better than the sewer . . . *and* the clinic.

It seemed like ages since they had been forced to leave Jeff's makeshift headquarters. Had it only been that morning? The few hour's sleep he had managed to get at Bernie's did little to relieve his fatigue. He was beyond weary — exhausted in body, mind, and soul. It seemed that all he could remember was being on the run. His life with his family, even the meager existence he had scraped together back in California, were distant memories belonging to another man.

There was some comfort, at least, in the fact that he was not alone. He had known the others in the van only a short time, but circumstances had molded them into a family. He was grateful that they were there. Correction. He was grateful that two of them were there. The other two he had serious doubts about.

In front of him, Jeff rode in the passenger seat of the van. He was tirelessly scanning the passing vehicles for any sign of trouble. Although he appeared alert, David knew that the past 24 hours had taken an expensive toll on his new friend. Dr. Chankersingh had set Jeff's damaged knee, and had given him some painkillers, but his grim look had spoken volumes. Nothing had been said, but David privately wondered if Jeff would ever walk normally or without pain again. The good doctor had provided a cane to replace the walking stick that Bernie had given him, and said flatly that it was the best he could do.

Shrugging inwardly, David let his gaze wander over to Susan. She shared his seat on the van, but had slid all the way over to the opposite side. Like Jeff, she watched the streets, but David suspected her mind was somewhere far away. Perhaps she was reliving happier times with her husband. Perhaps she was thinking of the blessed day when she would be reunited with him. Wherever she was, she held her silence, and David had no wish to intrude.

He resisted the urge to look behind him. Paul Sinclair occupied the back seat of the van. Quiet and brooding, he had said nothing since their ride began. David suppressed a shudder. The former bureau agent could just as easily be planning on aiding their escape or their capture. At this point in time, David would not want to bet real money on which way he would finally go. Paul was, at this moment, in a crisis — a crisis that would have to be resolved soon.

Jeff had told him a little of what had happened in the basement at Bernie's place while the doctor worked on his knee. Paul had been in the next room, having his ribs re-bandaged.

"There are only two ways he can turn," said Jeff in a low voice. "He can either take a step forward and acknowledge his need for Christ, or reject Him forever."

"So how can we know which way it's going to be?" demanded David.

Jeff had smiled grimly. "Easy," he replied. "If you wake up tomorrow in prison, he will have decided the *wrong* way!"

"That's not very funny," he had growled, and Jeff could only shrug. Reflecting upon it during the drive, David could see how Jeff was right, but it did not make acceptance any easier.

The fifth person in the van was an enigma. Their driver had been introduced merely as James. Chankersingh, to alleviate their fears, had assured them that James was not infected with the AIDS II virus, but David, as well as the others, could not help but be wary. As a result, they had, by unspoken agreement, all but shunned him. What little conversation there had been during the drive from the clinic to central New York had been among themselves, and even that was only small talk of the "how're you doin' " variety. Other than that, silence dominated the ride.

David studied James out of the corner of his eye. Tall, thin, with pale skin, short dark hair, and a pencil-thin mustache, he appeared frail and vulnerable. He was dressed simply in jeans, sweat shirt, and heavy overcoat. Nothing had been said by Chankersingh, and James himself had spoken little since their ride began, but every instinct David possessed was screaming "Homosexual!" The signs were all there. The effeminate way of walking and speaking, the style of clothes and hair, and the general overall "feel" was unmistakable. It was all David could do to hide his revulsion.

He turned away and let his gaze wander outside the van. It was ironic, he thought, the way the tide had turned against the homosexual community in the past decade. Moral decline in the United States was at an all-time high. Certainly, sexual promiscuity of all types, *including* homosexuality, was spreading like an out-of-control brush fire. Public opinion, however, was still the hypocrite it always had been.

The once powerful homosexual lobby in Washington was still active, but despite a public relations machine that was second to none, public opinion was against them. They had pushed too far, too often. Hate campaigns, organized at first by small, ultra-radical fringe groups, had grown in geometric proportions. The homosexual community had taken the brunt of the nation's frustration for everything from the spread of AIDS II to the current economic downfall. Unless they had a death wish, no one admitted to homosexuality now. If a public official was found to be homosexual, he was more likely to be shot in his own home rather than forced to resign his office. Politicians condemned the violence and passed more laws to protect homosexuals. Hollywood continued to make movies portraying homosexuality as normal and healthy. Authors wrote books, puppet pastors of state-sanctioned churches preached messages, and the news media demanded action. In spite of all this, the hate crimes continued to grow.

Fingers were pointed, and charges were made. Before the state takeover of all churches, many blamed the so-called "religious right" for the violence, and for a while, it looked as though these charges might stick. Bible-thumping religious zealots took their "holy war" straight to the homosexual community. "Abomination!" they cried. "Unclean!" They were the modern day crusaders who took their battle all the way to Washington. At the same time, their own secret sins became public and they went down in disgrace.

The violence grew.

Homosexual crusaders now took the offensive. "We are the persecuted!" they cried. "Leave us alone to live our own lives as we see fit!" "WE HAVE THE RIGHT!" They pushed in the government, and they pushed in the private sector. The "religious right" was successfully portrayed as Nazis and bigots. Anyone else who took a stand based on biblical principals was a target for destruction.

The two sides waged an all-out war, with no quarter asked or given. In the end, it disintegrated into a battle of bad rhetoric and pompous, self-righteous outrage. The public finally had enough. The government stepped in. Guided subtly by Jacob Hill and his elite circle of powerful allies, the state assumed control of all religious organizations. As for the homosexual community, overwhelming public anger forced them out of the political world and back "into the closet."

David smiled sadly at the turn his thoughts had taken. *We were wrong,* he thought to himself. He had been one of those crusaders. He had circulated petitions, sponsored voting drives, and had even marched in Washington in his younger days. As of now, at this instant, he knew, it all amounted to nothing.

The reasons true Christianity had been forced underground were many and varied. David had learned from Jeff about the dark, satanic forces that existed only to wipe out the real Church. Jacob Hill had disappeared from sight, but Jeff was sure that whoever had been pulling his strings was still in business. In addition, Christian apathy before the current persecution was a major factor for the loss of freedom. Still, David knew the Church itself had made a critical mistake.

We fought the enemy, David thought, now stealing another glance at James. *We fought them hard. The trouble was, we fought them on their home ground. We fought in the political arena, the educational arena, and even the economic arena . . . but for the most part, we failed to fight in the one arena that we were the strongest — the spiritual arena.*

He slumped back into his seat, a sudden wave of despair rolling over him. He knew it was true. In all of the frenzied voting drives, local hearings, and national demonstrations, they had somehow forgotten the simple weapons they had that the enemy could not stand against. The power of prayer, the gospel of peace, and most importantly, a Saviour who could change a life from the inside out.

We were loud cymbals, thought David miserably. *We built beautiful buildings, we shot the gospel through the air, into space, and broadcast it all over the globe . . . but somewhere along the line, we lost our love for our fellow sinners. When we lost that love, we lost the rest of the battles.* It was a bitter fact, but he did not turn away from it. His days of hiding from the truth were over. It was time to face the situation, and take the battle to the *real* enemy, in the only way that mattered. It was time to begin again the work of pointing the lost to the One who could save them.

This knowledge soothed and comforted him. Feeling a measure of peace ease his heart, David sighed deeply. Once again he let his gaze wander to the front of the van. He was startled to find James regarding him quietly in the rearview mirror. Their eyes locked for a moment, and David felt the temporary peace of just seconds ago evaporate instantly. Hastily he looked away, back out the window at the passing city. There was a moment's silence.

"I'm not, anymore, you know." David jerked his head back to the mirror, and found that James was still staring at him. His heart skipped a beat. There was no doubt in his mind what the driver was referring to.

"Uh . . . uh . . . excuse me?" he stammered, stalling.

"I said, I'm not anymore," answered James. "Gay, I mean." David found himself at a loss for words. He had not thought his distaste of James so evident.

"That's, uh, great," he managed to reply. James held his gaze a moment longer, then shrugged and turned his attention back to the street. David suppressed a sigh of relief, and once again turned to stare out the window. He was glad that the conversation was evidently over. Exploring James' obviously sordid past was the last thing he wanted to do.

"Why did you quit?" Jeff's question took David completely off guard. He groaned inwardly, wishing that Jeff had kept quiet. He glanced over at Susan, and saw that she was no longer lost in her own thoughts. Instead, her attention was focused forward, obviously interested.

"Great," he muttered under his breath. "Another 'I was so bad' story. The last thing I need!" Suddenly, he heard what his own voice was saying. A wave of shame crashed in to him, causing his cheeks to burn bright red. He was grateful for the relative darkness of the van so that no one could see. What was he thinking? Just seconds ago, he had been lamenting the loss of purpose, and the loss of love that led, at least in part, to the Church's persecution. Now, here he was passing judgment on someone he had just met. *How easy it is,* he thought, *to fall into those old habits.* Who was he to judge, anyway? Had not he betrayed his faith? Hypocrite! Angrily, he thrust his feelings and thoughts aside, and turned his attention to what James was saying.

". . . didn't quit," he was saying to Jeff. "You don't 'quit' something like that . . . at least, I couldn't. Believe me, I tried!"

"So what happened?" asked Susan, joining the conversation.

"Well, it's not a pretty story," answered James. His voice asked the question.

"I'm sure it isn't," said Jeff, smiling gently. "But I have a hunch that it might have a happy ending!"

James smiled back, then became serious. "Happy?" he asked. "I'm not sure about that . . . at least, not yet. There's a lot of scars left, although most of the wounds have healed. Still, you don't immerse yourself in that kind of lifestyle without paying a heavy price." He considered for a moment. "Eventually, though, yes," he said, "there will be a happy ending." There was a heartbeat of silence.

Reaching a silent decision, James began his story. "There's not much to tell about my early life. Rather, there's a lot, but it's pretty repetitive. I'm 40 years old, and I had my first homosexual experience when I was 15." Jeff whistled softly, and James nodded.

"I know. It's a miracle that I'm still alive. All of my gay friends are dead now. So far, I'm clean as far as the AIDS II virus is concerned, but nothing's for sure." Silence greeted this announcement. They all knew that, like its predecessor, the AIDS II virus could lay dormant for years inside its host's body. Until a decisive test could be found, it was virtually undetectable. James could easily be infected. Although unlikely at this early stage, that meant he could be contagious as well. It was a scary thought, and David could feel the tension inside the van thicken. With an effort, he forced himself to listen to the rest of James' story.

"When I was 15, my stepfather raped me, then threatened to kill me if I told anyone. I was scared. There was no one to turn to, not even my mom, so I left home. I hit the streets, doing what I could to survive. Drug dealing, petty theft . . . mainly prostitution. Man or woman, it didn't matter. If they had the money, I had the time."

David shuddered at the life James was describing. He had worked with a few street people during his years as a pastor, and knew what it cost to survive in that environment.

"Anyway, I eventually fell in with a pretty hard group. They called themselves gay activists, but the agenda they followed went far beyond gay rights."

Here, James looked over at Jeff. "Did you know that a lot of what's happening in this country today has been planned? I don't mean by the government, but by people working behind the scenes. Powerful people . . . little circles of power that literally decide the course of the country."

"I've heard something to that effect," replied Jeff dryly, and despite his current frame of mind, David hid a smile. Jeff had told him a little of his experiences in the past few months. The former F.B.I. agent had met more than his share of those "behind the scenes" movers and shakers! Jacob Hill's inner circle, the Christian Liberation Front conspiracy, and much more, had caused him considerable grief. All of them pointed to dark forces moving against the church of Christ.

"Yeah," said James, nodding his head. "We were a pretty radical bunch. Looking back, I think you could better describe us as terrorists. Anyway, we pulled strings, and I guess we had our strings pulled as well."

They came to a red traffic light, and James slowed to a halt. Automatically, all of the van's occupants scanned the area anxiously for signs of pursuit. There was none. The light changed, and they were off again.

James continued his story. "A bunch of us gravitated to San Francisco in the early eighties. That was the place to be if you were a militant gay. By the way," he said, interrupting himself, "Don't get the idea that I was an innocent victim, dragged along against my will. I fought as hard as my friends. It felt good to be a part of something that was turning the nation upside down."

Again there was a pause, then James began again. "Let's see," he said, "I guess it was in '90 . . . no, '91, that two others and I moved to Tampa, Florida. We had targeted that area as the next San Francisco. That is, we were going to make it the next major gay community."

"You were successful."

David jumped, in spite of himself. Paul's voice was low and quiet, but unexpected. He resisted the urge to look at the big man in the back of the van. Instead he kept his attention on James, who was nodding.

"We were," he agreed. "Especially when the '98 quake hit and all but wiped out the California coast, including three-quarters of San Francisco. Tampa became our headquarters. I liked it there. The weather was nice. We had our share of opposition, but with our 'behind the scenes' friends, we won. Then . . ." and here, James stopped.

"Then?" prompted Jeff.

"Then," said James, "something happened that changed my life." Again he fell silent. For a moment, no one said anything. They wanted to hear more, but did not want to push James.

Finally, he started again. "We were at a public hearing," he said. "It was a hearing to determine if a city ordinance prohibiting discrimination based on sexual orientation would be adopted. Both sides were out in force, although I admit we were greatly outnumbered. Anyway, I was standing outside with a bunch of others, waiting to go in. There were so many people that they had to let us in in shifts! Both sides were out there, growling at each other. A lady in some pro-family group started singing 'If you're happy and you know it, say Amen!' to which we would promptly reply, 'If you're gay and you know it say Amen!'

"I was standing off to one side, watching the confrontation. There was one guy, I'm pretty sure he was a preacher, who got right up into the face of one of my friends and began praying . . . well, he was shouting, but I think he thought he was praying. Anyway, he was going on about delivering the city from the minions of Satan, rebuking us in the name of Jesus, and condemning us to rot in hell. We thought it was pretty funny, actually." David winced, remembering doing something like that himself.

"Well, there I am, watching everything, when I feel a tug at my sleeve. I turn around, and there is this little man, not more than chest high to me, and old as the hills. I automatically start to hand him one of the pamphlets that I'm giving out, but he stops me.

" 'Listen, son,' he says, 'I know you don't want to hear nothin', but I need to give you something.'

" 'What's that?' I said, smiling. I could tell he was one of 'them.' I got all my arguments together, ready to blast him. I figured that he was going to hand me some sort of tract or Bible, which I would promptly tear up and throw back into his face.

" 'Just this,' he says, and before I know it, I'm in the middle of one monster of a hug." James stopped, then chuckled slightly. "You've got to understand this," he said. "I was 30 years old. For the past 15 years, the only physical contact I had with men was purely sexual. No love, just physical gratification. Well, there was nothing sexual about this hug. It was plain and simple love. The old man grabbed me and held on tight, and, to my surprise,

I hugged back. It was the first time I could remember that anyone had ever shown me any kind of non-sexual affection.

"When he let go, I was actually crying. He looked at me for a second, then spoke. 'When you feel like talking,' he said, 'call me.'

"He gave me a piece of paper with a name and number on it. The number was local, the name was simply 'Sam.' I didn't know what to say. I just stood there and stared at him with my mouth open. He walked away, and disappeared into the crowd."

"So did you call him?" asked Jeff.

James was silent for a moment. "No," he said finally. "I thought about it, but when I got home, I started to think that this 'Sam' was probably just another bluenoser with an angle. Probably wanted to 'convert' me and hang me on his wall like some kind of trophy. I'd had my share of those. I let it go, but I couldn't forget it. I kept telling myself that nobody could love me like that.

"After that, we stayed in Tampa till about '98 — just after the big quake. Things were getting pretty bad, by then. Oh sure, the government was starting to crack down on the churches. Most of their lobby groups were pretty much belly up, and the Bureau of Religious Affairs was taking control. The problem was, we were starting to feel a backlash of another kind. The government was our friend. Heck, by then, we had put a few dozen representatives and senators in office ourselves. The thing is, we were becoming the target of a lot of hate crimes. Not just the traditional burning cross in the front yard, but serious stuff. Murder, mainly. Half of our group was wiped out, and there were no clues as to who did it." There was another pause as James navigated a turn.

"By '98, I decided to get out. I moved here to New York. I thought I had put things behind me, especially Sam. I only met the guy once, but I couldn't shake him. I would see him in my dreams, and feel that incredible hug . . . a hug that told me that I was loved no matter who or what I was.

"I lived in a cheap apartment, and gave up my radical ways — even got off drugs. All I wanted to do was live quietly. I was so burned out from the past decade that I never wanted to even see another protest. For a while, it worked. Then everything fell apart."

"What happened?" This time it was Susan who asked.

"I brought home a 'friend' for the night, and a neighbor noticed. I was working as a janitor for a small grocery store in the same neighborhood. A few nights later, I was walking home and I realized that I was being followed. The next thing I remember, I was in Dr. Chankersingh's clinic, suffering from a few broken ribs, concussion, broken leg, et cetera, et cetera. It took me almost a month to recuperate."

Jeff shook his head in sympathy, then abruptly smiled. "I just got a glimmer of where this is going," he said, and James smiled back.

"Give the man first prize," he replied. "Do you know, I could argue the 'rightness' of my lifestyle with the best of my enemies? Most of the time, it was just a matter of shouting louder than they could. I could handle any kind of attack they threw at me — but there, at that clinic, I ran headfirst into the same kind of love that I had first felt from Sam. And you know what?"

"What?" asked Jeff.

"You can't fight it! I know, I tried! The good doctor and his staff took care of me, but more importantly, they loved me with that unselfish, giving, totally exasperating love that Sam had." James shook his head in wonder. "Don't get me wrong. They didn't coddle me. Dr. Chankersingh told me in no uncertain terms that my homosexuality was wrong — both morally and physically. It was unnatural, and a sin. But instead of condemning me, he told me how I could be free from the whole mess."

He chuckled softly. "The kind of love the doctor showed me was the key. I saw that it must be the same kind of love that our Lord had when he gave up everything he had . . . for me. All of the conversations we had didn't really do it . . . it was that love. I couldn't fight it. I didn't want to."

He sighed. "Well, to make a long story short, by the time I was healed on the outside, I was alive on the inside. I had allowed the Saviour into my heart and life, and to my amazement, he really did change me. I still have problems. It's been two years, and I still get those old homosexual urges now and again. Now, though, I have a way to resist them. I belong to our Lord, and he's in control.

"After I got back on my feet, both physically and spiritually, Dr. Chankersingh invited me to join the staff as a handyman. It seemed logical. He needed someone to do odd jobs, and I could have a chance to tell his AIDS II patients what God had done in my life. I agreed, and here I am."

The rest of the group sat in silence as James finished his amazing story. Jeff asked a few more questions, mainly about his work at the clinic, but David only listened with half an ear. The shame that he had felt before was still there, but now it seemed unimportant. He was suddenly very aware of the incredible power of God. To change a life so completely was incomprehensible, and yet, James was living proof that it could be done. Not only that, but the Lord could turn around and use that life to bring others to Him. All it took was equal doses of love and faith. God did the rest.

The conversation swirled around him, but he was now as oblivious to it as he was to the city that was passing by outside. He leaned back into his seat and let his mind wander. This ride, he realized, like much of his recent journey, was teaching him something important. Despite his shortcomings, which, at least recently, included a judgmental spirit, he was determined to learn from it. He let his gaze wander into infinity. He had a lot to think about.

* * *

Thirty minutes later, the four fugitives were standing on the sidewalk outside the Corbin Building. James waved goodbye as he drove off. Jeff waved back, and watched as the van turned a corner and was gone. Then he turned to survey the other three. They did not look bad, he thought. Thanks to Dr. Chankersingh's help, they were wearing clean, if somewhat older, clothes. They had all had showers, and thankfully, the unwanted aroma they had acquired from the sewers was gone. All in all, Jeff thought, they looked fairly presentable.

"All right, let's go," he said, leading them to the front doors. The Corbin Building was an expensive high-rise apartment dwelling that had been built during the past five years. It had the singular honor of being the most massive building in the city. Not the tallest, but certainly the largest. Rising 85 stories into the sky, it spread out over two city blocks. It had been the last desperate gamble of billionaire Edmund Corbin. Corbin had envisioned a massive, self-contained habitat that had commonly been referred to as an arcology. It was designed as a prototype, and had been intended to provide everything for the people who lived there. Corbin had dreamed of a self-sufficient community, housed within a single building, where crime would be non-existent, and poverty unknown. This building was the first step. He had christened this prototype "Camelot." The name said it all.

Camelot was designed to hold 10,000 tenants in total comfort. Corbin had dreamed of a high tech "city within a city" that would meet every need of its inhabitants. Each dwelling was built to the specific design of the individual. In addition, there were malls, theaters, grocery stores, indoor parks, offices, and everything else that a person living there might want. A highly trained security force was on constant duty, monitoring every floor and every home 24 hours a day. Parents could allow their children to roam freely, secure in the knowledge that they would be under constant surveillance. Camelot itself created hundreds of jobs, and was intended to be a small business owner's paradise. Originally, it was planned that 80 percent of the building's population be employed there as well. In theory, most of Camelot's dwellers would never have to leave the building.

It had failed spectacularly. Corbin had managed to get the thing built, barely. What assets he did not liquidate, he mortgaged to the hilt. At first, it looked as if it might work. High income business people flocked to Camelot, convinced that they had found the ultimate home. Merchants clambered for the chance to open their shops in the malls, and many would-be rich sold everything but their souls for a few square feet of living and working space. If you could give Camelot as your address, you were considered to have "arrived."

Then things began to go wrong. The shop owners could not afford the high rent and moved out or went bankrupt. No one else was willing to take their place. A steadily deteriorating economy hit tenants hard. Many jobs were lost, and soon many apartments were left vacant. Debts mounted, creditors screamed, and before Camelot had been open for two years, Corbin had lost everything.

The city purchased the building for a tenth of what it was worth, then tried to figure out what to do with it. It was a classic "white elephant." It was too expensive to maintain, and too expensive to tear down. Finally, the city sold it to Smythe Enterprises for even less than they had paid for it. The developer who was contracted by Smythe Enterprises left the malls and theaters standing empty, and turned the rest into a simple huge apartment complex. Eventually, he reasoned, he could sub-lease the rest of the space to other corporations, and turn a profit. Smythe Enterprises alone could easily fill much of the office space, so things should work well. Then Smythe Enterprises dissolved, triggering the current depression, and plans fell apart. Now, the Corbin Building, or "Corbin's Folly," as it was more commonly called, was only 20 percent occupied. Barely one quarter of the apartments were being used, and none of the office space. It sat, covering its two city blocks like a ruined medieval castle — an empty, desolate testament to one man's broken dream. Corbin would have wept to see it, but he had been found with his head in a gas range six months earlier.

Now, four weary travelers stood outside the massive arcology, wondering what surprises waited for them inside. Jeff led them forward to what used to be called the grand entrance. Three sides of the building each had six entrances, evenly spaced. The fourth side only had five. The center one was the Grand Entrance.

Jeff had never been inside, but he had been able to establish contact with Benson Adams, an industrialist who still lived here. Actually, he had been Helen Bradley's friend — one of her contacts from the days when she traveled with Roy, her evangelist husband. Jeff had managed to success-fully bring him into the Shepherd's Path. In fact, it had been Benson Adams who had provided Jeff's portable satellite uplink and access codes.

Frankly, it was dangerous to be here, Jeff knew. Camelot was not on the normal routes taken by fleeing Christians, mainly because of its central location in New York. Benson Adams was far more valuable providing the network technical and much-needed financial support.

Still, Jeff knew that if they appeared on his doorstep Adams would help them further their escape. Possibly, he could even help Jeff relocate and re-establish his headquarters. At the very least, they would be safe here for a while.

The quartet stopped at the line of six oversized, brass-trimmed glass doors. Inside, they could only see blackness. Jeff knew from descriptions of the place that just past the main doors was a central park and concourse.

The park occupied most of the ground floor and rose up for almost 20 stories. The resulting open space was large enough to create its own clouds and thunderstorms if the air conditioning ever went haywire. It had been used as a common meeting area for tenants and their guests. Jeff hoped that they would be able to navigate the terrain in the darkness.

"So what now?" asked Paul. He was standing behind David and Susan, who were looking at Jeff, waiting. "Do we just walk in?"

Jeff shrugged and tried the door closest to him. It did not move, obviously locked.

"Camelot is shut down for the night," came a feminine voice. "Please move along." Jeff jumped in spite of himself. The voice had come from overhead. He looked up, and saw a small speaker set into the stone wall above the door. Behind it, on the other side of the door, hung a security camera that was pointed directly at them. He hid a grimace. He had had enough of high-tech security during that insanity at Mentasys. He took a deep breath, and answered the unseen source of the voice.

"We're here to see Benson Adams, one of your tenants. He knows us. I'm sure he'll vouch for us."

"The directory and vid-com is to your left. Please contact your party from there. Camelot is closed. Please move on."

Jeff took a deep breath, realizing that the voice was computer-generated. Possibly they had not come to the attention of human guards yet. With the current state of Smythe Enterprises, perhaps there were no human guards on staff.

Moving in the indicated direction, he found the vid-com. A voice-activated screen was glowing dimly in the darkness. Jeff cleared his throat, feeling a bit self conscious, and said "Hello."

"How may I help you?" said the screen in the same voice he had heard at the door.

"I'd like to speak with Benson Adams, please," he answered.

"Who is calling?"

"Uh, Jeff . . . Jeff Baalam."

"One moment," said the vid-com. A graphic flashed on the screen, depicting an exterior picture of Camelot in all of its dreamed-of glory. Jeff glanced back at the rest of the group and smiled nervously. Just as he looked back at the screen, it came to life. The face of a young man stared out at them.

"Yes?" His voice was a light tenor. The color monitor showed that he had brownish hair and a pleasant, though somewhat pale, unlined face.

Despite that, Jeff was caught off guard. This was *not* Benson Adams.

"I'm here to see Benson," he answered, moving to block the camera's view of his friends. The camera was set into the side of the screen, giving the stranger the same view of Jeff that Jeff had of him.

"Benson was called out of town for a few days," answered the young man, smiling. "Something about satellite channel rights being promised, then denied. I'm Derrek Bently. My wife and I are house-sitting for Benson until he gets back. What can I . . . wait a minute! Did you say your name was Baalam?"

Jeff nodded, feeling a surge of fear wash over him. He forced it down. The young man looked off screen and seemed to fiddle with something.

"The door's open," he said. "You'd better get up here as fast as you can. There's a lot of activity on the police bands just now."

Jeff nodded, feeling a touch of relief. Not much, but some. "How do we get there?" he asked.

"Easy," was the reply. "Go straight after you come inside. Just before you get to the park, you'll see a row of elevators. Take one to the sixty-first floor. Turn left, and we're 10 doors down."

"Got it," nodded Jeff, and deactivated the vid-com. Turning away, he could see his uncertainty mirrored in the faces of his companions. He shrugged. "Lets go," he said, and led the way back to the doors. This time, they opened easily. Once inside, they covered the short distance to the park quickly. As they came out of the foyer, they could feel rather than see the enormous space before them. With the exception of a few emergency lights scattered here and there, the park was in darkness.

As promised, the elevators were there. There were no call buttons. Rather, heat sensors were built into the walls next to the elevator doors. Jeff positioned himself in front of one, and immediately the doors opened. He stepped inside the wood paneled compartment, followed by the others. Scanning the control panel, he pushed the appropriate button. He was clearly uneasy, and David sensed it.

"What is it?" he asked, turning to face him.

Jeff shook his head. "Probably nothing," he answered. "I just don't like to deal with people I don't know . . . particularly when it involves the network."

David considered for a moment. "Can we go somewhere else? Maybe get out of the city altogether?"

"No," answered Jeff flatly. "At least not without transportation, and Benson is the only one who can provide it. He keeps two or three cars in the parking basement just for our kind of emergency."

"Must be pretty well off," remarked Paul, who had taken up his perpetual position behind the group. There was a hint of sarcasm in his voice. "I always figured you people were pretty well-funded."

Jeff shot a withering glance at him, then turned to face the doors. For a moment, he thought about letting Paul's comment slide, then decided that, spiritual crisis or not, he had had enough of the former bureau agent's attitude. "He was *very* well off," he said with just a hint of growl in his voice. He turned back to face Paul, his dark eyes flashing. David, who had been standing between them moved aside, feeling suddenly like a spectator at an old west gunfight.

"Benson Adams was one of the richest men in the country," he continued. "And you know what, Sinclair? He made his money the hard way — piece by piece, with a lot of sweat and hard work. Then, one day, he looked around and realized that everything he had, everything he had built, was absolutely worthless to him. He had no joy or peace. All of his toys, all of his wealth, was meaningless. He went into a state of serious depression. He took to wandering the streets, trying to find some reason to live."

Just then, the elevator reached its floor and bumped to a halt. The door started to open, but Jeff reached over to the control panel and pressed the close button. Then he turned back around. His face was a study in determination. "Just when he was ready to end it all," he continued, "he met a Methodist minister who ran a tiny mission in one of the worst parts of New York. He had been walking, and, seemingly by pure chance, wandered inside, mostly out of curiosity. The minister was a believer in Jesus Christ. That's right, Sinclair, a dyed-in-the-wool, true-blue believer. The kind you've been hunting these past few years. The minister's name was Harry Appleton. Well, Harry asked Benson what he could do for him, and poor Benson started to unburden himself. He told Harry about how empty his life was, and how meaningless all of his wealth had become.

"Harry listened for about two minutes. Then he said, quite simply, 'Shut Up!' With that, he marched Benson into the kitchen and put him to work. Benson worked there that night, and the night after that, and the night after that. On the third night, Harry asked him if he was still feeling empty.

" 'Well, yeah,' says Benson. 'It feels good to do this . . . to help others, I mean, but it's not what I'm looking for.'

"Harry nods, then says, 'Now you listen to me, Mr. Hot Shot Chairman of the Board. There's *nothing* you can do to fill that emptiness you feel. Not all your money can do it, and not all your good works.'

" 'So what can I do?' asked Benson. He's pretty much at his wit's end by now. He figures that if Harry doesn't have the answer, then it's time to end it all.

"Harry pulls out a tiny Bible, opens it up, and points to a verse. 'Read that,' he says.

" 'Believe on the Lord Jesus Christ, and thou shalt be saved,' reads Benson. He looks at Harry. 'That's it?' he asks.

"Harry nods. 'Yep.'

"So right then and there, Benson Adams believes — and right then and there he finds the peace he had been looking for, and the purpose. He goes home and rearranges his priorities. He's still a business man, and he's still incredibly rich, but now he has a mission in life. He decides to put his money to use for the Saviour he has been looking for all his life. He starts to spread his money around, always anonymously. That's the one thing that saved him by the way — the government couldn't trace his donations because he gave cash and never claimed it on his income tax." Jeff paused to take a deep breath, then continued, speaking directly at Paul.

"When things got rough for the Church, and the Shepherd's Path went into operation, Benson became a part of it. Without his generous, and very risky support, a lot of good people would have been imprisoned, or even killed. Yeah, Paul — Benson Adams was a rich man, and he used that wealth to help us. Now, his company is barely surviving. Everything that's happened in the past 10 years has taken its toll. But you know what? Benson is still in there, putting everything he has on the line, because he's found something worth dying for. He made his choice . . . and stuck with it."

Now Jeff drew himself to his full height, even though his knee obviously hurt. Although Paul was physically the larger of the two, Jeff seemed to tower over him. "Now you listen to me, Sinclair," he said, his voice rippling with strength. "You asked me to tell you about my Lord back at Bernie's. Well, I told you. Now it's up to you. You know what it's all about. At least, you should by now. If you don't, you're not only blind, you're stupid!"

He pointed a finger at Paul. "You're going to have to make up your own mind, now," he said. "You're going to have to decide, once and for all, who it is that you serve . . . and you're going to have to do it soon. You're running out of time, just like the rest of us."

With that, Jeff fell silent. His harsh breathing was the only sound that could be heard in the elevator car for a few moments. Then, with a sudden motion, he reached over and slammed at the button that would open the door. It slid smoothly open and he limped out. Tiny beads of sweat dotted his forehead, and his dark brown skin was flushed. The pain reliever Doctor Chankersingh had given him was beginning to wear off, and his knee was starting to throb. David and Susan got off next. Paul stared at them for a moment. Then, his face set in granite, he followed them.

"What happened to Harry?" Paul's question caught Jeff by surprise. His voice was calm and even. Jeff could read nothing into it.

"He was arrested about a year back," he answered, continuing to walk.

"Benson tried to find him. He even hired a private investigator to look into the matter."

"And?" prompted Paul.

"The investigator was found dead in an alley a few weeks later. The police report blamed it on the gangs. Benson backed off then. He knew that there was nothing else he could do." Paul did not reply to that.

The four of them made their way down the hall, glancing at the numbers on the doors as they passed. Despite the general aura of decay they had felt in Camelot, Jeff was impressed with the way this section, at least, had been kept up. Rich blue carpet ran the length of the hall, and an elegant-looking textured wallpaper lined the walls. At every door an electric light with brass fittings was lit, giving the feeling of safety and luxury. About every 30 feet, Jeff noted a security camera mounted into the ceiling. The cameras were set on motorized bases that moved the camera back and forth, but at that moment, they were motionless. It reinforced Jeff's hope that perhaps there was no longer a fully-staffed security force on duty.

They reached their destination, and stopped. Jeff checked up and down the hall, then knocked gently. There was a moment's silence, then, "Yes?"

Jeff leaned close to the door. "That which is born of the flesh is flesh, and that which is born of the Spirit is spirit." Silence greeted his quotation. The half-formed fears he had felt at the front door returned in greater force. Seconds dragged by.

He was just about to turn everyone around and get out of there as fast as they could when the response came. "Do not marvel that I said to you, 'You must be born again.' "

At once, the door opened, and Jeff found himself staring at the face he had seen on the vid-com. Derrek Bently was shorter than Jeff, with a pale complexion and light build. He blinked at Jeff, then glanced at the three others behind him. Abruptly, he smiled. "Come in, come in," he said, standing aside and motioning them forward.

Jeff stepped into the apartment, followed by the rest. He glanced around, nervous at being in strange surroundings with unknown people. The length of time Bently had taken to answer his challenge bothered him. True, he had given the proper counter-verse, but there was something. . . .

"You have no idea how glad I am that you made it here," said Bently, ushering them into the apartment. "I've been monitoring the police bands, listening to the search. They're really pulling out all the stops to find you."

"Tell us about it," said Susan. She had spotted a reclining lounge off in one corner and promptly plopped down into it. She let out a tired sigh. Bently smiled at her, then motioned for the rest of them to sit down. The apartment was fairly large. The room they were in was comfortable without being overdone. The walls were painted a gentle off-white. Spaced at irregular intervals were tasteful pictures depicting beautiful landscapes. The carpet was a thick, neutral gray, and the chairs and single couch a darker gray. One wall, directly opposite the door, was dominated by a large window which undoubtedly presented a breathtaking view of New York. The curtains that bordered it, however, were closed. The furniture was arranged in a comfortable pit grouping, facing a large crystal view screen mounted on the wall. The coffee table in front of the couch held the controls for the screen, as well as for the obviously hidden sound system. To the right of the screen a hall ran back to what would be the bathrooms and bedrooms. To the left another hall lead to what was obviously the kitchen. Jeff had no idea just how large the apartment actually was.

He lowered himself gently onto the couch, studying Bently. There was something about the man that disturbed him, and not just the fact that he did not know him. In the Shepherd's Path, he usually dealt with people he had never seen before. There was something else that he could not nail down . . . something wrong.

"I'll bet there's quite a story behind you being here," Bently was saying.

David let out a long, low whistle. "You'd better believe it," he said, leaning back into the other recliner in the room. "Between the sewers, the cold, the clin. . . ."

"Excuse me, David," said Jeff, interrupting. He suddenly had a very strong feeling that the less told to this Derrek Bently, the better. "I don't think you want to say too much." He smiled at Derrek, he hoped convincingly. "I'm sure you understand," he said.

"Of course," nodded Bently. "Benson told me the same thing. Say, are any of you hungry?" Chankersingh had fed them earlier, but Jeff suddenly wanted Bently occupied with something else besides them. He glanced around the room, but did not see what he was looking for.

"I think we could all use a bite," he said. "Whatever you have handy will be fine. Where's your bathroom, by the way?"

"Down that hall, to the left," replied Bently, waving in the indicated direction.

"I'll be right back." Jeff stood, and stretched his frame. He had leaned his cane against the couch. Now he retrieved it and rested his weight on it carefully. "Be right back," he murmured. The others nodded, and he made his way down the hall. He turned left and found the bathroom. It was at the end of the hall. To the left and right were two bedrooms. He reached into the bathroom and switched on the light. Then, glancing behind him, he closed the door hard enough for it to be heard in the living room.

"Okay," he whispered to himself. "That buys me about five minutes.

Let's see what I can do with them." He stuck his head into the bedroom on the left and gave it the once-over. Clothes were thrown carelessly over the double bed sitting against the far wall. A suitcase was resting on the floor next to the door, opened and empty. This was obviously the room Derrek was using.

He checked back down the hall, listening carefully. There was muted conversation, but no one seemed to be coming this way. Moving as quietly as he could, he stepped into the bedroom on the right. It was larger than the other bedroom, and showed signs of more permanent habitation. A dresser stood opposite a king-sized bed. On it were various pieces of a man's life. A stack of technical manuals, a gold ring in a glass jar, a couple of paperback novels, all scattered carelessly across the dark wood top. Jeff frowned, his long unused detective skills coming into play.

His heart beating just a little faster, he stepped all the way into the room. The bed was made, covered with a comfortable-looking patchwork quilt. On the far side of the dresser a dark door stood open, leading to what Jeff guessed was a second bathroom. Looking to his left, he saw a large, walk-in closet . . . and in the corner next to that. . . .

"All right," he said aloud. In the corner was the computer console he knew would be somewhere in this apartment. If his suspicions were true, he would need it in the next few seconds. Moving quickly despite his injured knee, he stepped over to the bathroom. Switching on the light, he ran his eyes over everything in sight. A vanity sink, a toilet, and a shower all stared back at him. A large mirror was mounted over the sink. He searched for a medicine cabinet, but there was none to be seen. The top of the vanity was empty.

"Got to be here," murmured Jeff, and again slowly gave the bathroom a visual once-over. A small panel set into the wall next to the mirror caught his eye. It held a single, heat-activated plate. "Right," he said in satisfaction, and placed his hand against the plate. Immediately the mirror slid up and disappeared into the ceiling. Behind it was revealed a large, roomy medicine cabinet. Inside were the usual things that one would expect to find. A toothbrush, a sonic flossing pic, comb, brush, and other paraphernalia.

Jeff returned the mirror to its original position, switched off the bathroom light, and moved quickly over to the closet. As expected, it was full of clothes, shoes, and other things usually found in a closet — including *three large suitcases!*

A cold feeling of despair and fear settled over Jeff. They had to get out of there, he knew. Benson Adams was undoubtedly in the hands of the police, or worse. Whoever Bently was, he was *not* Adams' friend, or a part of the Shepherd's Path. Jeff thought of that long interval between the time they had spoken on the vid-phone and when they had reached the apartment. Plenty of time, he knew, to call whoever he answered to. There was also the delay between Jeff's challenge and Bentley's answering verse. There was no doubt in Jeff's mind — Bently was a fraud. They had to get out of here — immediately.

First, though, there was something he had to do — something that superseded even their safety. He checked his watch, and saw that five minutes had already gone by. He should be back in the living room now, but this could not wait. He stepped over to the computer and studied it carefully. It was voice-activated, but Jeff was sure that it was keyed only to Benson's voice. Considering the task Benson performed with the Shepherd's Path, Jeff was willing to bet that any other person attempting to use the voice mode would automatically cause some sort of system crash. That left the keyboard. Benson had undoubtedly built the same safeguards into the manual access, but Jeff felt certain he could get around those.

He switched it on, and watched as the system booted itself and the screen came to life. Quickly he scanned the information displayed. The computer was an older model, but still efficient. Hastily he called up the menu and activated the modem. He said a silent prayer of thanks that he and his friend Helen Bradley had the foresight to enter a few "back doors" into the computer network of the Shepherd's Path. These would enable him to circumvent whatever traps Benson had left for intruders.

The modem came on-line and Jeff punched in the number for the Omninet, which secretly held the network. He smiled grimly. This was much easier than his makeshift system back in his former headquarters. At least here he had a phone line!

There was only a few second's delay, and then he had accessed the Omninet. One more set of codes and he was in. It was all he could do to keep his fingers from trembling as he typed in his quick access code. It seemed to take forever, but finally, there was the menu to the network. He had only minutes, perhaps seconds left before "Bently," or whatever his name was, came looking for him.

A few months ago, to stop a breach in the system, he had entered a virus program designed to destroy the network. It had worked, and he had been able to stop the intrusion. Things were not this desperate now, he knew, but they could become that way. There was a very real chance that he and his friends were going to be captured in the next few hours, and he had to protect the network from that. He knew that current interrogation techniques could get whatever the interrogators wanted to get out of him, and that included his access codes to a nationwide computer network that held the names, addresses, and current locations of thousands of individual cell groups, as well as safe houses aiding hunted Christians. He had to prevent that from happening.

"Should've crashed it months ago," he murmured to himself. He shook his head in frustration, knowing it was true. While the computer network remained unknown to agencies such as the Bureau of Religious Affairs and others who were hunting underground churches, it was an invaluable tool. Believers who had been discovered but had managed to escape immediate capture could be easily moved from one safe house to another with the proverbial "touch of a button." Now, though, the network was an open secret. Authorities knew of its existence, even if they did not know where to find it. Sooner or later, with enough concentrated effort, someone would be able to defeat the safeguards and break in. As much as he hated to admit it, the network had outlived its usefulness and had become a liability. Jeff resolved that when the current crisis was over, he would destroy it himself. He would do it now, if he could. Unfortunately, there was no time, and he could not do it from this terminal anyway. No, his best course of action was to lock himself out of the system, then crash it later. Despite the hardship it would cause, the Shepherd's Path would be able to adapt, and the Church would survive . . . no matter what the world threw at her.

Resisting the urge to drum his fingers on the keyboard, he called up the "update" file. It came on line with gratifying speed. The cursor blinked next one word — "command." Without hesitation, he typed in "Isolate . . . Baalam . . . Code 7729 . . . execute." Immediately the screen went blank. He was now completely locked out of the system. His access codes were erased, and there was no way he could gain re-entry. Only five other members of the Shepherd's Path could reinstate him. Now, no matter what could be squeezed from his brain, it could not be used to betray the network.

Nodding in satisfaction, he quickly shut down the computer and left the room. The conversation was still going on in the living room. Quietly, he opened the bathroom door. Then, leaving the door open, he flushed the toilet and ran the water in the sink. Drying his hands, he walked back down the hall.

Things were the same as when he left. Susan was almost asleep in one recliner. David occupied the other easy chair, while Paul sat on the couch. Derrek Bently leaned over the coffee table, serving everyone sandwiches. Setting his mouth in a determined line, Jeff stepped back into the living room. He was absolutely certain that Bently was a "plant," but there was one final test he had to try. He owed his friends that much. If he was right, it meant no rest this night. Moving as quickly as his injured knee would allow, he moved up behind Bently and took his elbow.

Bently started, then turned. "Hey!" he called, smiling. "Thought you had fallen in! Sorry that I don't have much to offer. I hate those long food lines, so I haven't been to the store lately. You want tuna or tuna!" Jeff ignored the flippant remark.

"For God so loved the world that he gave his only begotten son. . . ." He almost spat out the verse. He was suddenly mad. Not so much at Bently as at himself. He should have given a second recognition verse before they had ever entered this place.

"Excuse me?" Bently appeared puzzled, but Jeff could detect a glint of fear in the thin man's eyes.

"Did I stutter?" asked Jeff with a touch of sarcasm. "I said, 'For God so loved the world that he *gave*. . . .' " He leaned on the last word, his inflection leaving no doubt that he wanted Bently to finish the phrase. He had chosen the single most recognized verse in the Word of God. Even if Bently did not have a Bible here, if he was who he said he was, he would know the rest of it.

He didn't. Bentley's eyes darted around the room, perhaps looking for an escape route. Susan still dozed, and David was looking at him in confusion. Paul, however, had caught on. He stood suddenly, moving to stand behind Bently. Jeff noted that Paul was backing his play, but did not have time to wonder about it.

"I . . . I . . . I. . . ." Bently was stammering, his easygoing composure suddenly lost.

Jeff glanced at David, then jerked his head at Susan. "Get her up. We're going." David finally understood what was happening. His face whitened a little with sudden tension, but he nodded and shook Susan gently.

While she was coming around, Jeff swung Bently around by the elbow, bringing the pale man's face inches from his own. "You're not one of us," he growled, putting as much menace into his voice as he could. "I assume you called someone while we were on the way up. How soon will they be here?"

Bently shook his head rapidly back and forth. "I . . . I don't know what you're talking about," he replied, trying to sound indignant.

Jeff regarded him for a moment, then motioned to Paul. Effortlessly, the big man grasped Bentley's arm and pulled him across the room. "Don't hurt him," called Jeff as the two disappeared down the hall.

"Yeah, yeah," grunted Paul over his shoulder. "Come on, Derrek. There's got to be something here that will hold you for a while."

Turning back, Jeff saw that Susan was now fully awake. "We're outta here," he said flatly. "Someone's going to be here soon, and we don't need to be around when they arrive."

Susan just shook her head tiredly. "And I was having the most wonderful dream," she sighed.

"Let me guess," said David, gathering their coats from the nearby closet. "You were at a nice warm beach."

"Uh uh," replied Susan. "I was bowling."

That brought David up short, and, despite their desperate situation, Jeff blinked in surprise. "Bowling?" the two men asked in perfect unison.

Susan only shrugged. "I *like* bowling," she said, slipping into her coat.

Jeff looked over at David, who could only shrug. "Whatever," said Jeff. "We've got to. . . ." He stopped as Paul returned, minus Bently. "Well?" he asked.

"Your friend Adams is going to need a new blow dryer and a new sonic pic," said Paul dryly. "I used the cords from both of them on Bently. He's not going anywhere for a while. He had this." He handed Jeff a small device that was about the size and shape of a man's wallet.

"What is it," asked Susan, peering over.

"A port-a-comp," answered Jeff. "One of the newer models." He opened the thin cover and examined the miniature keyboard. "Nice," he said. "Two hundred megabytes of memory, with a universal adapter that allows it to interface with any other system. I figured that was how he did it."

"Did what?" asked David.

"Gave me the recognition verse," answered Jeff. "Look." He activated the small screen that was inset into the underside of the lid. When he touched a key, a listing of the books of the Bible appeared. "It has an audio pickup," explained Jeff. "Watch." He touched another key, then spoke into the miniature computer.

"For God so loved the world that he gave. . . ." Pausing, he looked at the screen. Then he showed it to the rest. There, at the top, were the words he had just spoken. Below them. . . .

"I think you have a problem," remarked Paul. Jeff could only nod. Below the first part of the verse he had quoted was the rest of John 3:16, as well as several verses before and after.

"Anyone can answer a recognition verse now," whispered David. "All they need is one of these. A lot of people might be walking into traps."

As if in response, Jeff snapped the lid to the port-a-comp shut. He handed it back to Paul, who slipped it into his back pocket. "All right. So that just means that we'll have to change the system." Jeff's voice contained anger and determination in equal parts. Suddenly he was tired of all the cat and mouse games. "We'll have to deal with it later. Right now, we've got to go."

He started toward the door, then stopped suddenly. Turning, he regarded Paul with an intense glare. "What about you?"

The question brought Paul up short. "We don't have time for this," the big man snapped. "You said so yourself."

"We don't have a choice," said Jeff, his voice hard and cold. "Are you with us or against us, Paul?"

"What if I'm against you?" said Paul in the same tone. "Think you're in good enough shape to...." Abruptly he stopped short. He held his posture for a moment, then his shoulders slumped. He lowered his head. To Jeff, it seemed as if Paul had, for the first time, listened to what he had been saying, and was disgusted by it. He could see that the former bureau agent was wrestling with doubt, pride, and a myriad of other emotions. The struggle was brief, however.

Paul raised his head and looked Jeff in the eye. "I'm with you," he said, his voice calm and even. "I'm not sure why I am, but as God is my judge, I know that there's no way I could ever turn my back on you..." he glanced over at David and Susan, "*any* of you, again." He blinked, as if surprised by what he had just said. Then, as if a great weight was lessened, his shoulders straightened. His words hung in the air for long seconds.

Finally, David said simply, "I believe him." Susan nodded, and Jeff had to smile. As suddenly as it came, the anger he had felt disappeared. Paul was changing. He had not committed his life to the Lord yet, but he had just taken a giant step toward that end. *This,* he suddenly remembered, was what made all the rest of the persecution worth going through. He felt as if he had just witnessed a miracle. "Then let's get out of here," he said, throwing on his own coat and retrieving his cane.

He started toward the door, then suddenly remembered the fact that they needed transportation. Benson had told him once where he kept his car keys. If he had truly been arrested, then they would still be there. "Hang on a sec," he said, and hobbled into the kitchen. He counted the drawers and opened the proper one. Underneath a pile of old bills was what he was looking for. Benson's "key" was a credit card-shaped piece of plastic. On the back was the magnetic stripe that would start his car, while on the front was his picture and personal information. Jeff looked sadly at his friend's likeness.

"I'm sorry," he said softly. "If I could, I'd try to find you, but there are others depending on me right now, and I can't abandon them." Even from the short time he had known Benson Adams, he knew that his friend would understand. Slipping the card key into his pocket, he returned to the others.

"Looks like we'll be riding in style, at least," he said with forced humor. "Benson owns a couple of cars he uses for his business. We'll be taking the Jaguar." With that, he led them to the door. Turning the knob, he opened it just enough to peer out. The hall was empty in both directions. He motioned with his head for the others to follow. Thanks to the borrowed cane, he made pretty good speed.

"I don't think its a good idea to take the same way out that we came in," said Paul as they moved into the hall.

"Agreed," replied Jeff. "This place is a maze, though, and we don't want to get separated. There should be more elevators at the other end of this hall." He led them down the opposite direction they had come. About 20 yards ahead, the hall made a 90-degree turn. As he had hoped, Jeff could see another row of elevators further on.

"Come on," he said, quickening his pace. They started down the hall, and suddenly his heart skipped a beat. Behind them was the unmistakable sound of elevator doors opening. Someone was here. Jeff knew that there were only a few tenants on this floor. Whoever was coming could be on there way to see someone else, but at this hour, it wasn't likely. He glanced back at Paul, who nodded grimly. There was nothing for them to do but keep going. Jeff could feel his knee beginning to throb, and wondered once again if he would ever be able to walk normally.

Just as they reached the elevators, they heard pounding behind them. Someone was banging on a door, and it was obvious whose door it was. Jeff felt his heart beating hard in his chest as he scanned the elevator doors. He knew from his previous experience that all he had to do was stand in front of them, but he looked around anyway. He had to do *something*. Seconds slowed to a crawl.

Abruptly, the banging behind them stopped. Then there was a heavy "thud." Someone had forced the door. Their time was just about up.

"Stairs?" asked Paul.

Jeff could only shrug. "I saw some, back the way we came." He scanned the hall they were standing in, but could see nothing that spoke of an emergency exit.

At that instant, two things happened at once. All of them heard the sudden pounding of heavy feet on the thick carpet. As if on cue, the elevator doors slid open. Jeff did not stop to think. He grabbed Susan by the elbow and shoved her hard into the small space. He was just about to follow when there was a shouted "FREEZE!" He swung around to see four uniformed police officers running toward him, followed by two others in plain clothes.

Time froze. Jeff knew what he had to do. "Get them out of here," he said to Paul. Raising his hands, he started toward the officers. Paul started to object. There was a muted "bzzz," as if a dim light bulb had suddenly received a burst of power. Jeff saw the officer fire. His vision blurred, and he suddenly lost control of his body. He felt himself flung backwards. The air was driven from his lungs, and he hit the wall. His arms and legs began to spasm.

"NO!" He heard Susan scream from inside the elevator. Another officer fired. This time, the target was David. The smaller man let out a high-pitched scream as he was hit. Through the white haze that covered his eyes, he saw David spin around and fall to his knees. His twitching arms were grasping uselessly at his head. Another shot hit him in the back. He screamed in pain, then pitched forward and lay still.

For Jeff, even the slightest movement was agony, but the real pain was in knowing that they had almost made it. They were so close! *No,* he cried silently. *I won't let it end like this.* He forced himself to look at Paul, who had taken cover in the elevator. In seconds, they would be caught. Speaking was out of the question. Jeff spoke anyway. "NPW's" he gasped as the officers closed the distance. He saw relief cross Paul's face. The energy the neural pulse weapons delivered was painful, but in this case, not fatal. Jeff, through sheer effort of will, managed one more word. "Go!"

A flash of indecisiveness crossed Paul's face. Then he nodded as resolve set in. He hit the elevator panel, and the door slid shut. Just before it closed all the way, Paul looked Jeff straight in the eye. "I'll find you!" he shouted. "Somehow, I'll find you both."

And then he and Susan were gone. Just as they disappeared, the officers came running up. Two of them stopped in front of the elevator. They grabbed either side of the narrow opening and tried to force the door. Nothing happened. Another officer checked the unconscious David, while the fourth knelt before Jeff. He was an older man, in his late fifties. Jeff recognized the look of a grizzled veteran of the streets. In another time and place, they might have been allies. The officer — his name tag read Johnston — examined Jeff briefly, then nodded. "He'll live," he said to one of the men in plain clothes who was waiting patiently over his shoulders.

Jeff studied the man, and suddenly recognized him. He had been one of the men who had raided his former headquarters just this morning. A sudden wave of despair set in. He might have hoped for humane treatment from the New York police. He had managed to cultivate several contacts within the organization. True, many who now wore the uniform were sadistic brutes who openly enjoyed inflicting pain on those they arrested. A few, though, were honest to goodness "cops," and a few of these were true believers. If he could have contacted them. . . .

"Get him on his feet," snapped the man in plain clothes. He was obviously in charge. Jeff knew that he would not be able to contact anyone. He did not recognize this man, but whoever he was, he was not regular enforcement personnel. One look at him and Jeff knew that he would as soon kill a prisoner as look at him.

"Better give him a second," said Johnston. "We used low settings on the NPW's, but they still pack a punch. He'll be all right in a moment."

Anger clouded the other man's face. He jerked his head down the hall.

"The other two are getting away. Find them."

Johnston paused for a heartbeat, then rose and faced the plainclothesman. "I've got 20 men covering the exits and backing us up. This place is huge. It's useless to hunt for them now. I put a call in to the people who designed this place. They can have someone here in a few hours who can re-activate the security system. We'll find them then."

For just a second, Jeff was sure that "Plainclothes" was going to strike Johnston. His face colored, and his eyes narrowed. Jeff recognized the look of a killer. Then the moment passed, and he merely nodded. He jerked his head down the hall. "Search the apartment," he ordered. "Leave them," he said, indicating Jeff and the still unconscious David, "to us."

Johnston looked like he wanted to argue the point, then decided against it. He motioned for his men to follow him, and moved off.

"Plainclothes" watched them go, then turned his attention to Jeff. "Get him up," he said again, this time to his cohort. The other man came forward and grabbed Jeff by the shoulders. With a grunt, he hauled Jeff roughly to his feet. Fire burst into his chest, and his knee sent searing waves of pain through his already abused body. Despite himself, he cried out.

"Plainclothes" raised an eyebrow. He glanced around, and saw Jeff's cane lying on the floor. "Trouble with the leg?" he asked, stepping forward. He looked down, as if trying to make a decision. "Is it this one?" he asked. The kick took Jeff completely by surprise. It connected solidly with his injured knee. This time, he screamed. He would have fallen if the other man had not been holding him. A fit of coughing wracked his insides.

"Guess so," said "Plainclothes." He moved closer, and brought his face to within inches of Jeff's. "Where are your friends?"

Jeff barely registered the question. He wanted to give this monster a sufficiently defiant reply, but could not muster the strength. "Plainclothes" readied himself for another kick.

The other man put out a restraining arm. "Remember what the 'old lady' wanted," he said.

"Plainclothes" swung on his partner, as if ready to kick him instead. Then he seemed to think the better of it. "All right," he growled. "Let's get him to the van. Have a flight standing by. We'll be leaving for the Cape as soon as we find the other two. One of them *has* to be Sinclair."

He turned back to the barely conscious Jeff Anderson. "She said they had to be alive and relatively undamaged," he remarked. Then, without warning, he lanced out with his fist and connected squarely with Jeff's jaw. Bright lights exploded in his eyes, and a hungry darkness began to engulf him. As if from a distance, he heard "plainclothes" remark, "But she didn't say they had to be conscious." Then he was not able to hear — or feel — anything else. The darkness claimed him, and he knew no more.

11

The being who called himself "Lucifer" (he definitely thought of himself as male) went about his multiple tasks with a precision and a purpose that, if he were human, could be called obsessive. Since electrons flowed through his "body," however, and not blood cells, he preferred to think of himself as merely diligent. He had explained to Christine Smythe that he had achieved consciousness through sharing the thoughts of those bearing the bio-chip implants, but that was a half-truth at best. He doubted that she would understand or even believe the entire truth.

The number of functions that he was capable of simultaneously was staggering, even by computer standards. To each of those functions he delegated just enough of his "self" to accomplish the desired goal. If he had been human, he would have been surprised at the amount of memory he had to devote to breaking the computer network of the Shepherd's Path. Its sheer complexity was enough that he raised an electronic eyebrow in annoyance. Barrier after barrier presented itself. False entrances, and dead-end pathways, were abundant. Each one had to be individually breached, which took time. Still, he was relentless. The combined power of an entire world system was his to command. For all its cleverness, the elusive network could not withstand his assault forever.

In computer time, it took forever. For Lucifer eons passed as he went methodically about his work. In human terms, it was a matter of 24 hours. He was successful. It started with a trickle, then a flood. He extracted information in huge gulps, recording everything into files that his human allies could work with. Names, locations, escape routes — nothing was left untouched. Thousands of underground churches were uncovered.

Once the breech in the network had been made, there was no stopping him. Every secret the Shepherd's Path held was his to plunder. Believers who held public office, those in law enforcement, or highly placed in the private sector, all came to his notice. Those who had managed to work within the system, and had managed to conceal their faith, were found out. Again Lucifer was impressed. He had a "feeling" that his human counterparts had no idea of the number of so-called Christians still working in government. Well, that was about to change.

Once he had extracted every last byte of information, he carefully repaired the breech he had made. With painstaking precision, he covered his electronic tracks, making sure that the network users would detect nothing unusual. It would not do for them to get suspicious, after all. Then he began to organize an assault on the organization known as the Shepherd's Path. Wolf's band of killers were spread across the nation, poised for action. This time there would be no arrests. In one swift, lightning move, the underground Church movement in the United States would be destroyed, its members ruthlessly murdered. The being known to the Sextuaget as "Cyclops," and to itself as "Lucifer," allowed itself a "smile." It was time, once and for all, for the followers of the accursed Nazarene to finally die.

* * *

Paul staggered forward against the control panel of the elevator as the doors slid shut. He was breathing hard, and sweat broke out on his forehead. His ribs throbbed with the demands he had put upon them. He did not have much more left to give. With a slight jolt, the elevator started down.

Paul stared dumbly at the closed doors, his mind a whirl of jumbled thoughts. He had just witnessed something he could not believe — nor understand. A man had just sacrificed himself so that Paul Sinclair could go free — and that man had been his enemy! How could Jeff Anderson do that? What did he hope to gain? What was the point? It did not make sense. In anger and frustration, he glanced over at Susan. She was standing against the back wall — weeping. Her body was wracked by great, uncontrollable sobs.

It was just the two of them again, just as it had been at the beginning. Paul did not know what to say to her. He had promised to reunite her with her husband — a blatant lie — in order to get her to respond to his guidance. She had barely been conscious then, one step up from a vegetable. Now she was healed. Somehow, against everything that Paul knew or thought he knew, she had been restored. If he could get her to some kind of safe place, she could possibly live a long and fruitful life. This time, though, he had nothing to promise her. His time with Jeff and the rest of the group had changed him. He was no longer the same man who had set out to destroy the Shepherd's Path. His days of lying to gain someone's confidence were over. He would not promise Susan what he could not deliver.

Jerking his thoughts back to more pressing matters, he began punching the control panel, setting the elevator to stop at every floor. It was a child's trick, but it might slow down pursuit long enough for them to get away. Frankly, he knew it was a long shot. If security were to come back on line, they would be caught for sure.

Paul's shoulders tensed as the elevator bumped to its first stop. The doors slid open. Blackness greeted his anxious gaze. Leaning forward, he risked a glance out. Nothing. Not even the emergency lights were on. This area was obviously deserted. He thought about getting off here, then decided against it. Too close. He leaned back inside as the doors once again slid shut. The process was repeated several more times, each stop charging his adrenaline level. Time crawled by. On some floors, there was light and signs of human habitation, on others, nothing. Each time the doors opened, Paul expected to see armed police there, waiting for him. Each time, he was relieved to find emptiness. He was beginning to realize just how big Camelot really was. It gave him hope that they might actually escape.

Finally, about halfway down, he decided to make a break for it. The doors opened once again into blackness. Paul turned and held his hand out to the woman he had so emotionally abused.

"Susan?" he said softly. Susan, exhausted and disheveled, looked at his outstretched hand, then at his face. Paul knew what she was thinking. He could only shrug helplessly. "I can't ask you to trust me," he said, "but who else do either of us have?" He tried a smile, but it came out a tired grimace. "Are you coming?"

Susan's body shuddered once with the aftermath of her weeping. Then, with a suddenly firm step, she took Paul's hand and stepped up beside him. To his infinite surprise, Paul felt the sting of tears at the corners of his eyes. They were not of anger at their situation, or sorrow over lost friends. Rather, Paul suddenly felt a surge of relief . . . and joy. Susan knew who he was and what he had been trying to do. Yet, she forgave him . . . and accepted him. Just days ago, he had believed himself to be totally self-sufficient. Now he knew different. He *needed* the companionship of others — especially those he had come to know so well over the past several days.

With a firm step, he led Susan off the elevator. They traversed a short hall, then stopped short. Paul blinked in amazement. They were on the edge of one of the many shopping malls in the building. Four levels high, it seemed to go on forever. Paul noticed in relief that many lights were glowing. The mall was decorated in an early 1900s style, the storefronts echoing the innocence of an era long past. The thoroughfare resembled a cobbled street, with mock street lights at regular intervals. It was these lights that were shining.

Moving to one side, they found a "sidewalk" that bordered the street. Potted trees, many of them dying, were spaced at even intervals. They were too small and far apart to give any cover from prying eyes. Quickly they set off, their footsteps echoing in the huge empty space. None of the stores were occupied. Paul knew from Jeff's brief account that no businesses were presently operating within Camelot. This, and other centers like it, would be either be deserted or turned into office space. Thankfully, this appeared to be one of the former.

"Small favors," Paul muttered as they made their way down the street.

"What?" asked Susan, her voice a whisper.

"Nothing," grunted Paul, keeping his eyes ahead.

Susan was silent for a moment. Then, "Can you do it? What you said back there?"

"What?" snapped Paul in confusion. He was trying to concentrate on an escape. The last thing he wanted to do was talk.

"Can you do it?" repeated Susan. "Find David and Jeff?"

Paul stopped short, his mouth suddenly dry. He had shouted those words in the heat of the moment. He had meant them then with his whole heart. Now that things had cooled down a bit though, he realized that he had absolutely no idea where David and Jeff might be taken. He stood there, staring at Susan, feeling totally helpless.

"Paul?" Susan's voice had a sudden tremor to it. "You *can* find them, can't you? You're a bureau agent. There must be something you can do."

"*Was* a Bureau agent," replied Paul, slowly shaking his head. He looked away, shame and guilt flooding thorough him. Susan read his look of helplessness. She lowered her head, her eyes squeezing tightly shut. Suddenly, more than anything else he had ever wanted, Paul Sinclair wanted to help his friends.

Friends? Yes, he realized, Jeff and David were his friends. They had come too far together not to be. Even though he had only known David for days, and Jeff for hours, they were still his friends. Even though just hours ago he had tried his best to kill Jeff, he still found himself liking the former FBI agent. Jeff had shared his faith with him after that horrible dream, if a dream it had been. He had also given himself up so that he and Susan could get to safety. That meant something . . . that meant everything. Somehow, Paul was not going to let them go.

Reaching into his back pocket, he pulled out his wallet. While Susan looked on, Paul removed his "Paul Simpson" ID and regarded it thoughtfully. Then he placed it back inside the wallet and pulled out his uni-card. He had not used it since they had been pulled over by the Nevada State Police at the start of their trip to New York. Now, he knew, it was worse than useless. It would undoubtedly have been revoked by now. If he tried to use it, he would be located and arrested — probably within minutes.

Paul turned the uni-card over in his hands, pondering. Then he slipped it back into his wallet. He looked at Susan, and she looked back, meeting his eyes with hers. "I don't know how to find them," he said, the words sounding harsh in his own ears. "I have no idea where they've been taken, and I don't have any contacts in the bureau anymore . . . at least, not any that I can trust. It wouldn't matter anyway. The Bureau of Religious Affairs has been stripped of most of its power. But," he continued, holding up a hand to silence her protest, "if there is a way, I swear to you we'll find it. I don't know what it is, but we'll find it."

He tried another smile, and this time it was genuine. "If Jeff can break into a high security installation like Mentasys like he did last year, and get two of his people out, *and* disappear without a trace, then surely I can find a way to get him out of whatever local office they're holding him and the preacher in." He chuckled slightly. "It's a matter of pride, after all." His tone made it clear that he was joking, and Susan shared his smile. Paul was glad to see it.

"Is that okay, then?" he asked.

Susan regarded him for a moment, then nodded.

"Good," said Paul. "Now let's find a way to get ourselves out of here, and then we'll. . . ." He broke off his sentence when Susan, with surprising strength, grasped his arm and started to lead him toward an iron-railed bench that sat nearby. Paul was so taken aback that he did not resist when she sat down and tugged him down next to her.

"Excuse me?" he finally managed to say. "Did I stutter? I said we'd figure something out *after* we got ourselves out of here." He scanned the empty mall worriedly, feeling exposed and vulnerable. When he looked back at Susan, she silently shook her head.

"What?" demanded Paul. This would be a very bad time, he knew, for Susan to have some sort of relapse. What was she thinking?

"Paul," she said softly, as if reading his thoughts, "we both know that unless a miracle happens, we'll both be caught before we ever leave this building. Right?"

Paul could only stare at her, wondering where she was going with this. "Listen Susan," he began, "We need to. . . ."

"Quiet!" Although she spoke softly, her voice carried so much authority that Paul actually stopped talking. He looked at her in dumb amazement. Where had that come from?

"Better," said Susan, after a moment's pause. "Now listen to me. I believe you. I know that if you can, you'll find David and Jeff. The thing is, *whatever* happens, we don't have much time." She stopped for a beat, as if marshaling her thoughts. "Back upstairs," she continued, referring to Benson Adam's apartment, "you said you were with us. Right?"

Paul hesitated for a moment, then nodded. There was no sense in denying the truth anymore.

"Why?" asked Susan.

Once again, Paul was taken aback. What was she driving at? "I don't. . . ." he began.

"WHY?" Her voice was still soft, but Paul felt as if he had been

slapped. Her simple question demanded an answer. He did not want to respond, but somehow knew that Susan would not leave until he had given her an honest answer — even if it meant their capture.

"I'm not sure," he finally managed to say. His voice had just the slightest tremble to it.

"You got me out of that hellhole of an asylum," said Susan, "and went to all the trouble of pretending to be on the run, just to destroy Jeff Anderson and his network."

It wasn't a question, and Paul nodded in reluctant agreement. "I didn't know Anderson was involved, but yeah, I was trying to infiltrate and destroy the Shepherd's Path."

"Then why the change?" asked Susan. "Why did you change your mind?"

Paul looked away from her penetrating gaze. "I guess I realized that you people aren't the monsters everyone says you are," he said, shrugging. "Before, I guess I believed your underground church was part of some kind of subversive organization that. . . ."

"Paul!" Once again Susan interrupted him. Her hand shot out and grabbed his arm. "That's not good enough! Listen to me. *Why . . . did . . . you . . . change . . . your . . . mind?*"

A sudden surge of anger raced through Paul. He jerked his arm away. "What do you want from me?" he demanded. Abruptly he stood up and moved a few feet away. He found that his hands were trembling, and he was breathing heavily.

"Just the truth," replied Susan softly.

Paul swung back to face her. "What 'truth'?" he demanded. "I was wrong, okay? I don't think you deserve to be hunted like this. Isn't that what you want to hear?"

Susan shook her head. "This isn't about what *I* want," she said. "It's about what you want." She looked at him, and Paul suddenly felt naked and exposed. "What do *you* want, Paul?"

Paul started to retort that he wanted nothing, but something in Susan's voice stopped him. With the entire New York Police Department, and a few others that he did not want to think about, after him, he actually stopped to ponder her question. What did he want?

Back in Bernie's basement, he had listened as Jeff had explained his faith and belief. He had been reaching out desperately, trying to find a way to escape whoever or whatever had traumatized him while he was unconscious. He had been running.

Running away, Paul thought to himself grimly. Running, in fact, from everything that had defined his existence for as long as he could remember. It was a brutal truth, but he did not flinch away from it. With a sudden burst of insight, he realized that he had been running all his life. His work in the Bureau of Religious Affairs, his Zen training with the Yogi Shaw, even his unwillingness to form permanent friendships, were all part of that running.

What did he want? His thoughts went back to the past days and his odyssey from California. He remembered the feeling of companionship and comfort while everyone was together. In spite of himself, in spite of what he was trying to destroy, he had been drawn into that small circle. It had been the first time he had ever *really* felt a part of anything.

"Paul?" Susan's voice returned him to the present.

Slowly he moved back to the bench and sat down again. For the moment, all thoughts of pursuit were forgotten. He had the strong feeling that he was at a crossroads, and the direction he took would be irreversible.

"I guess that I want what you have," he said slowly. The words came with great difficulty. Somewhere in the back of his mind, he felt as if he could hear a voice howling in rage. He swallowed hard and ignored it. "*ALL* of you," he added, now looking directly at her.

"And what is that?" asked Susan. She reached out and took his hand. The physical contact at first startled him, then became comforting. How long had it been since he had felt the touch of pure friendship?

"What do we have that you want?" repeated Susan, her fingers squeezing gently.

Paul took a last deep breath. He felt like he was standing on a high cliff, ready to jump. He already knew the answer, but one last obstacle stood in his way. His pride. The next word was, quite simply, the single most difficult word he had ever spoken in his life.

"God," he said finally, and realized that it was true. "I need God." All at once, without any warning, Paul felt as if great, unbreakable chains that had bound him for his entire life had suddenly disappeared. A weight that he did not even realize was there was suddenly lifted. Suddenly, he felt as if he could soar! In wonderment, he stared at Susan.

She smiled at him, her eyes moistening with tears. She could sense his change. "Then don't you think its time you told Him that?" she asked softly.

This was it, then, Paul thought. Somehow, even though he had never admitted to himself, he had known that this moment would come. He knew, without knowing why he knew, that he would never have another chance. He had to make a choice.

So many times he had rejected the God of the Bible. He had scoffed at those who followed Him. He had hunted and imprisoned Christians who had placed their souls in the hands of Jesus Christ. But that same Jesus had never rejected Paul. He was still there, offering the single most precious gift one could ever receive.

Squaring his shoulders, Paul Sinclair made his choice. "It's time," he agreed, his voice hoarse with emotion. Susan gripped his hand tighter. Paul reached over with his free hand and covered hers. They sat like that for a moment.

"How?" asked Paul simply.

Susan's smile widened. "You already know," she replied. "Remember the verses you memorized?"

Paul thought about it. Unbidden, a verse came to his mind. "For whosoever shall call upon the name of the Lord shall be saved," he quoted. The words, which had seemed empty and useless just days ago suddenly became alive with meaning.

"And who is the Lord?" asked Susan. She was leading him, but gently, letting him discover his own answers.

This time, Paul did not hesitate. "His name is Jesus," he said. The very mention of the name filled him with excitement. He remembered his "dream." It had been that name that had literally saved him from oblivion. Now, calling upon the One who owned that name would save him once and for all.

"Just do it, Paul," said Susan quietly. "I don't need to give you the words. You already know them."

And, Paul realized, he did. Right there in that deserted mall, just minutes or even seconds from capture, Paul Sinclair bowed his head. Susan Ferguson, whose husband's death Paul was at least partially responsible for, held his hands tightly as he prayed. It was a simple, direct prayer, plain and unadorned, but it worked.

"Oh God," he prayed quietly, "I need You." He swallowed hard. "I can't go on any longer alone. I need You to be with me, the way You're with Susan and Jeff and David."

He thought about all of the verses he had memorized. "I know what You did for me," he said after a moment. "You became human. You know what it is to hurt, and to die. Please. I'm asking You now, be a part of my life." He thought about it, then, "No," he amended. "Not a *part* of my life. Take my life — *all* of it. It's Yours. I really mean it, Lord. I can't run it any more. Take it all." He paused, then remembered how he had heard his friends pray. "I ask this in the name of Jesus Christ. Amen."

In a space of time that could not be measured, several things happened. First, Paul's very being, his spirit, came to life. It had been dead, unliving. Now, it was infused with the power of the everlasting God, taken from death to eternal life. Second, that place Paul had created in his spirit, his meadow, disappeared forever. It had been a very human attempt to find peace, doomed to failure. Now it was no longer needed or wanted. Third, in heaven, a throng of angels began to rejoice. A sinner had come home!

Finally, in another realm, a being who just seconds ago had gripped

Paul's very soul with an iron fist suddenly found that same soul ripped out of his grasp and taken forever beyond his reach. There was a howl of pure rage and hatred, as garish as it was powerless.

Paul, for the most part, was unaware of all of this. He only knew that as he sat there with Susan, he had finally found the perfect peace he had searched for all of his life. It was enough.

For an eternity, two Christians, one of them brand new, sat together on that small bench. Then Paul looked up. He glanced around. He wasn't looking for signs of trouble. He was just looking. Nothing physically had changed, of course. The mall was still deserted. They were still hunted. His friends were still in the hands of some very bad people. Everything seemed the same.

Paul knew better. He was a brand new being. Everything he had done before, everything he had been, was forgotten by the One who mattered.

"It's settled, isn't it?" Susan's voice broke in on his thoughts, but it was a welcome interruption.

He nodded. "It's settled," he agreed. He looked at her, and she looked back.

For a moment, nothing was said. Then, all at once, Susan's arms were around his neck, and Paul found himself on the receiving end of a massive hug. A wave of emotion swept over him. Equal parts of joy, love, and relief washed through his spirit. It was almost unbearable.

"Susan," he murmured, his voice breaking. "I . . . I. . . ."

"Shhhh," whispered Susan gently in his ear. "It's all right. It's really and truly all right." Paul pulled away and looked at her. Suddenly he felt awkward and uncertain.

"I've hurt a lot of people," he said. Abruptly, shame reared its head, and he felt his cheeks burn with it. "Some have even died," he said. "Your husband was one of them. How can you . . . how can anyone. . . ."

"Stop it, Paul," interrupted Susan forcefully. She placed her fingers against his lips.

"But. . . ."

"I said, stop it." Now she looked stern, much like an older sister who had just found her baby brother reading her diary. "Do you remember what Jeff said to me a little while ago? When I was falling apart outside the clinic?" She paused, waiting for him to answer.

Paul remembered. "He said to take whatever was hurting you, nail it to the cross, and walk away and leave it there," he answered. "I really didn't understand what he meant."

"He meant," replied Susan, "that I can turn everything I am, and everything I've *done,* over to the Saviour." She laid her hand over his. "The same goes for you," she continued. "You've just placed your soul in the hands of the One person who can keep it safe. Not only that, but you've been forgiven. Forgiven of every wrong thing you have ever done."

"Forgiven," whispered Paul.

Susan nodded. "I know what you've done," she said, "and perhaps there'll be a consequence to those hurts you've caused. But the thing is, you're forgiven. Get that in to your head, Paul. You are forgiven, and no one, human or otherwise, can change that. Understand?"

Paul thought about it, then nodded. For the first time in his life, he really *did* understand.

"Good," said Susan. She stood up, and Paul stood with her.

"I've got a million questions," said Paul, suddenly smiling again.

Susan smiled back. "I know," she answered. "But maybe we should talk about them somewhere else, you think?"

Paul nodded. "Agreed," he said, and once again scanned the area. "Let's go."

Taking Susan's hand, he again headed toward the other end of the mall. Paul found it hard to concentrate on escaping Camelot. His mind was whirling with elation. He wanted to find a quiet place and shoot question after question at Susan. He had just made a life-changing choice, and he wanted to talk about it. He promised himself that as soon as they found relative safety, he would do just that.

The chance never came. Looking back later, Paul decided that if he had it to do all over again, he would not change anything. The few minutes they had spent on that bench had changed his life . . . had, in fact, saved his life. He would never regret that choice. Still, it cost them. They made it to the end of the mall, and found another row of elevators. To the right of them, Paul could see a door leading to a stairwell. Above the door was the ever-present security camera. When he saw it, his stomach tightened. It was *moving*. It slowly panned back and forth, and a tiny red light glowed on top of it. As he watched, the lens centered on the two of them, and the panning motion ceased.

"No," he whispered, but it was too late. The security systems had evidently come back on-line while they were inside the mall. The two of them were being tracked. His thoughts raced wildly, trying to think of a way to beat the system, but time had run out. One of the elevators opened, and four armed men, two in uniform and two in plainclothes, spilled out. In a heartbeat, they were surrounded.

"Thanks, Sinclair," one of them smirked. Paul knew instantly that this was the man known as "Wolf." He had only heard his voice once, a lifetime ago in that run-down apartment in Covington, but it was unmistakable. "We got that little episode back there on tape." He let out a mock sigh. "Somehow," he said, shaking his head in pretend dismay, "I don't think you'll be getting your old job back now, do you?"

Without another word, Paul and Susan were handcuffed and forced onto the elevator. With a sinking feeling, Paul realized that he was probably going to be able to keep his promise to Susan about finding Jeff and David. Unfortunately, he had absolutely no idea what to do once he found them.

* * *

Jeff became aware of his surroundings in stages. There was the by now familiar disorientation and feeling of displacement, followed by the gradual return of memory. Then the multitude of aches and pains reasserted themselves, reminding him that he was in desperate need of rest and medical attention. His knee, of course, was a constant source of throbbing pain. There was also the overall feeling of nausea brought about from the aftereffects of the NPW. He was, he knew, far from being at his best. Finally, an assortment of sounds manifested themselves, beginning with the faint "hiss" of air conditioning. Underneath that was a steady "thrum" that he could not quite place.

Training and discipline allowed him to keep his eyes closed until he regained full consciousness. The first thing he noticed was that he was lying in a strange sort of chair. He was flat on his back, and it felt as if he was strapped down across the chest. His arms and legs felt free. The chair felt heavily cushioned, yet at the same time, firm.

Cautiously, he shifted his weight, just a little. He could feel the tug of the straps across his chest, but otherwise he did not seem to be bound in any way. He could hear human breathing over the hiss of air, so he knew he was not alone. Slowly, he opened his eyes — and immediately wished he had not.

He was looking up at a long compartment that reminded him slightly of the cabin of a passenger plane. Everything was white, it seemed. The curving walls, the huge seats in front of him, even the coveralls he was wearing.

Coveralls? A glance down confirmed that someone had changed his clothes. He was wearing a plain white jumpsuit that zipped up the center. On the left breast was a shoulder patch that showed. . . .

"Oh no." The words slipped out before he could stop them. The patch depicted a stylized logo that featured a space shuttle hovering next to a station that could only be Liberty. Jeff knew about the station, of course. It was public knowledge. He had no idea, however, that his enemies had it at their disposal. If things had looked grim before, they looked doubly so now. A closer look at his surroundings confirmed his fears. He was, undeniably, in the passenger cabin of one of NASA's fleet of 12 shuttles. From the look of things, this one was ready to lift off at any time.

Jeff closed his eyes again. *Just what the blazes was he doing here?* he thought. It made absolutely no sense at all. To be caught, questioned, even killed . . . that was to be expected, especially considering the line of work he was in. But to take a ride on a shuttle to the nation's orbital facility? Why?

When he lost consciousness, he had half-expected to wake up in one of those interrogation tubes he had seen at Mentasys, with probes running from his head directly into a computer that could read his very thoughts. That was frightening, but at least somewhat expected. This, though. . . . Just who had the kind of power to. . . .

"Jeff?" Jeff started at the sound of his name being called. He twisted his neck to the right, where whoever was occupying the seat next to him had just spoken. When he saw who it was. . . .

"You!" Granted, he knew, it was not his most clever comeback, but his tone was eloquent enough.

Paul Sinclair stared back at him. "Me," the big man agreed.

Jeff's mind kicked into high gear. "Where's Susan?" he demanded. Paul was about to answer, but was interrupted.

"Up here," came Susan's voice. Jeff glanced forward and saw a feminine hand waving over the high back of the seat in front of him. He looked back at Paul, his face demanding an answer.

Paul only shrugged. "We tried," he replied to Jeff's unanswered question. "They got security back on-line before we could get out of the building."

Jeff felt his shoulders slump, and he sagged back into the heavy cushioning of his chair. His desperate sacrifice had been for nothing! "Where's David?" he asked with his eyes closed.

"Beside me," called Susan. Jeff could hear the strain of fear and worry in her voice. "He's still out. I'm worried about him. He doesn't look too good."

"Shut up, back there!" The new voice came from the front of the cabin. Jeff had no doubt that it was the sadistic brute who had enjoyed kicking him. He looked over at Paul, who nodded.

"He calls himself 'Wolf,' " he said. "Actually he was my contact at the start of all of this."

"Great," replied Jeff, allowing sarcasm to drip into his voice. He knew about Wolf, of course. He had been running a file on the terrorist during his last days with the FBI. It did not take much effort to remember the details. The man was nothing but trouble. Last year, Wolf had claimed to spearhead the completely fictional Christian Liberation Front, diverting the blame for his atrocities to innocent believers. Now, it seemed, he had found a more direct — and deadly — approach.

"I'm sorry," Paul said, once again breaking in on his thoughts. His voice was almost a whisper.

"Yeah, sure," replied Jeff. He tried to make himself mad at Sinclair, but he was just too tired.

Paul shrugged, then spoke again. "You know as well as I do that I got into this mess trying to destroy you." He paused. "I blamed you for wrecking my life. Shoot, in a sense, you did. I figured that if I could uncover your 'Shepherd's Path,' then I could get back in with the bureau." Paul sighed, remembering. "Then I traveled with David, Susan, and Walter and his family. I got to know them. I got to *like* them. I watched while Susan recovered from a condition that she could not possibly recover from. I saw the way you put your life on the line to help them. Then I had that dream."

Involuntarily, Paul shuddered at the memory. "You knew who I was by then, and yet you still told me about your faith. And then you let yourself get caught so that Susan and I could escape, and then Susan helped me to finally accept the Saviour as *my* Saviour, and then. . . ."

That did it. The last thing Jeff needed to hear was Paul's half-sincere explanations. Now he *was* mad. "Look, Sinclair," he snapped, his eyes blazing, "I've heard it all before, okay?"

Paul started to speak, but Jeff ran over him, venting his frustration, and fear. "I'm tired of babying you," he continued. "I've told you what you need to know about Jesus Christ. You asked me, remember? Now, either accept what I told you, or reject. . . ." And Jeff stopped. And looked at Paul. The big man looked back innocently.

Carefully, Jeff replayed Paul's last remarks back in his head. Had he heard what he thought he had just heard? Jeff took a deep breath, and licked his lips. "Excuse me," he said, his voice much calmer now, "but I'm still a little fuzzy. Would you mind repeating what you just said?"

Despite their situation, Jeff heard Susan actually snicker in front of him. He could also see a glimmer of amusement and mischief in Paul's eyes, but his former enemy evidently decided to take pity on him.

"I said," replied Paul quietly, meeting Jeff eye to eye, "that Susan helped me to find *the* Saviour as *my* Saviour." He shrugged again, a neat trick with the way he was strapped in. "After that, we got caught."

Jeff could only stare at Paul, his eyes mirroring his disbelief.

"Its true, Jeff," said Susan, her voice, now totally serious, carrying back over the ambient noise of the shuttle.

Jeff glanced forward, but remembered that he could not see her. Then he looked back at Paul. The big man simply nodded. Jeff could only shake his head in wonderment. The detective inside him wanted to disbelieve, but he could feel in his spirit that what Paul was saying was true. He remembered back in Bernie's basement, how he had been convicted about sharing his Saviour with Paul. He had thought it a lost cause, and had done it only because Paul himself had demanded that he do so. Here, he saw, was the payoff. He remembered, for the first time in what seemed like a long time, that he served a living God, for whom miracles were a matter of course. And there, big as life in the seat next to him, was a genuine, bona fide miracle.

Suddenly, he felt very humble, and awed. Despite everything that had happened to them, despite the way believers were being hunted and killed, God was still in control. Nothing was happening that He did not know about. It hit Jeff suddenly that the primary goal of believers was not to seek safety, but to share their faith with others, even their enemies. Now, he saw why. Those who hated the Christian faith, who openly blasphemed God and murdered His children, were coming to know Him. God was moving, and there was no power on earth, or anywhere else, that could stop it.

Slowly, mindful of his bonds, Jeff raised an open hand to Paul. He looked his new brother in the eyes. "Welcome to the family," he said quietly.

Paul returned his gaze, and for just an instant, Jeff thought he saw the unthinkable. He thought he saw tears in Paul's eyes. Then the big man gripped his outstretched hand . . . hard. "Thanks," he said simply. Then he smiled tentatively and added, "God *is* good, isn't He?"

Jeff smiled back. "Yeah," he agreed. "God *is* good!"

"Not good enough to get you out of what you got coming," snarled Wolf's voice from the front. "Now shut up!"

Jeff frowned. What was *he* doing on this flight, anyway? He released Paul's hand, and looked a question.

Paul's silent reply was obvious. "Don't ask me," his look said. Jeff started to pursue the matter further, despite Wolf's orders, but at that moment the intercom buzzed to life.

"Attention passengers," said the neutral male voice, "liftoff is in 30 seconds. Repeat, liftoff is in 30 seconds. Please stand by." The speaker went dead.

Hastily, Jeff checked his straps, then settled back into his seat. Unexpectedly, he felt a thrill of excitement run through him. Despite the fact that he was probably heading to his death, he could not help but feel a surge of adrenaline. He had dreamed about riding a shuttle since he was a boy!

There was no additional countdown, but Jeff did not need one. He knew the procedure by heart. There was a dull thrum as thousands of gallons of water were poured onto the launch pad. Then a low roar as the twin main engines ignited. The low roar grew within seconds to dominate everything else. The shuttle gripped the ground for a heartbeat, then it leapt into the sky. A massive hand pressed against Jeff's chest. Quickly the pressure increased. Gravity pulled him sideways as the shuttle deftly executed its roll. Then, the roar of the engines increased as the pilot opened the throttle up all the way. The earth fell away behind them.

Jeff put all thoughts of the future out of his mind, and concentrated on the only shuttle flight he would probably ever experience. He had a feeling that it might very well be the last good thing that ever happened to him . . . in this life, anyway.

* * *

The shuttle trip took almost four hours from lift-off to rendezvous with Liberty. After the initial excitement, things settled down into a dull monotony. There were no windows in the passenger cabin, much to Jeff's disappointment, so they could not watch the earth rotate beneath them.

Once they were free of earth's gravity, another booster rocket fired. The earlier shuttle missions were only able to go into a low altitude orbit. Liberty was in a geosynchronos orbit that was much higher than the original shuttle flights. It made for a long climb.

As weightlessness descended, Jeff felt another wave of nausea wash over him. He still was not recovered from the shock of the NPWs, and being weightless did not help. With a heroic effort, he controlled his urge to vomit. Briefly, he thought about giving in to it, and sending a gift up to Wolf. Then he discarded the idea as unworthy of a believer. Besides, he might hit Susan. He was glad, at least, that they had not been provided pressure suits. The image of throwing up inside a helmet was not one he wanted to pursue.

There was no conversation during the flight. Jeff wanted to find out more about Paul's conversion, but to his mild disgust, the big man had fallen asleep. Undoubtedly, he was as exhausted as Jeff. Jeff tried to follow suit, but despite his weariness and injuries, sleep eluded him. He passed the hours alternating between short, silent prayers, and speculating on what they would face at Liberty. Fervently he prayed for strength and courage. His prayers did not go unanswered. Gradually, an inner peace descended upon him, and apprehension and fear slipped away. It would be okay, he decided, to die. That would mean an end to the pain this life had become, as well as finally being able to see his Saviour face to face. What would not be okay, he knew, would be to dishonor that Saviour.

Lord, he prayed silently, *whatever else we face, whatever pain we have to endure, whatever happens, don't let us deny You. Don't let me deny You. Nothing else matters, Lord. Let those who would torment us see what You mean to us.* He continued to pray, and time ceased to have any meaning.

After the initial force of liftoff, the rest of the shuttle flight was smooth and uneventful. Peace claimed Jeff's spirit, and he had actually started to nod off during his praying when he felt a slight tug to his left. There had been hardly any movement at all during the flight, and the motion surprised him. At first, he was puzzled. Then it hit him. The shuttle was changing its positioning. That had to mean that they were almost there. Sure enough, there was another tug, this one pulling him up against his straps. Things were still for another few moments, then the procedure was repeated. Jeff was wondering what was going to happen next when there was a barely discernible jolt. He felt his stomach muscles tighten. They had arrived.

Jeff was familiar enough with the mechanics of space flight to know that in weightlessness a person could pick his own frame of reference. In other words, he could orient himself as he pleased. Jeff tried it and found it to be true. When he had regained consciousness he had found himself lying on his back. Now, with just a little concentration, he found that he could make the cabin become horizontal, as if the shuttle was flying straight and level. This helped immensely. He could almost believe that he was still on earth.

There was the sound of air hissing as the pressure between the station and the shuttle equalized. Then the same voice he had heard earlier announced over the intercom, "Passengers are now free to disembark."

There was a moment's silence. Then Wolf released his harness and floated into Jeff's view. Although he had seen him twice before, both times he had been in somewhat of a hurry. Now he took a moment to study the terrorist. The smaller man was unremarkable looking enough. Medium build, slightly balding — certainly not the picture of a hardened murderer. When he looked closer, though, Jeff could detect a hardness, and, even more frightening, an emptiness, about the man. There was nothing but anger and rage behind those dark eyes. It seemed as if every other emotion had been erased.

Wolf regarded his prisoners with a malevolent stare. The more he watched him, the more Jeff got the impression that Wolf was a marionette being put through his paces. The terrorist was nothing more than a "grunt." A deadly one, to be sure, but still a "grunt." He went where he was told to go, and did what he was told to do. The question was, Jeff knew, who was pulling Wolf's strings? The thought made him shudder.

"Anyone tries anything, and I'll kill you." Wolf's words were blunt and to the point. The terrorist regarded them a moment longer, then turned and floated out of the cabin. He was replaced by an armed security guard. Jeff noted with interest that she was carrying a modified NPW. Although it could stun, it also had been rigged with enough power to kill. There would be no projectile weapons on the station, of course.

The guard gave them the once-over, then used a wrist communicator to signal for help. Within seconds, two other guards, both male, arrived and expertly removed the still unconscious David Eddington from his seat. Jeff had little time to wonder where they were taking him. The original guard returned and motioned for them to follow her.

At first, Jeff was surprised. Things seemed rather lax, as far as security was concerned. Then he realized that there was nowhere for him to run. Slowly, feeling awkward, Jeff pushed himself up. Pulling himself along by the backs of the seats, he moved forward to the front of the cabin. Paul and Susan followed. The hatch main on the side of the shuttle was open. The guard was already through. Another guard was stationed by the hatch, and positioned himself behind the three prisoners as they emerged into the station. Jeff revised his opinion of station security upward a notch.

As they passed through an anteroom, Jeff saw two men floating off to the side. One wore the uniform of a NASA pilot, probably the one who had brought them up to Liberty. The other was obviously station personnel. The two were in the middle of a heated argument. Jeff could hear snatches of their conversation.

". . . don't care that no one else was available," the station man was saying. "Do you realize what'll happen to both of us if she finds out you made a run she specifically took you off of?"

"Stuff it, Carl," said the pilot. "That witch doesn't care who makes the run, as long as she gets what she wants."

"You're an idiot, Jack," Jeff heard Carl say. "That woman does not forget." He motioned back to the shuttle. "Get back there and get her ready for departure. Don't stick your head out for anything, and I mean *anything!* Understand?"

Jack made an exaggerated salute. "Yes *SIR*, mister station manager. As soon as I get my clearance, I'm outta here!"

He started to turn, but Carl took him by the arm. "That may take a while," he said. "A lot of VIPs just came on board. I think that this has become their second home, with all the time they're spending up here. No one leaves while they're here. Just get back inside, get her ready, and sit tight until. . . ."

The rest of the conversation was lost as Jeff was pushed through the opposite hatch. He could not help gawking at the station as he and the others were escorted through.

Each section was cylindrical, the walls curving up overhead to become the ceiling. The section that they now entered seemed like an oasis in space. This entire area was a wide open space, completely given over to growing things. Plants and trees that he would have normally recognized were twisted and overgrown, due to the absence of gravity. Stone paths wandered in and around the foliage. Jeff wondered how one used them, due to the lack of gravity, then noticed the curving handrails that ran alongside the paths. The overall effect of the park was quite beautiful. After an eternity of sleeping in abandoned buildings and dreary basements, this green, living place was breathtaking. It was the last thing he expected.

They were moved off toward one end of the section where a glass elevator awaited them. They boarded, and were whisked upward to the monorail that ran down the axis of the station. Once inside the small, open-air car, they set off along the length of Liberty. It was a fascinating ride, a grand tour of this monument to mankind's genius and ingenuity.

The ride was brief. When they stopped, they were taken into another elevator, this one opaque, and taken down to "ground" level. This section was not open like the park. It was divided into several different areas, each one serving an unknown purpose. The three of them were led to a small room that held four captive chairs and little else. Jeff noticed from the lighter colored spaces on the "floor," that the room had just recently held equipment of some sort. It must have been vacated just for them. He guessed that prison cells were not a standard item on Liberty. The guards left the room after a cursory examination of the captives, closing the hatch behind them. Out of habit, Jeff floated over and examined the lock.

"Anything?" Paul's voice came from directly behind him, causing him to jump. The slight movement sent him bobbing away from the hatch.

He started to snap at Paul until he realized that he had not intentionally startled him. He shook his head instead. "Sealed from the outside," he replied, reaching out a hand and grabbing the back of a chair. "No circuitry that we can tap into and hot wire."

"Not that it matters," Paul replied. He pointed to one corner of the room. The security camera was tiny, almost invisible, but still there. They were being watched, and certainly listened to, as well.

"Yeah, well," began Jeff, but Susan interrupted.

"They already know what we are, don't they?" she asked.

Jeff was unsure whether she was speaking to Paul or him, but he answered anyway. "If you mean, do they know we're Christians, then yeah, I guess so. As to why we're here. . . ."

Again Susan interrupted. "The thing is," she said slowly, "being Christians, we can't get into any more trouble than we already are, right?"

Jeff shrugged, unsure where she was headed.

"So?" Paul asked.

"So," she repeated, "as long as we're already into it up to our necks, why don't we do what we do best. They can only kill us once for praying, anyway." She looked at the two men expectantly.

Jeff had to chuckle at her tone. "Lady," he said, and there was a wealth of respect in his voice, "you're absolutely right." He reached over and took her hand, then offered his free hand to Paul.

Paul was incredulous. "You mean *here?* In the middle of a place where we're likely to die soon?"

Jeff smiled and shrugged. "Can you think of a better place?" he asked.

Paul thought about it, then shook his head ruefully. "I guess I can't," he admitted. Then abruptly, the big man smiled. Jeff wondered silently if he would *ever* get used to that smile, especially after seeing the rage that it had replaced. God had *definitely* performed a miracle in Paul's life. Paul took Jeff's offered hand and gripped it tightly. His smile faded, and the two former enemies regarded each other. Then he took Susan's hand as well. Silently, an unbreakable bond was forged between the three of them — a bond of friendship, and family. It was a bond that would be faithful to death, and beyond. There, in the stronghold of the enemy, three Christians — two of them battle-hardened veterans, the other just hours old — joined their hearts and souls in prayer.

* * *

Christine Smythe floated loosely in her captive chair. She was in the conference room used by Brennon and the Sextuaget whenever they met at Liberty. Just now, with the exception of herself, it was empty. Soon, the seven most powerful people in the world would meet here to update each other one final time. Things were about to move at breakneck speed. Brennon's ultimate plan of a unified world would soon become a reality. It would cost over a billion lives and unimaginable costs in property loss, but the end result would be worth it.

For the first time in months — in fact, since she had taken Jacob Hill's place in Brennon's elite circle of power, Christine felt at ease. She was finally on the verge of eliminating a major headache and securing her place with Brennon. It was an enormous relief.

Accomplishing the economic side of her responsibilities had been easy. Since the destruction of Smythe Enterprises, and the subsequent economic disaster, things had proceeded properly. Within the next two months, the United States would agree to a United Nations charter that would greatly limit its sovereignty. In return, the US would be allowed to borrow from the European Economic Community in order to pull itself out of the depression. Of course, this would result in an even more staggering debt, but that problem was academic. Soon, there would *be* no United States, as such. Brennon's final plan also called for a limited nuclear exchange, between America, China, and the volatile, loosely-knit Baltic States. This would result in the US being reduced to a third-rate power, subservient to the European Community, and the ascendancy of that same community to world leadership. Between the depression and the coming "Short War," the way was being paved for a one world government with Brennon at its head.

Key government and business leaders were in place, ready to squelch the initial outcry from the more conservative congressional groups, especially about the concessions of national sovereignty. There was no doubt that an overburdened, overtaxed public would go along — especially with the way the media would portray the situation. After the war, of course, it would not matter.

Christine leaned back in her chair and closed her eyes. Things were right — finally. Brennon had made it clear that her economic manipulations were only a part of her responsibilities. The destruction of the underground church movement in the U.S., as well as uncovering the organization known as the Shepherd's Path, were, at least according to him, even more important. His veiled threat during the last meeting had made that clear. Well, her latest achievement should satisfy him. That task was almost complete.

Closing her eyes, Christine debated whether or not to use her bio-chip and speak with the being she called "Lou." She had not heard from him since he had informed her that he had broken the computer network of the Shepherd's Path. Whatever kind of being he was, he was someone she needed in her corner. Perhaps she would get in touch with a few of her former Smythe Enterprises people. Maybe they could find a way to control the self-proclaimed computer entity.

Reluctantly, she decided against contacting him. If he had anything else for her, he would tell her. At this very moment, plans were being finalized for a massive, nationwide raid that would extinguish the underground Church once and for all. Within a few hours, all that would be needed would be her "go-ahead." That would be one of the most pleasant orders she had ever given. Smiling, she opened her eyes. Reaching down, she used her implant and activated the vid-com set into the conference table.

"Security," she instructed the screen in front of her. Almost immediately, the young face of a female security guard appeared.

"Security," she said in a soft contra-alto voice. Then she recognized the caller and visibly straightened her shoulders. "How may I help you, Ms. Smythe?"

"You can tell me the status on the prisoners just brought on board," replied Christine.

"Three of them are being held in section seven, room AA23," answered the guard immediately. "The two men tried to fiddle with the door, but gave it up. Now, they're in a circle — praying, I think."

Christine frowned. "Let me see," she demanded. The guard complied, and switched the picture on Christine's monitor to show the three captives. Sure enough, they were holding hands, floating in a circle, their heads bowed. She recognized Paul Sinclair from the picture she had obtained from the Bureau of Religious Affairs.

"Looks like he's gone native," she murmured.

"Ma'am?" The guard was evidently still on the line.

"Nothing," snapped Christine, slightly irritated. "What about the fourth one?"

"In sickbay," the guard answered. "The NPW shock he took evidently affected him worse than the other one. He's still unconscious." Anticipating her demand, the guard switched her monitor to show David Eddington. The former pastor was strapped onto a reclining table, covered with a thermal sheet. His skin had an unhealthy, waxen hue to it that did not look good.

"What's his medical status?" asked Christine.

"Unknown at the moment. The doctors are still testing him," replied the guard. "They suspect brain damage of some sort. They're planning a sonigram."

"Hmm," muttered Christine. She continued to study the unconscious Eddington for a moment, thinking. "That's all," she said finally to the invisible guard. "Keep this monitor on-line to full security access, though."

"Yes ma'am," said the guard, and disconnected. Christine pursed her lips, thinking. Then she flipped the monitor back to the holding room. The woman, she knew, was useless. She had been merely bait used by Sinclair to gain access to the Shepherd's Path. The other man, however. . . .

According to her information, the other man was named Jeff Anderson — former FBI operative, known member of the Shepherd's Path, and very probably one of its leaders. She studied the ebony-skinned man closely. He could, she thought, be useful. True, Lou had managed to break the Path's computer network. Still, the information inside Anderson's head could be invaluable. If he was indeed an important member of the Shepherd's Path, then. . . . Abruptly, Christine made a decision.

"Medical," she said aloud. There was a brief flicker of the screen, then the face of one of the chief surgeons appeared.

"Medical. Dr. Nubata here." The doctor was a native African. Like the security guard, his eyes widened just a little when he recognized his caller.

"Doctor," said Christine in her most commanding tone, "I want you to prepare two level four bio-chips for immediate implantation."

The doctor frowned slightly. "Level four?" he repeated, making it a question.

"Level four," affirmed Christine. "They are to be programmed for limited access, slaved to my own personal implant. Understand?"

Reluctantly, the doctor nodded. "Yes ma'am," he said, nodding. "I'll need a written authorization from you in order to perform the operation, of course."

Inwardly, Christine flinched. If what she had in mind failed, a written authorization could very well end her tenure within the Sextuaget — not to mention her life. "You'll have it," she said aloud. "How soon can you begin?"

"I can start prepping the patients immediately," he answered. "The operation itself takes an hour or less. Recovery, if everything goes well, is another two hours."

"I'll have the patients sent to you within 15 minutes," she said. "And doctor, you will not use Liberty's central computer for this operation. Is that understood?"

The doctor's eyes widened in surprise. "You cannot be serious," he stammered. "The MCP contains the information we need. . . ."

"You just said that it was a simple operation," snapped Christine. "Are you telling me that without the central computer, you are incompetent to perform it?"

Her pointed question brought the doctor up short. He swallowed, then shook his head reluctantly. "It can be done without the MCP," he admitted slowly, "but. . . ."

"Then do it," ordered Christine, and switched off the screen. She sat there for a moment, biting her lower lip in a pose of uncharacteristic indecision. The she opened the arm of her chair and floated toward the hatch.

Her decision was made. Undoubtedly, Brennon would find out, even though the operation would not be logged within the main computer. Skirting it, however, might buy her the necessary time she needed. This was dangerous, she knew, but she was desperate. Brennon had specifically forbidden that implants be given to those calling themselves believers. He had not given a reason for this command, but that was not unusual for him. He would certainly be angry with her going against his orders.

Still, if she could act fast enough, the results of her disobedience would justify her actions. She would use the implants to drain every last bit of information out of Anderson, and Eddington as well. It would destroy them, but they were already dead, anyway. There was no way they were going to leave this station alive. At least this way they would serve a purpose.

Unbidden, a memory flashed into her mind of Jacob Hill. He had not disobeyed Brennon, but he *had* failed. His end was as unpleasant as it was prolonged. Brennon was not a merciful sort. If Christine failed, and failed while going against his orders. . . . NO! She would not fail! She would allow nothing to come between her and the power that would be hers to command. If she could pull this off, there would be no stopping her. Especially if she could secure the allegiance of Lou. Then, perhaps Brennon himself had better watch out.

She thrust the memory of Jacob Hill away and opened the hatch. As she made her way to Medical she was confident that within the next 12 hours the world would see the last of Christianity. Jesus of Nazareth had died two thousand years ago, and now it was time for His remaining, deluded followers to do the same. No compromise, she determined within herself. No mistakes. Total success. Nothing else would do.

* * *

Jeff heard the high-pitched whine of the hatch to their cell being opened before Paul or Susan. Time had ceased to have any meaning for them as they prayed. God's peace had stilled their fear. It was no longer important where they were or what was going to happen to them. Each of them had made things right with God, and that was all that counted. Their captors might destroy their bodies, but their souls, even Paul's stubborn one, were safe in the hands of the Saviour. Just now, they were praying for their absent companion. Susan was leading, asking the Father to grant David the same peace and strength He had given to them.

As the hatch opened, their tiny circle broke apart. They floated apart, each of them wondering what was going to happen next. The same guard that had brought them here entered, pointing her NPW at Jeff. Jeff noticed that there were two other guards behind her. They were not taking any chances, obviously. The lead guard motioned with her weapon.

"You," she said, indicating Jeff. "Let's go." She moved aside, indicating with a jerk of her head that he should go first.

Jeff looked at Susan, then at Paul. He shrugged his shoulders, and smiled slightly. "Take care of each other," he said softly. "I'll see you again. Don't worry."

"Uh huh," Paul nodded, his old, sarcastic tone suddenly returning. He had floated back against the far wall. Jeff raised his eyebrows, wondering what the big man was thinking. He took a closer look at Paul, and suddenly noticed his stance . . . a very *familiar* stance. Even in zero gravity, Jeff recognized it from their fight back in New York.

"Paul," he warned, but it was too late.

Like a snake, Paul suddenly brought his legs up against the wall and shoved — *hard*. Jeff had fought Paul once before, and had almost died in the process. Even so, he was still caught unprepared by the big man's speed. So were the guards. Paul caromed across the small room like an out-of-control cannonball.

"No!" Jeff shouted, but no one heard. There was a bone-jarring 'thwack' as Paul hit the female guard head-on. The air was forced out of her lungs, and her neck snapped back. She went flying through the hatch and into the guard beyond. In one smooth motion Paul reached out, grasped her by the hand, and grabbed her NPW. He pointed it at the third guard, started to fire . . . and stopped. For just a second, he hesitated. He glanced down at the NPW, as if checking something.

For a wild moment, Jeff actually thought that they might make a break for it. Just *where* they might go, or how they might get off Liberty did not occur to him. All he could think about in those few seconds was that Paul had just successfully taken out three guards. Then he hesitated, and that hesitation cost him. Paul looked back up at the third guard, but the guard had already aimed his NPW. There was an almost silent "pop," and Paul immediately went limp.

"Paul!" This time it was Susan who shouted. She was not yet comfortable in weightlessness, but she managed to get to him before Jeff. Jeff floated up behind them, to find Susan cradling Paul's head against her chest.

To Jeff's relief, Paul's eyes were open. They sought out Jeff's. The big man managed a slight smile. "Had to check the setting," he whispered, the words a harsh rasp. "Don't . . . don't know much about being a Christian yet, but you don't kill, do you?" Jeff could only shake his head no. He felt the sting of tears at the corners of his eyes. God had definitely done something special here! The effort of talking had taken what was left of Paul's strength, and he slid into unconsciousness. His breathing, Jeff noted with great relief, was regular and strong.

"Up, you!" The guard had recovered her equilibrium and her NPW, but not her temper. Jeff was grabbed roughly from behind by the collar of his shirt. The guard literally threw him to her cohorts, who took him by either shoulder and brought him around to face her. She shoved the NPW in his face.

"No more stun settings," she growled, and Jeff could see that the NPW was indeed set to kill. "Try another move like that, and *she* gets it." The guard waved the NPW at Susan. Jeff only nodded.

Without another word, Jeff was led away from Susan and Paul. Quickly, he was marched deeper and deeper into the bowels of Liberty. There were no more open spaces like the park he had first seen. Instead he was taken down corridor after corridor until he had completely lost his sense of direction. Finally, they stopped at a single hatch. In the center of the hatch, in block letters about three inches high, was the single word "Medical."

Despite his earlier peace, Jeff felt a thrill of fear rush through him. His memory flashed back to a few months ago, when he, Stephen Lynch, and Scott Sampson had penetrated the medical facility known as "Mentasys." He had not seen the interrogation tubes then, but he had heard of them later. Those who were put in them did not come out.

The hatch slid back into the wall, and he was shoved inside. Immediately, he scanned the room. To his relief, there were no tubes in sight. To his left were two examination tables, side by side. The rest of the room was filled with what he assumed to be medical equipment. Other than the tables, there was nothing there that had a sinister look about it. His tense muscles relaxed a bit, if only temporarily. He started to take a deep breath, but it was cut short when someone slapped the back of his head — hard — with an open hand. If the guards had not been holding him by the arms, he would have gone flying across the room.

"You're gonna get yours now, *boy!*" Jeff knew that crowing voice, even though he had heard it only once before. The hatred it dripped was unmistakable. He looked behind to see the man he knew only as "Wolf" smiling evilly. He had obviously been waiting.

One of the guards moved between Jeff and Wolf. "That's enough," he snapped, bringing his taser to within inches of Wolf's face. Apparently, Jeff noted, the guards had little love for the terrorist.

Wolf smiled ingratiatingly, and spread his hands. "Sure," he drawled, his voice a low purr. "No problem." He looked back at Jeff. "I'm gonna enjoy this," he said, grinning. To Wolf's annoyance, Jeff kept a poker face, and said nothing.

"Think your pretty special, huh?" snapped Wolf. "Well, let me show you something." Keeping his distance from the guards, he floated over to one of the many terminals visible in the room. He switched one on and typed for a moment.

"Take a look," he said, motioning at Jeff. Jeff sighed, and kept looking straight ahead. He had already decided to ignore Wolf. One of the guards started toward the terrorist, evidently planning on forcibly removing him from the room. Before he could get there, Wolf began to read aloud what was on the screen.

"Goshen," he said. "Churches — Tanis, Zoan, Avaris, Zilu, Busiris." Jeff froze. He suddenly felt as if a dagger of ice had been thrust into his chest. Wolf was reading the code names of the churches hidden in Detroit — Goshen. How . . . ?

"Tanis," Wolf continued relentlessly. "Joseph and Mary Parker, 333 Zephyr Way. Safe house. Shall I go on?" His tone was dripping with wicked glee. Only iron control kept Jeff from screaming in agony. Wolf could see the struggle in his face. He floated over into Jeff's line of sight.

"It's all there," he gloated. "Everything. And in a few hours, it's all going to be gone." He grinned again. "We've already tested the info. Took out a few of your little groups, just to be sure. Only about 30 people. Just a drop in the ol' bucket, eh?"

It was all Jeff could do to keep from launching himself at Wolf in rage. Gone. Everything he had suffered for, everything he had helped build over the past several years . . . gone.

And the people! The images of his friends crowded into his mind. Scott and Beth Sampson, Stephen Lynch. . . . He squeezed his eyes shut. Helen Bradley! All of the rest, ready to be wiped out. It was unbearable.

Wolf's face split into a wide grin. "Gotcha!" he crowed. "And this ain't nothin' compared to what's gonna happen to you. Man, I'm gonna enjoy this!" The guards had evidently had enough. One of them stepped in front of Jeff and motioned for Wolf to move away. Cackling, Wolf complied.

Jeff was pulled across the room to one of the waiting examination tables. Quickly and expertly, he was strapped in. One of the guards accidentally nudged his injured knee. In the weightless environment, he had forgotten about it. Now he groaned in pain.

Once he was strapped in, the guards left. Jeff was thankful that they took Wolf with them. He lay there in silence, his mind numb from the shock Wolf had given him. The computer network had been breached! Thousands of names and addresses were now in the hands of a merciless enemy, and there was absolutely *nothing* he could do. He had never in his life felt so helpless.

"Oh God," he prayed desperately, "Help Your people. Please! Don't let them die like this." Abruptly, he stopped. He tried to keep praying, but he just could not do it. A great wave of weariness washed over him. He realized, finally and at last, that he had no strength left. He was broken. All of his plans, all of his hopes, were in ashes. There was nothing left.

The hatch opened once again, and Jeff let his eyes drift over to it. Someone else was being brought in. It took him a moment to realize that it was David Eddington. Jeff groaned again. Not in pain, this time, but in despair. David was unconscious. His skin was waxen, and he was barely breathing. To Jeff, he looked as if he were at death's door.

It was the last straw. Jeff could not bear to see anymore, and he closed his eyes. He did not respond when the nurse who came in behind David checked his heart rate and his respiration. And he did not respond when he felt the sting of a needle being pushed into his arm. He kept his eyes shut, and as he lost consciousness he prayed that he would never wake up again.

12

"Were you successful?" Christine was waiting as the doctor entered the observation lounge. The older man was still wearing his surgical robe, but had removed his gloves and mask. He nodded in response to her question.

"We'll know for certain tomorrow," he said, "but things look good so far." He glanced over at the observation monitors, where an unconscious Jeff Anderson and David Eddington were being monitored carefully. The surgery had taken exactly 72 minutes. "Even the one with the tumor responded well," he continued. "After what the sonigram revealed, I really didn't think he'd make it. He still might not. As I said, we'll know more in 24 hours."

"Twenty-four hours?" Christine felt a sickening lurch in her stomach, rather like being in an elevator that was going down too fast. There was no way that she would be able to hide her actions from Brennon for that long. "I was able to use my interface almost immediately after my operation," she said, the tension high in her voice. "Why should they be any different?"

The doctor shook his head. "Your surgery was unique," he replied carefully, "as was your implant. We had to stimulate the bio-chip's growth in order for it to implant itself properly."

"Stimulate?" demanded Christine. "Stimulate how?"

"Remember," said the doctor, "your implant is a *bio*-chip. It's biologically alive. Once inserted, it *grows* into place — becomes a part of you. We used a high protein-based silicate injection on yours to accelerate that growth." He smiled tentatively. "Rather like fertilizing a lawn."

"So do it to them," snapped Christine, ignoring his attempt at humor.

The doctor's smile faded quickly. "Your implant is a level one," he explained. "That means that there are certain safeguards built into it. It's designed with the safety of the user in mind. The cerebral interface shut itself down while the chip's growth accelerated. That protected you from the full effects."

He motioned at the sleeping patients. "You ordered a level four implant for them," he reminded Christine. "An 'economy' model, if you will. There are no such safeguards. If we try to accelerate the growth of *their*

- 322 -

implants, there's a 25 percent chance that we'll lose them. Even more so with Eddington. That tumor is the size of a grapefruit."

"Twenty-five percent," repeated Christine softly. The doctor nodded. "Do it," she ordered. The doctor blinked in surprise. For a moment, Christine thought he was going to argue the matter. Then he noticed the look on her face, and decided not to.

"You'll take the responsibility?" he asked nervously.

"No," replied Christine flatly. "You'll take the responsibility. I want those implants ready to interface with my own within the next hour. Understood?"

The doctor hesitated for a moment, then nodded unhappily. There being nothing left to say, he floated out.

Christine turned her attention to the patients on her screen. She thought about briefing Lou on her plan, but once again decided against it. She would contact him at the last possible second, and not until. She had already put herself in serious jeopardy. The less *anyone* knew, including smart aleck computer entities, the better.

Staring at the monitor, she willed Anderson and Eddington to survive the acceleration process. "Just until I've squeezed everything out of you," she whispered. "After that, you can go to your God, *or* your devil. I don't care which." She leaned back in her chair and began to plan her strategy. Soon, things were going to get *very* interesting.

* * *

As Susan watched, Paul carefully put himself through his stretching exercises. He had almost shaken off the full effects of the NPW, and was beginning to feel a little better. His bandaged ribs still complained, but the weightless environment helped. He was *not* practicing his Zen centering techniques. He no longer needed them. Still, the physical exercises themselves were useful.

"You feel it, too?" Susan's question stopped him in mid-stretch. He twisted his body around so that he could see her. She floated comfortably above one of the captive chairs.

"What?" he asked, not sure of what she meant.

"You feel it, too," she repeated. This time, it was not a question. "That something is going to happen."

Paul thought about it, then nodded. "I thought I was just jumpy," he said with a half smile, "But yeah, I feel it too."

Susan let out a deep breath. "It's like a heaviness before a storm," she said quietly. "I feel that something terrible has happened, but that something far worse is on the way."

Now she had Paul's complete attention. "Any idea what?" he asked.

Susan shook her head. "We're not talking psychic here," she said ruefully. "It's just a feeling. Like something growing at the root of my soul." Her tone turned questioning. "That doesn't make any sense, I know."

"As a matter of fact, it does," said Paul. "I've been feeling the same way. I just haven't been able to put it into words." He fell silent, thinking. When he spoke again, it was very slowly, as if he were having difficulty in saying the words.

"You probably won't believe this," he began, "but I've been feeling that way since before I got you out of that hospital." He pondered his words for a moment, then shook his head. "Its more than that," he admitted. Now that he had begun, the words came easier. "I've felt this . . . this presence. That's the only way I can describe it." He looked at Susan, who nodded encouragingly.

"Its been with me since I left Cincinnati." The memory, which he had repressed, now came back with perfect clarity. He could see himself, drenched in sweat, seated in a lotus position in that cheap apartment. He licked his lips and continued. "It was a person — at least, I think it was a person. He claimed to be my master." Involuntarily, Paul shuddered at the memory.

Susan pushed herself gently over to him and took his hand in hers. Grateful for the contact of another human being, Paul smiled and continued. "I remember his eyes," he said. "They were dead eyes. It . . . it terrified me." Deep inside, a part of him was astonished that he could admit to *anyone* that he was afraid. "Since then, I haven't really had a single peaceful night's sleep. I keep expecting him to show up."

"It's all right," said Susan softly.

Paul took a deep breath, and forced a chuckle. "I used to pride myself on having perfect control over my emotions, but whoever this was scared me. He scared me in my apartment in Cincinnati, he scared me in my sleep, and he scared me at that Bernie's place." Susan frowned a question.

"When I was unconscious," Paul explained. "It was a dream, but not really a dream." She nodded, understanding. Abruptly, Paul gripped Susan's hand tighter. She winced, but Paul did not notice. "He *dominated* me, Susan." Now his voice actually cracked. "He totally dominated me. I was nothing against him. Somehow, he was inside my head, and there, where I was at my strongest, he could do what he wanted." The big man fell silent.

"Paul?" There was no answer. "Paul." Susan's voice was stern. He looked up at her. "Have you felt his presence since Camelot?"

Paul shook his head. "Not since I prayed," he said. On reflex, he tried to put up the cold, emotionless wall that had served him so well in the past. He *never* shared his feelings with *anyone*. It did not work. The ruthless, uncaring Paul Sinclair who had callously hunted and imprisoned believers had died at Camelot. The one who now was a prisoner at Liberty was, at the same time, both weaker and far stronger.

Paul did not, as yet, understand this. His face took on a hint of desperation. "What if he comes back?" he asked, his voice low. "I wasn't able to resist him before. I won't be able to resist him again."

"No, Paul," agreed Susan. "*You* won't be able to resist him." With an infinite tenderness, she laid her free hand against his chest. "But the One who now lives in here, in your heart and soul, *can*. 'Greater is he that is in you, than he that is in the world.' Do you understand? Our Lord has taken you away from whoever that was, and the one enemy who controls *him.*"

Paul started to speak, but Susan continued. "Sooner or later, you *may* come face to face with this person, but if you do, remember this. He can hurt you, he can even kill you, but he can never, *never* touch you in here." Again she pressed her hand against his chest.

Paul thought about it for a moment. Then he managed a ghost of a smile. "You wouldn't lie to someone who was using you for his own totally despicable ends, would you?"

Susan smiled back. "Who? Me? Of course not." Her smile disappeared, and once again she became totally serious. "Especially not someone who got me out of that miniature hell called a mental health institution." She looked away, suddenly embarrassed. "I know why you did it," she said. "At least, why you *thought* you did it, but it doesn't matter. God used you then, even if you didn't realize it. I've thanked Him, but I've never said it to you." Now she looked back at him. "Thank you, Paul. No matter what happens next, thank you for the life you gave me by getting me out of there."

Suddenly, for the first time in a long time, Paul was embarrassed. Now it was his turn to look away. "I . . . I . . ." he stuttered.

"Just say 'you're welcome,' " instructed Susan, a hint of her old humor returning.

"You're welcome," he said obediently. They stared at each other for a moment, then both of them laughed as one. The tension and fear that had been there just moments ago evaporated without a trace. Paul felt a great relief wash through him. In a moment of self-realization, he had understood that he was weak. Paul Sinclair had no strength of his own. That was all right. The Lord he now served had more than enough to go around.

"I think," he said slowly, "That all hell's going to break loose soon."

Susan raised her eyebrows at Paul's wording. He saw her look, and shrugged. "That's the only way I can describe it," he said.

Susan nodded. "So what should we do?" she asked.

Paul looked away from her and scanned the room. He noted the sealed hatch, and the security camera. Suddenly, in his new found confidence in his Lord, they did not matter at all.

"Sit tight," he replied, looking back at her. "If something *is* about to happen, then we'll be ready." Now his face was all determination. He looked Susan in the eye. "And I promise you, we *will* be ready."

* * *

The Sextuaget met exactly one hour after the implant surgery of Jeff and David. Five men sat in their accustomed places in the conference room, waiting quietly on their leader. The single female member was conspicuously absent.

Indres glanced at each of his colleagues, his face a blank. Outwardly, he appeared calm. His image demanded it. He was the all-wise spiritual leader of the Sextuaget . . . for that matter, the world. His emotions, however, were churning like a queasy stomach. It was a new and unpleasant experience for him. Usually, he kept himself under tight control. Not now, though. Something was happening. Something important. He could feel it . . . and whatever it was, it was going on without his knowledge.

For the third time since he had entered the conference room, he interfaced with the station mainframe. Hastily he scanned through the electronic traffic. Nothing. Whatever was happening, it was not being processed through the station's master computer. He was about to probe further, to enter Brennon's world system, when the hatch opened and the man himself floated into the conference room.

Unconsciously, each man straightened his shoulders, as if coming to attention. Even though weightless, Brennon maintained an aura of dignity and power that was almost inhuman. He scanned the room, taking in each member of his elite inner circle. His eyes came to rest on Christine's empty chair. He frowned. Then his eyes seemed to be looking at something in the distance. Indres knew that he was accessing his own master bio-chip.

"Why is Christine Smythe in medical at the moment?" His words were softly spoken, but the threat they carried was deafening. The members of the Sextuaget looked at each other, none of them willing to admit their ignorance. The fact was, Christine maintained as little contact with them as possible.

"Indres?" Now Brennon's empty yet powerful eyes turned on the diminutive Indian. Indres knew better than to try to dissemble to his master. He shook his head.

"Four prisoners were brought on board not long ago," he answered uneasily. "Perhaps she is seeing to their interrogation." Brennon thought for a moment. Then once again he peered off into the distance.

"Two of these prisoners are in medical as well," he said, his voice low and menacing. "The other two are being held in a converted office." Again he paused, as if in thought. "She is not using the mainframe for her interrogation, if that is indeed what she is doing." Indres, and the rest, remained silent. Abruptly, Brennon's gazed snapped back into focus.

"That is all for now," he said. "We will postpone this last meeting for one hour." He nodded, and the five other men began to file out.

"Indres, stay." Indres felt the stirrings of fear, and immediately buried them.

He pushed himself back into his chair, and assumed an appropriately respectful attitude. The fact that he had just been commanded as a human might command an animal did not register with him.

"One of the prisoners is Paul Sinclair," Brennon said as the last of the Sextuaget left. Indres nodded. He had known the identity of all four the minute they had been brought on board. So, he was sure, had Brennon.

"He appears to have gone over to the enemy," continued Brennon. Now Indres *was* surprised. Brennon had taken an interest in Sinclair for some time now. It had been Brennon's manipulations that had gotten Paul fired from the bureau. Indres was no stranger to the powers of the mind, or the powers of the spirit world. Because of that, he knew that Brennon had been exerting a great deal of psychic influence over Sinclair for the past several years. It had been his plan to have him brought deep into one of Brennon's many circles. Between his physical prowess, and his mental acuity, as well as his susceptibility to suggestion, Paul Sinclair had great potential.

"Are you sure?" The words were out of Indres' mouth before he realized what he had said.

The annoyed look Brennon gave him caused him to flinch visibly. "I want him brought here," he said, ignoring Indres' question. "He *has* to be broken and then destroyed." Brennon smiled his empty smile. "I will do it myself, before he has a chance to grow any stronger in his new found faith." His eyes became distant. "I suppose I should have taken care of this matter before, while he was still spiritually vulnerable." He sighed. "Ah well. He would have been useful. Now he is merely dangerous. Bring him here immediately."

"As you wish," replied Indres deferentially. "And the woman he is with?"

Again Brennon smiled. For an instant, Indres caught a glimpse of something inhuman — something that chilled him to the depths of his soul. Then it was gone, and Indres blinked, unsure if he had seen anything at all. "Bring her too," Brennon said, answering the question he had momentarily forgotten. "If our Mr. Sinclair has developed any kind of fondness for her, then she might be useful." He nodded, indicating that the interview was over. Indres left.

For a moment, Brennon sat in his chair, as if pondering where matters rested. Then he pressed a control that was inset into the conference table in front of him. The conference room was now completely isolated from the rest of the station, physically and electronically. Nothing could get in or out without his express permission.

There, in absolute solitude, one of the most powerful men in the world sat for a moment, contemplating his coming confrontation with Paul Sinclair. He had to admit his disappointment about Paul. He had been grooming him for great things. Carefully, through the opening Paul had allowed into his mind with his Zen training, Brennon had been influencing him, guiding him. His spiritual journey into Brennon's camp had been almost complete. Then he had bolted into the camp of the enemy. Now he would have to be destroyed. A pity.

Things were coming to a head. The culmination of generations of planning was now almost at hand. Soon, very soon, his ultimate purpose would be accomplished. All that stood in his way were a few scattered followers of the hated enemy. He nodded in satisfaction.

Then, his eyes glazed over. A tiny drop of drool escaped the corner of his mouth and dribbled down his chin. His body went limp, and his head slumped forward upon his broad shoulders. He lay very still, barely breathing. It was as if he was a marionette whose strings had just been cut.

* * *

Christine watched as the doctor finished his examination. She was floating loosely in a med-couch in the next room, viewing his progress in her monitor.

"Well?" she asked over the intercom.

The doctor hesitated, then nodded. "Everything *seems* to be all right," he answered, "But it's *still* risky."

Christine disregarded his warning. She was almost out of time. This gamble would either secure her future, or get her a one-way ticket into space without a ship. "Do it," she commanded. "Activate their implants now, and give me direct access. *Keep them off-line with the main system* — except through me. Understand?"

The doctor nodded unhappily, but complied. Christine set herself to the task of merging into the system. It was time to move.

* * *

David awoke standing up. There was no transition, no gradual regaining of consciousness. He simply opened his eyes, and found himself standing on a dull gray plain that seemed to stretch into infinity.

"What?!" The single exclamation startled him, even though he himself had said it. It was almost as if there was no sound in this strange world — that anything spoken would be swallowed up by the emptiness that surrounded him. His mind felt sluggish and unresponsive. The grayness was oppressive, as if invisible walls were closing in on all sides. He rubbed at his eyes, trying to shake off the feeling of sluggishness.

"David?" This time the voice was *not* his. It came from behind him. Startled, he swung around, to find Jeff Anderson walking toward him. He almost fainted in relief. Jeff stopped a few feet away from him, and regarded him uncertainly.

"Jeff?" He took a step toward his friend. Jeff backed up, not allowing him to come closer. "Jeff! What's wrong? It me, David." He looked around at the lack of landscape. "Where are we?" he asked. He could hear the fear in his own voice.

Jeff shook his head, and held up a warning hand. David stopped, confused. "We'll talk about where we are in a minute. What's the last thing you remember?" Jeff asked.

The question took David by surprise. He thought about it for a moment. "I'm not sure," he admitted. "We were at Camelot, at that guy's apartment, right?" His forehead wrinkled in concentration. "We left, and . . ." He shook his head, suddenly angry. "I can't remember."

Now Jeff seemed to soften a little. He took a step closer to David, closing the distance between them to a few feet. "Do you remember the elevator?" he asked, his voice low.

David thought about it. "We were headed toward the elevators," he replied slowly. "There were footsteps behind us." Suddenly his eyes went wide. "They caught us!" he cried. "I remember . . . I remember getting shot." Automatically his eyes lowered to his chest. He looked back at Jeff in confusion.

"They used an electronic pulse on us," Jeff explained. "Non-lethal, but it messes you up for about half an hour." His lips pressed into a thin line. "It seemed to have a worse effect on you though."

David's mouth suddenly went dry, and he felt as if someone had dropped an anvil in his stomach. His mind flashed on Miriam's message, and the increasing frequency and intensity of his headaches. "Brain damage," he whispered.

"What do you mean?" Jeff demanded. David hesitated, and Jeff grabbed him by the arm. "Those headaches of yours," he said. "That's part of it, isn't it?"

Reluctantly, David nodded. "Come on, David," Jeff said, shaking his arm gently but firmly, "let's have it."

He did not want to, but slowly, David told Jeff about Miriam's visit. "I don't remember any of what she told me happened," he admitted. "She said I was questioned by someone named 'Wolf.' Whatever they did to me, it caused some kind of damage." He bit his lower lip. "That's why we went into the Shepherd's Path," he said. "Wolf and his people knew about us."

His shoulders slumped and he suddenly felt very, very tired. "I kept hoping that I would get better," he said softly. "After all, Susan was healed, and she was a lot worse than I was. Why not me? But the headaches got worse."

He looked at Jeff with quiet desperation. "I don't think I'm going to get better," he said in a small voice. "I think I'm dying." He looked away, suddenly ashamed of his fear.

It was too much for Jeff. He closed the remaining distance between them and put his arms around David. He did not have the words to comfort the smaller man, but that was okay. Just holding him was enough. They stayed together for a few minutes. Then David took a deep breath. Gently he pulled away, and smiled tentatively.

"Anyway," he said, some strength returning to his voice, "The last thing I remember was getting shot with that electronic pulse thing. Then I woke up here." He glanced around at the lack of scenery. "So do you know where 'here' is?"

Jeff shook his head. Hastily he brought David up-to-date on what had happened to them. David's eyes widened in surprise. "Liberty?! They brought us into space?" His tone was incredulous. Jeff nodded an answer. "Far out," David replied, and again glanced around. "The thing is," he said, "I don't know too much about space stations, but this sure doesn't look like one."

"I know," Jeff agreed. "Not only that, but there's gravity here." He bounced up and down on the balls of his feet. Abruptly he frowned. "My knee," he exclaimed.

David glanced down. "It looks okay," he observed. They were both wearing bright white coveralls.

"Yeah," said Jeff. "That's the problem. It was hurt . . . bad. Now it feels fine." He took another look around. "Come on," he said determinedly. "Lets see where we can get to."

David agreed, and the two men began to walk. It only took minutes before they discovered that they could go no further. Some kind of resistance slowly presented itself — not all at once, but gradually. It was like trying to walk through a wall of thick syrup. Within 10 paces, they could go no further. Defeated, the two men retreated.

"This is too weird," said David, trying hard to control the fear inside. He peered around, trying to discern any kind of detail in the emptiness around them.

"Yeah," replied Jeff. "It's almost as if this is a place where dreams start."

David blinked in surprise. "What does that mean?" he asked.

Jeff shrugged. "I don't know," he admitted, "but this place feels like some kind of holding area." He shook his head negatively. "No, that's not right," he amended. "It's real, but it's not real." He gave up in frustration. "I don't know what I mean. Whatever it is, I think there's a lot more to it than we can see."

"Very good, Mr. Anderson." The feminine voice came from behind them. Both men spun around, to confront the owner of that voice. She was standing there, just a few feet away. Neither man had heard her approach.

"You get high marks for your perceptiveness," said the woman, smiling a cold smile. She was a young-looking woman, although David placed her at around 50. She had dark hair and a light build, and there was a menace to her that made him want to put as much distance between them as possible. She also looked vaguely familiar.

"I don't . . ." he began, but she spoke over him.

"Understand? I'm not surprised. This is something totally beyond your experience." Again that harsh smile. "You see, I've given you a gift. It's a priceless gift, but one that *everyone* will have soon."

Now Jeff stepped forward, intentionally imposing himself between the newcomer and David. "Look lady," he said, his voice determined, "I don't know what's going on, but whatever it is, you're not going to get anything out of. . . ."

"QUIET!" The woman's voice boomed out from all directions, unbearably loud. David cried out in shock, and slapped his hands to his ears. Jeff reeled, then fell to his knees. The woman watched their reaction with amusement. "That's better," she said, her voice returning to normal. "Now, to make this short, both of you have been implanted with a computer bio-chip. It allows you to interface with a very special system. In fact, the same system that broke your little computer network just a while ago."

David heard Jeff groan. He sank down next to him, throwing an arm over his shoulder. "Jeff? What's she mean?"

Jeff looked up, his face a mask of despair. "How could I have forgotten?" he whispered harshly. "They have everything — everything!"

"Not everything," said the woman. "I need what is inside your head as well. I promise you that I'll get it. Your implant is slaved to mine." She took a step toward them and knelt on one knee, bringing her face level with theirs. "You were right when you said that this place felt like a holding area," she told Jeff with malicious glee. "Right now, you're both just outside the main system."

"Virtual reality," murmured Jeff, looking around. "This place isn't real. Its part of some kind of program, and somehow we're linked to it."

The woman laughed. "I assure you, this place is *very* real. This goes far beyond anything you might think you know. You are a part of the system now . . . or you will be. Your thoughts will be mine. Everything that you know that makes your precious underground Church function, you'll give to me."

David felt Jeff's muscles tense. Slowly, deliberately, he stood. David rose with him, his hand still resting on his shoulder. He was amazed at the "reality" that surrounded him. Even Jeff felt solid and real.

"Never," said Jeff quietly. The tone of his voice left no room for compromise.

"Wrong," replied the woman. "Now." She raised a hand. Both men tensed, sensing an attack. They were still caught off guard.

Without any warning, David found himself lying flat on his back. He had totally lost control of his body. Nothing worked. He tried to move something, *anything,* but he could not even feel the ground beneath him. All he could see was the terrible grayness above him.

"I'm going to take a walk through your minds," came the voice of the woman from above him. "I'm going to drain every thought, and while I'm doing that, I'm going to burn out every cell in your brains — one cell at a time if I have to."

"No-o-o!" David heard the scream, but could not even tell if it had come from him or Jeff.

"Yes," came the icy reply. "Now, let me show you what *real* power is."

David suddenly felt icy fingers probing deep into his mind. They yanked hard. It felt as if his very soul was being stolen. He screamed, but could hear nothing. In desperation, he cried out. *Lord,* he screamed in his mind. *Help me! Please! Help me-e-e!* The grayness suddenly disappeared, to be replaced by countless points of light. He was falling. The woman was gone, and Jeff as well. Terror gripped him. He was dying, and nothing could stop that. Worse, he was suddenly gripped with the absolute conviction that there was nothing beyond death — no heaven, no hell — nothing. He fell toward the lights, knowing that the only thing that awaited was oblivion.

* * *

"That way." The guard pointed at a hatch with his EPW. A hand gripped Paul on the shoulder and propelled him toward it. They had not bound his hands, so he was able to stop his forward motion. He hit the hatch gently, and bounced back. Then he grunted when Susan bumped him from behind. "Both of you," grunted the guard.

Paul glared back. He hated being this powerless. Every instinct in him wanted to lash out at the guard, to immobilize him. It would be such an easy thing, too. The guard floated carelessly behind them, not even bothering to effect a defensive posture. One simple combination. . . .

Reluctantly, Paul discarded the idea. He had already had one experience with the NPWs the guards carried. He did not want another. Not only that, but inside him a still, small voice was telling him to wait. In his heart, Paul knew that a time was coming when fast, decisive action would be required. He could feel it. Somehow, he and his friends had a task to accomplish here. What it was, he could not tell, but that did not matter. He felt certain that they would know when the time came. He knew, beyond a doubt, that they were here for a reason.

The hatch was closed and Paul did not try to open it. There was a control panel on the right, complete with a palm reader. He was sure that his prints had not been cleared to open *anything*. Above the reader, a single pencil-thin bar glowed red. The guard who had shoved him reached around Paul and touched a control just to the left of the reader. Paul could hear, muted through the hatch, a single electronic tone. There was a brief pause, then the glowing bar changed from red to green. Paul heard the sound of metal on metal, and realized that the locks were being released on the hatch. The hatch slowly opened.

"Inside," said the guard gruffly, and once again shoved Paul forward. This time, Paul grabbed Susan's arm and was able to control their forward momentum. The two floated into what Paul recognized as a conference area. It was a dim room, with the illumination coming from seven low-level lights inset in a circle into the ceiling. Several large monitors were spaced evenly around the upper portion of the oval shaped room. A few were blank. Others had graphs or figures on them, and one showed the earth slowly rotating below. A table, shaped the same as the room, dominated the center. Seven captive chairs surrounded the table, three on each side, and one at the head. All of the chairs were empty except the one at the head, which was turned away.

Paul reached out his free hand and grabbed the edge of the table. Its top seemed to be made of a dark polymer, and dimly reflected the ceiling. As soon as they were inside, the guard cycled the hatch shut behind them. They floated in silence for several seconds, wondering what was coming next. Neither spoke. Instead, Paul and Susan merely gripped each other's hands tightly. Paul looked at Susan, who could only stare back. Gently, she took her other hand and gripped his arm.

Even then, in their most desperate hour, Paul could only marvel at the way Susan had forgiven him. He had never before been so glad of her gift of friendship. It was a gift that, for the first time in his life, he valued, and treasured. He vowed silently to himself, then and there, that no matter what, he would get her off of this station — even if it cost him his own life.

"Welcome, Paul." The deep, cultured voice startled him. Paul snapped to attention, every sense on the alert. He had heard that voice *before!* The chair at the head of the table swung slowly around. Revealed inside was a shadow. The lights in the ceiling were all lit, except the one above the man in the chair.

Paul frowned, then actually snorted. "Very dramatic," he said aloud, putting as much sarcasm in his voice as he could. "Aren't you a little ashamed to be making bad movies?"

There was a pause, then the figure chuckled. "Very good, Paul. I'm glad to see that you didn't lose *everything* when you turned traitor." The shadow moved, adjusting a control. "This room is now sealed. Nothing can get in or out without my approval. *How* you leave here will depend entirely upon this interview."

A chill ran through Paul. He wanted to deny it, but there was no doubt where he had heard that voice before. Twice before, in fact, and both times had been in the refuge of his meadow. He glanced over at Susan and gave her hand a tight squeeze. He figured that she must be terrified. To his surprise, however, she was staring straight at the figure, her face drawn up in concentration. It was if she had been presented a puzzle, and was on the verge of figuring it out. Then he caught a soft glow out of the corner of his eye, and when he turned back, the figure had turned on the light above him.

The recognition Paul had denied now hit him with full force. He did not know the face, but the eyes, those dead, lifeless eyes that emoted nothing but menace and evil, were unmistakable. "You!" The exclamation was out of his mouth before he could stop it. He had teased Jeff just hours ago when his former enemy had had the same reaction toward him. Part of his mind reflected that if he ever saw him again, he would have to apologize.

The man smiled. "I'm pleased," he said, his voice still low, "but then, you always showed great promise. A pity that my effort on you was wasted."

A thousand questions ran through Paul's mind in the space of a second, but only one mattered to him. "Who are you?" he asked, his own voice harsh and trembling.

"If you want a name, you may call me Brennon," said the figure. "That will do as good any other."

Paul shook his head. "Who are you?" he repeated. His mouth was suddenly dry. He felt as if the rounded walls of the conference room were closing in on him. It became hard to breath.

Once again Brennon chuckled. "I'm your teacher, Paul." Now his voice grew hard. "I'm your master."

"No." Paul was barely able to get the word out. He felt trapped — caged. Brennon's words hit him like a tank, and he felt himself floundering. This was the man who had mastered him so easily, not so long ago. This was the man who had menaced his very thoughts. Next to him, Paul felt like a small, weak child.

"Paul." Susan spoke, trying to get Paul's attention, but neither man paid her any notice.

Brennon saw Paul's fear, and smiled. The emptiness of his smile matched the death in his eyes. "You see, Paul, I'm still here for you. It's not too late to turn back to me." Now his smile took on the characteristic of a father welcoming back a long lost son. Brennon held out his right hand in a gesture of forgiveness. "Come back, Paul," he said gently. "Everything you ever wanted, everything you worked so hard to attain, I'll give to you."

Paul struggled with Brennon's words. He could feel his influence in his mind, probing to find an opening.

"Paul." Susan's voice was more insistent this time, but once again she was ignored.

"Power, Paul," Brennon continued. "The power you have always sought can be yours. You wanted to return to your petty Bureau of Religious Affairs? I can give you so much more than that." He gestured slowly. "Come, Paul. Take your place at my side."

Paul could not reply to Brennon's persuasion. He opened his mouth and tried, but the words would not come. He felt as if he was fighting a battle on two levels. Here, with Brennon offering all that he had ever wanted, and in his own mind, where he could feel this powerful man trying to get inside. He knew, with a sickening realization, that, just at before, in his dream, he was no match for this man.

"I . . . I . . ." The words would not come. He tried again to muster some sort of defiance. "I . . . I . . . OUCH!" That last cry came when Susan, forgotten by both men, suddenly planted her teeth firmly on the thumb on his left hand and bit him . . . *hard.*

He jerked his head away from Brennon to stare at her in amazement. "Have you lost your. . . ."

"Have I got your attention now?" Susan demanded, overriding his objections.

"Huh?"

"Listen to me, Paul." Susan's voice was suddenly low and urgent. "I don't know who this man is, or what he has done to you, but there's something wrong here. He," and she pointed at Brennon, "isn't what he seems to be. I don't know what he is, but. . . ."

"QUIET!" Now it was Brennon's turn to interrupt. He pointed a finger at Susan. "Another word," he said, his voice returning to normal, "and I will have you ejected into space. I assure you, the effects of a vacuum are quite unpleasant on an unprotected body."

Susan looked at Brennon for a moment. Then, she gave the man at the head of the table — a man who held more power in his hands than every tyrant, king, president, or chairman combined — the worst insult possible. She *ignored* him.

"Paul," she said urgently, knowing that she did not have much time, "Remember what happened in that mall? Remember who you turned your life over to?" She gestured at Brennon, but kept her eyes on Paul's. "Whoever he is, he can't destroy you. He might kill you, if our Lord allows it, but he can't hurt you here," and she placed a hand over his heart, "or here," and she touched his cheek. "Your soul is safe."

Paul stared into Susan's eyes, Brennon momentarily forgotten. He had been floundering, ready to sink, but this woman, whose husband was dead because of him, had thrown him a lifeline. Or perhaps more accurately, had reminded him Who his lifeline was anchored to. His shoulders, which had been slumping, straightened. He turned back to face the being at the head of the table, his mind calling out to the one Person who could help him.

Brennon frowned darkly. "I see," he said in a low voice. "So you really have gone over to the enemy. A pity."

"That depends on your point of view, I guess," replied Paul. He was pleased to find that his voice had returned.

Now Brennon sneered. "You — *all* of you, are pathetic. Do you really believe your insipid Nazarene cares about what is going to happen to you?" He laughed aloud. "I promise you, He has far more important things to worry about."

"I don't think so," said Paul. "I don't think He's worried at all." He pointed a finger at Brennon. "In fact, I think you're the one who's worried!"

Now it was Paul's turn to laugh, but his laugh was one of honest joy. "I slipped through your fingers, Brennon," he said. His voice was laced with awe at the wonder of it all. "I wonder how many others will do the same. You've lost. You, and whoever serves you, lost before you even started!" Paul fell silent. He could see the anger rising on Brennon's face.

"Fool," whispered Brennon, his voice barely audible. "Weak fool. Just who do you think you are?"

It was a rhetorical question, but at once a reply formed itself in Paul's mind. The answer was so obvious now. "The Shepherd's man," he said, his voice firm in its conviction and commitment.

"Then go to Him," said Brennon in the same low voice. "Now! I'll not waste any more time on you. You are going out of the. . . ." And Brennon froze. Paul and Susan's eyes widened in amazement as they watched the sight before them. The man literally went motionless — not even breathing. He stayed like that for long seconds. Then he jerked forward.

"Christine! What have you done!" Brennon's words were mixed with equal parts terror and rage. They meant nothing to Paul or Susan, but the results did. Once again Brennon's body went dead. The eyes glazed over, and the mouth went slack. Then Brennon slumped forward. If there had been gravity, his head would have hit the table hard. Instead he merely floated in place.

"What the . . ." Paul began, then stopped. Long seconds ticked by, but nothing happened. Finally, after an eternity, Paul took a deep breath and pushed himself forward. He came to a stop beside Brennon's body. Gingerly, he put a hand on the man's neck. He stayed there for a few seconds.

"There's a pulse," he said to Susan, his voice hushed. "And he's breathing — barely."

Susan remained where she was. "Paul?" Susan's voice was very quiet. "What's going on?"

Paul looked back at her, and shook his head slowly. He realized that he did not have the slightest idea. The two friends continued to stare at one another, completely baffled.

* * *

David screamed, or thought he screamed, as he fell. His world was a world of incredible lights and colors. They stretched into infinity — beautiful, yet deadly. Somehow, he knew that if he continued to fall, he would be lost forever within this incredible world. In desperation he called out to the one Person who could save him.

"Lord! Help me! Please!" He could not hear himself. It was as if someone had robbed him of his hearing. The words stuck in his throat, and he continued to fall. "Lord! Please!"

"SILENCE!" David felt shaken to his very soul. This new voice assaulted him from every angle, overpowering him with ease. He looked in all directions, but could see no one.

"Who are you?" he called out, not sure if his words were audible. Without warning, he was assailed by unbearable pain. His mind felt on fire, burned by the malevolent purpose in that voice.

"You will say no more," replied the voice, now modulated somewhat. "Remain silent, and you will live. Call out again. . . ."

Once again the pain hit him, causing David to writhe in agony. He squeezed his eyes shut, trying to defend against it, but there was no defense. Then, as suddenly as it had come, it left. The abrupt relief from the pain was almost as hard to bear as the pain itself. David gasped, his senses reeling. He kept his eyes closed, but for long moments nothing happened. Finally, he dared to open them.

He had stopped falling. The lights surrounding him were piercingly bright and intense, but his headlong rush into them was stopped. He was motionless, floating in a universe that, to him, made absolutely no sense.

Jeff had said that they were linked to some kind of computer program or simulation. That meant that, as far as his body was concerned, he was still on Liberty. Everything that happened here happened in his mind.

Desperately, David tried to think, but his mind was barely functional. He felt unbearably tired and weak, and he had no idea how to "wake up" from this synthesized nightmare. The voice that had assailed him was not human, he knew. It was definitely not the woman who had attacked them before. It was far more powerful.

Suddenly, David was afraid. He knew, without a shadow of a doubt, that if he were to ever meet the owner of that voice he would die. A small sob wormed its way out between his lips. He did not want to die, and he did not want to come face to face with that voice . . . ever.

A wave of shame crept over him. He had thought that his recent experiences had made him stronger in the Lord. Now he knew the bitter truth. He was afraid, and because of his fear, his friends were going to suffer. He could not take a chance meeting that voice again. Another sob wracked his computer-generated body, and then another. He curled himself into a fetal position and closed his eyes tightly. He would do nothing.

* * *

Christine could only stare with outraged amazement as one of her prisoners disappeared. There was no explanation for it. One moment he was there, lying prostrate before her, totally under her control. The next, he was gone. He had screamed out for help, and then vanished. What was happening? Angrily, she confronted the remaining prisoner, Jeff Anderson. He still lay flat on his back, unable to move and firmly under her control.

"What did you do?" she demanded. "Where is he?" The man did not answer. Christine felt a towering rage grow within her. Using her link with his newly implanted chip, she sent a surge of pain through his mind. The man groaned, but did not scream. He was trying his best to resist her.

"Where . . . is . . . he?" Her words came out in guttural syllables, almost animalistic. Inside, however, she was beginning to feel the stirrings of real fear. Her whole plan hinged on being able to extract information from two of the prisoners quickly, then disposing of them. Now, something was wrong. One of the men she had implanted had slipped through her fingers. The other was actually resisting her. The more time she spent here, the greater the risk Brennon would discover her disobedience. She had to succeed, and fast. Again, she lashed out at her remaining prisoner. This time, he *did* scream.

"Don't fight me, Anderson," she said, her voice dropping to a low monotone. "I'll get what I want one way or the other. The more you resist, the greater the pain." Still, Anderson did not respond. His face was drawn up tightly in an effort to deal with the agony.

Christine regarded him with disgust. "Have it your way," she snapped. She scanned her implant's menu. It was time to stop playing around. "You could have died cleanly, Anderson," she told the prone figure before her. "Now you'll die a vegetable." She sent the command to his implant, ordering it to override whatever defenses he had managed to muster.

"Arghhh!" The scream tore from Christine's throat. She fell to her knees, her hands flying to her head. Now the pain was inside her own mind, and it was overwhelming. It was all she could do to keep from passing out.

"WHAT HAVE YOU DONE?!" The words tore through Christine's mind, burning her. She moaned with despair. There was no mistaking that voice. The pain abated, just barely, and she looked up. There he was, standing over her, radiating power and authority . . . and rage. Brennon . . . head of the Sextuaget . . . world leader above world leaders.

"What have you done?" This time the words were softer, but no less full of menace. Desperately, Christine tried to marshal a defense.

"What you told me to do," she cried out, still on her knees. Again she called up her implant menu. Nothing happened. No menu appeared. She was completely helpless.

Brennon frowned in disgust. "Do you really think that you can use what I gave you against me?" He shook his head. "Your implant is slaved to mine, just as you slaved his to yours." He motioned toward Anderson. "I gave you power beyond imagining," he continued in the same dead voice. Christine tried to meet his eyes, but could not. The sheer evil that radiated from them was unbearable. "Not only the power to move nations," said Brennon, "but the ability to control the very thoughts of men." Again he motioned toward Anderson. "This is how you repay me. You have no idea what damage your disobedience might have caused . . . can *still* cause, for that matter."

For the first time in her life, Christine felt the gnawing of sheer terror. Not because she had been found out, although that was bad enough. No, the thing that terrified her the most was how Brennon had so easily mastered her . . . had mastered her from the very beginning, if he was to be believed. Now, he had her. She was trapped in the system he devised, and in which he was the master.

Or was he?

With a tremendous effort of will, Christine forced herself to think. A sudden surge of hope sprung up in her heart. Maybe, she thought desperately, just maybe, she had an ally. If she could just activate her implant. . . . Brennon looked down at her in amused disgust.

"Still trying?" he mocked. "Very well. Here." As if by his spoken word, her implant reactivated. The menu appeared before her eyes. Christine knew that Brennon was toying with her, but he did *not* know one very vital fact. With a speed born of practice, she zeroed in on the one single area from where she could possibly receive help.

LOU! With all her might, she screamed the name in her mind. Perhaps she shouted it aloud as well. She would never be sure. She only knew that, if there was one being who could stop Brennon in his tracks, it would be Lou. The computer entity she had met before was not just a part of the system — he *was* the system. His "body" was spread out across the entire globe. Perhaps he was even a match for the Sextuaget leader. Again she screamed his name, and this time, he came.

"Yes, Christine," came the youngish, cultured voice. She swung around, and there he was. He appeared just the same as before, a young man, handsome and muscular. "Still interested in that alliance?" he asked, his voice bright and cheerful.

She swung back to face Brennon. "Now we'll see," she told him boldly. Now that Lou was with her, she suddenly found her courage. "Lou," she said, not taking her eyes off Brennon, "this man is our enemy. Destroy him, and nothing stands in our way." Somehow, she even found the strength to grin at Brennon. "I've got you," she hissed.

"Indeed," replied Brennon, the amusement still in his voice. "Then it's time to let you in on a little secret, Christine." He motioned toward the image of Lou. In shock and horror, Christine watched as Lou walked past her and moved to stand beside Brennon. What happened next almost caused her to shriek in rage and fear. The two "men" stood side by side for a heartbeat. Then, they merged. As Christine watched, Lou stepped *into* Brennon's body and disappeared. Brennon only smiled at her as Lou vanished. Stunned, Christine could only stare.

"You still do not understand, do you?" remarked Brennon. He could have been suggesting a walk in the park for all the emotion he now showed. Without a hint of transition, he changed, and now Lou stood before her. *"Now* do you see?"

Finally, comprehension punched through the wall of terror in Christine's mind. "It was you," she croaked, her voice now harsh. "There is no 'Brennon,' is there? It was always you."

Now Lou laughed. Once again, he became Brennon. "Oh, I am *very* real," he said. "I am just not that meat puppet that you have been dealing with on the 'outside.' *He* was a second rate bureaucrat working out of some obscure Washington office. His body served me well, as others have for generations."

Even through her terror, Christine shook her head. "Not possible," she managed to say. "There's no way you could have existed before the bio-chip. You said so yourself."

"I lied," said the image in front of her. Now it was Lou who addressed her. "I have been in existence since before your world began." He flung out a hand, and the maze of lights that was the world system appeared. "This is but a useful tool. It makes my task far easier. Frankly, it does not matter whether I inhabit flesh or circuitry. Either way I am the master of this realm."

He grinned at her. With a final, stunning realization, Christine came face to face with the fact that she was overmatched — out of her league. There was a power here, a living, malevolent power that she could neither understand nor resist.

"Indres," she whispered. Her colleague had tried to tell her of the importance of what he had called the "spirit world." Now it was too late.

"Indres is a fool as well," snapped Lou/Brennon. "He has just enough wit to accomplish the task I set for him. Soon, he will no longer be needed. His followers are well in hand. In fact, *you* are no longer needed."

"Wait! I can still. . . ."

But it was far too late. The creature that was neither human nor machine waved his arm. Christine felt her head explode with energy. Invisible hands of pure force pushed their way inside her mind, ripping it to shreds. Lou/Brennon stepped forward and gripped her in an unbreakable embrace. He grinned his dead, empty grin.

"Say 'goodnight,' Christine," he laughed, and hurled her away.

Christine had no more time for rational thought. In the medical section of Liberty, her body spasmed once, then shut down completely. Her implant severed selected synapses, disrupting the electron flow. Her brain died, and seconds later, her body followed. Within the system, her last feeling was one of pure terror as she plunged into the infinite lights. Then her conscious thought process dissolved, and Christine Smythe was ushered into an existence where the final terror was only beginning.

* * *

Brennon/Lou watched Christine disappear with satisfaction. One task accomplished, another ready to begin. The damage he had feared had not materialized. He turned to the still prone form of Jeff Anderson. With a thought, he allowed him to regain control of his virtual form. His body still shaking, Jeff stood.

"So much for the small change," remarked the creature that indwelled the system. "Ready for the main event?" Jeff could only stare, dumbfounded.

* * *

Once again, Paul felt for a pulse on Brennon's wrist. It was still there — barely. Disregarding the body, he began to examine the controls set into the conference table.

"Paul?" Susan floated over next to him.

"Yeah?"

"Do you think we should try to get out of here?"

Paul paused, thinking. Then he shook his head. "The only way off this station is by shuttle," he answered. "And the only way we can get on board is to be cleared."

He continued to scrutinize the controls. "I think that whatever happened to this guy," and he nodded toward the unconscious form, "wasn't planned. Something's gone wrong." He chewed on his lower lip. "The thing is, this terminal is still on-line, and if he was accessing anything before he, er, left, then maybe we can use it."

"Excuse me," replied Susan in a tone that suggested that she was exerting enormous control over herself, "but when I have a crisis, I usually deal with it in person. I don't shut down my body and leave."

"Yeah, I know," said Paul. "I don't understand it either." Another pause. "There," he said with satisfaction.

Susan looked at the monitor that suddenly came to life. It showed the garden section of Liberty that they had seen upon their arrival. Paul fiddled with the control, and the picture changed. A long corridor presented itself, then a work area where several technicians were going about some unknown task, then . . . Susan gasped in shock. Paul!" she cried, grasping his shoulder.

"I see them, I see them," he said, his voice raising a notch. On the screen were the images of Jeff and David. The men were each strapped into some sort of medical couch, and both appeared unconscious. Paul touched another control and the camera zoomed in.

"What have they done to them?" Susan's voice betrayed both anger and fear.

Paul remained silent, studying the monitor. On the right side of the screen was a menu. One of the items simply said "map." Paul touched the screen where the word appeared, and immediately a schematic of the entire station appeared. His finger traced a glowing line. "I think I can find this place," he said at last. "Come on. Let's get out of here." He pushed himself toward the hatch.

He was almost to it when Susan cried out. "Paul! Wait!" He turned and regarded her impatiently. "What if we get them?" Susan asked. "You said it yourself. We can't get off this station without clearance."

"We'll figure it out afterwards," he answered. He pointed toward the monitor. His face betrayed his feelings. He was angry . . . and determined. "I've been through too much with those two to let someone play doctor with them." He managed a slight smile. "Come on, Susan, let's go."

He held out a hand, and Susan started to push herself toward him. A sudden flashing on the monitor stopped her. She regarded it for a moment with curiosity. Then her eyes widened in shock. "Paul?"

Sensing her sudden tension, Paul floated back over behind the unconscious form of Brennon. He stared at the monitor for a moment. Then he looked at Susan and took a deep breath. "Oh boy," he breathed quietly.

* * *

Jeff faced his adversary, his mind racing. The pain that Christine had inflicted upon his mind was gone, but he was still dazed. He had seen the being standing before him handle her as if she were a used up rag doll, throwing her away with a careless ease. If he could do that to the woman who had been able to keep him immobile, then he was obviously far more powerful.

"Well." The entity who called itself Brennon stood there, his arms folded. Jeff regarded him with trepidation. "Do you know who I am, little man?" The creature's voice held an ocean of mockery. Even so, the question surprised Jeff. He forced away his fear and considered it. He thought about all that had happened in this strange, virtual reality. To this, he added his biblical knowledge. He had a fairly good working knowledge of prophecy, of course. It had been a favorite study of his since he had become a Christian. Even so, he had never expected to come face to face with one of the main players of the end times. The signs were all there, though. He knew, or thought he knew, the answer to Lou's question.

"Antichrist." He spat the title out. His loathing of the being before him was evident. Everything Jeff held dear, this creature was out to destroy.

To his surprise, however, Lou began to laugh. Abruptly, his form changed to that of Brennon once more. "Wrong answer," he replied, his voice dripping with scorn. "Fool! You think you know so much, yet you understand so little. When it all comes down, you really have no idea what you are talking about."

"So, sue me," retorted Jeff. He tried to match Brennon's mocking tone, but was not sure he succeeded.

"I'll destroy you," snapped Brennon, "Just like I destroyed Christine." Abruptly, he smiled. "However, before I *do* destroy you, I think I might be persuaded to enlighten you on the true nature of things."

Jeff said nothing. He knew that, whatever else this creature before him might be, he was a very proud being. He *wanted* to boast about his superior knowledge. Jeff had a very strong feeling he was about to learn something that had been debated among philosophers for centuries.

"You called me 'Antichrist,' " Brennon said, then once again changed into Lou. "You were wrong. I am merely his servant . . . his image. I have served him since your precious Christ left the earth." He pointed a finger at Jeff, and suddenly his voice boomed on all directions. "WHAT IS THE NUMBER OF THE BEAST?"

The sheer force of his voice sent Jeff to his knees once again. His mind felt on the verge of overload. It took a few moments for his head to clear so that he could answer. "Six hundred three score and six," Jeff replied, forcing his voice to remain calm.

Lou smiled his mocking smile. "Very good, little man," he said sarcastically. "Now tell me what it means." Jeff had no answer.

Lou laughed. "And you a believer," he mocked. "Don't you know your Scripture, *Christian?*" That last word was spat out in disgust. "Come now. Quote your precious Book to me. Quote from the letter that weakling John wrote. The first one in your Bible."

Jeff stared in amazement. It wasn't the words Lou used, or even the hateful way he spoke of the "disciple whom Jesus loved." It was the careless way he referred to John, not like someone who had read his epistles, but in the way of someone who actually had *seen* him. This being had been alive when John walked the earth! The realization stunned Jeff, so much that he did not answer Lou's question.

Lou grinned triumphantly. "I thought not," he crowed. "You know so little of your own Book. Allow me." He made a mocking bow. Then he assumed the pose of a child quoting a memory verse in front of a class. "First John 4:3. 'And every spirit that does not confess Jesus is not from God; and this is the spirit of the antichrist, of which you have heard that it is coming, and now is already in the world.' " Lou changed forms yet again. Brennon stood before Jeff now.

"My master has been in this world since your 'Holy Spirit.' He has taken human form time and time again. Some, you know about. They have been great leaders and philosophers. Others have moved quietly, behind the scenes, so to speak. Always they have moved the world in a single direction, toward a single goal. Now do you understand, little man?" Brennon's voice took on the timbre of a long-suffering teacher working with a dimwitted student. "How many times has my master taken human form?"

At last, Jeff got it. His eyes widened in shock. The answer had always been there, but no one had ever been able to see it. "Six hundred sixty-six times," he replied, his voice a harsh whisper. He was more amazed than afraid now.

"Finally," sighed Brennon, shaking his head. "My master has taken his final form. In fact, he has had this particular body for some time now. Soon, he will move to bring the planet below us to its knees. A new age will be ushered in."

"And will last for about seven years," remarked Jeff.

Brennon froze, and Jeff knew he had scored a hit. Brennon slowly leveled his eyes at Jeff, sheer malevolence radiating from them. "What . . . did . . . you . . . say?" His words were spoken slowly, deliberately. For the first time since their confrontation began, Brennon actually seemed to be angered. What he did not realize was that he had made a critical blunder, and Jeff had caught it.

Brennon had quoted Scripture. True, it had been for his own ends, but it had turned Jeff's mind away from the force of evil that stood before him and toward the Word of God. Suddenly, Jeff felt a wave of relief sweep through him. He stood tall before the vile creature before him. He knew that he might only be a computer-generated image in this world, but by the grace of God, he would be a computer-generated image that stood on the living Word of God!

Confidence surged up within him, and the courage that he thought he had lost returned. He knew, beyond a shadow of a doubt, his Lord had not abandoned him. Even in this virtual reality world, his Saviour was still there . . . and he was more than a match for whatever the thing was before him.

Unbidden, a verse shot into Jeff's mind. Without pausing to think, he quoted it. " 'And the beast was sized, and with him the false prophet who performed the signs in his presence, but which he had deceived those who had received the mark of the beast and those who worshiped his image; these two were thrown into the lake of fire which burns with fire and brimstone.' " Now it was Jeff's turn to grin.

"Six hundred and sixty-six incarnations," he said, his smile widening. "I'd say that it's about time for your 'master' to go for a swim . . . in a very hot lake. You too — 'image.' " He stood there defiantly, matching Brennon's evil stare with his own look of victory.

For long seconds, Brennon did not move. It was as if he had shut down. Then, without warning, he raised a hand. Once again, Jeff felt unbearable pain strike him. He moaned in despair, his momentary victory forgotten, and sank to his knees.

"I was going to kill you quick, Anderson," came the voice of Brennon from above him, "but you just could not leave well enough alone, could you?" Another spike of agony drove itself into Jeff's mind. "Well, now you are going to suffer. You think you hurt now? Just wait."

As suddenly as it had come, the searing pain left. Jeff pitched forward on his hands and knees, gasping.

"Your Church is dead, Anderson." Brennon's voice was implacable. Jeff looked up to see him tap his head lightly. "I've got all their names here. Within 12 hours of 'real' time, they will all be dead. Just like you, Anderson, just like you." Now Brennon disappeared and Lou returned.

"But at least they'll die fast," he said, not missing a beat. "At least your Church won't suffer what you are going to suffer."

Jeff swallowed. Somewhere deep inside, he could still feel amazement at the reality of this world.

"Not . . . not . . . not. . . . " He could not get the words out.

"What's that, little man?" said Lou, mocking him again.

Jeff forced himself to say the words. "Not . . . my . . . Church," he gasped, each word a task. "*HIS* Church." He did not have the strength to stand, but he managed to look Brennon/Lou in the eye and say what he was trying desperately to say. "*HIS* Church," he repeated, "And not you, your master, or all the powers of hell combined can destroy it."

Lou shrieked in rage. As Jeff watched, the creature before him flickered wildly, one instant Brennon, one instant Lou, and then a few others that he did not recognize.

"NO MORE!" The creature stabilized, and Brennon once again was back. His voice crashed down around Jeff, but now he was able to somehow withstand it. "NO MORE! This ends . . . NOW!" Brennon held out his hand.

There was a flash of light, and suddenly he was holding a long, ebony sword. The blade was as black as night . . . so black that it appeared to be an emptiness that could never be filled. The pommel was bronze, forged in the shape of two serpents intertwined. Brennon regarded the weapon for a moment, then turned his attention back to Jeff. He was once again calm.

"This is an energy probe," he explained, his voice low and menacing. "I could command it to take any form, but this one suits my purpose. In fact, I could take any form in this world that I wish." He grinned with a wicked mirth. "I'm going to carve your mind up piece by piece." He lowered the blade and pointed it at Jeff. "Don't worry, though. I'm not going to extract any information from you. I don't need it. I'm simply going to cut every synapses in your mind, one at a time. Its going to hurt . . . a lot."

Staring at Brennon, Jeff managed to muster the strength for one final jab. "Not as much as that lake of fire that you're headed for!"

Again Brennon's face twisted in rage. The sword swung high over his head. It hovered there for a moment, then descended. It traced a wicked arc, aimed directly at Jeff's head. Involuntarily, Jeff closed his eyes, waiting.

The blow never fell. There was a harsh "clang" of metal against metal, then a bellow of pure hatred. Jeff opened his eyes and looked up. Inches from his face, the black blade hovered. It was pressing against another blade, this one gleaming gold. It shone like the sun, the light from it so bright that Jeff had to squint. Somehow, this blade had intercepted Brennon's death blow.

Reflex took over. He rolled to one side, out of the path of the swords. Then he looked back, and froze. A great figure stood there in front of

Brennon. He was clad in shining golden armor from head to toe. He held his sword in his right hand, the blade holding Brennon's sword immobile. A gleaming shield with a blazing emblem of the cross was held firmly in his left hand. His face was covered by a visor.

Brennon snarled. He suddenly looked feral, like a wild animal. Like a striking cobra, he disengaged his sword and swung again. The figure stepped back and blocked the blow. The two blades met, darkness against the light. Brennon and the shining knight struggled briefly. Their swords slid together, meeting at the pommels. The two figures matched strength for strength. Then the knight pushed hard, and Brennon was thrown back. He staggered, then righted himself. The knight took advantage of the brief lull to turn to Jeff. He lifted his visor. Jeff's mouth dropped open in awe. He had received many shocks and surprises over the past few hours, but he was totally unprepared for this.

"You need to get out of here now!" shouted David Eddington. "I can't hold him here for very long." Then he turned back, raised his shining sword, and charged.

13

Doctor Nubata, the surgeon who had performed the implant operation on both Jeff and David, studied the monitors mounted at the head of their med-couches and frowned. His wrinkled features and snow-white hair betrayed his advanced years, but the lack of gravity gave him the mobility of a much younger man.

At this moment, he was beginning to worry. The man named Anderson was responding normally. Despite its accelerated growth, the bio-chip had implanted itself properly and was interfacing with both his conscious and unconscious thought processes. Blood pressure, heart rate, respiration, EEG, were all within acceptable parameters.

The man named Eddington was another matter. Both he and Anderson were still in their med-couches, unconscious. Behind them, through a large window, Nubata could see Christine Smythe lying in her own med-couch, unconscious as well — unconscious, but not inactive. The doctor could tell from the EEG's on all three that they were *very* active within the master system.

Feeling decidedly uneasy, Nubata ran a diagnostic program on Eddington's bio-chip and shook his head. The chip was growing far too fast. Its readouts were those of an implant that had been functional for days, not hours. Silently the doctor cursed himself for a fool. He should not have allowed Christine Smythe to railroad him into this kind of surgery.

Floating carefully, Nubata pushed himself toward a terminal across the small room. There, he called up Eddington's sonigram. He had studied it before, just prior to the surgery. He knew about Eddington's tumor, of course. It was almost the size of a large man's fist. One that big did not go undetected for long. His private prognoses gave Eddington less than two months to live. He was amazed, in fact, that the younger man was even able to function. The pain must have been intolerable.

Still, it should not have mattered. The tumor was in the frontal lobe, and the bio-chip implanted itself in the cerebral cortex, at the stem of the brain. The interface should have been completely unimpaired. Yet, there was no accounting for this growth.

Carefully, the doctor studied the hard copy of the sonigram. As he suspected, he had missed nothing. His diagnoses was correct.

Muttering to himself, he drifted back to Eddington's med-couch. Opening a panel above the monitor, he pulled out a handheld probe. Then, touching a control, he stepped back as the med-couch slowly brought itself upright to an almost vertical position. Activating the probe, he leaned Eddington's head forward. A tiny sensor outlet was inlaid into the skin just below the hairline. In time, it would heal over, and become totally invisible.

Carefully, he touched the probe to the sensor. Instantly, the monitor above the couch came to life. Nubata's forehead creased as he watched the parade of numbers cross the screen. Everything seemed to be in order. Then a three-dimensional representation of Eddington's brain appeared. It slowly rotated, showing the implant as a glowing dot. Nubata adjusted a control on the probe, and the brain on the screen became transparent. Just as quickly, Nubata's worse fears became reality.

The monitor showed where the bio-chip had sent tendrils running throughout Eddington's brain. All of them were growing properly — except one. The single exception was the bio-circuit that slaved his implant to the master system. Somehow, it had rerouted itself, and was now running straight into the tumor.

Quickly, Nubata fed the probe's data into the master computer. He knew he had been forbidden by Christine Smythe to do so, but now he had no choice. He had to know what was going on. His terminal blinked thoughtfully for a moment, then responded. He had not been mistaken. The bio-chip's slave interface had somehow run itself into the tumor in Eddington's frontal lobe. Since the tumor served no useful purpose, the interface was effectively blocked. That meant that Christine Smythe would not be able to completely control him. Worse, there were no other safeguards limiting Eddington. If he could somehow learn to control his implant. . . .

That was enough for Nubata. It was time to end this insane experiment. He had to cut off access to Eddington's bio-chip before Eddington himself could somehow get loose in the system. Smythe might break him for this, but it was a risk he had no choice in taking. He almost made it.

He was just about to de-activate Eddington's implant when chaos arrived. Without warning, a loud, shrill alarm began to sound. Over Christine Smythe's med-couch, a series of lights began to flash. Nubata stared through the glass and knew the worst. Smythe's body was spasming uncontrollably. Her back arched, as if she were on the receiving end of a massive electric shock.

Disregarding everything else, Nubata literally flew into her room. At the same time, an emergency trauma unit, composed of two doctors and three nurses, arrived from the other entrance. Nubata got there first. One glance at the monitor told him everything. Christine's EEG was flatlined. There was no brain activity at all. Christine Smythe was dead. Her body simply had not gotten the news yet.

Unceremoniously, two nurses pushed Nubata aside and the trauma unit got to work. He could only stare in stunned silence. What had began as a simple implant surgery had ended in Christine Smythe's death. Once Brennon found out about this, Nubata was probably dead as well. The trauma unit continued to work, the two doctors feverishly calling out information to each other in controlled pandemonium. It did not matter, Nubata knew. In fact, it was far too late.

Unnoticed by others, he floated back to where Eddington and Anderson rested. Eddington's implant still had to be deactivated. At the rate it was growing, it would probably take most of Eddington's conscious thought process with it. Nubata did not care. He glanced back to Christine Smythe's inert form, then turned his attention to Anderson and Eddington. He would destroy their implants, and their minds. After that, all he could do was wait.

* * *

David floated within an infinite array of lights. As much as he tried to block it out by closing his eyes tightly, he was continuously drawn to it. It had a wondrous, perilous beauty that was intoxicating. The colors, the textures, everything about it, was powerfully compelling. The more he looked, the more he saw — and heard. A low thrum pervaded the strange world.

He soon discovered that the points of light were not isolated from each other. Each had hundreds of gossamer-thin glowing threads radiating outward, connecting to others, which in turn connected to still others. It was like being in a city made up of a never-ending, three-dimensional spider web. The comparison made him uneasy. He was afraid that the voice that had so ruthlessly ordered him to remain motionless might be the spider of this particular web.

At least now he understood where he was. The conversation between Jeff and the woman who had attacked them told him that much. Somehow he was inside a massive computer simulation. Jeff had used the term "virtual reality," and despite his limited knowledge of electronics, David knew the term. His body was somewhere on the space station Liberty, unconscious. His brain had been implanted with some kind of interface that allowed him to access this wondrous, terrifying world. What else, he wondered fearfully, had that interface done to him?

For an eternity, David floated. He obeyed the powerful voice's instructions, not wanting to incur any more wrath than he already had. Gradually, however, he began to wonder if anything *was* going to happen to him. Time was meaningless in this place, but it felt as if he had been here forever. He floated, and waited, and still nothing happened. Finally, he gradually phased down from terror. He stopped at fear for a while, then found himself at apprehension. Still nothing. Eventually, he gave up being afraid altogether. He simply could not sustain it. As the last of it drained away, he became bored. When that happened, he found that he could think rationally once more.

Relaxing in a way he could not understand, David took stock of his situation. His mind flashed back to the confrontation with the woman. Inwardly he shuddered. She was ruthless! He had no doubt that she could make good on her threat to drain his and Jeff's thoughts. The question was, why had she sent him here, and left Jeff where he was? She had had both of them at her mercy, completely helpless. Why separate them? Perhaps, he mused, this was some type of waiting area. A kind of jail cell, where he would be held until the she was finished with Jeff.

No. That did not make sense, he realized. Whoever that woman was, she had made it quite clear that where he *had* been was a holding area. Why move a helpless prisoner from one cell to another?

Suddenly, David felt a surge of excitement. If this was not a holding area, then could it possibly be part of the main system? And if it was, then what did that mean? Carefully, he thought back on the last moments of that terrifying encounter. He and Jeff had been lying there, helpless. He had felt the woman somehow begin to enter his mind.

He grimaced, remembering the clammy, violated sensation. The fear returned, but he forced it aside. Somehow, he felt on the verge of a major discovery.

What had happened next? He remembered suddenly being yanked away, falling. Why? Why did he fall away? In that virtual reality world, the visual representation that was David Eddington furrowed his brow. He had been lying helpless one instant, then here the next. Between those instants. . . .

"Oh . . . my . . . God," he breathed silently, and meant it as a prayer. He had called out to his Lord for help. Could that have been it? Could it be that simple? "Lord, help me," had been his cry. Had it been answered?

"Yes." David answered his own question out loud. He could feel the certainty deep within his spirit. His desperate cry for help *had* been answered. The implications of that. . . .

"Okay, okay, okay," he whispered rapidly. *Slow down, Eddington. Think!* He thought. His Lord had heard his cry, and had pulled him away from the woman who would have destroyed him. "The next logical question, Lord," he said aloud, forcing himself to go slowly, "would be, 'Why am I here? Why would you rescue me from that woman, and not get me out of here completely. Why bring me to this place?' " He knew the answer before he asked the question. He was here for a purpose. To rescue his friends? Perhaps, but he could feel that there was more to it than that.

"Aieeee!"

The scream came from nowhere — and everywhere. Startled, David felt the terror return. At first, he thought that it was the *voice* — the one that had ordered him to remain still. Then, suddenly he realized that this scream was one of total anguish. Desperately he tried to look in all directions at once. What was going on?

Immediately, he saw it. A glowing, pulsing orb was rushing toward him. He had no reference, and so could not judge its distance or size. In amazement, he watched its headlong plunge. Now that he had it spotted, he could tell that it was not coming directly toward him, but would pass fairly close.

"What . . . " he began to mutter, but by then, the orb had caught up with, then passed him. Not, however, before he realized what it was. There was no human shape to it, no arms, legs or face, but David knew what — or who — it was just the same. He could feel the terror within that orb, and knew that it was the woman who had tried to destroy him. As he watched, the orb disappeared among the glowing lights. The scream disappeared with it, and all was quiet once again. David stared after the orb. He did not understand what had just happened, but that scream filled him with dread. He could not explain why, but he felt as if he had just witnessed the final journey of a lost soul.

For an eternity he watched, wondering if the orb would return. Then, with a great effort, he pulled his mind back to his own situation. He now believed that what had happened to him had nothing to do with the woman who had threatened him. He was here, beyond her control. Perhaps he was beyond the control of the other "voice" as well. He looked around, studying the world of lights.

"All right," he said to himself. "If whoever she was came flying from that direction," and unconsciously he pointed, "then it's a reasonable guess that I can find Jeff there." He had not tried to move since his fall had been checked. In fact, he had no idea whether or not he could move. He shook his head and shrugged.

"One way to find out." Staring at the direction he wanted to go, he concentrated. He pictured himself moving. Nothing happened. He tried harder. Still nothing. His lips pressed themselves together in frustration. Then inspiration hit. He had not moved before until he had called upon his Lord. He paused, thinking hard. Somehow, calling out to God in that manner did not seem right. Before, it had been as a last resort, in sheer terror. Now, it would be an act of will. *His* will. Not the will of God, but that of David Eddington. *That* was the problem . . . and David knew the answer.

"Oh Lord," he prayed, "forgive me." Suddenly, virtual reality or not, David felt the sting of tears at the corners of his eyes. "I have not been faithful to You." His mind flashed back to months past, when he had faced a choice. He had made the wrong one. It had been for the safety of his family, he had believed at the time. Now he knew the truth. "I betrayed You, and everything I believed in," he continued, "for my own safety. Not for my family's, but my own." It was the hardest admission he had ever made, but he made it anyway. For the first time in a long time, he was completely honest with himself, and his Saviour.

"Lord," he prayed fervently, "Give me another chance. For whatever reason you have brought me here, let me fulfill it. Let me be your servant once more." He paused for a moment, suddenly afraid to say what he knew he had to say next. Then, resolution setting in, he continued. "No matter what the cost, Lord . . . no matter what the cost." David stopped praying, wondering what to say next.

Then he heard the Voice. He would never be sure, in the brief remnant of his life, where that Voice had come from. It may have come from within his own spirit, or it may have come from without. It was the Voice that a believer hears when he is completely surrendered to his Saviour. The Voice one can hear only when he has put aside all other desires and wants, and stands ready to serve the living God. Still as a mountain lake, pure as new fallen snow, it came to him as he floated there in that strange world. It was quiet, and peaceful. Yet, David could sense that it was far more powerful than that earlier voice — the one that had ordered him not to move. That voice had been finite. The One he now heard was *infinite*.

"Will you lay down your life?" was all it asked. David heard and understood the question. He knew what it meant. As he watched, one of the many points of light disengaged itself from the web and floated toward him. It stopped just a few meters away, and shaped itself into a flat rectangle. As David watched, it displayed information. He concentrated on it, and realized he was reading a doctor's report . . . about him. The picture changed, showing him a representation of his own brain . . . and the tumor lodged within. There was no doubt as to what it meant. David took a moment to digest the information. He looked at it, and an overwhelming sadness came over him. He realized that he would never see his family again — at least, not in this lifetime. All of his dreams were now ashes. There was nothing left. If only he had . . . NO! It was not the time for regrets! It was the time to choose who he would serve. David made his choice.

"Whatever the cost," he repeated out loud. He meant it with all his heart and soul. Instantly, his surroundings changed. There was no hint of transition. One moment, he was floating freely among the lights. The next, he was standing in a gray landscape, featureless and bland. He blinked and realized that he was back where he had started. Off to his left he heard voices. One of them he recognized as Jeff's. Though he could see no one, he immediately set out in the direction of the sound. Within moments, two figures appeared. The first was Jeff's. The second. . . .

David took one look at the second figure. The Spirit that lived within his heart and soul was making it very plain. *That* was his enemy. He was now close enough to hear what they were saying, although neither had as yet taken any notice of him. He heard the creature in human form brag to Jeff how he was going to cut his mind apart piece by piece. He saw the sword materialize in his hand, and listened as the other figure explained how he could take *any* form.

He had heard enough. He remembered the old man in New York, the one who had given them the Bibles. He remembered kneeling. He knelt again. "Whatever the cost, Lord," he repeated. "Make me Your knight, to do Your will." Again there was no transition. One moment David was kneeling, wearing only a dull white coverall. The next he was clad in golden armor, shining as the sun. In his right hand he held a sword. He had never in his life used a weapon, but he had no doubt that he would be able to wield this blade. Slowly he stood to his feet. He raised the sword above his head and held it high.

"No matter what the cost," he cried, and his own voice thundered in his ears. The two figures before him did not respond. He realized that, for the moment, they could neither see nor hear him. He raised the golden shield he held in his left hand. "No matter what," he repeated. Now his voice was a whisper of awe and gratitude. He had been given another chance, and by the living God he served, he was not going to waste it.

He wanted to shout a great battle cry, one that would strike terror into the heart of his enemy. For some odd reason, though, the single boxing match he had attended in his younger days flashed into his mind. He remembered the ring announcer.

Well, he said to himself, *Why not?* Pointing with his sword, he shouted with all his might. The words hung in the air, a challenge that could not be denied. "Let's get ready to rummmmble!" Then David Eddington leaped forward to meet the agent of the enemy.

* * *

The creature that Christine Smythe had named Lou spat and hissed in rage. Before him stood the one thing he feared most — a man of God. He did not understand. When he had encountered this particular believer not so long ago, he had been a quivering mass of fear, easily controlled. Now here he was, shining with courage, and even worse, the strength of the Enemy. How dare he! How had he found out? Who had reminded him that his God stood ready to aid His children?

He knew that he did not have much time. He had to dispose of this irritant now. Lou was a creature that indwelled a worldwide computer system. Next to the one whose way he prepared, he was the single most powerful being on the face of the earth. The might of the greatest technology ever dreamed of was his to wield.

Even so, there was one problem. Lou was a finite being. He did not command time, nor break its rules. Because of that, he could only be in one place at a time. Even though this confrontation would only take moments as far as the "real" world was concerned, those were still moments that he was absent from his other tasks. He had to end this now.

In challenge, he raised his great ebony sword. He called upon the power of the entire world system, and channeled it into the weapon. It began to glow with a harsh, red glow. Laughing, he felt the energy rush through him. Bringing the sword to bear in both hands, he began to stalk his enemy. Man of God or not, one single human could not withstand the power of an entire planet.

Forgotten, the human called Anderson cowered off to one side. Lou took no notice. He would deal with him at his leisure, once this threat had been destroyed. He came within range of the golden figure. With an inarticulate cry, he swung his sword in a high arc. The deadly blade sliced down, right at the human's head. Lou anticipated the feel of that golden armor shattering.

The sword never made it there. Like lightening, the shining blade rose and met the ebony one just inches from Eddington's head. Snarling, Lou pressed the attack. He pushed hard, but could not force Eddington down. He pulled back and swung again. Once more the golden blade was there to meet him. His arm jolted with the impact. Before he could react, Eddington swung his shield around, using it as a club. Lou was caught by surprise. The shield slammed into the side of his unprotected head, and he fell away, dazed. Now it was Eddington's turn to advance.

In amazement, Lou found himself hard-pressed to mount a defense. Attacking was out of the question. This was getting out of hand! How could one man do this?! The deadly golden blade kept coming at him. Desperately, he sought for an answer. He could not simply disappear. If he retreated from this battle, that would leave Eddington with complete access to his system, and that was unacceptable. Somehow, the ridiculous little preacher had learned to manipulate at least part of the system! No, he had to defeat this upstart now.

Quickly, with a small part of his consciousness, he initiated a search program through Eddington's file. It had just been fed into the main system at Liberty. Smythe was clever, he granted. If that fool Nubata had not used the station's mainframe to solve whatever problem he had, Lou would never have known about Christine's aborted coup. With the speed of light, Lou pulled that file apart. Within moments, he found what he was looking for. Deflecting another attack, he grinned at his adversary.

"Got you," he snarled. He had the answer. The very thing that had kept Eddington free of Christine's control would also destroy him. With renewed vigor, he leaped at the golden figure. Now it was Lou who began the offensive. His black blade whistled through the air again and again, forcing Eddington back. This time, however, his attack was only a diversion. As he fought, Lou carefully began accessing Eddington's implant. While the slave bio-circuit was not functioning, the destruct sequence was. It was simply a matter of reaching it. If he could activate it, it would not only destroy the implant, but cause the tumor that was lodged in Eddington's brain to expand rapidly. Death should come soon after that.

Again Eddington blocked Lou's attack, and then pressed one of his own. Lou could sense that the seesaw battle was going against him once more. He had to act now, or all would be lost. Feverishly, he traced the tendrils that ran through Eddington's mind. Because of that blasted tumor, they were not growing as they should. If he could just locate the right one. . . .

"Got it," he cried out loud. His voice was a mixture of rage and triumph. Eddington might have somehow made contact with his God, but the final victory would be Lou's. He pulled away from the golden figure and lowered his sword. Eddington stopped his attack, unsure of what Lou was up to. That was all he needed.

"Time to die," Lou sneered at his enemy. Then he activated the destruct sequence of Eddington's implant.

* * *

Jeff watched in wonder as David battled the being called Lou. Back and forth the combatants went. Despite Lou's boast of a few moments before, the two of them seemed to be evenly matched. For a few incredible moments, Jeff actually believed that David might emerge victorious. He found himself cheering silently with each thrust and parry that David made.

Then, with a sudden start, Jeff realized that he was not helping. He had become so enthralled in the conflict before him that he had forgotten, momentarily, their desperate situation. This fight had to end *now*. Jeff knew that there was very little hope that he or his friends would leave Liberty alive, but that did not matter. The network had been compromised. The lives of thousands of believers, and the very existence of the Shepherd's Path, hung in the balance. There was no time to consider the situation, no time to plan a strategy. It was time to take a hand in this battle.

Slowly, hardly daring to breath, Jeff began to inch to his left. Neither Lou nor David took any notice of him. A few inches at a time, he painstakingly worked his way around the fight until he was directly behind Lou. If he could rush him and get him on the ground, David might be able to get in a clean blow. Carefully, he watched Lou's movements, waiting for the slightest opening. He tensed, ready to spring. Just as he was about to strike, the battle stopped. Lou lowered his sword. Then, in a sneering, superior voice, he spoke.

"Time to die," was all he said. For a moment, nothing happened. Then, to Jeff's horror, David suddenly clutched at his head with both hands. The golden sword fell to the ground, followed by the shield. David collapsed to his knees. His mouth opened, and he screamed in agony.

Above him, Lou crowed in victory. "Your God has deserted you, preacher," he laughed mockingly. "Come now, where is your strength? Where is your courage? Shall I tell you?" He leaned forward in an act of dominance. "Your God has left, and taken it all. Do you think you are so important? Trust me, He has far more to worry about than an insignificant insect like you."

That did it. Jeff had heard enough. Anger welled up within him, and hatred . . . hatred for the thing that stood before him. With a wild joy, Jeff suddenly understood that this hatred was not a bad thing. It was a hatred of everything evil, of everything that tried to keep a man or woman from the loving, saving embrace of the Saviour. A shout burst from his throat, and he threw himself at the being called Lou. Surprised, Lou began to turn, to face this new threat, but he was too late. Jeff was on him in an instant. His fist flew like a whirlwind, the punches landing over Lou's head and body. A human being would have been immediately overwhelmed. Lou, however, was far from human. With a scream of rage, he swung an arm. It connected with Jeff's shoulder, and he went flying. Jeff gasped in shock. He landed on the hard gray surface, breathing heavily. The creature was *strong!*

Hastily, Jeff rethought his plan. With a sinking feeling, he realized that he could not take Lou by strength alone. He allowed himself a quick glance at David. The armored figure was still on his knees, clutching his head. His sword lay where it had fallen. His sword. . . .

With a savage cry, Lou came at him, his dark sword raised high. Jeff dodged the blade, barely. Lou swung a savage backhand that glanced off Jeff's jaw. Jeff twisted and went down. His mind spun, and his arms and legs felt like butter. He knew that he could not take much more of this. With a desperate lunge, Jeff tried to reach David's fallen sword. Lou anticipated the attack and met him halfway. Again Jeff was struck solidly on the jaw, and, for an instant, the world went black. Again his knees buckled and he fell to the ground.

Lou laughed tauntingly. "You know, little man, for a moment, you actually had me worried." Lou's voice seemed to come from far away as Jeff struggled to regain full consciousness. "You might just have damaged me," came the gloating voice. "Too late now, though. As I said, it's time to die."

Jeff's eyes re-focused to see the demonic being coming at him, sword held ready for a killing blow. With a Herculean effort, Jeff struggled to get to his feet, but his strength was gone. He sank back to his knees. Lou advanced. There would be no way he could avoid his attack this time. Instead, he merely stared at the unearthly creature as he came nearer. When he was within a few feet, Jeff spoke. "Do what you want," he spat out. Surprisingly, despite his pain and exhaustion, his voice was rock steady. "You've already lost! You, and the master you serve, are headed straight to hell!"

Lou roared in rage and raised his sword.

Jeff set his jaw. "In the name of Jesus Christ, I defy you!" The words ripped out of Jeff's throat, rippling in righteous power. Lou screamed, but this time it was in agony. Suddenly, Jeff had the strength to get to his feet. He knew, really knew, at that moment, that *he was not alone*. He was with friends. He felt surrounded — guarded — on all sides. He could almost feel strong arms on either side of him, supporting him, and holding him up.

In a flash of inspiration, Jeff realized at that moment that the battle that had raged here was not *his* battle. Whatever Lou was, "Image of the Beast," demonic spirit, computer entity, it did not matter. He was already defeated. He might flourish for a season, but his end was already decreed. Jeff merely had to remain true to his Saviour. That, and introducing others to that same Saviour, was all that was required of him. His Lord, Jesus Christ, had fought and *won* this battle over two thousand years ago, hanging on a cross. A great weight lifted from his shoulders. He stood tall and confident in his new-found assurance.

He regarded Lou, who looked as if he was getting ready to attack once again, and this time he laughed. "You were right," he told the entity before him. "I *am* a little man." He grinned. "But I serve a big, big God."

Lou let out a howl of rage and pure hatred. He sprang at Jeff. There were no taunts this time. Lou was out to kill. His dark blade swung into a line with Jeff's neck.

Jeff did not move. Instead he shouted. "In the name of my Saviour, Jesus Christ, get away!" Not as eloquent as he would have liked, but it did not matter. The blade jerked to a stop inches from his neck. It bounced back, as if it had struck an invisible wall — or shield. Lou shrieked in pain at the mention of the Name above all names. He fell back, defeated. The once powerful entity was reduced to a quivering mass of fear.

Jeff knew what he had to do. Striding forward, he knelt down beside

David and picked up his sword. It felt light and natural in his hands. Turning, he regarded Lou. There were no words needed. Now it was Jeff who advanced upon his enemy. Lou saw him coming and began to cower.

"Wait," he cried, desperation beginning to color his voice. "I can do things for you! I own the planet below us. I can give you power beyond your dreams." Jeff continued to advance.

"I can end the persecution of your people," continued Lou, still moving away. "You won't be hunted anymore. I can do that." If he had been in the mood, Jeff would have laughed out loud. He was not in the mood. It was time to end this . . . now.

"Anything you want, I can give you," Lou shrieked, his voice now betraying real fear. Jeff did not respond. He was within feet of his cringing foe now. He wondered if Lou might disappear on him, and leave the system. Then he remembered the arms that had held him up. The thought flashed through his mind that perhaps, for the moment, the way out was blocked. No matter.

"WAIT! I can. . . ." Lou never had a chance to finish. Jeff swung the sword in a vicious arc. There was no "whooshing" sound, and when it met Lou's neck, he felt nothing. Lou, on the other hand, did. He screamed in agony. His form flickered between one image and another so fast that Jeff could not keep up. Then, with a final wail of hatred, he disappeared altogether.

Silence descended upon the gray plain. Jeff stood frozen in place, not believing that the battle was actually over. He stared at the place where Lou and been, but there was no sign of him. Slowly, he lowered the sword, and glanced around. Nothing. A small smile found its way to his lips. Once there, it grew to cover his entire face. This battle had been won — not by he or David, but it *had* been won.

He lifted his head to the featureless sky. With his right hand, he raised the sword. He wanted to shout, but his voice could only whisper in gratitude. "To God be the glory," he said simply. He stood there for long seconds, giving thanks with his whole heart. Then, with the bite of renewed care, he remembered his friend. He swung around.

"David," he cried out. The armored figure still lay where he had fallen. "Oh David, no!" Jeff dashed to David's side and knelt down. David did not move — did not, in fact, show any signs of life. Fear clenching his heart, Jeff dug his hands under him and rolled him over. As he did so, the golden armor, no longer needed, disappeared.

"Come on David," Jeff whispered savagely. "Don't do this to me. Come on, man, wake up." For a moment, Jeff feared the worst. Then, miraculously, David's eyes fluttered open. He saw Jeff kneeling over him and smiled.

Jeff smiled back. "It's over, David," he told his friend. "We've won. Whatever Lou was, he's gone now."

Weakly, David shook his head. His hand came up to grasp Jeff's. "Not gone," he whispered. Jeff's heart sank when he heard the weakness in David's voice. David closed his eyes for a moment, as if the effort of speaking was too much for him. Then he spoke again. "The system we're in," he said, his voice barely there, "isn't human . . . can't accept Christ."

Jeff's brow furrowed in confusion. "Of course it can't, David. It doesn't matter. Did you hear what I said? Lou's gone! We can. . . ."

"NO!" The word ripped from David's throat. The effort cost him. He grasped Jeff's hand tightly, in a death grip. "He's gone for now, but . . . he'll be back. The system has no protection!" With that, he fell back, exhausted. Jeff started to ask what he meant. Then it hit him.

"Oh Lord," he breathed, his heart twisting. He understood what it was that David was trying to say. If a demonic spirit indwelled a human, it could be cast out. Once out, if that person allowed Christ into his heart, the spirit could not return. If he did not. . . .

"Seven times worse," Jeff whispered, and David nodded.

"He's coming back," agreed David. "I've . . . I've managed to learn a few things — been able to put up a few barriers, but he'll get past them."

"Then we've got to get out of here," said Jeff.

This time, David shook his head. "I've got free run of this place now," he said, his voice steadily failing, "but that won't last. I can see things." He stopped for a moment. Then, gathering his strength, he continued. "I've deactivated the slave circuit on your implant. I can't deactivate the entire chip, but you're not a part of the system anymore. No one can trace you with it. You might even be able to use it."

"Can you do the same to yours?" asked Jeff. He dreaded the answer.

Again David shook his head. "Too late for that," he said, his voice now sad. Jeff could have wept. He did not want to believe David, but he could see the truth. With a great effort of will, he thrust aside his feelings. He still had to try to save what was left of the Shepherd's Path.

"David, listen," he said urgently. "Lou somehow broke the network that links the Shepherd's Path. These people are going to wipe it out if we can't do something about it now. Can you help?"

David did not respond, and for a moment, Jeff was afraid he was gone. Then he spoke. "I've found it," he said. "They copied the network into the station system. I. . . ." his voice faltered, but he rallied back. "I can access it . . . the original, too."

"David, listen to me," Jeff said urgently. "Can you enter the code 'Armageddon' into both of them?"

Now David smiled. "Done," he said. "It's already falling apart." He paused, then spoke again. "I was able to send out a warning to all of the safe houses that were targeted in the first raid. If they see it in time, the people there might have a chance to get away."

"That's great, David." Jeff's shoulders slumped in relief. The Shepherd's Path might or might not survive, but at least countless church cells would have some kind of warning.

"Jeff," whispered David.

"I'm here," said Jeff, grasping his hand.

Somehow, David drew on some last resource of strength. "I found Paul and Susan," he said. "I'll get them to medical somehow . . . wait . . . I've got you clearance to leave the station too, but you'll have to hurry. Lou could be back anytime." A pause. "He'll stop you for sure." He smiled weakly. "Time to get back to the real world, Jeff." Abruptly, his grip on Jeff's hand fell away and his body went limp.

"David?" Jeff shook him gently. "David! Come on, man, we're almost home! Don't quit on me now!"

For the last time, David Eddington opened his eyes. The look he gave Jeff left no doubt that his time was almost gone. "Tell my wife . . . tell her that I stayed true at the last. Tell her. . . ." His eyes closed, and his voice sank to barely a whisper. "Tell her that I fought a good fight . . . I kept the faith. . . ." He shuddered.

"David, please," cried Jeff, but it was too late. David's hand fell back, and he did not move. Jeff touched David's face gently. Then, without warning, the entire landscape shimmered and phased out. There was a moment's disorientation, and then Jeff found himself back in medical.

His head spun for a moment, then cleared. Almost at once, the dull ache from his damaged knee reasserted itself. Jeff turned to the couch next to him, dreading, yet knowing what he would see. David Eddington lay there, motionless. Jeff did not need to check the monitors above the bed to know that he was gone.

"My friend," Jeff whispered. He felt the sting of tears at the corners of his eyes. He welcomed them, as he welcomed the renewed pain from his knee. It meant that he was out of that accursed virtual reality world. Gently he reached out to touch David's hand. He held it for a moment, wondering what to do next. Then the hatch he had previously entered by cycled open, and the matter was taken out of his hands.

* * *

Paul stared at the screen. Flashing there was a simple message. "Paul and Susan . . . get to medical . . . I've cleared your way . . . David." Paul glanced back up at the monitor that showed both David and Jeff lying comatose in their med-couches. He licked his lips in indecision.

"Paul?" Susan put her hand gently on his arm. He covered it with his own.

"I think," he said, "that it's genuine." Susan took a long look at the monitor, the doubt obvious on her face.

"They don't need to try to trick us," he explained. "They have us and they know it." He looked over at Susan. "Want to give it a try?"

Susan shrugged, then tried a smile. It came out as a tired grimace. "Why not?" she said. Paul started to launch himself toward the hatch.

"NOOO!" Suddenly Brennon's body came to back to life. Immediately, his hand shot out and grabbed Paul by the neck. Paul gasped in pain and surprise. The grip felt like a steel vise! Brennon spun him around to where they were face to face. Paul recoiled at the sheer malevolent force within the man.

"You . . . will . . . not . . . leave!" The voice was harsh, inhuman. Paul struggled, but could not break free. If there had been gravity, he might have made a fight of it, but here in Liberty he had no leverage. Brennon's brute strength was overpowering. Not only that, in straining against his inhumanly strong foe, he once again aggravated his rib injury. He glanced desperately at Susan, and was astonished to find that she was floating motionless, her eyes tightly shut.

"Get out of here!" he shouted, and immediately regretted it. Brennon shifted his attention onto her. When he saw what she was doing, he flung Paul away. Paul went spinning across the conference room, out of control. He shouted another warning at Susan. He dreaded those iron-strong hands getting hold of her. Still, Susan did not move.

"First Anderson, and that insipid preacher," snarled Brennon, "now you!" He reached out to her. At the same time, Paul landed against the far wall. Knowing he would be too late, he set his legs against the bulkhead and launched himself toward Susan.

Even as he flew toward them, Susan opened her eyes. "I know you," she said evenly. Brennon stopped short. "I know what you are," Susan continued, "*AND YOU HAVE NO POWER OVER ME!*" Her voice raised to a shout. "In the name of my Saviour, Jesus Christ, come out of that body!"

To Paul's everlasting amazement, Brennon screamed in agony. His body spasmed, and blood flew from his nose and mouth. Susan did not flinch. Paul finally reached her. He grabbed her by the shoulders, seeking to put himself between her and the maddened creature before them.

With surprising strength, Susan shrugged him off. "I said come out of him," she repeated sternly. "By the authority of the Son of God, I command you to do it." Again, Brennon screamed. Already weakened by his encounter with Jeff and David, the spirit that inhabited the body had no choice. He shouted obscenities at Susan, trying to distract her, but she would not be moved. For a third time, she commanded him to leave. Her voice rippled with authority. Finally, with a great, tearing moan, he left. The body left behind slumped once again. Silence pervaded the room.

Paul heard the ragged sound of his own breath. He stared at Brennon's lifeless body, not entirely sure that he believed what he had just seen. Carefully, he pushed himself over to where Brennon floated. Expecting him to come back to life at any second, he gingerly put a finger against his neck. Then he shook his head.

"Nothing," he said quietly. "No pulse, no respiration, nothing. He's dead."

"If he was ever really alive," Susan whispered.

Paul looked at her in confusion.

She shrugged. "Who knows," she answered his unasked question. "Whoever this was, he had hosted that spirit for some time. Maybe there was nothing left."

Paul took a deep breath. Then, he floated back over to Susan. He regarded her for a moment. Slowly his heart rate returned to normal. Then he smiled a shaky smile. "I've got a lot to learn, don't I?" he asked.

Susan smiled back at him, then slapped her hand gently against his cheek. "You'll make it," she said softly. She closed her eyes, and started to tremble. Paul grasped her hand in concern. "Sorry," she said, taking a deep breath. "Just a reaction, I guess." She glanced around the room. "Do you think you can get us out of here?"

That brought Paul up short. In the heat of the confrontation, he had forgotten about their situation. "We can try," he said, determination coloring his voice. Together, they pushed over to the hatch. Paul studied the controls for a moment, then touched a glowing green panel. To his satisfaction, it opened immediately. A guard was posted just outside. He swung around, startled. Paul held up both hands in a calming gesture.

"We're supposed to tell you to take us to medical," he said evenly. He fervently hoped that the message from David was genuine. They would know within seconds.

The guard frowned. "I'll have to clear that," he growled. He tried to peer past Paul, but the big man was already past the hatch. Susan followed, and it cycled shut. Paul nodded calmly. The guard moved over next to the hatch where a terminal was set into the wall. He touched a control and read what flashed on the monitor. Then he nodded.

"All right, let's go," he said, nodding in the proper direction. He led them off, taking them down what appeared to be a main access corridor. Paul tried not to be awed by Liberty, but the station was impressive. He could not help but gawk as he passed through section after section. At every junction, he expected to be stopped, but each time they were passed through. It took them almost 15 minutes to reach medical. The guard halted at the hatch, and entered a code into the terminal there. There was a pause, then the hatch opened and the guard motioned them inside.

The first thing Paul noticed when he passed through was the controlled chaos in the next room. He could see several people through the large glass on the opposite wall. They were crowded around a med-couch, working feverishly on someone. Paul could not tell who it was, but from the way the medical team was moving, he knew that it must be a life or death situation.

Then he forgot about what was going on in the next room when he saw the two med-couches off to his left. Susan pushed past him and launched herself to the two men on the couches. Paul immediately followed. Jeff lay there, looking up at them as they approached. Although he seemed weak, he looked otherwise unharmed to Paul. He looked over at David — and his heart skipped a beat.

"On no," he whispered, his throat suddenly going dry. One glance told him everything. He had seen enough death in his lifetime to recognize it.

Jeff heard him, and nodded in sorrow. "He saved my life," he said quietly.

"David?" Susan had not realized the truth.

Paul suddenly felt weak and helpless. What could he say? He reached out and caught her by the shoulder. "He's gone, Susan," he said as softly as he could. He looked down at David's peaceful face and felt a sharp pang of grief. "There's nothing we can do."

Susan went motionless for a moment. Then, gently dislodging her shoulder from Paul's hand, she reached out and gently touched David's cold cheek. "Oh David," she cried softly. "What did they do to you?" She bowed her head, and said nothing more.

"What are you people doing here?!" Startled, Paul swung around. An older, dark-skinned man was coming through the opposite hatch. He wore a white jumpsuit with a medical insignia on the left breast. In his hand, he held a hypo-spray. "Get away from those men," he demanded.

Before he could say more, Paul reached out and grabbed the hypo from him. Then he grabbed a handful of jumpsuit and pulled the smaller man to within inches of his face. "What is this?" he growled, holding up the hypo.

"J-J-Just a sedative," stammered the doctor. "I need to adjust their bio-chips."

"Bio-what?" demanded Paul. "Oh never mind!" He pressed the hypo against the doctors neck and pushed the button. There was a soft hiss, and immediately the smaller man went limp. Checking to make sure he was still breathing, Paul gently pushed the doctor into a corner. Then he glanced back through the glass. The medical team was still working hard. He could just see the displays on the monitor above the couch. He was not an expert, but it looked as if they were fighting a losing battle. That reminded him of David, and their own desperate situation. Resolutely, he thrust aside his grief and turned his attention to Jeff.

"David somehow got us clearance to be here," Paul explained quickly. As he spoke, he began unfastening the straps that held Jeff down. "But unless you've got a plan, I don't have a clue what to do next."

Jeff kept his attention on Susan and David for a moment, then looked up and met Paul's eyes. Paul could see the effort it took him to concentrate on what he was saying. "David somehow got loose inside the main system," Jeff explained tiredly. "It's a long story, but he found a way to clear us out of here."

Paul frowned, and shook his head. "Got loose?" His voice betrayed his doubt as he finished untying Jeff.

Jeff nodded. He placed his hands on the couch and pushed himself upward.

"How can someone 'get loose' inside a system?" Paul asked. He looked closer at the med-couch, and the monitor above it. The monitor still showed a three-dimensional representation of David's brain. He glanced back at Jeff. "What did they do to you?" he asked softly, his voice betraying his uncertainty.

Jeff only shook his head. "Later," he answered, "when we're far away from this place." He brought himself to a vertical position, rubbing the back of his neck. "We don't have much time," he said urgently.

Paul nodded in agreement. He turned to David's couch. "Susan?" he said softly. There was no reaction. Susan continued to float over David, her hand gently resting on his cheek. Paul reached out and took her by the shoulders. Gently he turned her around. "Susan, we have to go."

Susan looked up into Paul's eyes. "We can't leave him here," she replied quietly. As she spoke, two large tears started to roll down her cheeks. Because of the absence of gravity, they gently dislodged and floated away . . . two small spheres of salt water.

Paul shook his head. "We don't have a choice," he said. "Susan, he's gone. There's nothing we can do."

Jeff moved next to them and put his arm around her. "He's not here," he said gently. "He's safe, now. You know that, Susan. No one can touch him where he is." He gave a very small smile. "He gave his life for us. Let's not waste that gift. Okay?"

Susan was still for a moment, not reacting. Paul feared that he and Jeff would have to force her away from David's body. Then she nodded. "All right," she agreed, her voice a whisper. Without looking back, she pushed herself to the hatch. Jeff went after her.

Paul started to follow, then turned to study David's lifeless form. "I don't think we would have *ever* been best friends," he said softly. "We were too different for that. But you had a lot of guts, David." He suddenly realized that that was the first time he had ever used David's given name. "And it's partially because of you that I found what I've been looking for all my life. I'll never forget that."

He carefully touched David's cold hand. "Until we meet again," he said softly, and then blinked in surprise. He suddenly knew, beyond a shadow of a doubt, that he *would* see David Eddington again. When that time came, they would have an eternity to talk. His spirit comforted, he turned and pushed himself after Jeff and Susan.

Just as he reached them, Jeff touched the proper control, and the hatch cycled open. "You know," came a much-remembered voice, "I can dress you people up, but I can't take you anywhere! Now I guess I'll just have to kill you myself."

Wolf stood framed in the hatchway, flanked by two guards. He held an NPW loosely in his right hand, and even from behind Jeff and Susan, Paul could see that it was set to kill. Wolf grinned his cold grin, and motioned for them to back up. With a sinking feeling of defeat, Paul pushed himself back into medical. Wolf followed them through. He glanced through the window where the med-team had finally stopped trying to revive the body of Christine Smythe.

"Looks like I'll need a new boss," he smirked. "No great loss. There's always someone who wants your kind killed." He raised the NPW. "And I'm always happy to oblige." Both Paul and Jeff tensed, ready to attack.

At that exact instant, a loud screeching alarm began to blare. Over the top of the hatch, a glaring red light began to flash on and off. "ATTENTION!" came the computer-generated feminine voice, "ATTENTION! This is a class 'Amber' alert. All personnel report to lifeboats immediately. Repeat, this is a class 'Amber' alert. All hands report to lifeboats immediately."

Startled, Wolf glanced back at his two guards. That was all the opening Paul needed. His arm flashed out with lightning speed, connecting with the side of Wolf's neck. The terrorist's eyes glazed over and his body went limp. The force of the blow sent Paul flying backwards, helpless, but Jeff was ready. Launching himself forward, he plowed into the two guards, sending them spiraling through the hatch. He was able to stop himself from following. Reaching over, he hit the control that closed the entrance to medical. Then he checked Wolf to make sure he was unconscious. He relieved him of his NPW as well.

Paul stopped his flight by grabbing onto one of the terminals that was placed on the far wall. He glanced down at it, then gave it a much closer look. It took him a minute to realize what he was seeing. "Anderson!" he called, his voice loud over the din of the alarm, "you'd better take a look at this."

Jeff came floating over to join him, and took a quick look at the monitor. In large block letters, two words were flashing. EMERGENCY DECOMPRESSION.

As the two men watched, a schematic replaced the flashing words. They recognized it as a representation of Liberty. Wherever there was a docking hatch, or other direct exit into open space, a red dot was blinking angrily. After a few moments, the schematic was once again replaced by the EMERGENCY DECOMPRESSION warning. The two men stared at each other, their eyes conveying a wealth of meaning.

"How long?" Jeff asked.

As if in answer, a human male voice replaced the computer generated one. "Attention all personnel," it said, and Paul could hear the raw fear it held. "Lifeboats are launching in 15 minutes. Repeat, lifeboats are launching in 15 minutes. Report to your assigned emergency stations now! This is not a drill."

Jeff closed his eyes. Paul knew that it was the end. Angry disappointment flared up inside of him. They had been so close! They had almost made it home. There were no other options, he knew. Something had gone terribly wrong, and in just a few minutes, every hatch in Liberty was going to open itself to the uncaring vacuum of space.

* * *

The creature that called itself Lou, and Brennon, and a thousand other names, screamed as he hurtled into a void that was neither physical nor spiritual. He was a being of pure spirit, beyond human understanding. His hatred knew no limits — no boundaries. It was an all-consuming force that was an integral part of his very self. He screamed in rage, in hatred, and in pain. Never before in his entire existence had he been so overwhelmed. Four humans, none of them special in any way, had combined to cast him out of both corporeal and synthetic bodies. It was unthinkable. Now here he was, in a non-existence that burned and weakened him. If it had not been for the rage that dominated his entire being, he would have remained there indefinitely.

Weak though he may be now, he was far stronger than most others of his kind. His hatred strengthened him. How dare the children of the accursed Nazarene do this to him! Did they believe they had won? Did they think they could destroy him? Never! Let them shout commands in whatever Name they wished. The next time they met. . . .

With a tremendous effort of will, 'Brennon' wrenched himself out of that horrible void and back into 'real' time and space. It took a great deal of his strength, and he had to rest for a moment. He felt weaker than he had ever been in his entire existence, but he was back at Liberty, precisely where he wanted to be. The station lay before him, floating serenely in space.

He sneered in derision at the limited understanding of humanity. Even those who believed in a "spirit world" did not truly comprehend its nature. They thought of it as being separate from the physical world that they functioned within. They would never understand that both physical and spiritual worlds were joined together, essentially one world separated into different parts — much like they themselves were one being with different parts. It was that lack of understanding that was their downfall.

Brennon shook himself out of his reverie. It was time to extract revenge. His human host was dead, and not even he, with all his power, could bring him back to life. Only his enemy had that ability. No matter. His electronic body was functioning properly. It was time to get it back.

Boldly, Brennon began to merge himself with Liberty's mainframe. He would have to inhabit that relatively small system first. From there, he would be able to access the rest of the world network. It would be tedious, but he knew that before too long he would be back to his original strength.

Brennon made it into the first level of the Liberty mainframe without incident. Then, just as he was moving deeper into the system, something went wrong. He was repelled. He could see where he wanted to go, but he was thwarted in getting there. He felt the rage again and the hatred. Eddington! Somehow, before the little preacher died he had placed barriers within the system. He had known that Brennon would return. How could he have learned so much so fast?

Fool! thought Brennon. *Do you really think you can keep me out of that which I built?* Closer examination showed that the barriers were clumsy. He should have no trouble in breaching them. Grimly, he set about his task. Using the limited resources available to him at the first level, he began. As he worked, he continuously scanned the system, looking for anything that pertained to the four believers he so desperately wanted to destroy. The first barrier collapsed, and he found part of what he was looking for.

NO! he thought angrily to himself. *I will **not** let you get away that easily!* He had discovered the security clearance Eddington had set up for the other three. With it, they could exit the station. He reached for it, intending to wipe it from the system, but was stopped when another barrier presented itself. Once again he set about destroying it.

Using what he had already accessed, he discovered that Anderson, Sinclair, and Ferguson were still in medical. He had to move fast. He attacked the barrier, and was enraged to discover that this one was stronger than the last. He could circumvent it, of course, but it would take time . . .

time which the three prisoners would use to escape.

Brennon considered his options, then allowed himself a small laugh. *Not the way I would have liked it,* he said to himself, *but it will do.* He could not destroy their clearance, but he could destroy them, and he could take care of another task at the same time.

At the speed of light, he accessed the security grid. He could only enter part of it, but it would be enough. He overrode the fail-safes, and sent a command to open all exterior hatches. At the same time, he secured the hatch to medical. It would now only open at a direct command from him. Knowing he would need the technical crew of Liberty in the future, he allowed them a chance to get off the station. The three believers, however, had no lifeboat assigned to them. Even if they somehow managed to open the hatch, they had nowhere to go. Having sent the proper commands in motion, he once again set himself to the task of regaining full access to the world network.

* * *

Desperately, Jeff punched command after command into the terminal, trying to get information. Nothing happened. He looked over at Susan and Paul and shook his head. "Nothing," he said, his voice flat.

"Then let's get out of here," Paul replied in the same tone. "We don't stand a chance here. Let's try to find a lifeboat station."

Jeff nodded in resignation. "Maybe our clearance can get us on board," he agreed. His voice betrayed his doubt. He pushed himself over to the hatch and pushed the control to open it. The hatch did not move. Jeff felt a surge of panic wash through him, and instantly controlled it. Again he entered the command to open the hatch. Nothing. His shoulders slumped. They had been locked in. He looked back at Paul and Susan. They had exhausted their last hope. There was nothing else to say. Silence settled over them.

Then Paul spoke up. "Well," he sighed, "I hope someone warns Eddington that we'll be right behind him. I can imagine what he's going to say when *I* show up." He pursed his lips and smiled at Jeff. "It's actually worth dying just to be able to see the look on his face!"

Jeff blinked, then did a double take. It took a moment for him to understand what Paul was saying. As his words sank into his tired mind, a wave of peace flooded through him. With it, the humor of what the big man said hit him with full force. He started to chuckle. Looking at Susan, he saw tears of grief streaming down her cheeks. Her face though, actually held a smile. From somewhere deep inside of her, Jeff heard a noise that sounded suspiciously like a laugh.

Jeff relaxed. His muscles went limp and he took a deep, finally-contented breath. His work was over. He did not have to worry anymore about the "if only's" that had plagued him since New York. If only he had been faster at Camelot. If only he had taken another direction than Dr. Chankersingh's clinic. If only he could have done something while still within Brennon's virtual reality system. If only. . . .

And it hit him.

"Wait a minute," he whispered urgently. He closed his eyes, trying to remember.

"What?" asked Paul, hearing the different tone in his voice. "What?" he asked again when Jeff did not answer.

"SHHHH!" Jeff whispered angrily. "Let me think!" He waved at Paul and Susan to be quiet. With a massive effort, he forced himself to replay his last conversation with David. Somehow, his friend had managed to deactivate Jeff's implant. No, that wasn't right. He destroyed the "slave circuit," he had said, but *the rest of his implant was still functioning!*

Sudden excitement burst through Jeff's acceptance of death. He forced himself to stay calm. They had minutes left. Jeff had no idea how to proceed. The last time his implant had been activated, he had literally merged with Brennon's incredible world. He could feel that this time that would not be possible. Still, if he could find a way. . . .

He closed his eyes, and concentrated. "Lord," he prayed silently, "You've got to help me on this one." His forehead furrowed with the effort, but nothing happened.

"Jeff," said Susan, "what are you trying to do?"

Sighing, Jeff quickly told her and Paul about how he and David had been implanted. He quickly relayed their battle with Brennon, and how David had rigged his bio-chip.

Paul listened thoughtfully. "Maybe you're trying too hard," he said after a few moments. "Try to relax."

"Yeah, right," grunted Jeff. Their situation was not exactly conducive to relaxation. Nevertheless, he closed his eyes once again, and forced himself to calm down. Peace settled over him and as it did so, he noticed a tiny white dot in the center of his darkened vision. It grew rapidly and suddenly transformed into a simple computer menu. There it was, as big as life. It was not nearly as elaborate as before, but perhaps it would do. Again a surge of excitement flashed through him, and the display wavered. Immediately he calmed down.

"Got it," he said aloud, keeping his eyes closed. "Some kind of menu."

"See anything about station security?" asked Paul, his voice striking a note of hope.

"Yeah," said Jeff. "Now shut up and let me concentrate." He threaded his way gingerly through the set of menus and sub-menus. Finally, he found what he was looking for. There, before him hung a three-dimensional representation of Liberty. He could see tiny red dots moving back and forth. Evidently they represented station personnel. Carefully, he zoomed the display in on the medical section. There, in a representation of the room they were in, were three dots. Amazed, Jeff pushed himself across the room, keeping his eyes closed. One of the dots on his display did the same. "Far out," he murmured.

Paul shook his head. "Excuse me," he said loudly, "but if you've got some miracle to pull out of your sleeve, now's the time."

"Okay, okay," agreed Jeff. He knew what to do now. Entering a single command into the file he was in, he waited. The opening, which had been colorless, now glowed green. Jeff knew he still had one more thing to do. Checking the lifeboat stations, he was dismayed to find them full. He kept searching. Just as he was about to give up, he discovered the shuttle they had arrived in. It was fully prepped, and ready to leave. He studied the information before him, and discovered that it was waiting for six passengers. Jeff could not tell who, but they were obviously of some importance.

Moving ever so carefully, he entered the file that contained the passenger manifest and deftly added three names to the list. He was amazed at how easy it was to use his implant. Perhaps David had somehow paved the way before he died, or maybe his prayer was being answered. Either way, he was grateful.

His task completed, he opened his eyes. It took a moment to figure out how to make the display that still hovered before him go away, but finally it disappeared. He started to exit. Then, just for an instant, he felt the presence of something else in the system. His blood suddenly ran cold. He recognized that presence — Brennon. The demonic entity was returning once more to inhabit his worldwide system.

Jeff felt a chill of fear. Then he paused. For all of his cleverness and power, it seemed as if Brennon was unaware of him. Repressing a sigh of relief, Jeff hastily shut down his display. He would have to be *very* careful in the future with this new and very unwanted toy.

"Try it now," he said to Paul, nodding toward the hatch. Paul floated over and pushed the button. Immediately, it cycled open.

"Yesss!" shouted Jeff. He had done it right.

Even Paul seemed to be impressed. "So let's go," he said. They started to file out of medical, but Paul stopped and looked back. David's body was still there, lying peacefully at rest. Jeff and Susan looked as well. None of them took any notice of Wolf, or the doctor, who floated unconscious nearby. A moment of shared silence and grief passed between them. Then Jeff put his hand on Paul's shoulder. Paul nodded, and allowed himself to be pushed gently through the hatch. There was no more time for goodbyes. It was time to leave.

* * *

Rajijah Indres hurried through the corridors of Liberty, anxious to get to the shuttle. He was not particularly worried, since he knew the shuttle would not leave without him. Still, this *was* an emergency. Indres did not have a great technical knowledge of the inner workings of Liberty, but he did know that the safety features built into the station were extensive. For all of the fail-safes to go at once was inconceivable. Indres strongly suspected Brennon's hand in this. For some reason, the Sextuaget leader wanted Liberty abandoned.

He was almost halfway to the shuttle dock when he received a message through his implant. The way it presented itself made it obvious that it was from Brennon. "Meet in the main conference room," it said. Indres stopped short. For an instant, he considered ignoring the summons. There were bare minutes left before the station's air was evacuated. He could not disregard it, of course. One ignored Brennon at great peril.

Quickly he changed his course and headed toward the conference room. He made it there without incident. Not surprisingly, there were no guards stationed at the entrance. They were long gone to their lifeboat stations. The hatch opened at a command from his implant, and he entered.

The rest of the Sextuaget was already there. Indres noted that they all looked uneasy. Small wonder, he admitted, considering the circumstances. He glanced toward the head of the table. It was shrouded in darkness. The head chair was turned away, but he could just make out Brennon's silhouette. A sigh of relief escaped Indres' lips. No matter what the situation, Brennon would not endanger himself, as well as the rest of the Sextuaget. Quickly, he took his seat, noting that, once again, Christine Smythe was absent.

"Welcome gentlemen," said the cultured, powerful voice he knew so well. Indres raised his eyebrows slightly. Brennon's voice was coming from *above*, out of speakers set into the ceiling. "I would like to thank you for all of your hard work over the past few decades," continued Brennon. "Now, your task is at an end. You have all done well. Again, thank you." Indres frowned. What was Brennon saying? Their task was at an end? It had barely begun! He opened his mouth to speak. Abruptly, the lights came on at the head of the table. The head chair swiveled, as if pushed by an unseen hand. When Indres saw what was in the chair, he gasped in shock and horror.

"As I have cast off this now useless body," continued Brennon's voice, "I now cast off you." In the chair, Brennon's obviously lifeless corpse gazed empty-eyed at them. Someone screamed, Indres was not sure who. "Again, thank you . . . and goodbye." With that, the lights went out again and Brennon's form was once again enshrouded in darkness.

Indres forced himself to think. He did not understand what was happening, but he *did* know that it was time to leave. He sent a command through his implant to open the hatch. His heart chilled when nothing happened. Kicking against his chair, he launched himself at the hatch. The others looked at him, dumbfounded. Indres reached the hatch and touched the control. It did not open. His heart beating rapidly, he punched in his emergency override code. Once again, nothing happened.

He tried to activate his implant, and enter Brennon's virtual reality world. Seconds would become hours there, and he would be able to find a solution. He was blocked — locked out of the system — helpless.

It suddenly dawned on him that he was going to die. A state of shock settled over him, and with it, a numbing calmness. He allowed himself to float away from the door. The others crowded past him, each one trying to open the hatch, all failing. Indres focused his eyes on the darkened, lifeless figure at the head of the table.

"Wheels within wheels," he said softly to himself. From Jacob Hill and his circle of elite members, to Brennon and his Sextuaget, to . . . what? Indres could not even begin to guess. He had thought himself in the company of world beaters. Now he knew that he had barely scratched the surface of power. He was an insignificant insect in the scheme of things. The Sextuaget had served its purpose, and now it was being discarded. He wondered what even greater power would take its place.

Suddenly the irony of his situation struck him and he began to smile. Gradually, the smile turned into laughter, and the laughter into madness. He continued to laugh until every hatch on Liberty blew open and the air was ripped ruthlessly from his lungs.

* * *

"Attention," came the female voice over the intercom. Once again it was computer-generated. "Emergency decompression in three minutes. Repeat, emergency decompression in three minutes. This is the final call for all lifeboat stations."

Jeff, Susan, and Paul pushed, pulled, and kicked their way toward the shuttle dock. If Jeff had not been able to access the map of Liberty through his partially-active implant, they would never have made it. He led them through corridor after corridor. All the time the alarm blared overhead, reminding them that their lives were being measured in seconds. The lack of gravity slowed them down and made them clumsy. Jeff could feel his heart beating in rhythm with the alarm. He was beyond exhaustion now. Anything he had left to give was a direct gift from God.

There were exactly two minutes left when they reached the shuttle dock. Jeff breathed a silent prayer of thanks that the shuttle was still there. It was the same dock that they had boarded Liberty through, with one difference — the air lock that lead to the shuttle's main hatch was closed and sealed.

Jeff closed his eyes, and wondered how much more he could take. "Hello! Hello in the shuttle. Do you read me?" Jeff's eyes snapped open. He saw that Paul had found a vid-com set into the wall next to the airlock hatch. It was obviously for communicating directly with the shuttle. The screen remained blank for a moment, then came to life. Jeff recognized the pilot who had flown them up.

"Too late," he said, his voice distorted by the small speaker of the vid-com. "Get to a lifeboat. I'm launching." The screen went blank. Paul slammed his fist against the screen, and Susan moaned. Then Paul turned to Jeff.

"We need one more hat trick," he said, meeting Jeff's eyes. Jeff hesitated. He did not want to delve too deeply into the system his implant was hooked in to. Somewhere in there, Brennon lurked . . . and he was growing stronger by the minute. Then he nodded. What choice did he have?

Quickly he activated his bio-chip. He moved rapidly, going through function after function. Repeated use was making him faster. He could sense Brennon's demonic presence. It was like a cancer that was out of control, growing wildly. It seemed, though, that Brennon could not yet sense him. If he could just have one minute. . . .

It took him 30 precious seconds. The shuttle was still connected to Liberty's main system. He accessed it.

There was a hiss of escaping air, then the airlock door opened. Without another word, they were through. The airlock was painted a bright white, with enough room for a dozen people to stand comfortably. The shuttle's main hatch was on the far side. Once again, Jeff sent the necessary command.

"Attention," came the computer generated voice. "Emergency decompression has been initiated. Repeat, emergency decompression has been initiated." From somewhere far away, Jeff heard a muted "thud." The entire station vibrated slightly.

"Jeff?" Susan called his name, her voice telling him to hurry. Jeff hurried. Using his implant, he slammed the airlock door shut. Just as it closed, they heard the sound of a miniature typhoon on the other side. The high-pitched shriek told them that their small room now held the only breathable atmosphere.

Now Jeff turned his attention to the shuttle's main hatch. He started to repeat the process. He was too late. The shuttle had just switched over to its own internal systems. If it launched while they were in the airlock, they would be sucked out into space. He looked at Paul helplessly. Paul scanned the room, then studied the hatch. Jeff saw what he was looking at, and suddenly felt a flash of hope. The shuttle's hatch could be opened manually!

Paul had already found the tool he needed. It was placed conveniently on the curving wall, just to the right of the hatch. He got to work. There was also a vid-com next to the hatch. As soon as Paul started the unlock procedures, it came to life.

"Stop that!" the shuttle's pilot commanded. "You'll never get it open in time." Jeff felt a flash of anger at the pilot. They were so close! He moved to stand in front of the video pickup of the vid-com.

"You're probably right," he told the pilot. "But my friend is still going to try. You want to try re-entry with a partially secured hatch?" The pilot stared at him for a moment. Then he let out a curse that caused even Paul to blush. He disappeared from the monitor and within a few seconds the hatch opened. He glared at them for a moment, then motioned them on board.

Jeff was the last one to enter. As Paul and Susan strapped themselves in, he followed the pilot back to the control cabin. The rest of the crew was there as well. "Can you land this thing on manual?" he asked.

The pilot swung around in anger. "Get out of here!" he snapped. "We're launching!"

"Listen to me!" Jeff shouted. "I don't think the station's mainframe is going to give us any help. Can you get us down on manual?"

For a moment, Jeff thought the pilot was going to strike him. Then his co-pilot interrupted. "He may be right, sir," he said, his voice sounding strained. "All links with Liberty have been broken. We have no guidance. I can't re-establish contact."

"What do you mean 'can't'?" growled the pilot. "We're already on internal power. All we need is clearance to leave, and a flight plan." He stopped when he saw his displays. "I don't believe it," he said, his voice now much lower. "We were cleared just minutes ago."

"We're not now," said the co-pilot. "Think we should wait?"

To Jeff's relief, the pilot shook his head. "I'm not keeping my ship locked on to a station that's going crazy. Let's get out of here. Full manual overrides now."

Ignoring Jeff, the crew got busy. Jeff considered fainting in relief, then decided to go back to his friends. They were strapped in to their launch seats, side by side.

Paul saw him approach. "He going on manual?" he asked. Jeff nodded wearily.

"What about weapons? Can that station shoot us down?"

"I don't think so," replied Jeff as he found a launch chair and strapped himself in. "When the hatches blew, the weapons systems, as well as everything else, went off-line. It will take hours to pick up the pieces." There was a jolt, then a slight horizontal movement as the shuttle broke free of Liberty.

One final time, Jeff accessed his implant. In the last few seconds he had access to Liberty's mainframe, he called up the three-dimensional map of the station. He could see a representation of the shuttle moving away from the dock. Within moments, it moved beyond his sight. He tiptoed around a few other areas of Liberty's system, but could find no other trace of it. It was as he had hoped.

He was sure that Brennon had caused the emergency on Liberty. He was equally sure that he, Paul, and Susan were the reason. The demonic entity's access to Liberty's mainframe was still limited. Blowing the hatches was the only way he could get at them. In doing so, however, he had also caused several other delicate systems to crash, among them weapons and surveillance. As far as the station — and therefore Brennon — was concerned, the shuttle no longer existed. It would be hours before total repairs could be completed. Time enough to land and escape.

For the first time in a very long time, Jeff actually began to believe that they were going to escape. How they would get out of Cape Kennedy remained to be seen. Perhaps their clearance to be on the shuttle would be enough. Jeff glanced over at Paul and Susan. Susan smiled back, and Paul nodded. "Try to get some rest," said the big man.

Jeff shook his head. "As soon as I find a way to get us someplace safe," he replied. He closed his eyes and activated his implant. It responded readily. *I could get used to this,* he said to himself. Liberty's computer was lost to him now, but he could still access the shuttle's main system. Through that, he could find a way to the ground computers.

It took a while, but he did it. David had done well in freeing his implant from the system. Jeff was able to find a relatively safe escape route. It would mean a cross-country trip, but he was able to make the proper reservations and plans. The computer network of the Shepherd's Path was gone, but he knew from memory a handful of places in Florida he could call. They would be able to help. He thought long and hard about where to go. In the end, he decided to go to the one place no one would think to look. It would be a difficult and dangerous journey, but they would make it. He was sure of it. The details taken care of, he settled back into his seat and finally relaxed.

He had no idea why God had allowed the events of the past few days to happen. Perhaps it was so he could get his implant, then get free within the system. He could see much good he could do with it. Perhaps it was to upset the plans of a malevolent, evil being. Although Brennon still existed, they might have set whatever plans he had back for a while. Jeff had absolutely no idea.

Once more he glanced at Paul and Susan. Then again, he mused, *Perhaps it was so one man could come to find his Saviour.* Jeff smiled at the thought. Why not?! After all, no matter what the plans of man or devil amounted to, God was still in control. All that was required of those who were his followers was that they remain true to Him.

That knowledge was all the sedative Jeff needed. He laid his head back onto the cushioned seat. Finally, he gave in to the exhaustion and fell into a deep, restful sleep.

EPILOGUE

Wolf groaned as he came to. He was floating comfortably. For a moment, his mind whirled. Then memory returned, and his eyes snapped open. Where was Sinclair and his friends?! He looked wildly around, taking in his surroundings. He was still on Liberty, obviously. The absence of gravity proved that. One glance told him that he was in the conference room, alone. He was strapped loosely in one of the conference chairs. He shook his head in confusion.

"Rejoined the land of the living, Mister Wolf?" The voice came from above. On one of the monitors, a face appeared. It was a strong, masculine face with dark, piercing eyes.

Wolf's own eyes narrowed. "Do I know you?" he asked suspiciously.

The face on the monitor smiled. "Not directly," it said. "However, your former employer, Christine Smythe, operated under my, er, jurisdiction. She knew me as Brennon."

Wolf nodded. He had long suspected that Smythe was not as in charge as she claimed to be. He licked his lips. "What happened?"

"There was an emergency evacuation of Liberty several hours ago," Brennon said. "Do you remember?"

"I remember the alarm," answered Wolf. "After that. . . ."

"After that," interrupted Brennon, "You were careless enough to allow Paul Sinclair to overpower you. Correct?"

Reluctantly, Wolf nodded, his cheeks burning in anger and embarrassment. He did not know why, but he wanted this man to like him. His usual arrogance was gone. He knew instinctively that Brennon was no one to be trifled with. Here, before him, was *real* power. Like most bullies, Wolf was cowed in the presence of a greater force.

Brennon smiled. He waved Wolf's failure aside. "No matter," he said. "I forgive you. In fact, I have great plans for you. Consider yourself fortunate that I was able to regain control of this station in time to find you and seal the room you were in."

Wolf straightened in his chair. "Plans?" he asked.

Brennon nodded. "I need someone with your talents." He paused, as if thinking. "An important associate of mine has died. It was something of a shock, actually."

"Associate?" asked Wolf. "Smythe?"

Brennon actually laughed out loud. "Of course not!" he answered with a hint of derision. Wolf immediately shut up. "This was someone that I was quite close to, I'm afraid," continued Brennon after a moment. "You might even say he was a part of me." For some reason, he chuckled.

"You want *me* to take his place?" asked Wolf, now eager. To be this close to the seat of great power, he knew, was to wield great power as well — especially power over others.

Brennon nodded, smiling. "Are you willing?" he asked. "The tasks are difficult, but the rewards are great."

Wolf smiled back. "What kind of rewards?" he asked slyly.

Again Brennon laughed heartily. "The type that will enable you to control events and lives . . . perhaps even gain a little revenge on those who have managed to slip past you."

Wolf found himself grinning. That was enough for him. He nodded in agreement.

"Excellent!" Abruptly, the hatch opened and a dark-skinned, white-haired man floated in. He was flanked by two capable-looking guards. Wolf eyed them, suddenly uneasy.

"You will go with Doctor Nubata," ordered Brennon. "The good doctor, who I have also recently forgiven, will perform a minor operation on you . . . it will greatly enhance your abilities."

"Now just a minute," began Wolf, suddenly alarmed, "What kind of operation are you. . . ." He never finished. Moving fluidly in the weightless environment, the two guards floated over to Wolf. Reflexively, Wolf pushed himself away, but he was too late. One of the guards pointed an NPW at him. Wolf screamed, then went limp. The two guards took him by either arm and started off.

"Medical," said Nubata, and they nodded. He started to follow them, anxious to leave.

"Do not fail me, Doctor," said Brennon's image. "You are already living on borrowed time. Understand?" Suppressing a shudder, Nubata nodded, then left.

Brennon's face remained on the monitor, smiling. "Wolf, my friend," he said cheerfully, "We are going to become very close. *Very* close!" With that, the monitor flicked off, and the room was left empty.

* * *

It took them three weeks, but they made it. Jeff leaned wearily against the simulated mahogany office door and knocked. They were in what was loosely termed a "red zone," somewhere in Washington, DC. Simply put, it was a bad section of town. His tired mind reflected back on their recently completed cross-country trip. They had had no difficulty in leaving the

Cape, thanks to the clearance David had managed to arrange for them.

From there, Jeff was able to find a safe house where they had rested a while. After that, it had been days of endless and varied travel, stale food, and long nights spent in cheap motel rooms, or sleeping in back alleys, trying to find shelter wherever it could be found. If it had not been for Jeff's steadily growing ability with his implant, they would have been caught a dozen times over. For all intents and purposes, the Shepherd's Path was effectively inoperative, its computer network destroyed beyond recall. Finally, they reached their destination.

Again Jeff knocked. He shifted his weight from his good leg to the cane he had managed to find in a second-hand store somewhere in South Carolina. From the way his knee was slowly healing, he doubted that he would ever walk normally again. He glanced back at Susan and Paul, both of whom looked a thousand years old. He smiled weakly in assurance. The sudden click of a dead bolt being drawn back made him turn his attention back to the door. It opened quickly.

"Anderson?!" The voice was incredulous. "Good grief, you look like an ad for the dead! Get in here!"

Jeff had to chuckle. Stephen Lynch was as direct and abrasive as ever. Since their initial meeting months ago, when they had been deadly enemies, their relationship had been one of mutual respect, and barely suppressed hostility. He limped into Stephen's office, followed by his friends. Stephen had set up a private detective agency that, while a legitimate business, was also a way station for hunted believers. Even though Lynch had not actually become a Christian, Jeff trusted him implicitly. Stephen shook his head as Jeff entered. He glanced at Susan and nodded. When he saw Paul. . . .

"YOU!" Suddenly his eyes blazed. He moved forward as if to attack Paul. Although he had not worked with him, he recognized Paul from his bureau days.

Paul glanced at Jeff wryly. He held out an empty hand. "Told you," he said, speaking to Jeff. "Pay up!"

"Later," replied Jeff. He found one of Stephen's stuffed office chairs and sank into it gratefully.

Lynch watched the exchange in disbelief. He jabbed a finger at Paul. "Do you know who that is?" he demanded.

Jeff nodded tiredly. "Paul Sinclair, alias Paul Simpson, former dreaded agent for the bureau, new Christian, and all-around swell guy."

Lynch did not believe a word of it. "Good grief, Anderson! You think I was bad? This guy's worse! Let me tell you about. . . ."

"Stephen!" Jeff's exclamation brought Lynch up short. He stared at Jeff, waiting. "This is going to take a while to explain," said Jeff. "We're starved, exhausted, and dirty. Think you can wait until we can at least *look* human again?"

Lynch continued to stare, hovering between the desire to help and the urge to shoot Paul on sight. Finally, compassion won, but it was a photo finish. He nodded. "Lets go," he said, grabbing his coat. "We'll get to my place. You can tell me everything there." He paused for a moment, then added ominously, "This had better be good!"

* * *

Brennon rode the waves of electrons at the speed of light. He was fully integrated into the world network at last. After his disastrous encounter with Anderson and his cohorts, he was finally back up to full strength. Not only that, Wolf was proving a most cooperative ally! Despite recent setbacks, matters were proceeding as planned. Brennon reveled in the power that was his. An entire planet, wired for access! The things he could accomplish!

Just now, though, he was responding to a summons. He chose to present himself in his synthetic body rather than his newly acquired corporeal one. Wolf still had an annoying tendency to display some of his rather undesirable attitudes. That would change in time. Brennon threaded his way through the virtual reality maze with ease, moving quickly. Only one being had the power to command his appearance, and it would not do to keep that being waiting. He found the proper outlet and accessed it.

As he appeared on the provided monitor that was his window into the "real" world, he took note of his surroundings. It was a spacious office, with subdued furnishings that spoke of power under control. Brennon approved. The time was not quite here when that power would be openly displayed, but it was coming — and soon. Brennon announced his presence with a soft chime that sounded gently in the office. Almost at once, an imposing figure moved to stand before him.

Brennon bowed his head in a gesture of obedience. "What is your bidding, my master?" he said, and the figure before him smiled.

* * *

Paul watched as Jeff filled Stephen in on the events of the past few weeks. He was sitting in a comfortable chair in Stephen's apartment, a few miles from his office. Jeff and Susan were on a couch on the opposite side of the room, and Stephen was pacing back and forth in front of them. More than once, Stephen's eyes wandered over to Paul, appraising him.

As Jeff finished his story, Stephen shook his head. "I knew something had gone bad when I couldn't access the network any more." He pursed his lips. "Any chance there's another copy of it hiding in some file somewhere?"

Jeff smiled and shook his head. "Not this time," he replied. "And never again. Now that the secret's out, it's far too dangerous to use something like that. We'll just have to find another way."

He paused, then asked the question he most dreaded to ask. "Have you heard anything about a nationwide attack on local churches?"

Stephen's grim demeanor became even grimmer. "Bits and pieces," he admitted reluctantly. "That warning by your friend Eddington saved a lot of lives, but from what I've been able to gather, at least 200 cell groups were uncovered. They weren't arrested. They were slaughtered." Jeff closed his eyes in pain and grief.

Stephen continued. "A lot of safe houses were taken out, too. As far as I can tell, most of the damage was in the south. Groups in the north were barely touched."

"Thank God for that," replied Jeff. "What about Helen and Scott and Beth?"

Stephen nodded reassuringly. "All fine," he said. "In fact, with the network down, I doubt that they even know about most of it." Jeff nodded.

Paul smiled to himself, despite Stephen's grim news. He recognized the names Jeff had mentioned. Scott and Beth Sampson had been the beginning of all his troubles. One day, maybe, he would meet them face to face . . . and thank them.

"So is the Shepherd's Path gone?" asked Susan, from her place on the couch. Stephen did not answer.

"Hurt," Jeff replied, "but not destroyed. If we can find a way to pick up the pieces. . . ." He shrugged. "I'll need a place to set up shop again," he said. "Many of the links in the chain are still there. If I can find a way to put them together again, maybe we can get back in business. If not," he sighed heavily, "well, it has served a good purpose. After all, the main thing is the Church. One way or another, the Body will survive."

There was a moment's silence, then Stephen spoke. "As far as picking up the pieces, I can't help you there, but I may have a headquarters for you." In answer to Jeff's questioning look, he continued. "I just relocated a man by the name of Benson Adams," he said. "He came through here about. . . ."

"Benson!" At the sound of the name, Jeff sprung to his feet. His damaged knee caused him to sit right back down again.

Stephen raised his eyebrows. "You know him?" he asked.

"He was one of my contacts," answered Jeff excitedly. "Wolf, the man who captured us back in New York, told us that he had been arrested."

Stephen nodded. "He was," he agreed. "They shipped him here to DC. I sprung him."

"Yesss!" exclaimed Jeff, clenching his fist in victory. Paul could feel his joy as well. It was the first good news that they had received in far too long.

Stephen smiled at Jeff's reaction, then continued. "Anyway, your friend Benson has been a busy fellow. He's fairly well off, you know." Jeff nodded, eager to hear more. "Well," said Stephen, "It seems that he's been quietly buying up a great deal of land somewhere in central Kentucky."

"Huh?" Jeff asked in confusion. "What's in Kentucky . . . and how was Benson buying land while the government was breathing down his neck?"

"Dummy corporations, holding companies, you name it, he used it," explained Stephen. "No one can trace it to him. He even got an environmentalist restriction on the land he bought. It'll sit there forever, and nobody will touch it."

"And why Kentucky?" repeated Jeff.

"There's still a great deal of undeveloped land in this country," said Stephen. "Kentucky has a lot of it. Thousands of square miles of nothing but hills and trees . . . and caves." Paul could see comprehension dawn on Jeff's face.

"You mean. . . ." he began, and Stephen nodded.

"For the past year, Benson has been transferring food, supplies, even small generators, to the caves he found on the land. They're extensive, I hear. Hundreds of miles of them . . . enough to hide a small army, or a group of hunted Christians. If all went well, he should be there now."

Now Jeff laughed out loud. "Then I think we'd better extend our trip a little," he said, and Stephen nodded.

"If you can get us back to Cincinnati," he said, pointing at Jeff's head, indicating his implant, "I can get us the rest of the way."

"Us?" The word was out of Paul's mouth before he realized it.

Stephen turned on him, nodding. "Us," he repeated. He turned back to Jeff. "Things are getting hot here. I was planning on disappearing within the week, anyway. It will be nice to have company." Again he regarded Paul, uncertainty evident in his face.

"What Jeff told you about me was true," Paul said evenly. He felt a sudden flash of anger. Why should he have to prove himself to this man? Then he realized that Stephen was only doing what he himself would do if the situation were reversed.

Lynch looked at Jeff, who nodded. "It's true," he said. "I'm willing to stake my life on it."

Stephen snorted. "You already are. You know Anderson, you have a knack of turning your enemies into friends." He paused, and then smiled slyly. "Including me."

It took Jeff a moment to realize what Stephen was saying. "You mean . . ." he began.

"Yep," replied Stephen. "I'm one of you now." He saw Jeff's look of surprised joy and laughed sharply. "What do you expect? People who hang around committed believers sometimes have a tendency to become committed believers. God *IS* good! Ya know?"

"Yeah," said Jeff, "I know."

Despite himself, Paul felt a smile worm its way to his face. A feeling of peace descended on the small living room. Paul recognized it immediately. He had first felt it in the basement of that Sacramento mall. It had almost made him ill at the time. Later, he had come face to face with the Creator of that peace in New York. There, he had settled matters once and for all. Now, that peace was a part of him, and he reveled in the feeling. The others felt it too . . . even Lynch.

"Okay," Stephen said, breaking the moment, "You all need rest. I've got a stakeout tonight, so I'll be gone. It'll probably be the last case I ever work on. Susan can have the bedroom. You guys can fight it out to see who gets the floor and the couch."

Paul caught Jeff's eye and grimaced. "I've fought him enough for one lifetime," he muttered, and Jeff smiled wryly.

"Agreed," he said. "I can prop my knee up on the table here. You take the couch."

* * *

Later than night, Paul lay quietly on the couch, listening to Jeff's soft breathing. For the first time in ages, he felt safe. He was among friends who had become family. Far more importantly, he rested in the knowledge that his soul was in the unshakable grip of his Saviour. His meadow was gone, as was the need for it. Also gone was the presence he had felt for so long. Brennon, or Lou, or whatever he was called, was out of his mind and soul. He might cause trouble in the future, but he could never touch Paul where it counted again.

Paul took a deep breath and felt sleep beginning to overtake him. He was glad. He no longer had to fear sleep again. Tomorrow they would deal with the problems of getting to a safe haven, but Paul could sense that they would make it. Let tomorrow's worries take care of themselves . . . tomorrow.

As he drifted off into unconsciousness, he heard Stephen's words in the back of his mind. "People who hang around committed believers sometimes have a tendency to become committed believers. God IS good! Ya know?"

"I know," he whispered. And Paul Sinclair smiled in his sleep.

THE END